# The Boy on an Eagle

## A fictional biography of a pioneer aeronautical engineer in peace and war

## Robin H. Meakins

Cover and Map designs by Tim Meakins

iUniverse, Inc.
New York   Bloomington

**The Boy on an Eagle**
**A fictional biography of a pioneer aeronautical**
**engineer in peace and war**

*iUniverse books may be ordered through booksellers or by contacting:*

*iUniverse*
*1663 Liberty Drive*
*Bloomington, IN 47403*
*www.iuniverse.com*
*1-800-Authors (1-800-288-4677)*

*ISBN: 978-1-4502-6207-1 (sc)*
*ISBN: 978-1-4502-6208-8 (ebk)*

*Library of Congress Control Number: 2010914125*

*Printed in the United States of America*

*iUniverse rev. date: 11/16/2010*

# Acknowledgements

I wish to thank my wife Victoria for her support throughout this project and for editing the text. I am grateful to my sons for their help, Timothy for the design of the cover and the maps, and Dominic for some photographs of the Supermarine S6A.

All the characters in the book are fictitious and in no way reflect any person alive or dead. However the main character is based on the life of my father, the late Herbert Meakins.

# Dedication

This book is in memory of my father Herbert Meakins and my maternal grandfather Alfred Peckham. It celebrates their pioneering work as early aeronautical engineers and also I hope the work of those who have served, and still serve, the aircraft industry.

## Other novels by the author

A Paradise Lost – The Jade Tree. 2006. Athena Press, Twickenham
...And None were Innocent. 2007. AuthorHouse, Bloomington, Indiana
Target: London 2012. 2010. iUniverse, Bloomington, Indiana

# Frontispiece

One of the few documents about Sebro.

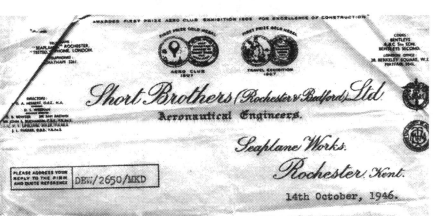

Short Brothers (Rochester & Bedford) Ltd
Aeronautical Engineers.

Seaplane Works.
Rochester, Kent.

DEW/2650/MKD

14th October, 1946.

TO WHOM IT MAY CONCERN at the Ministry of Labour,
London Appointments Office

MR. H. MEAKINS was Chief Inspector of our
subsidiary Company, Sebro Limited, Cambridge, from
March, 1941, to August, 1946, when the establishment
was closed.

During that time he was responsible for an
Inspection Department of considerable size, handling
the repair and overhaul of military aircraft.
During the period mentioned above, over one thousand
4-engined military aircraft passed through the
establishment, and it is a tribute to Mr. Meakins
that the work was handled most satisfactorily, in
spite of all the difficulties associated with wartime dispersal and shortage of skilled labour.

Mr. Meakins is leaving us of his own
accord, and he does so with our best wishes for his
future success.

(D.E. WISEMAN)
MANAGING DIRECTOR

# Preface

The author was born during the Second World War in Royston near Cambridge. His father was at the time the Chief Inspector of a major Civilian Repair Organisation known as Sebro, short for Short Brothers Repair Organisation. Sebro was where all the badly damaged RAF and USAAF Short Stirling and Liberator four-engine bombers in England were repaired from 1940 until 1946. From the frontispiece it is clear that they repaired over one thousand such aircraft under extremely difficult conditions. Some still say that Sebro and other CROs played a major role in saving the RAF and Britain.

For some unknown reason all the records and papers relating to Sebro were destroyed in a fire in 1946. So having inherited the reference for H. Meakins the author started to find out more including his father's work with R.G. Mitchell building the Schneider Trophy winning Supermarine S6 and S6B float planes. From these aircraft Mitchell designed the world famous RAF fighter, the Supermarine Spitfire. However the records concerning the men who actually built the aircraft are poor. So the author had to rely on information learned from strangers and his own memories of his father's friends.

The historical basis for this story is what was told to him by his father, the late Herbert (Bert) Meakins and maternal grandfather Alfred (Alf) Peckham. Both men met as aeronautical engineers while working at Supermarine Works at Woolston, Southampton. They built the Schneider Trophy winning S6, S6A and S6B aircraft. Later they worked for Short Brothers in Rochester before Alfred Peckham left to be Chief Inspector in the Short Brothers factory on Lake Windermere building Sunderland flying boats and Herbert Meakins went to Sebro in Cambridge. Alfred's son John started to work at Supermarine on the Spitfire. Later John Peckham went to Australia where he designed the successful Jindivik and Ikara missiles.

My father was born in Eastleigh and his father was a Sergeant in the British Army until after Irish Independence. As a young man Bert and his friends raced motorbikes, mostly Norton, and toured Europe before the Second World War. He was a talented pianist but did not play anymore as he grew older, though he still loved Tchaikovsky's music. His last contact with Supermarine Spitfire and Seafire fighters was when working for the Union of Burma Air Board between 1959 and 1960. Maybe Bert's advice helped the Union of Burma Air Force (UBAF) Spitfires commanded by Brigadier Tommy Clift fight the Chinese MIG 15s over northern Burma. Many of the surviving UBAF Spitfires were years later presented to the RAF by President Ne Win and some were sold privately to people in the USA. Some still fly.

Information on the history of Short Brothers is to be found in Shorts by Mike Hooks (1995)[1]. A Solent Flight by Ivor J. Hilliker (1990)[2] shows a wide range of aircraft associated with the aircraft companies operating on the Solent. In both books the illustrations are excellent. Details of the Schneider trophy races are described in the well illustrated Schneider Trophy Diamond Jubilee Looking Back 60 Years by Alan Smith (1991)[3]. Additional information on the S6 aircraft was provided by the author's son Dominic Meakins who photographed her being prepared for display at the Goodwood Festival of Speed. Today the surviving papers concerning Supermarine and other Solent aircraft manufacturers are kept in Southampton by Solent Sky in their Museum.

Many parts of the story are purely fictional and all the names of the characters imaginary and in no way reflect any person living or dead. A V1 missile did land in the upstairs of the house next door so that father had to rescue an old lady and a Messerschmitt Bf 109 did strafe the village causing a baby, the author, to be pushed into the ditch and cut his tongue. There was a huge German aircraft repair organisation based in Heidelberg. It is no great secret that the Germans wanted to destroy the RAF and all repair organisations, so that the attempts to sabotage Sebro are founded on fact. Likewise the modification and repair of enemy aircraft for use by the SOE can be verified by visiting the Imperial War Museum at Duxford. There are many substantiated stories of the Irish living in the Republic helping Britain during the Second World War even when their leader was adamantly pro-German, or at least neutral. To what extent the Irish helped Britain unfortunately is not recorded.

The truth remains that without aeronautical engineers and mechanics, the RAF could not have operated as they did and we may not have won the war. What the author asked his friends is would you drive a car that was badly maintained? Sadly it is even more true today especially in aeronautics and those working on the frontier of high performance work. In the 1930s few people had degrees and so most manufacturers preferred people like Mitchell who had done their apprenticeship and were licensed engineers. As the author finished writing this book he asked himself why our nation is so bad at acknowledging those ordinary heroes who kept our aircraft flying, our ships sailing and our machines operative? None of them were extra special indeed few had degrees and most just worked every hour God gave to keep their nation's forces operational.

Lastly he wishes to thank all those ex-RAF pilots who told him about RAF Bomber Command and Sebro. Through his father he met many pilots and engineers who talked about flying in the war. While at school in Abingdon, he attended a parachute course at RAF Abingdon held at the No 1 Parachute Training School. There he met General Roy Urquhart who told him how his father, Herbert Meakins, organised the gliders for Operation Market Garden, the attempt to capture the bridges over the Rhine that ended in defeat at Arnhem. While teaching at a school in Cambridge the author was surprised to meet two people who knew his father. One was a Polish Professor who had, in his own words, flown for his father and the other a lady whose sister had been his father's secretary at Sebro. Unfortunately they, like so many of the author's sources, are no longer alive and so he cannot ask them what they meant by some of the things they said. What the author does know is that they operated as a team who celebrated their successes together with a beer and mourned their losses as good friends do. In fact he owes his name Robin to one of his father's RAF friends and maybe his life to their eggs.

Thank you.

Robin H. Meakins

# Prologue

We all know that no newborn animal can fly. Even insects take a few hours to spread their wings and birds many weeks after their feathers are fully grown to learn. Man took millennia to develop a simple flying machine based on a bird's wing to glide a few miles. Then there developed powered flight and with it the conquest of the air. So that today even with all of the modern training techniques and equipment it still takes a human many months to learn to fly safely, years to be a very good pilot even longer to be an aeronautical engineer.

The development of flight has made global travel possible changing both the face of communications and travel. Today we expect aircraft to transport us around the world cheaply and whenever we want without any delays. In our rush for cheaper airfares too many do not care how reliable and safe or even how old are the aircraft. So that regularly aircraft have to make emergency landings because an onboard system fails or in extreme cases something falls off! In fact most people do not realise that to keep an aircraft airworthy it must be regularly serviced and maintained by highly skilled aeronautical engineers certified to work on that specific type of aircraft. This is very expensive and takes time to do properly so that some less responsible companies tend to keep this down to the minimum, while the best airlines check each aircraft before and after every flight. It is said that you get what you pay for and maybe that is why even today some aircraft fall from the sky.

This novel is fictional but based on the true life of an aeronautical engineer famous for building the S6B Schneider Trophy winner from which was developed the famous WWII fighter the Supermarine Spitfire.

He helped run the Civilian Repair Organisation known as Sebro that repaired over two thousand Royal Air Force (RAF) bombers during the Second World War. Unfortunately most of the information on Sebro has been lost in the mists of time, as at the end of the war a fire destroyed the records in the parent company Short Brothers. It is well understood by logistics experts that without specialised repair organisations such as Sebro, the RAF would have been unable to keep airborne many of her bombers during WWII. It was a time when the RAF required as many pilots and aircrew as possible but the real shortage was for trained engineers and mechanics needed to keep the planes airborne. Often people mistakenly mix up the ground crews who re-arm and refuel aircraft with the engineers who service and repair them. They are very different though both essential in any Air Force.

Even today more aircraft crash due to mechanical failures than are shot down in combat. Without dedicated aeronautical engineers no aircraft can safely stay in the air for very long. It only takes one loose bolt, worn out unit or badly maintained part to destroy any machine especially aircraft. Sometimes simple things like dust and small stones damaging the rotating rotor blades of a jet engine or a major instrument failure can prove fatal. The military wines and dines their officer pilots like kings while taking their engineers for granted. In 2010 the average age of a combat helicopter in the RAF was over ten years and because of being constantly flown in conflict zones were showing their age. Yet politicians and the Ministry of Defence continuously failed to supply newer and more efficient equipment. One of the most outrageous errors in management was the deployment of the Nimrod surveillance and control aircraft. The Nimrod was based on the excellent but dated 1950 design for the world's first commercial jetliner, the de Havilland Comet. It outlived its usefulness and desperately needed refurbishment as it leaked fuel and was prone to explode. It was reported that the connections and valves controlling the refuelling system may have caused the Nimrod MR2 XV230 to crash on 2nd September 2006 near Kandahar, Afghanistan. In May 2008 the Oxford coroner suggested that the aircraft's refuelling system may have been responsible for the fire, possibly due to poor maintenance, that killed the fourteen servicemen on board. The replacement for the MR2 Nimrod is the Nimrod MRA4 which was to be in service in the RAF by April 2003 but the first will not be delivered until 2010. However on 26th March 2010 after a public outcry all MR2 Nimrod aircraft were taken out of service with the RAF for safety reasons.

This fictional story is based on fact. It is dedicated to the aeronautical engineers and workers from the wartime Civilian Repair Organisations (CRO) and the RAF. For a hundred years they have kept our aircraft flying and helped make them safer. In peacetime minor mistakes can be easily rectified when they occur. However during war it is very different. Then aircraft are flown for hours without a break, often in very testing conditions varying from desert storms to hostile fire. Under such circumstances the smallest error may kill both crew and passengers. In severe cases poor maintenance can make air forces inoperable.

The reader is taken from the First World War and the twenties to the Second World War when aircraft development radically changed.

# 1

## From de Broyen to Brown

The French and the British are the same people born of the same blood only separated by the sea, their history, arrogance, misunderstandings and language.

On a hill eight miles north of Hastings during the day of 14th October 1066, a battle raged that was destined to change England forever. It was when the King of Anglo-Saxon England Harold II, Harold Godwinson was confronted by the invading army of the French Norman Duke of Normandy known as William the Bastard and his men. It was a conflict between seven thousand Saxons experienced foot soldiers versus eight thousand Norman foot soldiers, assisted by cavalry and the new revolutionary crossbow. Throughout that day the Saxons successfully held the high ground on Senlac Hill repulsing all of the Norman attacks with their nearly impenetrable wall of shields. For most of the day the contest was equal. Indeed anyone could have won the battle until a Norman arrow killed King Harold's horse. The sight of their King's horse falling and fearing the King dead, caused some of the Saxons to panic and flee. This allowed the Normans to advance through a smaller Saxon army led by Harold's loyal bodyguards, the houscarl, who fought by his side to the death. Then the Norman knight Guy de Broyen rode through the weakened Saxon wall of shields to capture King Harold's Red Dragon flag and with it all of England.

Next morning the seriously injured Guy de Broyen lay on the ground on Senlac Hill guarded by his loyal men. He was in that place called limbo that is between life and death and struggling to survive. All around him the noises of war were replaced by the terrible cries of the wounded asking for water or just someone to help them. Among them were priests and physicians tending the wounded and, of course, the usual bands of scavengers. The latter stole all the valuables they could find while nearby birds pecked at the bodies of men and horses undisturbed. Guy did not remember the details of the battle except that it was a hard fought, closely run contest in which anyone could have won.

Being neither alive nor dead Guy was guarded by his squire as a priest tended his severe wounds to stop the bleeding. It was then that something magical happened. While unconscious Guy saw through the eyes of an eagle soaring in the sky above the battlefield and cried out in horror at the carnage. He saw that both once brave Saxon and Norman warriors were now reduced to identical grotesque dead figures lying where they had fallen. All of these once fine men were now merely mutilated bodies some without arms, legs and even a head. It was Hell on Earth caused by the greed and ambition of Guy's master William the Duke of Normandy. Then, as life flowed back into his wounded body, he opened his eyes to see a large black eagle soaring in the sky, so majestic and so powerful. It made Guy vow that one day a de Broyen would fly like that eagle for when men flew like the birds they would control the world. It is the dream of inventors, scientists, engineers as well as power hungry kings and despots.

Guy never forgot his eagle so that when he became an Earl and the Lord of the village of Puddlestree, his new coat of arms was simply a golden boy riding on the back of a large black eagle. Like many other Normans, in time he anglicised his name to Browen that later became Brown. On his estate, he built a fortified manor house from which he could survey his lands that stretched out over fertile fields and forests to the horizon. There he bred both eagles and falcons for sport and as a reminder of his dream on Senlac Hill. By Norman custom the eldest son inherited everything while the younger sons left the estate on their sixteenth birthday and the daughters remained until they were married. All the children on leaving the family home received a horse, some money and a copy of the family's crest so that they knew their heritage. If they became sick, or fell upon hard times, they could return but only after renouncing all their claims to the land.

For eight hundred years the Browns and their birds of prey flourished. Some said that the eagles and falcons kept the lands free of rats and other vermin so that even the village cats went hungry. So that when the deadly Black Death and its plague of rats ravaged the country it completely missed Puddlestree. Meanwhile the fertile soil proved bountiful yielding, year after year, disease free crops and good cattle. The grain fed man and beast throughout the year and the excess sold. In time the village had a blacksmith, thatchers, weavers, carpenters and builders who were encouraged to produce good work that would last centuries and indeed most have stood the test of time. A watermill produced flour of such a high quality that city traders purchased all that was offered for sale. Unlike many other noblemen, the Browns became popular as they wisely shared some of their wealth with the villagers. They built a chapel, a school to which they sent their own children alongside the village folk, and paid for a teacher, priest and village nurse. Even the village ponds were well stocked with fish and ducks, while geese patrolled the manor house's grounds. Of course the Lord of the Manor had the pick of the geese for Christmas and Easter feasts and the other old geese were shared among the villagers. It made a happy village where most people were well fed and content.

In time, many of the Norman Lords wed Saxon women often for their dowry, sometimes for love. For if the truth were known, the Lords had little money except what they earned from selling their harvests. In 1830 Jeremiah Brown a second son left to become a potter in Stoke selling fine chinaware from his The Boy on an Eagle Pottery. Later his elder son and daughter became potters, while the younger son Simon went to sea. Simon eventually became a merchant trading in everything from spices to slaves, from coal to gold. When he discovered the horrors of slavery it made him feel so sick that he sold every slave ship. It was a timely and popular move as it was just before slavery was abolished in 1833. Like many others Simon always found it difficult to morally differentiate between a slave and a bonded worker as both worked without pay and lacked freedom. The bondage of people mostly as payment of debt, his wife told him, was the work of the Devil even though she paid a pittance to her young maids who took care of her every need. For all her pious nature she never educated anyone though she made them attend church on Sundays and learn the liturgy. Maybe this was because she was illiterate and signed her name with a badly made cross.

Many Browns became priests or ordinary soldiers. Most were not rich enough to buy a commission to become an officer. A few soldiers were highly decorated and sociably acceptable, but most lived a quiet life. Like all families there were the dishonest ones. Jacob Brown had a brief, but spectacular career as a highwayman before being caught, sentenced and deported to Australia, where in time he became a respectable businessman. Mathew Brown joined the Honourable East India Company to make a fortune selling spices and jewels, some not his for the selling. No one ever proved his dishonesty partly because anyone who became too inquisitive was discretely paid off or disappeared. For the princely sum of a rupee any man could be made to vanish in a land where the Indian stranglers, the *Thugi*, successfully traded in death.

In 1880 Jonah Brown left The Boy on an Eagle Pottery to work in the growing south coast shipyards. He did not argue, drink, gamble, or have any vice except an ability to work eighteen hours a day, six days a week. After two years he purchased a house, married and in time taught his children to read and write. In 1886 Jonah's son Enoch Brown was born, who like all his children he taught to read, write and calculate. At fourteen the restless Enoch left home to join the army looking for excitement. Soon he stood out in any military parade as always having the shiniest boots and the best pressed uniform. His ability to read and write helped him rapidly progress from a Private to Regimental Sergeant Major in only ten years. Then he purchased a house in two acres of land in Hampshire near Eastleigh, married Elizabeth and together happily raised four children.

When in 1914 the Great War began RSM Enoch Brown kissed his dear wife Elizabeth goodbye as he went to do his duty for King and Country. As if it was perfectly normal Enoch happily embarked with his men on a paddle steamer to cross the Channel to go off to war to fight against Germany in the fields of France. He was not afraid of anything because he believed that he was invincible unless the bullet had his name on it, and then all the pain would be over. Officer or no officers, Enoch was in charge of his men and come hell and high water would never let them down. He was their father, priest and leader to be followed through gunfire and mayhem without question and they loyally did. Those men who survived the bloody slaughter on the Somme followed Enoch first to Mesopotamia and then to India. When the war ended many of the survivors went to Ireland where the war for an Irish Free State still raged.

# 2

## Memories

"Before a midnight breaks in storm,
Or herded sea in wrath,
Ye know what wavering gusts inform
The greater tempest's path;
Till the loosed wind
Drives all from mind,
Except Distress, which, so will prophets cry,
O'ercame them, houseless, from the unhinting sky."
**Rudyard Kipling, "Dedication".**[4]

Early one morning Bert was woken up by the sounds of thunder coupled with the smell of burning, as smoke filled his bedroom and red and yellow lights danced on the walls. Very worried, he looked out of the window to watch, like a moth trapped in the light, the smoke and sparks rising from an old apple tree near the house. As the fire devoured the sap juices it began to slowly die down, helped by the effects of the heavy rain. Soon he saw that all that remained of the once magnificent tree was a smouldering trunk that occasionally sent sparks harmlessly high up into the air.

It was a sobering thought that in minutes the well loved tree had been turned into a dead trunk barren of its former glory. Was this what war was like? Was it an omen of the future? Maybe it was a reminder of the hell his father was in fighting in the trenches? Bert was never a very religious man, but he made the sign of the cross and prayed for all those in peril wherever they may be. Then he put on his dressing gown to go downstairs where his two sisters and brother were staring through the kitchen window at the burning tree. They were excited and a bit scared at what they saw.

'Good Morning Bert, that lightning was a bit too close for comfort. A few feet closer it would have struck the house and heaven knows what would have happened,' Joyce, his eldest sister said cuddling the two younger children.

'It wasn't that bad, but it did wake me up,' commented Bert with a smile.

'Don't you think someone should go outside to see if anything is burning?'

'Well as the man of the house I'll go. I expect we're alright, but better safe than sorry.'

'Thanks Bert. I'm worried the fire will spread to the house,' Joyce answered relieved that she did not have to venture out into the rain. She always relied on Bert to do the things she didn't want to do in a house with no adults. It wasn't that she was fussy or arrogant. It was simply that since their mother's death and father being away at war she felt that Bert as the eldest should play his part as man in the house. Anyway she knew that Bert liked the role of being the strong man who kept the family together even though he was legally only a child.

Once outside, the only damage Bert found was a small bit of paint on the kitchen door scorched by the heat from the smouldering tree. So all he could do was watch as the rain extinguished the fire. At intervals he noticed that from inside the tree came a few sparks that rose into the sky as the fire gradually died. Then he returned to tell the others they were safe when satisfied the danger was over,

'There's nothing to worry about. The old tree is just smouldering and soon the remaining fire will die.'

'Thanks Bert. Do you want your breakfast now or at the normal time?' asked Joyce.

'I'm going to get some more sleep and will eat later, thank you,' Bert replied as he started to walk up the stairs to go to bed.

The fire reminded Bert of the nights when the silent German Zeppelin bombed the nearby Southampton and Portsmouth docks. Then the sky was filled with columns of black smoke mixed with flashes of red and orange flames. No one heard those cigar-shaped airships come or see them go. It was rumoured that a Zeppelin was shot down by an aircraft of the Royal Flying Corps – but no one knew for certain. This war was different to the previous ones as it had reached England. Now there was no safety for civilians as the conflict consumed all in its path. Whether on purpose, or by accident, most of the Zeppelin bombs missed the dockyards to fall on residential areas. The economic damage was small but it destroyed many homes and terrorised the local community. In a twinkle of an eye innocent women and children asleep in their beds were burned to dust, just casualties of modern total war.

They say when talking about the weather that March comes in like a lion and goes out like a lamb. On 18th March 1906 Enoch's first child Herbert, usually shortened to Bert, was born during a violent storm at home in the Hampshire town of Eastleigh. The young Bert had a happy childhood as he was well fed, clothed and cared for by loving parents. During those early years life was a round of doing simple chores, playing football, and trudging to and from school. Sadly, when he was only twelve his Mother Elizabeth died while Father was away at war. Bert and Joyce found themselves having to grow up fast or else all of the family would be put into an orphanage. They vowed to stay together to run the home as well as any adults, hoping to be left alone. Somehow they looked after each other so that to all onlookers the family thrived. However they missed Mother's gentle touch and soft voice, her kindness, and above all her optimism – for even when she knew she was dying she smiled. She had taught them all to sew on a button, repair and iron their clothes and above all how to cook. Every Sunday she had taken them as a family to church and when Bert took his first communion she gave him a silver cross that he always wore around his neck. Instinctively when in danger, or just in need of love, he would touch the cross to feel her near him. Not only was Bert her son in flesh and blood but he also had her intelligence and spirit living inside him. Above all she gave Bert a deep sense of what was right and what was wrong that helped him throughout his life. Mother instilled into all her children a belief in God, the King and above all of loyalty.

Mother was well educated and so taught her children to read, write and do sums so that they did well at school. In her spare time she played the upright piano in the sitting room, sometimes to amuse her children, to accompany them singing, or to escape into her own private world. Sometimes she taught the children to play the piano with various degrees of success. Her best student was Bert, while Joyce who had a lovely voice could not play a note. Mother also explained to them that the family crest said that the eagle was the king of the skies and one day a Brown would be that child sitting on an eagle soaring through the sky. Many years later Bert could say that the ancient dream had come true when he flew in an aeroplane like the boy riding on Guy de Broyen's eagle. It is surprising how ancient ideas have a habit in time becoming a reality. Like a loyal Brown everywhere he lived a copy of the family shield of The Boy on an Eagle was displayed above the fireplace in Bert's sitting room. It was both his connection with the past as well as an omen for the future that he desperately sought.

Bert enjoyed playing the piano and dutifully learned each composition note by note including the Tchaikovsky Piano Concerto Number 1 in B flat minor, which he played to professional standards. Probably because, when he played the piano he remembered Mother, he used a delicate touch that enthralled his audience. Whenever he played Tchaikovsky he found an inner peace and happiness. Even in old age he could remember every note. When he listened to Tchaikovsky's 1812 overture it removed all bad thoughts from his mind. It left him relaxed and at the same time feeling excited. He revelled in the composer's brilliance at portraying all of the City of Moscow's bells ringing and the canons firing in celebration as Napoleon's army retreated from the captured city harassed by the Russian army. It was a joyous celebration of unexpected victory that signalled both the saving of Moscow and the beginning of the end of the rule of Emperor Napoleon. When listening to the end of the music Bert saw people cheering their soldiers as they returned home knowing that they were free. This was inspirational. It produced within Bert a feeling that made him thankful for all the good things in life.

For many years after Mother's death they only knew that Father was alive because they received payments from the Paymaster General's office. A letter from Father was so rare that it was read out loud many times to absorb every precious word before being placed carefully in the sideboard. Father never said where he was or what was happening; only that he sent his love to them all and told them to be strong. Probably the censor did not allow him to say anymore. When Mother died Father simply wrote telling Bert to look after everyone until he returned. The next born Joyce became their mother by running the home, caring for the younger brother Henry and the baby of the family her sister Olive. Somehow they all survived without an adult though the food was not very appetising or the clothes of good quality – but they never asked for charity. However as they had been taught by Mother that it was a sin to be proud, they accepted gifts from friends and neighbours of old clothing, homemade cakes or vegetables from their gardens. While in their back garden were fruit trees and a large vegetable patch with potatoes, peas, leeks, carrots, cabbages, runner beans, marrows and rhubarb. Everyone helped dig the ground, sow the seeds and when they were mature uproot the potatoes and carrots or pick the peas. No visitor to their house would ever know that no adult lived there or visited as it always looked neat and tidy. With Joyce's good cooking they were all healthy in all seasons - though some might say a bit on the thin side. Often after school and at weekends, Bert did odd jobs for neighbours to earn extra money. This was used to repair their shoes and most importantly to have strawberry jam thickly spread on bread on Sundays after church. Winter was hard as they had to buy everything except for the potatoes and apples stored in the attic. When the ice was thick on the ground and the house cold they gathered in the kitchen to keep warm by huddling around the stove. Some nights they all slept together fully clothed and wrapped in as many blankets as they could find. It was probably unhygienic but warm and helped the children bond together like glued paper.

Sundays were family days and the time to rest. At dawn, the old metal bath was filled with warm water that was boiled on the kitchen stove, for their weekly bath. The two girls always bathed first while the boys waited. Bert and Henry had to share the water by standing up in the metal tub which was just big enough for a large baby. Still they enjoyed it. Then the bath water was thrown on to the garden before they dressed in their Sunday best clothes to walk to Church. Once inside the church, while singing and praying to God, they were never far from the horrors of War. During every service the vicar read out the names of the members of the congregation who had died and to pray for their immortal souls. Sometimes the list was short, but it was long after another great battle in some foreign field. Then the whole congregation cried out in torment praying for God to save the souls of their departed loved ones.

For the Brown family life was a continual rush from one place to another with never a dull moment or time to moan. All around them a growing number of widows wore black, while working hard to keep their families united and healthy. No one was ever heard to complain about their lot, only occasionally about the weather. Everywhere one looked there were mainly women of all ages and children to be seen as the only men around worked in the docks or factories, or were too old or sick to fight. So the church was filled by people praying that their trials and tribulations would soon pass as does the winter snows and storms. It was a time when that killer called poverty stalked the land and yet when asked, everyone denied they were poor. Though to tell the truth when fed at school or during a church lunch they would, like Oliver Twist, ask for more.

At fourteen, Bert started as an apprentice at the London and South Western Railways Eastleigh (LSWR) Works along with Dominic Falcon whose father ran the local garage, Tim Watkins from Eastleigh, and Fred James from Chandler's Ford. They all started by making tea for the older men and fetching the tools, materials and anything that was required. Here they were well treated and even the Trades Union officials left them alone while harassing the older workers to pay their dues. The LSWR Works was a closed shop where only union members could be employed even for the most menial task. The possession of the Union card gave the worker the right of representation during industrial disputes and promised them all financial assistance if they became unemployed. Some used to say that the unions collected money for the Communist Party to start a revolution in Britain, but there was never any proof. In fact it was just a continuation of the ancient guilds that had existed for centuries to protect skilled men from being exploited by the rich.

At fifteen, Bert learned carpentry by working on the coachwork of the carriages before graduating two years later to the iron foundry to learn how to cast molten metal into moulds. The castings varied from small metal rods, to links and joints, and to the large wagon wheels and their heavy axles. Then he learned how to cut metal sheets, bend them and rivet them together. This involved hammering white hot rivets into the holes cut in to the sheets. A skilled riveter made all his rivets form a straight line of the same shape and only slightly raised above the metal's surface. When each piece of work was finished it was inspected by the supervisor. If the work was rejected as being done badly they were severely reprimanded or had their meagre salaries reduced. So everyone tried to produce work of the highest standard so as never to have to redo anything. This emphasis on the highest quality of everything he worked on stayed with Bert all his life to make him an excellent engineer. One thing that he never forgot was when a careless workmate lost his hand when cutting steel sheets with the very sharp guillotine. It was not the sight of so much blood that was shocking so much as it was an unnecessary mutilation. The guillotine had a safety grill to pull down before operating the cutting blade. However to save time many workers left the grill up and cut a few more sheets than before. But was it too great a price to pay for a few extra sheets? For days afterwards Bert found himself brooding over the incident and swearing that if he was ever in charge of any men working in dangerous conditions he would sack anyone who took risks.

Life in the metal works was hard and the fellow workers were a tough breed of men who fought over any trifle. What made life bearable was that the foremen knew who the unruly men were and if they misbehaved too often, they were fined or dismissed as another bad egg and soon forgotten. While working there Bert learned to defend his corner and keep his nose out of other people's business. By nineteen he was five foot eight and muscular with a tendency to readily get into fights, something that Mother would never have approved. However his cheerful nature and willingness to do any task, however small, without objection made him very popular among his friends and colleagues. One of his supervisors commented that Bert was a treasure because he was hard working, learned new techniques quickly and above all inspired others to be proud of their workmanship. He then added that Bert was one of the best examples of a Master Craftsman who developed his skills by innovation and genuine inventiveness. The supervisor assessed

Bert as an apprentice who showed signs of becoming famous. Indeed he would succeed where so many others had failed to develop new engineering techniques.

He earned extra money by doing errands for the neighbours, especially the young widow Doris who was trying to raise her new born baby without a husband. Bert liked her cheerfulness as well as her lovely long blonde hair and brilliant dancing blue eyes. In fact he was in love with her and would do anything she asked. Inevitably the day came when Bert saw her sitting in the lounge feeding her baby from her full breasts. She told him to stay as she knew that he was mesmerised by her and liked being admired by a handsome young man. So after putting her baby back into the cot she kissed Bert fully on the lips while putting his hand on her naked breast. He had never felt so good or so confused.

'You're so beautiful,' he stammered.

'Shush! I need you to love me as much as you need me. Just like Eve was made for Adam I am here for you,' Doris softly whispered in his ear.

Bert was lost in an exciting new world in which friends became lovers. It was gentle at first until he learned how to satisfy her and at the same time to feel fulfilled. Their love lasted for over a year until she met and fell in love with the local butcher Wilfred. When Bert heard that Doris had married Wilfred, he was glad someone would look after her and the child, but inside felt a deep sense of loss. He would always remember his first love dear Doris for her kindness, generosity and above all for showing him how powerful and beautiful a woman's love could be. Doris had shown Bert that if he was to be complete he had to work hard, save as much as he could and then when he could afford his own house he would marry. He knew that he was not in a hurry to start a family but sometime wanted a son to keep the family name alive. First he wanted to become famous or rich or at least have money in a bank. Was that too much to ask for in life? He hoped not but was very aware that others would place obstacles in his way out of jealousy or sheer spite. It did not bother Bert as he was going to succeed if only for his own pride. He found engineering exciting but was not sure that building trains and their carriages gave him a big enough challenge. Still it would pay the bills until he found something more suitable and stimulating. Of course he hoped that Father would soon return from Ireland and run the house again. Then Bert would be free to explore life when no longer being the main wage earner and only man about the house.

# 3

## Ireland and Partition

Two nations divided by history and misunderstandings.

Like many other British soldiers Father did not return home after the war but went to fight and try to maintain peace in a troubled Ireland, where a large independence movement was gaining ground. He found his time there very difficult as there were no identifiable enemy to fight, only large numbers of irregulars on both sides without uniforms and looking like any normal peaceful civilian. For hundreds of years the Irish had tried to expel their British rulers to be free to rule themselves. Then during the First World War the republican Sir Roger Casement who had helped form the Irish Volunteers obtained support for the movement from Britain's enemy Germany[5]. He returned to Ireland at night from a German submarine U-19 on 21st April 1916 to be arrested, tried for treason and hanged. He was unaware that the Irish Republican Brotherhood (IRB) together with the Irish Volunteers and Irish Citizen Army was going to attack Dublin castle on Easter Monday 24th April. They did and for the next seven days the Republicans armed mostly with rifles and pistols held the Post Office and nearby buildings against massive British attacks. Eventually the brief uprising was put down but only after some five hundred British Army and Police were wounded or killed against up to two thousand five hundred Irish fighters and civilians supporters. Afterwards the British arrested three thousand five hundred Irish men and women just for being Republicans of which ninety were condemned to death for treason. In the end fifteen men were executed by firing squad including Patrick Pearse, Joseph Plunkett and James Connolly who had signed the Proclamation of the Republic that had been read out on the steps of the Post Office on 24th April. Other signatories such as the American Éamon de Valera avoided execution because they were not regarded as British citizens and therefore not punishable for treason. The severity of the British response only encouraged the feelings of the people for some degree of independence.

The Irish Independence movement grew to win the majority of the Irish seats in the 1918 general election. Afterwards at a meeting in the Mansion House in Dublin they secretly set up their own government called the Dáil. The former republican Irish Volunteers became the Irish Republican Army under Richard Mulcathy who continued to fight the British. Soon they were reorganised and led by Michael Collins[6,7], while the political movement in the Dáil was led by the eloquent American Éamon de Valera[8,9,10]. The British ruling government were supported by the mainly Catholic Royal Irish Constabulary (RIC) and the protestant northerners. The situation came to a head when de Valera prematurely declared Ireland independent in January 1919 effectively ending any negotiations. Then to support the RIC, Britain unwisely recruited units of ex-soldiers known as the Black and Tans. Within a matter of weeks the ruthless actions of the Black and Tans and some members of the RIC alienated the majority of the Irish population. So the British had no alternative other than to arrest and execute some of their own people for murdering innocent civilians, though many escaped unpunished. The fact that many Black and Tans operated freely outside the law was a major mistake that increased the popular support for the IRA. The British then responded by passing the Government of Ireland Act in 1920 setting up one parliament in Northern Ireland and the other in the South. Nobody accepted this solution so the Pro-British James Craig on an official visit to Dublin, secretly met Éamon de Valera to settle the conflict. The two men had so little in common that the meeting proved fruitless. So the fighting continued until a settlement was drawn up in London. It divided Ireland into the southern Republican Irish Free State consisting of twenty-six counties and the much smaller northern

Ulster or Northern Ireland formed from only six counties. Then all sides reluctantly agreed to the settlement and the fighting calmed down. Having signed the agreement Michael Collins took over as Chairman of the Provisional Government and Head of the Irish National Army. Then there started a different conflict as Collins' group became effectively at war with the anti-Treaty IRA headed by de Valera.

It was during this time that Enoch Brown was stationed near the new border to guard the railway linking Belfast to Dublin. It was normally a quiet duty since the civil war appeared to be over and Michael Collins was due to take over running the Irish Free State and arrange with the Ulstermen in the north to agree on the actual borders. The conflict nearly over, the number of men on guard duty was reduced as no one expected any trouble. One night when the wind blew squalls of rain so hard that it soaked Father to the skin, he decided to shelter under the bridge. Though he was alone he knew that he could see anyone approaching the bridge and lay back to rest, maybe he started to sleep. Then he heard the sounds of people walking nearby. After rubbing his eyes he saw twenty yards away two men placing dynamite against the bridge supports. Immediately he raised his rifle to the firing position prepared to shoot.

'Stop what you're doing and put your hands up or I will fire,' Enoch shouted out.

There was no answer. Then the older man shot Enoch in the left arm as he fired back hitting the man in the leg. As Enoch reloaded his rifle and bound his wounded arm, the injured man escaped into the night abandoning his companion, a young lad to his fate.

'Dear Holy Virgin Mary Mother of God I beg you to save me,' cried out the boy kneeling as tears streamed down his face. Through the rain he saw Enoch approach and expected to die or at least be arrested.

Enoch knew that he should arrest the boy for attempted sabotage knowing it meant the lad would be sentenced to death by firing squad. He did not like what he had to do even though his arm hurt, so he just stood there with his rifle pointing at the lad. Would letting him escape be treason or just showing some humanity where normally there was so little?

'Why are you trying to blow up the bridge, maybe to kill people in a train especially now that peace has come?' Enoch asked the lad bewildered at what was happening.

'Patrick the older man told me that Ireland expected us to blow up the train along with all the bloody Ulstermen and British negotiators going to finalise the peace settlement in Dublin castle,' the boy replied; bowing his head in shame.

'Thank God it was me that stopped you being a murderer. For that is what you nearly became. So bugger off as fast as you can before I change my mind and decide to do my duty by arresting you. Remember never listen to murderers and try to live a good life helping others,' Enoch said giving the lad a gentle slap on his head.

'God bless you sir,' the lad said running away to disappear into the night. All the way home he thanked the Holy Mary for his deliverance and not once dared look back.

When his duty was finished, Enoch Brown reported shooting the older man and handed over the dynamite while forgetting to mention any lad. Two weeks later Ireland was divided into the southern Republican Irish Free State and the smaller northern British Northern Ireland, sometimes called Ulster. Like most soldiers he forgot the whole nasty incident under the bridge except when his left arm hurt. Now all he did was count the days until he would be demobbed and return home. It was a strange time for there were fewer regular British soldiers on the new border since most had been replaced by soldiers from both sides. While waiting Enoch spent his last few days in Ireland going for walks and having the occasional drink at a friendly local pub. It was in the pub that a handsome man in his twenties, wearing the uniform of a captain of the new Irish Free State Army came and sat by his side. Officially they were at peace so there was no reason why they should not be friendly.

'Am I right in thinking that you maybe the same Sergeant Enoch Brown who stopped some silly people blowing up the nearby border railway bridge?' the captain inquired softly without any malice in his voice.

'Yes sir I'm he,' Enoch replied wondering what was going to happen considering the war was over. 'I hope that I did not cause you any offense, but I was only doing my duty.'

'There's no need to be alarmed as you did the right thing. Sergeant Brown it's a privilege to meet you. I'm Captain Liam Gallagher ex-IRA and now in the Irish Free State Army. That night by the bridge you did me a great service by not arresting my younger brother. He had been misled by a stupid man who wanted the war to continue. Sadly there are still many who want war and back Éamon de Valera against my Commander-in-Chief Michael Collins. So I've come here tonight to thank you for your humanity in saving the lad's life and can tell you he will always remember your kindness. We Irish can always tell a good man from the way he walks and talks to others and so I see that you are such a man,' Liam Gallagher said.

Liam smiled firmly shaking Enoch's hand.

'I don't kill lads if I can help it, sir,' a very surprised Enoch Brown replied.

'Thank God for that. We need more people like you over here to help keep the peace we all greatly need. Please let me know if there's anything I can do for you before you leave or if you ever return to the Emerald Isle. I am sure you know that we Irish are a proud lot who stay loyal to our friends and know how to say thank you.'

'I am glad we're at last at peace and can go our own ways. Maybe we have a chance to prosper as friends rather than enemies,' Enoch added.

'I hope so. De Valera's men wanted to blow up a train full of Ulstermen and their British escorts. They were travelling to Dublin to discuss the implementation of the peace treaty and if they had died we would be back fighting each over. Thanks to you the Ulstermen went and returned safely. Again thank you for being such a decent man, indeed for stopping a tragedy,' Liam replied.

'Captain Gallagher there is no need to thank me as I only did what I thought was right. Anyway after all these years of fighting around the world I'm very tired of war and the killing. So let's be friends and toast to peace for all.'

'That would be nice, but I insist you call me Liam as everyone else does and may I call you Enoch. Indeed I'm glad to join you in the toast but first let me buy us a real Irish drink,' Liam commented. Then he turned to the barmaid to order a bottle of the finest Bushmills whiskey and two glasses. Within a minute their glasses were full with that fine Irish spirit.

'Peace to all people,' Enoch said lifting his glass.

'Peace to you my friend Enoch and to all people,' Liam responded to be joined by all the people in the pub. Everyone wanted peace to raise their families without fear, hoping that the new treaty would give them all hope for a better future.

The two men talked for a while before Captain Liam Gallagher said 'goodnight' to walk out of Enoch Brown's life. However Liam was never far away and secretly made sure no one bothered Enoch. Two weeks later Enoch left Ireland on a ship to Southampton together with the few remaining members of his regiment to be demobilised. Only when the ship entered Southampton water did Enoch worry about what lay ahead. Would he get a job? How would his children react to his presence and could he cope with civilian life after all those years in uniform? Only time would tell.

# 4

## War Heroes Return to Unemployment

"If England was what England seems,
An' not the England of our dreams,
But only putty, brass, an' paint,
'Ow quick we'd chuck 'er! But she ain't."
**Rudyard Kipling, "The Return"**[11]

Long after the last bullet was fired the British soldiers started to return home. Talk of war was replaced with hope of a new world where everyone was equal even though they knew it took time for the effects of peace to be felt at home. Even then many soldiers were transferred to Ireland or to distant parts of the Empire. Demobilisation involved being transported to England, surrendering all weapons and uniforms before receiving one's final pay, mass produced civilian clothes, train ticket and allowed home. Once completed the old warriors had to leave barracks and never return, unless invited. Most returned to try to find work as civilians. A few were kept in the smaller peacetime army dispersed throughout the Empire or remained in Britain for mainly ceremonial duties[5].

In October 1922 Bert's father, Sergeant Enoch, came home from Ireland. He was shorter than Bert remembered and much more serious. In fact Bert was a full four inches taller than Father but not as solidly built. Father was not fat but solid meat and bone, neat and tidy with the looks of a prize fighter entering the boxing ring. After being demobbed he made straightaway for home without telling anyone that he was returning. It was one of his many mistakes as he should have at least written. So Enoch arrived on the doorstep of his home standing in his demobilisation suit and knocked firmly on the door.

The door opened to reveal Bert in overalls having just returned from work.

'Hello Bert. My God you've grown,' Enoch stated with a magnificent smile.

'Father?' a surprised Bert commented.

Enoch just nodded.

'Come in. Pardon the mess but we weren't expecting you. If only you had written to say that you were returning home.'

'Sorry son, I should have at least written,' Enoch stated as Bert carried his small suitcase into the house.

In seconds Father was surrounded by his children and enjoying every second. The house seemed different without his dear wife but it was tidy and well run.

Soon it was clear that he had a tendency to demand too much and often descend into a world of his own. However the children were wise enough to accept his behaviour and learn to live together as a family without Mother to keep the peace.

At first Bert found Father difficult as nobody had warned him about the effects war has on men. Father was older and frailer than Bert remembered and only strong enough to work as a railway porter. Slowly Bert discovered that Father was wounded in the right leg while fighting on the Somme, lost an eye in Mesopotamia and had recently been shot in his left arm while serving in Ireland. Enoch was a man who never complained and carried on life as best he could. Unless you looked very closely you could not see that he was disabled. When he turned his head to look left he moved it more than a normal sighted man for he had only one good eye, the left one was made of glass. When it was very cold he walked with a limp with his left arm hanging loosely down. However every morning, whatever the weather, Father got up with a smile rejoicing at being alive and greeting all his children with a simple Good Morning.

Five days a week Father worked hard. Only on Friday night did he go to the Army Club. A drink of bitter with fellow ex-soldiers followed with a game of draughts was his idea of a good time. It was always only the one drink, never any more, then back to the house within two hours. Unfortunately, Enoch was a strict disciplinarian who demanded everything done exactly as he wanted. In his room he was surrounded by souvenirs, such as sword-like bayonets, medals, pictures of him in uniform surrounded by his sergeants. His shoes had to be polished to a fine shine and his trousers immaculately pressed with creases down the middle. Even his oak rocking chair was placed by the fireplace next to a side table holding his tobacco pouch and a pipe. To be fair, everyone now had better clothes and more food and he let Bert keep some of his earnings. Sometimes the memory of the burning tree reminded Bert that Father was a changed man – who in time gradually recovered his sense of humour. Father was again the head of the family while Bert remained his loyal right hand man. Bert secretly hoped Father would marry again or have a lover, but instead he kept Mother's picture by his bed to grieve in silence. Every now and then, especially when bolts of lightning and the accompanying roar of thunder filled the skies, Father descended into a depression as if transported back into war. Once when half-asleep in his rocking chair Father cried out 'Dear Jesus, stop this slaughter. We can't take any more.' Then his body shook, as if he had been struck by something, to wake up looking very old and vulnerable.

The second memorial Poppy Day was observed on the third anniversary of Armistice Day, 11th November 1922. In Eastleigh, as across the whole Empire, people gathered around war memorials in a Service of Remembrance and exactly at the stroke of 11 am stood silently for two minutes. From that year forth Father usually accompanied by his children attended the Remembrance Day parade proudly wearing his campaign medals. Only when the lone trumpet sounded The Last Post did he show any emotion as he could not help but shed a tear for his many fallen comrades.

One night, when all the others were asleep, Father talked to Bert about things that worried him such as the war, vanity and racism.

'Bert nothing prepares you for war when at any moment one's life may be extinguished and the only thing keeping you alive is your rifle and fellow soldiers. Never let anyone tell you war is full of glory and brave men saving the world from the evil ambitions of others. Alas dear son, it's never so simple. The Great War was fought because the leaders were unable to discuss their differences. What they needed was a good father to bang their heads together until they saw sense. Unfortunately none existed. So for five long years we fought just for national pride. Too many men needlessly died capturing some useless piece of land that was too often lost.'

Father took a few puffs from his pipe as he contemplated what to say and then, with his eyes half closed as if reliving the conflict, he continued.

'War is the Devil's work where death, torment and pain lurk behind every door and smoke filled cloud. We were led to believe that our officers knew best and would lead us to victory while protecting us from our enemies. Unfortunately most were just young men that were either not properly trained or too inexperienced in trench warfare. So we were ordered to dig miles of trenches while our officers looked at badly drawn maps before moving us like toys against an enemy we should have easily destroyed. We either never attacked in strength or were not supported when we did capture the enemy fortifications. All too often our upper class young officers armed with a whistle and pistol were easily identified so that the enemy marksmen shot them first. Conditions in the trenches varied a lot depending on how they were built and the weather. The best were dry and lined with sand bags and wood to protect us from the enemy fire. The bad ones were muddy hollows filled with water and infested with rats. Many of the trenches were only separated by a hundred yards from the enemy positions. The artillery bombarded the enemy to destroy their defences before we attacked, but it also warned them we were coming. As soon as the guns stopped firing we climbed out of our trenches to walk through that hundred yards across No Man's Land. This was a terrible time as we always came under heavy enemy fire often loosing half our men before we had gone a few yards. I learned to ignore the orders to walk tall and instead made my men keep low while running at a decent trot through the mud, riddled with bomb craters and the remains of both men and animals.'

Bert was spellbound by his Father's words that were so different to the images of heroes walking through fire to capture the enemy as portrayed in most books and the newspapers. Father stopped to relight his pipe and gather his thoughts.

'Son, promise me that you'll never consider anyone, whatever his race or creed, as being beneath you. During the Great War I fought with many a good foreigner such as the French, Indians and Africans. They all fought hard and were the best of brothers in those horrific seas of blood. If anyone should be bitter it is those Indians and Africans forced by their colonial masters to fight in a White Man's war. I pray all that survived will live a happy life, never to be used again in another European war where kings are protected from their folly by us like pawns in a deadly game of chess.'

'From what you say we should ask them to forgive us for making them fight for our flawed nationalism,' Bert solemnly replied.

Father took out of his pocket a bright deep green stone set in a gold ring that he pushed onto Bert's small finger of his left hand.

'Wear this jade ring to protect you from harm. It is from that part of India they call Burma and given to me by a saffron robed Buddhist priest for saving him from a Bengal tiger. It was no great act of bravery on my part, for if I hadn't shot the fierce beast he would have attacked me. The priest said that when I returned home I must give this ring to my eldest son to protect him from the evil dogs of war. So I give it to you to fulfil my promise but hope that you may never experience the hell that is war. Maybe the Buddhists are correct that one should not kill any animal, especially man, nor eat of his flesh.'

'Are you saying we should not have beef for Sunday lunch? If so then I had better warn Joyce,' Bert ventured curious to find out how Father felt.

'Good God no thank you! I don't share the idea of eating nothing but plants. In fact I love my roast beef served up with Yorkshire pudding, roast potatoes, Brussels sprouts and horseradish sauce,' he responded with a hearty laugh.

Bert said nothing but was relieved that Father still had the same appetite for good English cooking. Then he thought that maybe for his birthday he would get a brace of well hung pheasant that Father had always loved. They were cheap enough if he got them from a local poacher he knew from school.

It was a Saturday night and so they spent most of it talking in a way they had never done before. Father believed that if all people served a forgiving God such as Jesus or Buddha the world would be a haven of peace. In his opinion, only when the rich valued the poor and all greed was relegated to the rubbish dump could this happen. Goodness and peace does not come from war or revolution, but from the willingness of all men to live as brothers.

The poppy of Flanders fields became the symbol of remembrance because of a poem " In Flanders fields the poppies blow between the crosses, row on row" by the Canadian, John McRae[12]. The poppies first appeared after the shelling and fighting stopped. It was as if out of the horrors of war came forth peace because the beauty of the red poppies would last forever. The sight of a battlefield covered in poppies when seen could never be forgotten.

Britain had too many serious wounds that no medicine alone could heal. Ex-soldiers were bitter at not being hailed as heroes when the government did not know how to employ or receive their men returning home from hell. Over eighty thousand combatants suffered from mental problems, dizziness, insomnia, and inexplicable paralysis that was together called Shell Shock. Many had lost one or more limbs while others were blinded from the clouds of Mustard gas that engulfed whole trenches. This chemical poison destroyed the linings of the lungs reducing once strong men to mere shadows of their former selves. When the war was over and the allies had won, no one cared about those who had fought. Many had been conscripts who were quickly trained then forced to fight in conditions from Dante's Inferno. Conscription won the war but it sent men to foreign lands from which many never returned and those who did were changed forever. Some scars were physical, while people's minds were tormented by what they had seen or done. Nobody was prepared to see a friend blown to pieces or climb through fields of mud strewn with parts of man and animals. The worst was the sounds of the injured in No Man's Land crying for help while hoping to die. Or perhaps it was the smell of Mustard gas and the shaking of the ground as shells burst all around. It is said that you never forget the faces of those you killed. Their eyes always stare at you.

It was a time of enormous changes where old regimes disappeared as a reaction to the destruction caused by the Great War. Many watched as Vladimir Lenin's Bolshevik Revolution swept across Russia empowering the workers and destroying the aristocracy. Many thought the pro-Tsarist White Russian Army would defeat the socialist forces but they failed as the huge Red Army mercilessly defeated all opposition. The fear of a Russian Type workers' revolution made the frightened British government pass the Emergency Powers Act authorising the use troops to maintain essential services in the event of civil unrest and strikes. Many ignorant politicians and the thoughtless rich feared that their loyal workers were planning a revolution that would endanger their privileged positions. The feelings became so deep that even the wealthiest families became divided, as many of their sons returning from war rebelled against the old ways and wanted change. If the Great War did any good it was to teach the mighty, the rich and the arrogant that the poor also bled and died the same as they did.

Only a few ex-soldiers returned to their pre-war lifestyles as they had changed. The shortage of fit men meant that large country estates never again had so many servants. Some had died in the trenches and others did not wish to go into service. For many calling someone 'Sir' was unacceptable so they pronounced the word to sound more insulting as 'Cur'. Gone was the arrogance of the old moneyed aristocracy as both Lords and Ladies learned to tie their own shoelaces or, heaven forbid, had to dress themselves without help. Of course there remained the old trusted servant who was too old to fight and so never changed his or her ways. However, a well-trained butler, cook or lady's maid became someone to cherish or pay well enough to stay on. For a few years, they were better treated but never allowed to get above their lowly station, while keeping the households running with as little interference from their masters as they could manage. Meanwhile the rich masters were busy hunting, gambling, or living the high life while many of their loyal wives remained at home sewing or attending social gatherings.

It was not long before the countryside again resounded to the traditional sound of the hunter's horn. Then packs of fox hounds followed by the red jacketed gentry on horseback chased the elusive red fox. The excitement of the chase and the killing of the fox re-enforced their status as rulers. It was made heinous by the ancient rite of rubbing the fox's blood on the faces of the children to make them accept and even enjoy blood sports. In many ways the red foxes and their hunters were equally ruthless. Sadly when some ex-soldiers refused to go hunting they were told to grow up and stop feeling sorry for themselves. It was a reminder that those who have never seen war cannot understand the feeling of those who have and sadly do not want to.

One would like to think that the old fashioned, heartless society suddenly was replaced by an understanding generation, one that did not forget the sacrifices of others. Unfortunately as unemployment grew and the poor desperately needed work the old ways crept back. Then even the slightest error by an employee was met with thunderous retribution by the employer as if a murder had taken place. Often the master of the household would say to his servants, 'If you don't like it here you can always leave. You and I both know that there are many others who would like to do your job. So don't let me hear any more of your pathetic complaints and do your work as I direct.'

Now the rich enjoyed all that money could buy while the poor suffered. It was only by the grace of God that they survived the rightful wrath of the masses. Many of the wealthy lived a life of sheer debauchery often carefully hidden behind well closed doors. What the butlers saw was secret as all around them history repeated itself. The rich and powerful behaved with the same excesses that only a century before had cost the lives of their cousins, the French nobility. In fact the idle rich had nothing to fear since all that the workers needed was a job to earn enough money to feed their families.

It was a time when Britain descended into the evil world described by Charles Dickens. Men peddled matchboxes to earn a penny while cripples begged for alms or polished shoes for a pittance. As things became worse, people sold everything they owned including their hard won medals and wedding rings. The growing number of pawnbroker's shops paid a few pence for items worth ten times as much, while the ruthless banks and moneylenders grew richer. The idea that the Jews were to blame was used by the fascists to encourage the poor and ignorant to join their cause. It was not long before many an ermined lord and lady openly supported fascism as a defence against communism and a method of retaining their class privileges. Steadily the hatred of all foreigners and banks increased to dangerous levels that endangered the stability of the state. For just a few pounds anyone could arrange for a rival to be beaten, his business burned, and him left dying in the gutter. So the tough and the ruthless removed most of their competitors or took what they wanted as ruthless capitalists exploited the nation.

The Christian doctrine of love and caring for each other disappeared except on Sundays and even then the powerful sat in the best pews in church while the others sat behind them. Now the spectre of the Mosley's Blackshirts and fascism with all its xenophobia grew. In 1939 the fascists invaded their neighbours to start the turmoil that is total war, death and the loss of freedom.

# 5

## The Age of Motorcycles

There is absolutely nothing so exciting or so exhilarating
as riding my motorbike fast though long winding roads.
The breeze washes away the cobwebs that cloud my mind.
Then I am alive, to feel clean and full of hope everlasting.

Bert forgot about The Boy on an Eagle as he learned about repairing
and riding a motorcycle. In fact he never for one minute thought he
would fly or have anything to do with aircraft. Now was the time that
he like all great people had to learn and grow the same way that a small
acorn becomes a mighty oak tree. However he would do anything to
gain experience, qualifications and improve his lowly status.

His first motorbike was an ex-army Norton he reconditioned at
Jack Falcon's garage. At the back of the garage was Falcon's scrap yard
that contained hundreds of unwanted vehicles, mostly left over from
the war. Most were in good condition and saleable, the others were
gradually cannibalised for spare parts. If you had the time, the cash, and
the ability you could buy whatever you wanted. It was the time when
some pilots bought two ex-fighter planes, one to fly and the other for
spare parts. If you had the money you could legally buy most ex-army
equipment ranging from tents of all sizes to ships, army boots to rifles,
tin hats to bayonets, guns with ammunition, and pistols at a time when
there was no effective gun regulation. This was partly because most

rural people traditionally kept shotguns and rifles to control vermin such as rabbits, rats and foxes. While the gentry owned very expensive hand crafted shotguns for shooting game birds during the season and poachers whenever they were seen. Most houses had a gun, some from the war but many hundreds of years old that were family heirlooms. Bert's father had an immaculate working Winchester 1894 lever action rifle that he kept above the fireplace next to an old English Bohemian flintlock pistol embossed with silver. Many unscrupulous dealers bought any weapon they could find to sell to anyone at a vast profit with no questions asked. The large numbers of army surplus guns and ammunition fuelled revolutions and armed gangsters around the world that enriched the ever growing merchants of death – the international gun runners.

In their spare time Bert and his friends worked in Falcon's Garage to learn about maintaining motorcycles and cars. They were taught how to re-build an engine and make new parts when the original part was damaged or too expensive to buy. Most of the work was on ex-military motorcycles that fetched a good price when reconditioned. Each bike was stripped down to its frame, carefully cleaned and painted before the wheels were attached with good tyres. Every engine was carefully dismantled, cleaned to remove any old oil or rust and re-assembled. Once finished the engines were run and carefully tuned so that they looked and sounded as good as new. It was not long before Falcon's Garage gained a fine reputation for being the place to buy good reconditioned motorbikes and trucks.

After a few months work, Jack Falcon presented each of his part time workers with a motorbike from the forty they had re-built. He knew that without their help he would have not made so much money so quickly and wanted to encourage them to continue working for him. Bert and his three friends were delighted with such a handsome reward that few of their friends could afford. So they cautiously learned to ride their motorbikes on the waste ground behind the garage. Initially they fell down when turning a corner too fast to be rewarded with bruises all over their bodies. However this did not put them off as the excitement was worth all the pain. With Jack Falcon's guidance they improved their riding techniques making them more confident. Having seen how often they fell off the bikes, Jack Falcon insisted they buy proper leather riding boots, gauntlets and goggles. Of course he sold them to the lads at a reduced price.

Bert spent hours at home polishing his bike and making sure she ran as smoothly as possible. The black paintwork shone brightly so that she looked as good as new and he could clearly see his face reflected in the paintwork. Of course he finely tuned the engine so that it fired perfectly to show that his bike was one of the best in the world. Bert wanted everyone to see that he was now a proud owner of a motorcycle. A modern man on the move up the ladder of success, though he was very aware of the pitfalls that lay ahead for a working class lad. Within weeks they were good enough to race each other and drive on the winding country roads around Eastleigh. It was exciting as there was little traffic and the only hazard being the occasional herd of sheep or cows. Bert loved the feeling of air brushing his face and leaning through the bendy roads. It did not matter if it rained or shined as long as he was riding his motorbike. Whenever Bert wanted to be alone he rode his bike through the surrounding countryside knowing that whatever the season there was always something to see. When the snow lay deep on the ground he would walk over the fields trying to identify the tracks of the animals in the snow. He learned to tell the difference between those made by cats and dogs and others from foxes, badgers, ferrets, and pheasants. As the snow melted and the days became longer he spent hours watching the horse drawn ploughs prepare the soil for sowing. When spring arrived he revelled at the sight of the new shoots breaking through the ground and yellow buttercups covered fields. It was the time whenever possible to go fishing or lay by the river watching the fish jump and the otters with their cubs play in the shallows.

Summer was the best time. The sun shone, the flowers blossomed and everywhere the sky was full of birds and butterflies. This was when they dined on freshly picked peas and new potatoes with a lump of butter and a piece of mint or ate the apples and blackberries ripening in the garden. Too soon the warm days became cooler as the leaves on the trees turned yellow/brown announcing autumn. In the fields the famers hurried to harvest the crops before the rain came to spoil them. Teams of oxen pulled the wagons carrying the cut wheat from the fields to the willowers who separated the grain from the chaff. Then the grain was sacked up for milling and the stalks tied together in sheaves for drying before being collected to be stored in haystacks for use as winter fodder for the livestock. It was an ancient sight of a man driving the oxen with a stick, another on top gathering the hay, and men throwing the sheaves from the fields up onto the wooden wagon. Harvest time was when rabbit was readily available and cheap because the farmers shot them as the harvesters cornered them in the fields. Often if you helped bring in the crop you were not only paid but also given a few rabbits for the pot.

Every evening during the working week Bert and his friends started to attend evening classes at The University College of Southampton to advance their careers. They knew that certificates in Higher Maths, English, Engineering Drawing and Physics were passports to better jobs that could change their lives. By now most well paid jobs required higher qualifications on top of passing an acceptable apprenticeship. This was often very tiring after a long day at work but proved inspiring. The four friends helped each other master complex ideas such as using a slide rule, understanding new mathematical techniques and some of the previously unknown theorems. To the surprise of his lecturers Bert often was top of his class producing better work than their degree students. These excellent results were to help Bert get the better paid experimental work when so many others were rejected. In fact they were to become his passport to a new adventurous life that would be full of challenges.

First he had to develop the skills needed in the new world waiting to be discovered. One in which new innovative engineering would change everything as they conquered the new frontier, the open skies. When Bert was not working he liked to enjoy himself. He was happiest when at weekends he raced his motorbike in cross-country competitions or played the piano in local pubs and parties. On busy weekends he did both making his sister Joyce ask if he was still part of the family. This was not surprising as often at weekends Bert appeared only to eat, sleep and sometimes didn't return home until Sunday night. In fact he was starting to use home like a hotel where he came and left whenever he wished. Only years later did he realise the hardships he placed upon Joyce who kept everyone calm and rarely complained.

# 6

## The 'Ampshire 'Ogs

Jazz is a spontaneous expression of one's inner self. It warms our souls as it did for the creators of this great art. It is the music of freedom that often expresses the vulnerability of the human condition where most people have to work to eat and pay the rent.

Jazz was king as the rich enjoyed the 'Roaring Twenties'. This was not what today we call Jazz – but any piece of music with a syncopated rhythm. It was an age of frivolity where the rich danced the night away drinking American cocktails made from mother's ruin, gin, shaken with that Mediterranean drink, vermouth. Often the barmen added fruit juices with a cherry or a slice of lemon, a drop of aniseed or angostura bitters. Fashion ruled everything as dance crazes changed as regularly as the season of the year. First there was the Jog Trot followed by the Twinkle, the Vampire, the Camel Walk, and the Shimmy. However the Charleston became the dance of the decade. No one took life seriously but celebrated being alive.

Bert and his fellow apprentices formed the 'Ampshire 'Ogs musical group to perform in pubs and at social events. As their reputation grew they were invited to play at private functions that paid well and showed the hidden side of society. At all the performances Bert played the piano, Tim the base, Fred the trumpet and Dom the drums. They thought that by dropping off the H it showed them to be local lads and appealed to the snobbery of those who could afford their fee. It certainly worked with the women some of whom chased them after each session. Mostly they politely ignored their female fans, though they socialised with the prettier and less demanding ones. Everyone present spoke the King's English with that distinctive BBC accent while dressed as if royalty, of course some were just ordinary people.

Each performance started at 8PM with Bert playing a medley of popular music on the piano. This kept the audience content as they waited for the room to fill or to be told to start. Like all paid servants they did as requested.

Then Fred introduced the band.

'My Lords, Ladies and Gentlemen please take your seats so that we can begin our entertainment! Welcome to the world of modern music, the world of syncopated rhythm we call Jazz. So please sit back to enjoy the music or feel free to dance to the satisfying beat. Let the rhythm run through your veins and make you feel alive and above all - be happy. Maestro let the music play and everyone who wants to dance.'

So Bert and the others started playing and the adventurous started to dance with a fury and passion as violent as it was extreme. People threw away their inhibitions to let their bodies swirl in time to the beat that encompassed everyone in an exciting glow. The 'Ampshire 'Ogs performed to rapturous applause all of the latest songs such as Charleston, Yes Sir! That's My Baby, Baby Face, Fascinating Rhythm, and When the Red, Red Robin Comes Bob, Bob, Bobbin' Along[13]. Around them the ladies were dressed to kill in high heels, black silk stockings, and but short tight dresses. Few people danced the steps as they were invented, preferring to improvise each move as if it was something special. If they played the wrong note or made an error no one cared as long as the music kept on coming. All mistakes or variations to the well known tunes were considered to be improvisations known as scat jazz. The music, dancing, drinking and loving did not stop until when exhausted, everyone took a break. Then the party continued. During the intervals some of the couples went outside for fresh air while others disappeared into darkened corners to explore each other. Some stayed and drank while others talked to the lads about music and life in general. Perhaps it was because they were young that the rich accepted them. Maybe it was to make the lads feel relaxed and play until the cock crow announced a new day.

This was a time when clothes were a sign of beauty and wealth. Fashion replaced years of old, dull wartime designs. Ladies showed off their wealth by wearing expensive dresses with long chains of pearls. Bright colours appeared on everything from cloth to shoes and even buildings. Woman painted their lips bright red with lipstick while men wore fashionable check pullovers and tweed trousers. The Edwardian concept of female beauty was long legs, flat chest and sleek hair combed back over the head often covered with a little cap or bonnet. Brassieres were designed to reduce womanly breasts to make them look more like young boys. Stylish dresses were tubular where the waistline dropped below the hips. On every occasion there were always more women than men and it would remain that way for years to come. Sadly, many of the less forward or plainer girls were forced to watch the dancing from the chairs that lined the walls like wallflowers, hoping that someone, anyone, would ask them to dance. Too many ended up alone as spinsters when in pre-war days they would have made good wives and mothers. So to avoid being a wallflower the women set out to impress the men in any way they could. Many danced with complete abandon letting their body's move with the music and showing as much of themselves as allowed. Some even went so far as to dance on the piano and tables. While a few more daring women performed erotic stripteases and couples made love wherever they wanted to. Others sniffed cocaine, smoked opium or cigarettes in long cigarette holders.

It was surprising how many women at each event were working class. They were often stunning beauties dressed in the latest fashion and accompanied by well-to-do or aristocratic men. They always spoke as if they had emerged from the finest private school, speaking the best form of the King's English. However when talking to Bert they often dropped their H's or used common slang.

Always the band was paid before each session. If things went very well and their employer was generous they sometimes received a bonus at the end of the evening. It did not happen often, but when it did it was gratefully received. As their reputation grew they became selective to perform only for the generous and polite patrons. Indeed they developed a loyal following among the upper classes many of whom provided them with as much work as they could wish for. So nearly every Friday and Saturday night they were playing at some private function often in very exclusive venues and large county mansions.

After one country house party Bert gave Alice a lift home on the back of his motorbike. She was very pretty with short hair and sparkling eyes that simply devoured him.

'If a girl is going to get on in this world she has to make the best of what she's got while her looks last. I'm pretty so rich men buy me the things I could never afford,' Alice said while sitting on the pillion seat and holding him tightly.

'What happens when they tire of you, or they get married?' Bert enquired.

'I count my earnings and either find another rich toff or settle down with a nice lad and start a family,' Alice replied.

'Don't you get worried about losing your reputation?'

'Heavens above you're an old stick in the mud! Do you think King Teddy's mistresses suffer for their royal fun and games? Of course not, they get rewarded with gifts to set them up for life. Believe it or not I earn more than you will ever see.'

'I'm sure you do and I bet you're worth every penny.'

'That's something you can be sure of my dear. I'm beautiful, have a supple responsive body and know when to keep my mouth shut,' Alice replied.

'Yes, you're right. Make hay while the sun shines but remember we're not rich like them. I'm sure you will be because you deserve a rich man.'

'I'm not sure that I want to bring up children with a rich man. A good man yes, but how many good rich men are there in this world?'

'I expect you're right, but there must be some decent rich people.'

'That's as maybe! It's a pity you're not rich as you're a nice guy that many a sensible girl would gladly marry.'

'Thanks for the compliment, but I cannot marry until I find true love and can afford to keep her.'

'What a load of dribble. It could take you a hundred years. Life is for living and not for waiting for a dream that may never come.'

'Maybe you're right. However I've just finished raising my brother and sisters and don't want to think of starting my own brood,' Bert commented not happy discussing marriage. All he needed was friendship with the occasional cuddle, and if lucky, sex.

For the rest of the journey Bert enjoyed feeling Alice's large firm breasts pushing hard against his back as she held on to him very tightly. When they arrived at her home he was invited indoors to be rewarded with all the loving that he needed and much more than he expected. She proved to be as good in bed as she was beautiful so that when he reluctantly left at sunrise he felt excited. Indeed he remembered her warm sensual body for many days. From that day onwards Bert often took Alice to the cinema or enjoyed her ripe body hoping that she would love him. But he knew that she wanted to get rich and could never marry him unless she was pregnant. So he tried as often as he could to give her a baby but unfortunately he failed.

The wealthy drove cars while others rode motorcycles or pedal bicycles. In 1923 the cheapest car was an Austin Seven costing two hundred and twenty-five pounds which was the first of the light cars designed for the middle classes. Gradually as they became more available when the prices dropped so that by 1930 an Austin 7 cost only one hundred and twenty-five pounds, a Morris Minor just one hundred pounds or a racing Bentley the large sum of five hundred pounds[13]. However because a motorcycle travelled five times more miles on a gallon of petrol than any car it was the younger man's chosen vehicle.

The rich adored all things continental as shown in the new glossy magazines such as Vogue and the cinema. People queued for hours in all weather to watch the latest stars on the silver screen. The silent film cartoons such as Felix the Cat, who walked up and down with his hands behind his back, became popular. Going to the cinema was not cheap, as a ticket cost six pence - the price of twenty cigarettes or two pints of beer. However on paying to see the film each customer was given a free copy of Film Fun magazine that advertised coming attractions. Women loved the real or imagined stories about their stars and simply adored Rudolph Valentino in silent films like The Sheik. Everyone liked the stunts and antics of comics like Charlie Chaplin, Harold Lloyd, Buster Keaton, and the Keystone Cops. Then in 1927 the first talking film The Jazz Singer arrived in Britain to rapturous applause. It was about this time that the latest fashions came from the Paris *Exposition Internationale des Arts Décoratifs* to be known as art deco. This meant that everything had to have clean-cut angular shapes and geometrical curves with daring and bright colours. Simply stated art deco was a fusion of cubism and futurism with the art of the ancient Aztec and Egyptian period.

It was a period when Bert decided to improve his education by reading the famous classical novelists. So he subscribed to a leather backed series of reprinted classics produced monthly by Odham Press of London. When each book arrived in the post Bert would read it from cover to cover starting with Charles Dickens' Christmas Stories and ending with Charles Darwin's The Origin of the Species. He enjoyed reading when alone in bed and felt that it was improving his mind so that he could communicate with others who were better educated. In fact reading became an obsession that helped him pass many long hours waiting for things to happen and taking his mind off the problems that surrounded him. He thought that Dickens above all others understood England warts and all better than any others. Indeed he felt Dickens cared for the poor and the underprivileged in a way that he hoped he tried to do. Slowly he started to develop a social conscience after reading of the hard times experienced by most people in Victorian England.

Bert's family was doing well. Father was promoted by the Railway from a porter to a better paid guard, Joyce worked part-time and young Olive studied to be a school teacher. Only Henry was still at school before starting as a trainee in a local solicitor's office. They were grateful that they were not among the multitude of unemployed people. Everywhere people hoped that slowly the country was getting back on her feet and the good, old days would return. The nation was nearly bankrupt and the exports were so poor that there were few jobs. The cost of running the Empire was becoming too much for Britain to pay for especially when so many territories owed the government millions of pounds. The country was effectively penniless because the war had drained most of the nation's wealth and killed too many of her young men. Contrary to public belief, wars make countries poor while enriching the arms manufacturers and money lenders. For most people life was about survival and earning enough to keep both body and soul together. No one trusted politicians or banks as the ordinary man in the street learned to place his or her meagre savings under the bed or in a jar on the mantelpiece for safekeeping. Father collected gold sovereigns that he kept in a box with his valued, hard won medals. He told Bert that because gold was a precious metal it would always be valuable and did not deteriorate. He added that you always paid cash for what you needed and only replaced an old item when it failed to work and was not repairable. It was Father's way of telling Bert not to buy the latest motorcycle he had seen in the local garage. Spend not, want not was his motto. Followed by a warning to his children to never be a lender or borrower as in his opinion it was a road to ruin. It did not please his bank manager but he didn't care. He owed no one and that is how he intended to spend the rest of his life.

# 7

## From Trains to Aeroplanes

The cheapest and most efficient way to move goods is by train, the fastest by plane and the most popular way by road. So why are so many heavy goods moved by road? It is because no government dares charge the heavy trucks the real cost for using the roads.

Most nights Bert dreamed of running a large engineering works where hundreds of workers built strange, exciting machines to fly men and their horses as far afield as Ireland and France. Sometimes his lovely thoughts were troubled by a sinister figure dressed in black who suddenly appeared knife in hand as if trying to kill him. Sadly he always woke before the man in black with short black cropped hair attacked so that he never knew if he lived or died. Maybe he was just an undertaker or the result of listening too often to Father's tales of war. If so, did it mean he or someone near was about to die? He hoped not.

It was one Saturday night when Bert and Tim were tuning Tim's motorbike that a smartly dressed, middle-aged man approached them.

'Sorry to bother you chaps, but do you know where I can find a mechanic to fix my car?' he asked. 'It's a brand new Bentley whose engine for some unknown reason suddenly spluttered and stopped?' he asked.

'Sir, the nearest garage is Falcon's at Eastleigh, but at this time of night it's closed. Maybe we could be of assistance as we often work there. So if you like we can take a look at your car,' Bert replied.

'Well if that is not too much bother it would be marvellous,' he said.

'We'll have a go but can't promise to fix the problem,' Tim answered.

'Any chance is better than none, so please follow me. The car is just around the corner,' he said.

Bert and Tim felt excited at the chance of working on the epitome of modern cars, the luxurious and fast Bentley. They were as rare as gold coins and in their eyes twice as attractive. She was a very fast car rivalling the famous continental machines such as the Italian Ferraris and German Auto Unions for both speed and looks. Within minutes they found the British Racing Green Bentley waiting at the kerbside. So with some trepidation Bert and Tim opened the bonnet to look in amazement at the immaculate 3 litre engine. They first checked there were no lose leads before trying to start her using the starting handle. Though the engine turned over it did not run.

'Is it going to be difficult?' the man asked.

'I don't think so, sir. Looks to me like you may have a blocked fuel pipe that we can clean and try to start her again,' Tim responded.

'Please do what you think is necessary as I really have no clue as what to do,' the man replied.

So they carefully dismantled the fuel lines and cleaned the carburettor. Bert had the distasteful task of blowing through the fuel leads to remove some dirt. Oh he really hated the taste of petrol, but that was unfortunately part of the job. While Bert drank some water to get rid of the taste, Tim started putting everything back in place. Then with fingers crossed they again tried to start the engine. This time it started first time to keep on running smoothly without a hiccup.

'Sir, it looks like you've been buying fuel from someone who doesn't keep his storage tanks clean so some dirt entered the engine. Hopefully we have found and removed the dirt before it caused any serious damage,' Bert remarked.

'Well removing the blockage was all she needed. May I suggest you put a filter in your fuel inlet to catch any dirt or buy petrol from a reliable supplier,' Tim commented.

'Thanks a lot chaps. I'll take your advice and do both. Sorry I didn't even ask your names. So how about coming for a drink and we can introduce ourselves properly,' the Bentley owner said pointing at a nearby pub.

'That sounds like a good idea,' the lads replied in unison.

'Then I can get rid of that horrid taste of petrol still in my mouth,' Bert added.

'Sorry about that. It can't be nice,' the Bentley owner replied.

'It's not but one gets used to it.'

'I suppose so. So let's go as its getting chilly and Bert can taste something nicer.'

The lads nodded as they crossed the road to the Elizabethan pub The Prince of Wales. Once inside their host ordered a round of the best beer and hot steak and kidney pies.

'By the way my name is Samuel Hartley but folks call me Sam or Mr Hartley. Your choice', the car owner said handing them each a pint of Strong's best ale.

'I'm Bert Brown and the more reliable one is Tim Watkins.'

'Of course you know that since the war it's difficult to get good engineers and mechanics. I hope you don't mind me asking who you work for?' Hartley enquired.

'We both work for the London and South Western Railways Works at Eastleigh. It was where we served our apprenticeships and like it as we're well treated,' Bert replied.

'I am glad to hear you're happy where you work. However maybe I can both help you and myself at the same time. I am in the position of being able to offer both of you lads a chance in a lifetime that few would turn down,' Hartley continued.

'That is very kind of you, but we're doing well and don't need another job. I've always found that the only way to get on in life is by hard work and not by gambling on the off chance,' Tim intervened defensively.

'Maybe you're right as hard work and skills always bring their own rewards. However let me tell you that Sam Saunders' company on the

Isle of Wight is looking for engineers to refurbish some de Havilland DH9a bombers for the RAF[2]. The work is expected to last for at least two years and is well paid, probably double what you currently earn. In addition to this we are expecting some private work to convert other DH9s to carry freight and passengers. Before you decide anything let me remind you that only twenty years ago most people thought aircraft were either a rich man's joke or a passing fad. Indeed few thought they had any commercial importance. We've all heard it said that if God had made Man to fly he would have given us wings. Now the world has changed. As you know today aircraft are both important war machines and civilian transports that are making international travel possible. I tell you chaps that there is an exciting and rewarding future to be had in building aircraft,' Samuel Hartley advised.

'Well, how do we find out more about the work and will they recruit local lads like us?'

'Yes I know they will recruit local men as I'm Sam Saunders' recruitment manager and can select anyone I want. I must warn you that if you join us you'll have to prove yourselves. We pay good salaries along with the fees for you to take engineering courses and all the union dues. Then, depending on how well you do, you'll earn your licenses as an aeronautical engineer issued for every type of plane you work on. No two are the same and so you must be certificated for every new model before you can work on it. It sounds hard, but it is the safest way. I need not tell you that nowadays they are worth an arm and a leg when qualifications are so hard to get. If you want to know anymore about us why not come and visit the works?' Hartley said.

'Sir, I'm certainly interested,' Bert replied. 'I always wanted to work on aircraft.' Bert then wondered if his dream was coming true and then shuddered at the thought of the man in black attacking him. It was only a dream, wasn't it?

'Sir, you can count me in too,' said Tim.

'We have two fellow engineers who may want to work at Saunders,' Bert added.

'That's fine. Come along on Tuesday and make a day of it. Then we can see what we think of each other,' Samuel Hartley added.

'We'll be at the works at seven on Tuesday morning, if that's alright?'

'Splendid, Tuesday it is. Better make it eight as by then everyone will be at work. Here's two pounds for another round and for your expenses. This breakdown was a blessing in disguise as I now know where the carburettor is and have met you chaps,' said Hartley with a warm smile. Then thinking about what he should tell the lads he added. 'I want you to be fully aware that working on aircraft is very different from building trains. For one thing there are few heavy steel and iron structures as all the metal frames are usually made of alloys. So the work presents different problems that I'm sure you will soon learn.'

'Learning about new metals and construction is what we all want to do. So please understand that we will be excellent students and useful workers.'

'I'm sure you will Bert. I just wanted you to know what new frontiers you will face.'

'Thanks.'

That night Bert discussed the job offer with Father who was puffing at his pipe while rocking slowly in his chair by the fire.

'Bert I'm honoured that you have asked me what to do, but I know you're old and wise enough to make your own choices in life.'

'I know that Father but what would you do?'

'You know I would try anything that is new and adventurous. To get on in this world you must take risks but always think before you jump into anything and then don't, whatever you do, look back. I've never found it a good idea to say 'if only I had done this or that'.'

Bert nodded knowing that Father, for better or for worse, had joined the army looking for adventure and the chance of seeing the world.

'Soon the horse and cart will be replaced by the motorcar. Indeed the railways and ships will compete with aeroplanes to take people long distances. If life has taught me anything it is that all things change whether we like it or not. So if I were in your shoes I would move with the times and work on flying machines. I remember when we sailed back from India I saw aircraft fly over us and envied those aboard who would be home months before us. Mind you it will be difficult learning new skills and keeping your job,' Father added.

'Thanks Father, I promise I'll work hard so that you'll be proud of me.'

'I know that you will, as always, do your best. Remember the family coat of arms, maybe Guy de Broyen saw you riding on an aeroplane. If the eagle is a plane and you the boy, then his dream will come true. Our ancestors never lied in their prophecies, they just didn't know where or when they would come true,' Father said with a grin that lit up his wise old face.

'That's quite some thought but first I must learn to build aircraft before I go up in one,' Bert said happy at the idea of fulfilling their ancestor's dream.

'Be successful for yourself and don't care what others say. I've always been proud of you working harder as a boy than most men ever do. Your dear mother would have been delighted at the way you have grown,' he said as he took out his handkerchief to blow his nose and wipe a tear from his good eye. It was touching how that every time Father mentioned Mother, he would go quiet and a carefully concealed tear would appear. He always said big men don't cry, but he knew, as Bert did, that even the strongest man cries for his lost loves.

Dom decided that he wanted to devote his time working on motorbikes and so only Bert, Tim and Fred joined Saunders. They started as fitters refurbishing DH9a aircraft for the RAF and converting others to carry cargo or passengers in luxurious cabins built inside the fuselage. It was a good life as they enjoyed their work, staying together in lodgings where the landlady provided breakfast, sandwiches for lunch, and supper. In their spare time they all learned to sail in one of the many small yachts that Saunders had built that could be used by the staff. It was an idyllic place to work where the hangers overlooked the majestic waters of the Solent where both the rich and the ordinary people mixed while sailing the calm waters. Craft of all sizes sailed by from the small sailing dinghies to the twenty metres racing yachts and large steam boats.

Bert wanted more. So he grew restless at Saunders wanting to work on the latest form of metal aircraft, for he felt they were the future. So Sam Hartley helped Bert and his friends to get work on experimental metal aircraft at the A.V. Roe works situated on the banks of the Hamble. What the lads did not know was that Saunders and Roe were in the middle of discussing a joint venture.

They soon discovered that A.V. Roe built aircraft for the RAF and commercial interests eventually selling over eight thousand units. They also operated a passenger service aboard their Avro 504O floatplanes that carried the rich and famous to London or France[2]. This was so successful that it kept company financially sound especially when aircraft sales were poor. The flights were the height of fashion advertised in newspapers and expensive shiny fashion magazines with pictures of the fashion models and film stars boarding or flying in the Avro 504. Occasionally the engineers were given a brief flight to experience the sensation of flying. It was exciting hearing the noise of rushing water when the float planes landed and the thrill of being in the air. Tim and Fred paid for flying lessons subsidised by the company which were too expensive for Bert, though he did take the free ones. The Chief Inspector told them that every engineer should fly in a machine to understand how they worked and get acquainted with some of the problems involved. On Bert's first flight he learned to overcome his fear of flying as the little plane rolled around one minute flying in a straight line and the next suddenly dropping a few feet causing Bert to feel sick. As soon as he settled down he watched through the windows to marvel at how different things looked when viewed from the air. Houses looked like matchboxes and people became as small as ants. Once airborne everything looked bright and clear allowing him to see for miles in any direction. Now for the first time in his life he understood what a bird saw of the world beneath them. It made him proud to be the first Brown who soared above the ground riding his eagle. It made Guy de Broyen's dream of seeing through the eyes of an eagle a reality. Perhaps more importantly this new experience helped Bert understand how aviation would and could change the world. Now he knew that aircraft and flying were his first true love closely followed by racing his shiny motorbike. He decided that being a top aeronautical engineer was what he wanted to be and set out to fulfil this ambition. Nothing could stop him once he had decided.

It was not long before Tim obtained his commercial flying licence and appointed as a pilot delivering the new aircraft to their clients. Meanwhile Fred moved from engineering into management as a trainee executive. Now that the gang had broken up Bert decided to leave A.V. Roe after applying to work at the nearby Supermarine works. There he would have the marvellous opportunity to build the latest metal racing aircraft in a company that was famous for producing fast racing aircraft and modern seaplanes. Indeed some of the fastest planes in the world! This suited Bert as he intended to be the best engineer that he could be, make money, and above all be successful. Someone his father could be proud of while he hoped still being modest. Then he would be famous, have new friends, make enemies and change the world. He never understood how easy it was to make enemies and how hard to make real friends. Indeed his nightmares reminded him of the man in black who would become his nemesis. Indeed the one man who would try to kill him.

# 8

# Supermarine and Reginald J. Mitchell

In life Reginald Joseph Mitchell was poorly appreciated by the public. In death he was immortalised as the designer of the Schneider Trophy winning planes especially the Supermarine S6B and its successor the more famous RAF fighter the Supermarine Spitfire.

In 1928 Supermarine Aviation (Vickers) Works was situated on the east bank of the River Itchen at Woolston just outside Southampton[2,3]. It was now owned by Vickers Ltd (Aviation Department) so that the Supermarine Chief Designer Reginald Joseph Mitchell worked alongside Vickers own Chief Designer Barnes Wallis. It was Mitchell's genius in making seaplanes versus Wallis' experience on landplanes. Indeed a clash of the Titans. Luckily for both men the new company's management decided to run Supermarine as a separate business to Vickers. This meant that Barnes Wallis would return to Vickers (Aviation Department) headquarters in Weybridge.

Reginald Mitchell was born in Talke in Staffordshire. On leaving school he served his apprenticeship at Kerr-Stewart locomotive works in Stoke. At the same time he studied engineering and mathematics at night school before joining Supermarine. He quickly became their Chief Engineer and later their Chief Designer. Then his modified Supermarine Sea King II amphibian fighter powered by a 450 horse power Napier Lion engine won the 1922 Jacques Schneider Trophy Race held in Naples[3]. However if Supermarine was to help Britain keep the trophy Mitchell had to produce an even faster aircraft. He realised that the Americans, Germans and Italians were developing very fast aircraft that could easily win the next race. Therefore he needed engineers experienced in metal work who thought like him to help develop the best aircraft. After looking for such people he found Bert, gave him an interview, and liking what he found recruited him.

In December 1912 the French financier and aircraft enthusiast, Jacques Schneider announced a new race for seaplanes. Each seaworthy aircraft had to take off and land in the sea and fly two hundred and eighty kilometres without refuelling Therefore each race consisted of two parts: a seaworthiness test and an air speed trial with each aircraft separately racing against the clock over the course. Many aviation experts now feel that this challenge was the main reason why aircraft speed started to increase so rapidly. Between 1913 and 1934, the world speed record rose from 72 km/hr to an astounding 655.67 km/h (407.5 mph). Jacques Schneider believed seaplanes were the ideal way to transport people around the world because of their capability to land on rivers and lakes in places where there were no suitable terrestrial airstrips. The races initially were between individual pilots before the regulators decided that they should be between national aero clubs. Therefore each trophy race was organised by the *Fédération Aéronautique Internationale* and the Aeronautical Club of the hosting nation. The first race was held in Monaco during 1913 where the French Déperdussin piloted by Maurice Prévost won at a speed of 72.6 km/h. The winner was awarded the *Coup d'Aviation Maritime Jacques Schneider trophy* and the equivalent of one thousand pounds. The trophy was to be retained by the winners until the next race. It was twenty inches wide consisting of a silver sea wave of Neptune and his three sons, over which was poised the winged female spirit of flight mounted on a marble base. Anyone winning the competition three times in succession would keep the trophy and the competition would end.

To cover the required distance of one hundred and forty nautical miles over the sea and not be too far from land, most races were flown over six or seven laps. Each course was different but was either triangular or in a diamond shape with every turn clearly marked so that all the competitors could easily see the markers. This involved a lot of careful planning and cooperation with the local maritime organisations to provide the necessary course and naval tenders to look after the aircraft.

When Bert arrived at the Supermarine works, he found a large painted wooden board that showed all of the Schneider Trophy results.

It read:

**The *Coup d'Aviation Maritime* Jacques Schneider Trophy Results.**

| Year | Place | Pilot | Country | Aircraft | Speed (km/hr) |
|------|-------|-------|---------|----------|---------------|
| 1913 | Monaco | Prévost | France | Déperdussin | 72.6 |
| 1914 | Monaco | Pixton | Britain | Sopwith Tabloid | 139.7 |
| 1919 | Bournemouth Cancelled | | | | |
| 1920 | Venice | Bologna | Italy | SIAI S.12 | 172.6 |
| 1921 | Venice | Briganti | Italy | Macchi M-7bis | 189.7 |
| 1922 | Naples | Biard | Britain | Supermarine Sea Lion II | 234.5 |
| 1923 | Cowes | Rittenhouse | USA | Curtiss CR-3 | 285.5 |
| 1925 | Baltimore | Doolittle | USA | Curtiss R3C | 374.2 |
| 1926 | Hampton Roads | Bernardi | Italy | Macchi M-39 | 396.6 |
| 1927 | Venice | Webster | Britain | Supermarine S5 | 453.3 |

An older mechanic touched Bert's shoulder to introduce himself.

'Hello I'm Alfred White though most people call me Alf and I guess you're Bert Brown,' the older mechanic said.

'I'm pleased to meet you, Alf,' Bert replied shaking the older man's hand.

'I've been told to show you around the works and give you a brief history lesson about the company. Our job mainly entails building every design of aircraft the governor, Mr Mitchell, gives us. Sometimes it involves modifying an existing plane or building a new one completely from scratch. From experience I can say that no two jobs are exactly the same.'

'Well this sounds like my sort of work. I like challenges.'

'Mind you the pay is good but when there is no work we get laid off until the next job,' Alf added.

'Does that happen very often?'

'Not often. Last time it happened I took the family to Devon. It was my first holiday and I hope it will not be my last,' Alf said with a smile that lit up his face. He believed that every cloud had a silver lining.

'That's not so bad. Good jobs are hard to find as most are only piecework or part-time. Jobs for life went with the war.'

'I can honestly say this is the best job I've ever had. I served my apprenticeship in Portsmouth dockyard repairing and building ships. When my apprenticeship was over, I received my papers and had to join the other qualified men lining up against the dock wall hoping to be selected by the foreman. If he didn't like you, you could wait until hell froze over for the smallest job. Glad to say that there is none of that nonsense here,' Alf commented.

'Thank heavens for that! I would find it demoralising to have to line up against a wall every morning waiting to be selected for a chance to work. It's just like cattle being selected for the slaughter.' The idea of such a thing offended Bert's sense of human rights as how could the selector by just looking at your face know if you were worth employing?

'Then of course you know that we are not to discuss our work with anyone outside the factory,' Alf stated. 'The management believes that some competitors would steal our ideas if they knew what we were doing.'

'That's just like when we were re-furbishing aircraft for the RAF their security men patrolled the works looking for spies, saboteurs and other trouble makers.'

'Did they find any?'

'If they did we were never told,' Bert replied. Then he thought for a while. 'They must have caught someone because security was a major cost. Saunders never spent more than he had to.'

'I am sure there are spies as have you seen at every air display people taking photographs of all the aircraft and making notes.'

'Of course I have. In fact most of the photographs and notes are made by enthusiasts like us. However I get your point because I am sure that among the genuine plane spotters are probably a few agents.'

'The racing planes you will be in charge of building are the very ones that make Supermarine famous. Since they won the Schneider Trophy with the S5 in Venice we have been awarded a contract for the next RAF racing aircraft,' Alfred said with pride as it had been all his own work.

'Wasn't that an all wooden construction?' Bert asked worried that he was working on old types of aircraft.

'No you're mixing it up with the old S4. The S5 had a semi-monocoque fuselage of duralumin with the wings made of spruce-ply wooden ribs covered in plywood.'

'It was still partly wood,' Bert said feeling disappointed. 'Is the new plane the same?'

'It's not! Mr Mitchell is designing an old metal aircraft for the next competition to hold a larger engine.'

'Wow, that's a relief. I came to work on metal planes and build the fastest ones.'

'Then you came to the right place. Now I better show you around so that you know where things are.'

Bert nodded.

Alf showed Bert where everyone clocked in at the beginning of the shift and out at the end of the day, where the numerous stores were and the general layout of the works. All the work tools were kept in one store and in another the larger parts such as sheet metal. All the tools were only released to each engineer against his signature and had to be returned at the end of the day. Likewise, each piece of metal, screw, or rivet was only issued against an order signed by the Leading Hand – that now would be Bert. When Bert started work very few supplies went missing as he checked every item. Anyway no one wanted to be sacked. Every piece of metal was measured with Bert's own micrometer screw gauge that he kept in a felt lined wooden case. Every weld was checked and double checked by eye and then under a magnifying glass. Perfection was what Mitchell wanted and Bert made sure that it was what he got.

Like all the other engineers and mechanics Bert wore a protective blue full length overall with strong boots. When he went outside he put on a trilby hat while those junior to him wore cloth caps. What one wore was a sign of one's status. Therefore as junior management he arrived in his sports jacket and trousers changing into overalls before starting work. It was regarded as important that one dressed in the position one held. It certainly was not a classless society but one in which everyone knew their position.

One day Mitchell asked Bert in his position as Leading Hand to comment on the design of his new aircraft. This was because Bert was responsible for the construction of the aircraft overseen by the Chief engineer. Often the Chief was supervising other aircraft under construction leaving Bert in charge.

So Mitchell spread out a roll of blue prints showing how he wanted the aircraft built. It showed every weld, bolt, rivet and spar. Nothing was omitted however small.

'As you can see the new S6 is basically an improved version of my cup winning S5. I've retained the two pontoons as it's the fastest way to fly and be able to take off and land on water. Everyone uses them since the American Curtiss CR-3 won the 1923 race on them. However I'm sure Jacques Schneider believed that all seaplanes should land on their hull.'

'I see it is now an all metal construction,' Bert commented with a grin.

'Well observed. I want her stronger than the S5 but still light. To win we will need a larger engine and so the need for an all metal construction. It is a true monocoque with all the strength in the walls of the fuselage and no cross members,' Mitchell stated with pride.

'I like that,' Bert replied.

Mitchell stopped for a moment and pointing at a blue print, continued. 'A fast aircraft must have a powerful engine mounted in a strong streamlined fuselage. Every part however small must be tested so that in the end she is the best in the world.'

'So we need a water cooled engine with large radiators.'

'I don't like large radiators because they are usually mounted in front of the engine and slow down the plane. Instead, I always place my water cooling radiators inside the leading edges of each wing and the oil coolers along the sides of the fuselage. It is simpler and makes my aircraft more streamlined.'

'It's a very good idea but it means that all of the connections in the cooling systems must be very strong. Also there must be very efficient circulating pumps driving the coolant around the fuselage and the wings,' Bert dared to comment.

'Of course, all the connections must be as light as possible but so strong that there is no leakage of coolant,' Mitchell said with a smile.

'Maybe we should experiment with different linkages as well as try to find more efficient oils.'

'Yes, try different types,' Mitchell replied. 'Beware when testing oils as you know they are inflammable. One small fire could be enough to send all our reputations up in smoke. Accidents to aircraft can ruin even the biggest companies.'

'So is that why the fuel tanks are inside the floats?'

'Well, yes, it is silly to leave a space in the aircraft unutilised. The fuselage is already filled with the cooling systems and the cockpit holding the pilot with the controls. The other reason is that when the fuel is inside the pontoon it is cooled by the surrounding water.'

'That's brilliant, but I don't understand how the pilot sees ahead?'

'In my plane the pilot can't see ahead but navigates by instruments and looking down over the side. If I placed him any higher in the fuselage it would slow the plane down to a snail's pace.'

They were silent for a while as both men tried to understand each other. Bert was unlike most aeronautical engineers as he appeared to be a perfectionist who would try to improve anything that he thought was not the best.

'I'm going to visit the Royal Aircraft Establishment at Farnborough to test a model of the S6 in their wind tunnel to detect any faults. I would like to have your opinion on my new modifications. Would you like to come along?' Mitchell asked Bert.

'Yes Sir, I would be honoured to come.'

'So it's settled. Be here at 6 on Tuesday morning and we will all travel together,' Mitchell said. 'Bert do you have any more comments?'

'The design of an aircraft is critical. I can tell their performance just by looking at them. Sometimes I notice silly little things that shouldn't be there,' Bert added.

'Yes, careful observation can tell you a lot about an aircraft, but you still require a powerful engine mounted in a very strong fuselage.

Don't think building racing planes is easy. It is a race to build the best against many rivals who produce very fine aircraft. So we must use all the latest techniques to produce another winner. Unfortunately there is no prize for coming in second.'

'Will the new engine make that much difference if we have to make the fuselage heavier to accommodate it?' Bert ventured.

'Changing engines is always a risky business. However, Sir Henry Royce of Rolls Royce has promised to develop for us a completely new engine that will deliver one and a half times more power than the Napier Lion. I believe he will. In my opinion he builds the finest engines in the world. Let's hope he continues to do so.'

A month later when the fuselage was finished Mitchell came down from his office to inspect every inch. He ran his hand along the metal work to feel that all the rivets were as flat as possible leaving no dangerous edges. In fact the work was as good as it gets.

'Bert, your lads have done a good job. I can see that you have lengthened the fuselage for the larger engine.'

'She is built exactly to your specifications. However as you know we can extend the nose if necessary. I must admit that I'm a bit worried about how well it will all fit together. You see I don't like building a fuselage around an engine that I can't measure,' Bert volunteered.

'Well that's always one of the problems of developing completely new machines. One must always plan for all eventualities as you have done while keeping the costs down so that the company makes a profit on the contract. There's no sense in building a world beater if one goes bankrupt doing it. I want my aircraft to last for decades as examples of excellence. I hope she will be the envy of the whole world. The world watches the latest developments and speeds achieved by our racers.'

'I think that the development of faster aircraft is greatly enhanced by the research that is the basis for your aircraft,' Bert commented.

'That is probably why the government backs our work,' Mitchell replied. 'Do you know that since the competition started in 1913 the speed of the winner has increased from 73 kilometres per hour to over 450 by 1927?'

'Yes I have noted the remarkable progress. It is nearly unbelievable,' Bert replied.

'I believe it is the greatest triumph of modern aviation and there is more to come,' Mitchell commented as he returned to the drawing board.

Sir Henry Royce's new V-12 engine used a supercharger to force more of the fuel-air mixture into the cylinders than in a normally aspirated system. It was designed to develop 1,500 horsepower (hp) or four hundred horsepower more than the rival upgraded Napier Lion VIII engine. Developing the new revolutionary engine had many problems. In the Rolls Royce factory at Derby, the new engine had a dozen failures before a version finally ran for the required sixty minutes. It was no good being fast if the engine blew up especially during the race! Many racing engines burned out or broke a cylinder as easily as any eggshell. One of the Rolls Royce prototype 'R' engines reached 1,545 hp at 2,750 rpm before completely destroying itself. Engine development was dangerous and very expensive. When something went wrong the engine parts, usually the pistons flew through their casings at high speed destroying everything in their path. Luckily no one was injured, though the testing shed must have been littered with deadly metal splinters. Bench testing an engine was and is still a major part of her development. It allows the engine to be run at different speed in varying conditions to find out how well it performed. Because overheating was always a problem running the engines under differing conditions was essential. The best engine had to survive working when run at high revolutions in all weathers for hours, if not days, on end. However a racing engine only had to last for the time of the race plus warming up time. In the case of the Schneider Trophy Race this would mean about one to two hours.

When complete the fuselage, wings and floats of the new S6 was given a thick layer of paint to protect the metal and the cables were covered with grease. Only then were the numbers painted on the tail fin next to the British red white and blue squares. Finally, every part was approved by the Air Inspection Department (AID) inspector as he stamped his AID number on a plate next to its identification plate. Then they waited for the engine to come before the flying tests could begin.

Within hours of the first 'R' engine arriving at Supermarine, it was carefully lowered into the fuselage and the controls, fuel and coolant piping carefully connected. Luckily it slipped in like one's feet into a good shoe – snug but tight. When the aircraft was finished, inspected and given its certification of airworthiness Bert relaxed for the first time for weeks. However only time would tell if she was the winner they wanted. Now the completed aircraft was handed over to the pilots of the RAF High Speed Flight.

On 5<sup>th</sup> August 1929 the first S6 complete with her new 'R' engine started her proving flights after which a few minor problems were corrected. Everyone watched the flight anxiously only too aware of the dangers involved in high speed flying. They all remembered that in 1928 Flt Lt Kinkead had died testing the S5. Racing aircraft could prove as temperamental and dangerous as riding a thoroughbred race horse in a classical race.

It took months to build and test the finished aircraft. This was no problem as the work was funded by the Air Ministry in London under its high speed research programme. They wanted faster engines and more experience in airframe construction to compete with the latest advances coming out of USA, Germany, France, and Italy. It made economic sense to keep up with, if not ahead of, one's competitors in what was rapidly becoming a major commercial industry.

# 9

## The 1929 Schneider Trophy Race

All races are won by the person who has the best designed and manufactured machine on the race day. Often fate plays a major part in victory.

The 1929 Schneider Trophy Race was held on the Solent with all of the competing aircraft held securely on the RAF base on Calshot Spit[3]. The RAF High Speed Flight supplied the pilots and servicing while Supermarine engineers were there only for support. Bert felt uncomfortable watching others fiddle with his planes. There was nothing he could do about it as it was a done deal. The RAF would both fly and service the aircraft. By the time of the race, the only competition was between two of the Italian Macchi M.67s and one older M.52R, three British Gloster IVs and an older Supermarine S5 and two S6 aircraft. The expected German and American entries did not materialise.

Calshot Castle is situated on the end of Calshot Spit built to guard the waterway and the base for RAF 201 Squadron equipped with Supermarine Southampton II flying boats. It was a very secure site as the only way on and off the spit was on The Calshot Express. Contrary to its name, the train was a narrow gauge tank engine that pulled wooden open trucks with crude wooden seats. It was uncomfortable, but efficient. Landwards from the castle were a series of hangers and quarters to house the aircraft and crews taking part. The race was to

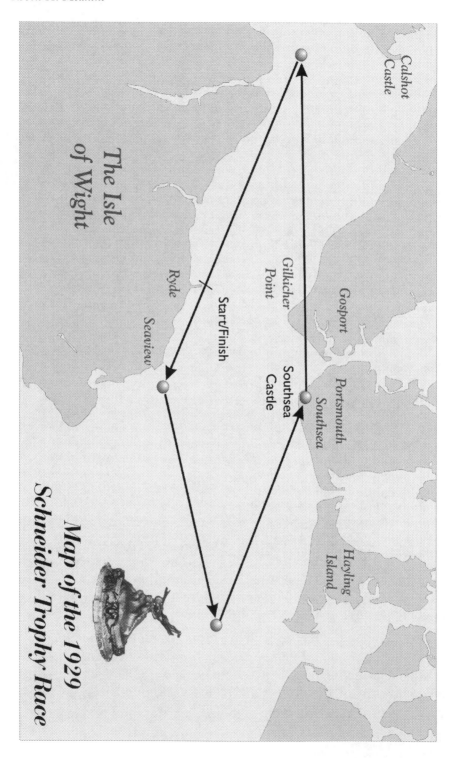

The Isle
of Wight

Calshot
Castle

Gilkicher
Point

Ryde

Seaview

Start/Finish

Gosport

Southsea
Castle

Portsmouth
Southsea

Hayling
Island

*Map of the 1929
Schneider Trophy Race*

run over a diamond shape fifty kilometre long course starting and finishing near Ryde pier on the Isle of Wight. All of the turning points were clearly marked by large yellow and black painted pylons held high from the decks of anchored Royal Navy destroyers. Each aircraft had to complete seven laps of the course totalling three hundred and fifty kilometres, without cutting corners. At the end of the day the plane with the fastest time was declared the winner. Thus the race was a test of speed and careful navigation.

For weeks before the competition, the teams arrived at Calshot to practice flying over the course and to get used to the Solent. So the security increased with armed guards protecting the aircraft from interference. The news of the Schneider Trophy Race spread throughout the world. Then the flagship for the event the battleship HMS Iron Duke was anchored offshore. By the time the race started, the Solent was full of boats of all sizes including cruise liners carrying spectators. While thousands more waited along the seashore to watch the fastest aircraft in the world compete. The first part of the competition was the seaworthiness and navigability tests. These were complicated because the large HMS Iron Duke got in the way of the pilots. One of them the Italian Lt. Monti was forced to land his Macchi M67 first ahead of the ship and then astern of her.

Around the world Schneider Trophy Race made headline news. On everyone's lips were the questions, who would win the race and how fast would they go? The international press regarded the Italians as favourites and the Gloster VI Golden Arrow as the most beautiful aircraft. In fact the Supermarine S6 was not even in the running, but little did these so-called experts know about flying. The winner would be the aircraft that flew over the required course in the fastest time. In Italy, aeroplane enthusiasts eagerly listened to each broadcast knowing that their beautiful red painted Italian Macchi M67 was fast. In fact a M67 flown by Captain Motta had reached a speed of 362 mph over Lake Garda before tragically plunging into the lake and killing the pilot. Apparently he was overcome by exhaust fumes and so new ventilation tubes were fitted in the M67's for the Schneider Trophy Race. The M67 was not the Italian's first choice as they wanted to enter the twin engine Savoia-Marchetti S.65. The organisers disallowed this saying that only single engine aircraft could compete in the competition. Then quite unexpectedly, the British Gloster VI aircraft were withdrawn before the start of the race scheduled for 7th September 1929.

Like every good engineer, the night before the race Bert and Alf with the RAF Engineer officer Eric Moon and his staff checked their aircraft.

'Bert, please come over here and look at this engine oil. It looks like there are traces of metal in it,' Alf commented while examining one of the engines.

In seconds Eric Moon and Bert were looking down at the oil to confirm that there were traces of metal. It indicated disaster.

'Well this engine has to be removed and replaced,' commented Moon. 'Doesn't it?'

'Well yes, but it is easier said than done,' Bert replied.

'Why is that?'

'Simple answer is that we don't have any complete spare engines so we had better strip this one down and fix it.'

'But that could take all night,' Moon commented.

'Well, unless we do examine it and repair the damage, we will never know whether it is faulty or whether someone has sabotaged it,' Bert replied. So they removed the engine from the fuselage and started to dismantle it. It was lucky they did as they found a cracked piston that had sent one or more pieces of metal into the cylinder block.

'Bert, can you fix it? What I mean is do you have the parts and enough time to make the aircraft ready for the race?'

'Yes we can replace the old cylinder block and pistons with new ones, but it will take time.'

'Don't worry about needing help as my men will work through the night if necessary. We can't have an aircraft that's unable to compete tomorrow. Just imagine what the press would say if we cannot compete with a full team. It appears the more people crash or someone dies, the more the newspapers have to print,' Moon added.

'No need to worry sir. No one wants bad publicity. You know as well as I do that what is bad for the RAF is bad for Supermarine,' Bert added trying to instil an air of confidence.

Then Bert, Alf and the RAF engineers started to strip down the engine and replace the damaged parts. Someone suggested that it was sabotaged by the Italians but they knew that accidents were always possible in experimental engines tuned to give their maximum performance. It was just after two in the early morning when Bert stopped working on the aircraft. As Bert walked away he saw Mitchell looking on and in his own quiet way said nothing. Then Bert and Alf found a quiet corner in a hanger to rest. They managed a few hours sleep before getting up to watch the race from the seawall at Calshot.

Next morning, the sun was shining with no clouds to spoil the view and the water was slightly choppy. It was all that they could have hoped for. If the water was too still the float planes had problems taking off. It was now up to the pilots and Lady Luck. Each plane was taken out to the start aboard a naval lighter to be launched into the water near the starting line off Ryde pier. The first was S6 number N247 flown by RAF Flying Officer H. Waghorn. The strangely beautiful humming noise of the Rolls Royce engine and the blue of the aircraft kept everyone transfixed as they counted the required seven laps.

'Isn't he flying an extra circuit?' Bert asked Alf.

'Maybe they have changed the rules and no one told us. Remember he's the first to fly the circuit,' Alf replied.

'I hope not. The engine won't last much longer without burning out,' Bert commented.

'Stop worrying Bert as I expect it will last. Anyway there's nothing we can do about it from here except cross our fingers and pray.'

'Alf as always you're right,' Bert answered Alf. 'Tell me how did you know that I've crossed my fingers?'

'I know you much too well. I'm surprised you're not touching the cross around your neck.'

Before Bert could reply things changed. They saw the engine splutter as it ran out of fuel forcing the S6 to land safely. It was just short of the finishing line after flying an extra eighth lap! However, because he had flown the required distance his average speed of 328.63 mph was valid. Then the Italian Warrant Officer Dal Molin in the Macchi M52R recorded 284 mph followed by Flight Lieutenant D' Arcy Greig in the S5 at 282 mph. Next to fly was the Italian Lieutenant Remo Cadringher in his revolutionary three-bladed propeller driven Macchi M67. He started well but at the first turn, the exhaust pipe fractured pouring fumes into the cockpit forcing him to land half-blinded and choking. He was badly shaken but not seriously hurt. Then Flight Lieutenant

Atcherley flew the second S6 N248 at an average speed of 325.54 mph only to be disqualified for cutting a corner. Yet again poor navigation let the RAF down.

The last competitor took off for Italy. The only difference between the two M67 planes was that the second one had a standard two blade propeller. Would the Isollo-Fraschini 18 cylinder engine developing 1,800 hp last the race? If so, would the M67 beat the S6's 328.63 mph. Lt Giovanni Monti chased the title recording 301.5 mph on his first lap. But as he started the second lap a radiator pipe burst sending hot water over him. In severe pain he managed to land and be rescued by the safety boat. So the Italian challenge was over with only the older Macchi M52R finishing the course.

As everyone left to go home the results were released by the judges.

## 1st place went to Fl. Of. Waghorn (Britain) in the Supermarine S6
## 2nd was Warrant Officer Dal Monti (Italy) in the Macchi M52R
## 3rd Fl. Lt. D'Arcy Grieg (Britain) in the Supermarine S5

So Supermarine and the RAF had won the Schneider trophy for a second time and it would remain in Britain until the next race in 1931.

That night the Supermarine engineers celebrated their victory at the local pub totally unaware of the fact that their futures were in doubt. Meanwhile the RAF team were wined and dined as national heroes while the public forgot the aircraft designer, Reginald Mitchell, and Supermarine. If Mitchell was upset about the lack of recognition he never showed it. He knew that without him there would be no Schneider Trophy in the Royal Aero Club as the Italians would have won the competition. On the day, the S6 was the better aircraft but a few weeks later it could easily have been the other way round. In the aircraft business there is always someone developing a new idea, a bigger and more powerful engine, or a faster more durable body. Indeed could the Italian Macchi M67 aircraft have won if either the exhaust pipe or radiator pipe had not broken? No one knows for certain as it was a time when all great nations were busy developing faster machines, especially aircraft.

# 10

## A Compulsory Holiday

It is said that a change is as good as a rest.

When the celebrations were over, and the victory only recorded on the faded pages of discarded newspapers, it was announced that the next Schneider Trophy Race would be held in 1931. Then the new Labour Government under Ramsay MacDonald decided not to fund the production of an aircraft for the next race. So the new Schneider Trophy Race aircraft programme was halted until Supermarine could find another sponsor. Then Bert and Alf were laid off for a month after collecting two month's pay. Hopefully their jobs would be waiting when they returned.

'Bert, don't look so worried. I bet you that Mitchell will get some money for the next aircraft and you and I will build it,' Alf said in his usual positive manner.

'I'm sure you're right,' Bert replied deeply worried about the future. It was the first time that he had been unemployed and did not like the idea.

'I hear that due to lack of work Saunders-Roe is making their staff take a holiday at the same time as us,' Alf informed Bert.

'Then I'll contact the lads and go to Europe. Would you like to come?'

'It's very kind of you to ask Bert but I have the wife and three kids to worry about. So I'll spend the time decorating the house and doing a bit of gardening. Come and see us when you are free,' Alf responded.

'Of course I will. I hope you're right about our jobs. Still I'm worried by the rumours of the depression getting worse as more companies fail to make a profit.'

'I know that if any company survives these hard times it will be Supermarine and Vickers,' Alf commented. 'We will build the next Schneider Trophy plane and win it. Just mark my words, lad. Just mark my words.'

Bert knew that Alf was right and with Mitchell's efforts there was hope for the future. He would do anything to continue working on aircraft, even try to learn to fly or join the RAF. For now all he could do was hope for the best.

'Thanks Alf. Regards to the family and see you soon,' Bert shouted out. So he rode his motorcycle home with the two month's pay burning a hole in his pocket. Now he could have a real holiday.

Over the next few days Tim, Fred, and Dom decided to join Bert on a European motorcycle trip. So they went by the ferry from Portsmouth to Le Havre where they started their tour. Every evening they stayed in a small hotel and during the day rode towards the cathedral city of Rouen. It was very pleasant as people waved and they waved back. For the first half-hour they had to concentrate on riding on the right hand side of the road before it became automatic. It wasn't a problem as the traffic was sparse and the weather sunny so they made good time. Everywhere they survived by speaking poor French and spent many a happy evening in cafés drinking various red and white wines. In one village, an elderly Catholic priest showed Bert how to add a little water to the wine so that he could carry on drinking without getting drunk and enjoy even the poorer wines. They were pleasantly surprised at how many French people spoke some English and were interested in motorcycles and aircraft. For all their differences, most of the French people regarded the English as part of the same family and at worse good allies in time of war.

It was late autumn with the leaves turning to a beautiful golden colour, some were red and others a delightful pale brown. The days were warm but gradually the night air grew colder. Bert photographed everything he saw such as fields, villages, cathedrals, foreign cars, and people sitting in the cafés, whatever took his fancy. No one complained though some wanted a copy of their pictures posted to them. Bert did as requested as he thought it was only fair.

Slowly they made their way to Paris where they stayed for five days because there was so much to see. On arriving they rode their motorbikes down the magnificently wide Champs-Élysées right up to the bottom of the Eiffel Tower. They stopped for a coffee before climbing the hundreds of stairs of the Tower to the top platform from where they viewed all of Paris beneath their feet. Afterwards they found a small inexpensive hotel with a place to safely park their motorbikes. It was in the arty district of Montmartre where all the clubs and theatres were situated near the beautiful white domed Basilica of Sacre Coeur. So during the day they visited the museums and cathedrals while at night the lads went to the clubs to flavour the naughty delights of Paris. They had been told by older colleagues to visit the famous Follies Bergière that had started as a circus with jugglers, clowns, wrestlers, magicians and of course long-legged beautiful dancers. Now it was famous for the daring performances of the talk of all Paris, the black American dancer Josephine Baker. When she came on stage with her pet cheetah Chiquita, the whole audience was mesmerised. She wore only a pink flamingo feather between her legs and some feathers and a string of sixteen artificial yellow bananas around her waist as she danced on a large mirror. Every man and woman in the audience was enthralled at her sensual dancing and her very beautiful slim and nubile body. Somehow the mixture of the music, her dancing and the smoke filled theatre was so magical that they would remember it for years to come. Bert especially remembered her sensual soft singing voice as she swayed from side to side watched over by her cheetah. He had never before seen anyone as fantastic as her and like all present could have spent forever listening to her magical voice. Josephine Baker was born in Missouri, USA then settled in France. In comparison to Josephine, Bert thought that the Can Can dancers with their stirring, lively music, high kicks and swirling skirts were nothing special. It was like comparing a sparkling diamond to coloured glass. Both were pretty – but Josephine Baker was worth her weight in gold. Bert watched her three times totally captivated by her grace and her beauty. Many years later Josephine

Baker was honoured by the French Government for her work in the French Resistance fighting the German Occupation. For bravery she was awarded the *Croix de Guerre,* the *Rosette de la Résistance* and made *Chevalier of the Légion d'honneur* by the President of the French Fifth Republic General Charles de Gaulle [14]. This small cabaret dancer proved to be both a true beauty and a real heroine.

Bert loved the tree-lined wide streets of Paris, the busy street cafes, and the sculptures and paintings that were on display nearly everywhere. It was idyllic just walking on the banks of the River Seine by the Cathedral de Notre Dame on its own island, the Isle de la Cité. Here the beautiful stain glass windows were made resplendent as the sun's rays entered, giving the holy cathedral a special spirituality. Bert wondered why they claimed to have relics like the Crown of Thorns, a Holy Nail, and a fragment of the True Cross. Maybe they were real but their presence added little to the holiness of Notre Dame. The cathedral's huge stone towers peered down above the River Seine and the streets of Paris as her bells informed all of her presence. All around the roof were grotesque stone carvings or gargoyles looking very pagan and in Bert's opinion a little offensive. He loved Notre Dame but felt it was not as holy as his local cathedral, the ancient stone Winchester Cathedral that held the coffins of the old Anglo-Saxon Kings of England.

The four lads simply fell in love with cosmopolitan Paris where people of all races freely mingled along the wide tree-lined avenues. Everyone they met was friendly even when discussing politics, except for some Germans wearing brown shirt under a black military uniform – a bit like boy scouts. The lads were drinking vermouth with some French students when they were confronted by three German 'boy scouts' who forced themselves into their ranks.

'Move over, we want your chairs,' one said.

'Sorry but the seats are taken,' Dominic said politely.

'Bad luck. When we want something we take it. We National Socialists are God's chosen people and will rule over you weak Anglo-Saxons,' the taller one, Hans, said.

'How can Les Boche win anything?' added the French girl Annette openly defiant at the behaviour of the Germans.

'You French think you are the centre of the world because you won the last war. Next time will be very different because we will conquer all of you,' Hans replied.

'You chaps couldn't even win a boat race, much less a war. You're a toothless dragon - all full of puff with no real bite,' Dominic unwisely added.

This proved too much for Hans who without warning thrust a sheath knife at Dominic, who quickly moved sideways to let it hit the table. Then as if they were under orders the other 'boy scouts' took out their knives ready to fight. Now it looked like the lads had little alternative other than to hit the Germans hard before anyone was seriously injured. Not for the first time in his life, Bert was scared as an ugly silence descended and all sides surveyed the opposition. It was as if suddenly lines were drawn in the sand and the battle royal was about to commence. Luckily it did not happen. They were all stopped in their tracks by a loud bang that shook the street as Pierre, the café proprietor held a still smoking sawn off double-barrelled shotgun he had fired into the air.

'*Disparaître mes Boches* before the gendarmes arrive or face my Lupe that will make certain you never have children! Indeed I have waited since the war to shoot a few more of you evil people,' Pierre shouted for all to hear.

Just the sight of the serious looking, short but muscular Pierre holding a sawn off shot gun sent the aggressors scampering down the street as fast as their feet could carry them.

'*Merci beaucoup Monsieur Pierre*,' Tim said and kissed the unshaven hero on both cheeks.

'*J'ai le plaisir mon ami*. There is little love lost between France and England but we do not hate each other. How can we, as we are from the same stock? However these young uniformed Germans are arrogant little warmongers, so we really hate them as we do not wish another war,' Pierre replied in excellent English.

'Who are they?' Tim asked.

'They are the *Hitler-Jugend* that you would call the Hitler Youth. They are trained to become party members and serve Hitler,' Pierre replied reluctantly.

'It's strange that the French and English have the same heritage, but have adopted a totally different life style,' Fred said trying to change the subject.

'The English like their football, beer, women, and beef; the French their football, wine, women, and snails. So that is not very different. While the Boche like discipline, sausages, and being the boss,' Annette added.

'We call you English *L'Boeuf*, the beef, because you eat beef, while you call us frogs because we eat frog's legs. This little joke is really a sign of how close our two nations are,' the pretty Simone intervened with a charming grin.

'Maybe that is correct. However I think our differences are because the Germans have no real culture. We talk of Italian, French and British famous painters but there are few German ones except for Dürer. Of course I know of many great German composers but their music is often too martial for my taste,' Pierre commented.

'That's a strange looking shotgun,' Fred commented trying to change the subject.

'She is my Lupe who I keep under the bar in case of trouble. It belonged to my wife's grandfather so I call her by the Sicilian name Lupe. It is the sawn off shotgun used by Sicilian shepherds to kill wolves and occasionally their enemies,' Pierre answered with a wicked grin that lit up his face. He was proud of his weapon that had often sent thieves and trouble makers running away for their lives thinking Pierre was a Mafioso or a gangster. Maybe he was but it did not matter as he was a friend.

As the afternoon gradually drew into night they all talked, drank and ate together enjoying new found friends. The students and Pierre talked about the growing threat from Fascism in Europe. Pierre said that the Germans were followers of Hitler's National Socialist Party known as Nazis who first attempted to come to power in 1923 during the so-called Beer Hall Putsch. Now Hitler tried a different approach by wooing the aristocracy, industrialists and important people telling them how he would make Germany great again. He played on their anger about how they were treated after the Great War and at the greed of the money lenders and bankers that bled so many honest Germans dry. This was made apparent when more companies sacked their workers and even the once reliable banks failed people by losing their savings making them impoverished and desperate. Hitler grabbed the opportunity to turn this disaster into a hatred of foreigners especially the Jews and Gypsies, forgetting to tell anyone that he was Austrian by birth. Like many other Frenchmen at the time, Pierre thought the Nazis were just a fashion that would not last. He admitted that Hitler was a talented orator who orchestrated his mass meetings with music, light shows and marching people. In his opinion, all great orators were dangerous as they rally large numbers of easily influenced people to their cause whether it is justified or not. An organised mob would do what their masters wanted, even destroy, rob and kill their next door neighbours. According to Pierre there is nothing more frightening than the sight of an out of control mob on the rampage destroying all before them.

Now the holiday was nearly over so they rode from Paris through Picardy to Amiens and then on to Bruges in Belgium. The city of Bruges with its cobbled streets, old houses and women wearing lace bonnets was a pleasant place to visit. The food and chocolates were fantastic and the shops so quaint that Bert had to explore them. Everywhere he went people were selling fine lace, Dutch and Belgium clocks, and all sorts of paintings – some large and some small enough to fit into a motorbike pannier. Bert purchased some of the famous Bruges lace for his two sisters and for Alf's wife and two boxes of chocolates. Then he purchased three handsomely carved meerschaum pipes, one each for his father, brother and himself. Then he discovered at the back of a little shop a small dusty painting covered in cobwebs. He never knew why but he picked it up, blew away the cobwebs and purchased it. It was an old oil painting of an old man smoking a long clay pipe, leaning over a wall and looking out at the barges on a canal. The detail was so good that you can see the veins in his hands and the wrinkles around his eyes. It still hangs on the wall by Bert's bed next to a French Madonna. Once the painting was dusted, it revealed a signature that read Durer - but it meant nothing to Bert as he liked the scene. Maybe one day he would have it valued or sell it, but things that one likes are worth more than mere money. They have a beauty that makes one feel good.

When they arrived home they found everyone was very worried because of the Wall Street Crash in share prices that also affected many British companies and increased unemployment. It looked like the economic depression would continue and could even get worse.

# 11

## The 1931 Schneider Trophy Race

National pride and aircraft development came from the people's generosity and not from a disinterested, nearly bankrupt government. The RAF took all of the credit while those who built and designed the aircraft had to sit back and accept being second class.

Luckily for Bert on his return he discovered that Supermarine restarted full time work. This was after Reginald Mitchell had found financial backing for the building of a new Schneider Trophy aircraft[3]. During the difficult financial situation the sponsorship unexpectedly came from public collections and the generosity of Lady Lucy Houston. She was the widow of a shipping millionaire and a staunch capitalist who wanted to show the ruling Labour Government that Britain cared about retaining the Trophy. Lady Lucy Houston announced to the nation something like, 'I'm proud to have inherited the spirit of my forefathers, who considered one Englishman equal to any three foreigners. We are not worms to be trampled under the heel of Socialism but true Britons with a heart for any fate.' Her words were well received by many of those people who wanted the Schneider Trophy to remain in England [3, 13]. Little did most people know that the magnificent statuette was at that time being treated with ignominy at the Royal Aero Club where some members used it as a hat stand! However with the help of the publicity in the newspapers it was not long before Lady Houston's Fund exceeded

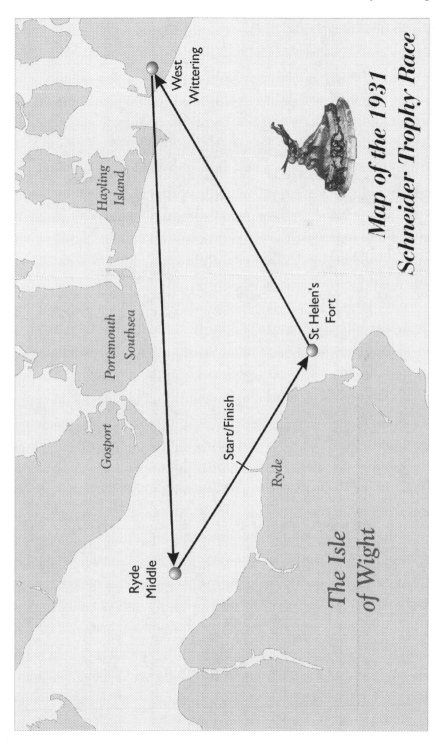

West Wittering

Hayling Island

Portsmouth

Southsea

Gosport

St Helen's Fort

Start/Finish

Ryde

Ryde Middle

*The Isle of Wight*

*Map of the 1931 Schneider Trophy Race*

one hundred thousand pounds that was shared between Supermarine and Rolls Royce.

In an attempt to save money Mitchell designed his new S6B by converting the now redundant fuselages of the old S6 Schneider Trophy aircraft. The S6B would be powered by an improved Rolls Royce 'R' engine modified to develop 2,350 horse power, an increase of 500 hp. Now Bert had the unusual task of rebuilding his own aircraft to meet the new specifications.

'Mr Mitchell is the old fuselage strong enough to hold the newer engine?' Bert asked worried about the task that lay ahead.

'I hope so Bert. If it does not I have made an enormous mistake that I expect you to rectify. However our stress engineer Nevil Norway has calculated that it should. To be on the safe side check each fuselage and replace anything you're unhappy with. In fact you can completely strip them down and check every part,' Mitchell replied.

'I will do my best. However we must remember the old S6 fuselages have already logged many flying hours.'

'I know, but when short of funds beggars can't be choosers,' Mitchell replied with a grin. He too was worried but was not going to show it.

The first of the old S6 aircraft to be converted were designated S6A and used to test the systems for the two faster S6B. Everything had to be done in a hurry because of the delay in funding. So Supermarine had only nine months in which to produce the new aircraft for the RAF team to fly in the race. To make matters more urgent, it was rumoured that the Italians were producing an even faster and more reliable aircraft than their Macchi M67. Then the French and Italians asked for the 1931 race to be postponed for a year, but this was rejected by the *Fédération Aéronautique Internationale.*

On 11<sup>th</sup> November 1930 the spectacular Dornier DoX flying boat arrived in Cowes on a visit to promote the revolutionary passenger aircraft. It was the biggest aeroplane of its day measuring one hundred and fifty-seven foot long with an enormous one hundred and thirty-one foot wingspan. Fully loaded it was expected to carry up to the previously unheard of load of one hundred and fifty passengers. While moored in the Solent many important people as well as some of the local aeronautical engineers including Mr Mitchell along with Bert and Alfred were invited aboard. They travelled together on a small motorboat to be warmly welcomed by the captain.

'Well Bert this aircraft will show you what can be built and the extent of the competition,' Mitchell commented as they neared the huge aircraft.

'I find it hard to believe that such a large aircraft can actually fly,' Bert replied.

'It must cost a fortune to keep her airborne,' the ever observant Alfred commented pointing at the engines.

'She's certainly a beautiful aircraft excellently fitted out with every luxury one could imagine. However one wonders if all the extra weight caused by such fittings limits her range and performance,' Mitchell stated in admiration. He was impressed by Cladius Dornier's fine design and workmanship but doubted if it would be a commercial success. Mitchell always was a man who appreciated good engineering and design.

On boarding the flying boat they were given a booklet stating the aircraft's dimensions, performance and capacity. It stated that flying boat had an all duralumin hull with wings made of steel and covered with fabric strengthened with layers of aluminium paint. The large fuselage was divided into three decks. The upper level was the flight deck with a captain's cabin and chartroom. The middle level housed the passengers, the galley and a sixty foot long dining room. In the lower level were the large fuel tanks needed to feed the energy hungry engines. She was powered by twelve Curtiss Conqueror 12 cylinder water cooled engines assembled in six pairs with a planned range of a thousand miles at 134 mph. One engine faced forward while the other was mounted behind it facing aft. At the time the largest British flying boat was the four-engine Short Singapore that was a minnow by comparison. The Singapore was only sixty-four foot long with a ninety foot wingspan or half the size of the Dornier DoX.

Next day back in Supermarine Mitchell came down from his office to talk to Bert and Alf during their morning tea break.

'Good morning gentlemen,' Mitchell said. 'I hope you enjoyed yesterday's excursion.'

'Thank you sir,' Bert and Alf replied nearly in unison.

'Don't thank me. The invite came from Dornier so I had to field my best team.'

'Well what did you really think of the DoX?' Mitchell asked while helping himself to a cup of tea from the pot.

'She was like a giant dream machine,' Alf replied timidly.

'Alf's right sir, she is so large that just maintaining her would take the work of an army of mechanics,' Bert added.

'I think you're both right,' Mitchell commented. 'In my opinion she is an example of excellent design and engineering but poor financial management.'

Very puzzled at his boss's statement Bert scratched his head and asked. 'Why is that?'

'Well she is so large and heavy that even with those twelve large engines taking off from the sea and staying in the air must be very expensive. She probably uses around four hundred gallons per hour. Few nations can afford that.'

'That must mean that she is uneconomical as a passenger carrier,' Bert added.

'I think that's totally correct. I even doubt if she can cross the Atlantic with enough passengers to cover the cost. If I was a gambling man I would bet that she will never cross to America in one hop.'

Like so many times before Mitchell hit the nail on the head. The beautiful Dornier DoX proved to be a huge commercial failure being too expensive to operate and never reaching its designed altitude of ten thousand feet. In 1931 she crossed the Atlantic in stages by hopping between the islands. Sadly the DoX regularly suffered from mechanical failures as well as using four hundred gallons of fuel per hour. Of the five aircraft built, two were sold to Italy. It was a design thirty years ahead of its time produced before anyone had developed more powerful engines. By 1944 Shorts in collaboration with Saunders Roe built the huge Short Shetland Flying boat. She was one hundred and eight foot long with a one fifty foot wingspan with a range of forty-six thousand miles when carrying thirty-eight ton payload. She never went into commercial production as the market ended with the ending of the war. Strangely the weight of flying boats limited their size because of the tremendous force needed to lift them free of the water's surface tension. Later aircraft with more powerful engines were developed though many were commercially uneconomical such as the Hughes Spruce Goose and the Saunders Roe Princess. After a few more years the USSR produced some successful large flying boats such as the Beriev BE 12 as did the Canadians, Chinese and Japanese. All were designed for use as antisubmarine, air rescue, or fire fighting aircraft. One unusual modification is the Canadair CL-215 of 1967 and Bombardier (Canadair) 415 developed in 1994 amphibious aircraft used in fire fighting. It scoops a ton of water at a time from nearby lakes to drop on fires.

On Sunday 13th September 1931 the only competitors in the Schneider Trophy Race were the three Supermarine aircraft. Therefore the organisers decided that all the S6B had to do to win the trophy was to complete the course at a new record speed. So Flt Lt John Boothman took off to fly in the S6B S1595 over the course completing the first lap in five and a half minutes at a staggering speed of 343.1 mph. As Boothman flew over Henry Royce's home at West Wittering, the old gentleman must have been happy to hear his engine work so sweetly to know it was a world record breaker. On the final lap the S6B listed to the left because John Boothman had failed to trim the fuel tanks so that one of the pontoon floats weighed more than the other. Still he managed to finish on schedule before flying a lap of honour. The crowds went crazy while ships blew their whistles and the church bells rang out in celebration.

That night the RAF team along with Mitchell were invited aboard Lady Lucy Houston's yacht Liberty where a group photograph was taken. Because Supermarine and the RAF High Speed Flight had won the race on three consecutive occasions, the contest ended and the Schneider Trophy remained in Britain. So it was placed in the Royal Aeronautical Club in London before being moved to the Science Museum.

Two weeks later the same Supermarine S6B now fitted with an upgraded sprint engine broke the world air speed record flying at 408.8 mph. This was the first aircraft to fly at over 400 mph. The record did not last long as on 23rd October 1934, the new Italian Macchi-Castoldi MC 72 achieved the remarkable speed of 440.68 mph. The MC72 had a revolutionary system of two pairs of propellers rotating in opposite directions to reduce the high torque produced by other systems. This speed has never been beaten by a piston-engine floatplane[15].

The Italian success should have sent a message to the British Government that Italy and Germany were catching up and even overtaking Britain in the field of aircraft manufacture – alas they wore blinkers and did not see the gathering storm. It was much cheaper to hide one's head in the ground or in their newspapers. Luckily the skills learned in designing and flying the Supermarine S6B was used in the design of the famous Supermarine Spitfire and its naval version the Supermarine Seafire[15,16]. The Schneider Trophy had resulted in the development of fast, monocoque aircraft powered by a new generation of engines that would prove important in the dark years to come.

*The Supermarine S6B at Calshot being checked by Supermarine engineers for the Schneider Trophy Race while the RAF look on. In the picture on the extreme right is Head Mechanic Herbert Meakins wearing overalls and a trilby hat and second left Alfred Peckham Bert's Leading Man wearing a flat cloth cap.*

Dominic Meakins holding the nose cone built by his grandfather Bert Meakins and his great grandfather Alfred Peckham.

The Supermarine S6 fuselage showing the company plate No 68 1096 and the AID Inspector's seal JA2.

Both photographs were taken by Dominic Meakins

# 12

## A Trip to Germany

A revitalised German economy was based on rearmament. Soon she had a large navy with powerful battleships, the best mechanised army and a superb air force. In fact all of the requirements for world domination, but Britain and France refused to see the danger.

After the success of the S6B, Mitchell produced a series of designs and even full-scale prototypes in an attempt to win the few government contracts on offer. Some were successful while others a complete disaster. Work was hard to find but Bert felt safe working with Mitchell. Now he rented his own flat nearer work and grew closer to Alf and his family. Meanwhile in Eastleigh Father and the other two children were now well looked after by Joyce and her new husband Edward in the family home. The new arrangement suited everyone and relieved Bert from some of his family responsibilities. So it was not long before Edward and Joyce purchased the house from Father while promising to keep everyone there for as long as they wished.

In 1931, the British political scene radically changed when Sir Oswald Mosley left the Labour Party to form the fascist New Party. A year later it became known as the British Union of Fascists (BUF) whose followers, the Blackshirts, terrorised foreigners. Bert wondered what politicians believed in, if anything, when an elected Member of Parliament can change from being a socialist to become a fascist in a blink of an eye. Was it really true that extreme socialism in the form of communism and extreme fascism were similar? He thought that maybe they were as both gave rise to absolute dictatorships that oppressed freedom of speech and censored all ideas other than their own. Everything around him was changing as the country went from crisis to crisis with growing unemployment bringing more hardship. The Labour government collapsed to be replaced by a coalition of all major parties to maintain a viable administration. Then, in an act of desperation, the government abandoned the gold standard so that the pound fell by 28%. At the scratch of a pen one pound fell from being worth four US dollars and eighty six cents to around three dollars and forty-nine cents.

Germany fascist *Nationalsozialistische Deutsche Arbeiterpartei* (NSDAP) or Nazi Party established the Third Reich (*Deutsches Reich*). The Chancellor Adolf Hitler, or the Führer, and the Nazis Party held spectacular torchlight parades throughout Germany where bands played martial music and people wore military style uniforms. The excitement generated was infectious especially when Hitler promised the German people a prosperous future after years of deprivation. They had a new national flag bearing the Swastika with the motto *Ein volk, Ein Reich, Ein Führer* (One people, one nation, one leader). Things changed as the speeches of Hitler and Sir Oswald Mosley encouraged xenophobia, especially a hatred of the Jews. The upper classes and the common mob became united in their support for fascism out of fear of a Russian-type communist revolution. Even the Oxford University Student Union declared that they would not fight for their King and Country. At the time on every street in Britain, Mosley's followers sold their newspaper Blackshirt for two pence and politicians preached the doctrine of peace at any price. Pacifism was attractive to many old soldiers who knew only too well the horrors of war and that Britain hadn't the will to return to the battlefield.

Bert and his friends carried on touring visiting Germany to enjoy drinking in the large noisy beer halls crowded with people and singing. Everyone they met was happy and optimistic about the future often being very helpful. While drinking they met some German pilots who were delighted to know that Bert had built the record beating S6B. So the pilots showed Bert around a nearby *Luftwaffe* base during a public air display. Here he saw rows of bomber, transport and fighter planes that varied from the very old biplanes to the latest streamlined single wing aircraft. To his surprise they even had squadrons of floatplanes that looked a bit like the S6B. Bert was very impressed by the sheer numbers and newness of everything he saw. The *Luftwaffe* officers were charming, showing him around their base and ending up in the officer's mess discussing the advantages of different aircraft. In the mess he met a design engineer Willie Weiss who invited him to visit the refurbished Bavarian Aircraft Works near Augsburg known in German as the *Bayerische Flugwerke* (Bf). The other lads were not interested in visiting another aircraft factory so it was decided that Bert should go alone and afterwards they would meet in Amsterdam.

At *Bayerische Flugwerke* Bert was met by Willie Weiss who arranged his accommodation in a nearby guest house. For the next two days Willie wined and dined Bert while showing him around the very modern factory. The two men got on like a house on fire as they were very similar in character and dedicated to building fine aircraft. Willie was especially proud of their Bf 108 *Taifun* (Typhoon) all metal four-seat touring aircraft that was as efficient as it was beautiful and a prototype of the Bf 109 fighter. Willie and his friends asked Bert many very complicated aeronautical questions such as what was in his opinion the best way to increase the range of their fighters while still making them fast. This was always a dilemma in building all fast aircraft. Simply the longer the range the larger the fuel tanks so the aircraft was heavier. Finding the right balance depended on what you wanted to use the aircraft for. So their questions puzzled Bert. In Britain most fighters were designed to have a three hundred mile range that was considered to be more than adequate for most defensive purposes. However it seemed from what Bert was told that the Germans wanted fighters with double the range suggesting they were being built for a more offensive role.

In his room after a challenging but exciting day, Bert had time to think about all he had seen. It was clear that all over Germany rapid modernisation was taking place as they built an impressive communications system of wide fast roads called autobahns, a network of high speed railways and an impressive airline network. The autobahns were unlike anything Bert had ever seen. The roads had two lanes going in one direction separated by a barrier from another two lanes running in the opposite direction. This allowed for large numbers of vehicles to travel at high speed between the major cities, something that Britain totally lacked. In every town and city, new factories appeared to be working at maximum capacity to produce everything from locomotives to sewing machines and tanks to bullets. But was all this industrial production driven by rearmament a good or a bad thing? Surely the German nation did not wish to fight another war and yet were apparently preparing for one. He shook his head thinking no one in the right mind would go to war so soon after the Great War. Then Bert felt disturbed that maybe they would, especially after seeing so many young children dressed in 'boy scout' militaristic uniforms while only being allowed to hear German folk music or Wagner. There was no popular music like jazz as it was regarded as the music of primitive people and the jungle!

After a very educational and enjoyable few days Bert sadly said goodbye to his new friend before driving to Amsterdam. All he carried with him were good memories and a camera full of pictures of the latest German aircraft. Many of the aircraft he had seen were excellent though a few were not so good. He was very impressed by their extremely high standard of manufacture with aircraft inspectors checking every stage of the assembly. However unknown to Bert a security officer Walter Brandt reprimanded Willie Weiss and his colleagues at Augsburg for speaking about their important work to a foreigner. Then the security officer ordered the police to search and interrogate Bert Brown before he left German soil.

At the time Bert had just arrived at a small village in western Germany to stay for the night at a traditional hotel. He enjoyed an excellent evening meal washed down with a fine, well brewed local beer before going to bed. Next morning after breakfast he rode out of the village and was stopped by a policeman.

'Mein Herr may I check your documents?' the policeman asked.

'Of course you can,' Bert replied handing over his passport.

The policeman carefully scrutinised the passport before putting it inside his pocket.

'Mein Herr you must come to the police station to explain a few discrepancies in your passport.'

'No problem,' Bert replied wondering what all the fuss was about but unconcerned as he knew the Germans could be very officious.

Then Bert and his motorbike were put into the back of a truck and driven to the nearby police station. To Bert's surprise he was searched before being thrown into a cell with only a wooden bench for a bed. Initially he was not worried as he knew it was all a mistake that would soon be rectified. However as the hours went by he started to wonder what horrors lay ahead and what he was accused of doing? Just when he felt like yelling for someone to explain what was happening, two men brought him a meal of bread and soup. Then they meticulously searched all his belongings to leave with his camera and films.

'Please tell me why I am in this cell?' Bert desperately asked.

'Be quiet, you are a dangerous foreign spy!' was the abrupt reply.

'Don't be so silly. I'm no spy. If you care to check I'm sure that the people I visited at the *Bayerische Flugzeugweke* at Augsburg will vouch for me,' Bert forcefully responded.

'Englander, eat your food and keep quiet. We will see what we find. If you are innocent you have nothing to fear,' the less bullish of the two policemen replied.

With those comments Bert was left alone to spend all night in the cell trying to get some sleep on the hard bench without a blanket or pillow. Every now and then he was woken by the sounds of people yelling out orders and the noise of leather boots goose stepping outside the door. Once he thought he heard someone scream out as if in pain but it was a long way off or maybe he imagined it. It is strange that when afraid we hear all sorts of strange noises, some of which are only figments of our imagination.

At daybreak Bert was taken to wash before being served a continental breakfast of coffee, dry brown bread and cheese. He wished it was a full English breakfast of eggs, bacon and sausage, but was glad as it filled his empty stomach. Afterwards he was taken to another room and asked to sit down opposite another officer.

'*Guten morgen Mein Herr*. Please state your name and nationality,' his interrogator asked firmly with no trace of menace.

'Herbert Brown sir, though my friends call me Bert. I am British born and bred.'

'Bert why are you visiting Germany?' the officer continued while lighting a cigarette.

'I'm on a motorbike tour of Germany and Holland with three friends.'

The officer merely nodded while writing down every word Bert said.

'Why did you visit the *Bayerische Flugzeugweke* at Augsburg?'

'I was invited by one of their engineers a Herr Willie Weiss to discuss with him and others the difficulties of building fast reliable aircraft. I am a well known aeronautical engineer who has built fast racing aircraft including the prize winning S6B,' Bert replied deciding that honesty was the best policy.

'Indeed your passport says you are an aeronautical engineer.'

Then the officer took some photographs out of an envelope and spread them on the table in front of them. They were the pictures Bert had taken of aircraft at the air display at the *Luftwaffe* base and during his visit to Augsburg. Luckily the detailed ones of the new prototype fighter were not there. Maybe they had not found that film or the pictures did not come out when developed.

'Do you think you can photograph the aircraft of the *Luftwaffe* without permission and get away with it?'

'I just behaved as I would at any air display in England. I have not seen anything that your people did not wish me to see,' Bert nervously replied before adding. 'In fact the *Luftwaffe* officers saw me take the photographs and often pointed out unusual aircraft for me to see. Why should I do anything to upset my hosts?'

'That is what I am trying to find out. Perhaps what you say Herr Brown is true or maybe it is not. But you have in your possession photographs of most aircraft ranging from the ancient to the most modern. One could think you have made a detailed inventory of our military strength for your government,' the officer continued with a menacing tone.

'It is nothing of the sort. I was fascinated to find out in what way your *Luftwaffe* has developed aircraft. I found that, like us in Britain, you have rejected the American large fuel guzzling radial engines for slimmer and faster V shaped ones. We discussed the problems of balancing the weight of an aircraft against the operational range and speed. It is a common problem when building and designing new aircraft. I also spent hours with their engineers trying to solve a few highly complex technical problems. It is something that always happens when a group of professional aircraft engineers discuss their work,' Bert suggested becoming aware that the interrogator may think that he was a spy. If this was the case he would probably be tortured, tried, found guilty and probably shot.

'*Unteroffizier* (Corporal) take this wretch back to the cell,' the officer remarked in English for Bert to understand.

'*Ja, Mein Hauptmann* (Captain),' the *Unteroffizier* replied clicking his heels and lifting up his right arm in the fascist salute before shouting; '*Heil Hitler!*'

The Hauptamnn replied, '*Heil Hitler*' with his left arm held out straight in front of him before turning to leave the room.

Then Bert was dragged back into the cell and much to his surprise systematically beaten with truncheons until unconscious. When he woke up his whole body ached from head to toe. Everything was very quiet as the only noise was the beautiful sound of birds singing their morning chorus. He tried to stand up but finding it too difficult, sat down overcome by nausea. Outside his cell the sun was trying to break through the clouds as rain hit the glass making a heavy tapping noise. He half-expected to see bolts of lightning strike all around while thinking of that tree burning in Father's house in Eastleigh. The memory of how the old apple tree stood erect even though half dead gave him hope. So he touched his crucifix to pray for guidance and protection from the hell that was all around. As if in answer to his prayers, a ray of sunshine suddenly lit the cell and a large red breasted robin came to sing on the windowsill. It was exactly as Mother told him – it was in the most terrible moments in life when the dear Lord and his angels appear to bring peace to all who truly believe in his love. Bert felt like Daniel in the lions' den hoping that even in this grim cell God would protect him.

He did not have time to worry as a guard brought in a tray with a cup of tea and some soup with brown bread for breakfast. Then he was escorted to the toilet and allowed to wash and shave. Afterwards Bert was made to sit in front of another uniformed policeman and an officer of the *Luftwaffe*.

'Good morning Herr Brown. Please sit down,' the new policeman said in excellent English while offering Bert a cigarette that he gladly accepted. There was another man with short blonde cropped hair wearing a long black overcoat and a black cap. He looked a bit like the man in Bert's nightmares, of course he could not have been. Could he?

'This is *Hauptmann* Walter Brandt of *Luftwaffe* security who has helped me try to understand your behaviour. We agree that you are an aeronautical engineer who enjoys looking at and discussing aircraft and their problems. After much discussion we have come to the conclusion that you had no intention of breaking any of our laws. In fact we feel that you are not skilful enough to be a spy and have not tried to conceal anything from us.'

Bert felt relieved that they thought him innocent.

'I'm pleased that you gentlemen realise I'm only interested in all things to do with aircraft and motorcycles. Is there any more that I can tell you or am I free to leave here to meet with my friends in Amsterdam?' Bert slowly replied.

'We think Herr Brown you have answered all our questions adequately. So I am pleased to inform you that you are free to leave. Please take your travel documents and most of your pictures as a reminder of your visit to our glorious Reich. May I wish you a safe journey and trust this little misunderstanding will not leave you feeling angry about our natural curiosity,' the policeman said handing over Bert's passport and firmly shaking his hand.

'Thank you gentlemen for your understanding and I promise not to photograph anything else on my way home,' Bert said with a smile. He was desperately trying to hide his anger and at the same time feeling relieved at being set free. Now was the time to control his temper as showing any hostility could be regarded as a sign of his guilt. Anyway on the open road no one would hear his angry swearing.

Then Bert walked over to his motorbike to slowly ride towards Netherlands. He could not believe that his ordeal was over and wanted to leave Germany as fast as possible. For the first hour he regularly looked behind to see if someone was following. There was no one. At the border there were no unusual difficulties just the casual examination of his passport, the compulsory dated exit stamp and then he was allowed to pass under the barrier to enter the Netherlands.

He felt free when everyone he passed moved around as always in an orderly, though carefree manner that is as Dutch as Edam cheese and wooden clogs. By the roadside were numerous windmills with their sails moving in the breeze and neat houses with high roofs and wooden shutters. Still he only felt normal again after meeting his friends in

Amsterdam. There they drank and ate in the street cafes as they had always done, but he said nothing about his problems. It was too personal to discuss and anyhow they would never have understood his fears.

On his return home, Bert discovered among his effects inside his motorbike pannier was an undeveloped film that had been overlooked. When it was developed, the prints showed details of the prototype Bf109 fighter that he copied and sent to a colleague in Farnborough. A week later, Bert was interviewed by Air Ministry experts from Farnborough at Supermarine wanting to know more about the Bf109. After two hours of discussing what Bert had seen at Augsburg they left thanking him for sending the photographs and telling them about the direction German aircraft design was going.

Later that day Bert had the chance to talk to Mitchell.

'Did you enjoy your holiday in Germany?' Mitchell asked more as a pleasantry than seeking information, while wondering why the Air Ministry men had visited Bert.

So Bert told him about the trip and the developments he saw in German aircraft.

'I've never seen so many different shapes and sizes of aircraft in all my life,' he told Mitchell. 'Germany is now one gigantic armaments factory. I noticed that in the design of their fighters, they are trying to achieve the balance between high performance, effective range and manoeuvrability. Strangely their fighter aircraft must have an operational range in the region of 500 miles.'

'What you say confirms what others have been telling me,' Mitchell commented while lighting his pipe. 'Did you see any of their newer aircraft?'

'At the *Bayerische Flugzeugweke* at Augsburg I was privileged to be shown around by one of their engineers. He showed me their latest four-seat touring aircraft called the Bf108 *Taifun* and the prototype of a single wing fighter the Bf 109 which was streamlined like our S6B. The small fuselage was built around a large engine. The wings were thin, I suppose for speed, with the Handley Page leading edge slats to reduce landing speed. They said that it would have a covered sliding canopy over the cockpit and a retractable undercarriage. I think it will be capable of beating most other aircraft currently flying.'

'A fast, manoeuvrable fighter with a strong retractable undercarriage is ideal and the sliding cockpit canopy gives the pilot a better chance of bailing out if he has to,' commented Mitchell.

'I agree,' Bert added.

'Is the plane an all metal construction or is it a metal frame covered with canvas?'

'It has an all metal monocoque construction that is strong and more resistant to bullet damage than those covered with fabric,' Bert answered carefully as he did not want to be misleading.

'Well, they think like I do, though I believe our new fighter will be faster and more agile in the skies than any other. It had better be as people are saying that another great war is coming and if they're right the RAF will need every modern aircraft it can get. Already Sydney Camm at Hawker is producing a new fast monoplane fighter for the RAF but I am sure that we can do better. Sydney's plane has a metal frame with a fabric covering to give it a decent range and speed. However I think that in my plane the losses caused by being heavier will be offset by it being stronger. Still given time the prototypes will prove what advantages one has over the other.'

With those words Mitchell returned to the drawing board to work on another new fighter. His first design for the RAF fighter under the specification F7/30, the Supermarine Type 224 was rejected by the ministry, so they had to start all over again[15,16]. After discussions with Sir Henry Rolls Mitchell decided to use the new Rolls PV12 engine designed to deliver over 1000 hp. The latter had developed as a private venture a faster engine based on a highly modified 'R' type that Mitchell used in the S6B. The PV12 was to become one of the most important engines in British aviation history under its new name, the Merlin. Now Mitchell straightened the wings of the old Type 224 and designed the new fighter around the latest Rolls Royce PV12 (Merlin) engine. Then he added a sliding cockpit canopy and a retractable undercarriage. Everything that Mitchell knew about design went into the aircraft together with the information gleaned from Bert, tests in the wind tunnels and his Stress engineers. He wanted his new fighter to look beautiful while being highly manoeuvrable and fast. After months of hard work and trials he produced the Supermarine K5054. Then the Air Ministry on seeing just how good it was decided to produce a new specification for their fighter F10/35 incorporating many of the features found in the K5054. After the prototype was tested by the Aeroplane and Armaments Experimental Establishment a few modifications were requested and the design approved. During the test flights the K5054 achieved speeds of up to 348 mph (557 km/hr) and proved so highly manoeuvrable that the test pilot remarked that nothing should be changed. The result was that in June 1936 the Air Ministry ordered three hundred and ten K5054 aircraft they named the Spitfire Mk IA. The Spitfire became famous when with Camm's Hawker Hurricane they proved their value during the Battle of Britain. However that was still a few years away.

During 1933 Reginald Mitchell was absent from work fighting cancer. His deputy Joseph Smith continued his work but Bert felt the atmosphere had changed. Sadly Mitchell died on 11th June 1937 knowing his new aircraft was a success, though he did not approve of the name Spitfire that he called silly. Today the Spitfire remains a tribute to Mitchell's genius. Some say it was the best fast single-seat aircraft of her day, indeed a world beater. Eventually over fourteen thousand Spitfires and its naval derivative the Seafire were built and flown by thirty-three air forces. The last Spitfires that flew into combat were probably the Union of Burma Air Force Spitfire Mk IX and a few modified Seafire Mk III fighters commanded by Brigadier Tommy Clift who successfully fought Mig15bis jets when the country was invaded by the People's Republic of China between December 1959 to January 1960.

*A reconditioned Supermarine Spitfire SM845 Mk XVIII. This photograph was taken at an air display held at Shoreham Airport in West Sussex by the author.*

# 13

## When Friends Part

True friends are for life.

Eventually the four childhood friends went their own ways. The first to work on his own was Dominic who opened a garage in Southampton selling and repairing the best motorcycles. Every year he raced as part of the official Norton team once finishing fifth in the Isle of Man TT. During his racing career he attracted many a young girl. It was not long before he became seriously involved with Rhonda whose father managed a private motorcycle team. After a romantic courtship surrounded by motorbikes, Dominic married Rhonda Jones in a small Welsh church in the valleys. On their wedding day Rhonda looked ravishing in a long white silk dress with Dominic dressed smartly in top hat and tails. Bert was there with Tim, but he found it strange watching one of his friends get married.

Tim moved to Hythe to join Imperial Airways as a pilot of their flying boats. His knowledge as a pilot and engineer made him highly employable by Imperial Airways who were developing long haul routes to new destinations. Soon he was flying on the first proving flights to previously remote places where an extra aeronautical engineer always proved useful. His timing was perfect as the government had told the nation's airlines to establish air links to most of the British Empire in order to improve communications. They felt the time had come when personnel and mail should be carried to their overseas posts as fast as possible by air instead of ship. However, they still relied on ships to carry heavier goods especially to remote places where there were no runways. Soon even some of the small Pacific islands had a flying boats service linking them with New Zealand, Australia and the USA.

Fred joined Vickers as a personnel manager at a factory producing bombers. All of a sudden he married an Irish girl in a quiet wedding. Then Bert heard no more as they wanted to live alone with little fuss. All she wanted was to be by Fred's side until death them did part. It was all very romantic but meant that Bert never saw Fred again and sometimes he wondered how his old friend was. For a few years they exchanged Christmas cards and then even that stopped.

It didn't bother Bert as he spent more time with Alf and his family to become quite fond of Alf's oldest daughter Jenny. When he first saw Jenny she was as thin as a rake and tall like a blade of grass. Her long shinning hair flowed gracefully down her swan like neck to touch her shoulders. In Bert's eyes Jenny seemed simply perfect. When she saw him come she always had a smile to greet him that was so captivating that Bert was happy being with her talking about nothing in particular. On the other hand Jenny had never seen such a handsome man with a short moustache, sparkling eyes and a body of a prize fighter. He was everything she had ever dreamed of in a man and indeed much more. When he spoke to her his voice was soft and gentle but when someone offended her he was quick to come to her defence with a firm strong voice that sorted out most people. The fact was that she felt safe with Bert as well as excited.

Alf was pleased that Jenny was happy while his wife Rebecca was far from amused. Why should a man ten years older than Jenny be allowed to turn her young daughter's head? To make matters worse he was not good enough for her because he raced motorcycles and was Alf's workmate. For all her humble beginnings as the daughter of a farm hand Rebecca was an enormous snob. No one was good or rich enough to satisfy her imagined high position in society and help support her horse gambling losses. When she won everyone had a feast, but more often they got by on the poorest joints as her gambling drained the family income. Rebecca told Alf that all motorcycles were dangerous and no respectable person would be seen dead on one. They were the Devil's chariots and Bert was the Devil incarnate. Luckily all of Rebecca's unsavoury remarks flowed over Bert like water off a duck's back. He was so besotted with Jenny that nothing and no one could stop him being with her. When he looked into her brown eyes he was lost. He knew she always kept the worst of the stormy clouds away and brought out the best in him. He did not realise it but he was gradually falling hopelessly in love. Now feeling alive and free his recurring nightmares stopped. Sadly in time they would return to haunt him.

As winter days got longer there followed the snow and then glorious spring bursting out with flowers and bird song. It was the time to be up and about inhaling the fresh spring air, so Bert took Jenny out into the country on his motorcycle. She sat in the brand new sidecar, having been forbidden by her mother to sit on the bike. The fresh air and the walks among the trees put colour in her cheeks and made her brown eyes sparkle. Bert didn't only think Jenny was beautiful, he knew she was perfect. When he was with her the world was a wonderful place where even blacked factory stacks spewing out plumes of obnoxious smoke appeared lovely.

Partly because Jenny's mother called men on motorcycles immature overgrown schoolboys, Bert decided to sell his Norton and buy a car. It was not going to be just any old car – but a gentleman's transport acceptable in the best circles and sporting enough to make people stare as he drove by. He could not afford a Bentley or a foreign made car but instead ordered a brand new, handmade, three-wheel Morgan directly from the factory. He never told anyone about his purchase even when he visited the factory to finalise the dimensions. All Morgan cars were a piece of art tailored to fit the client's personal dimensions and wishes, indeed built exactly to order. This meant that no two cars were exactly the same. In every case the client was measured so that the car was built around him. Every Morgan open top sports car was made by craftsmen with a light but strong steel tube chassis. The model Bert chose had one rear wheel driven by a JAP engine with two wheels in front. It was luxurious with two leather covered seats and a folding leather canopy. The three speed gearbox and small engine gave her both good acceleration and low fuel consumption. The car took many months to build so it was not until June before Bert collected his British Racing Green Morgan with fashionable bright red leather seats. He felt like a king when driving her from the factory on his way to show his car to Jenny.

For the next few years Bert and Jenny travelled all along the south coast visiting the seaside, local sites or just having a picnic. Jenny was as much in love with the Morgan as she was with Bert so that even her mother Rebecca became more pleasant. Often Rebecca would talk Alf into taking the family along with Bert to the seaside. So Alf bought a black Austin Seven saloon car in order to keep everyone happy and for a change regained control of the family finances. For the first time in years Alf no longer cycled to work in all weathers but drove like his bosses.

By a stroke of luck both Bert and Alf were offered senior jobs in the Rochester factory of Short Brothers who were busy building their commercially successful flying boats. Bert was promoted to the important position of Chief Aircraft Inspector of flying boats and Alf appointed as his deputy Senior Inspector. The job meant much better pay but less experimental work. However both Bert and Alf wanted a change so they accepted the offers. Unfortunately they were expected to start work as soon as possible. During Bert's last weekend in Southampton, he asked Jenny to be his wife. He half expected her to turn him down and was delighted when she said yes, sealing her promise with a long kiss. Life could not be any better and was proving Bert's creed that hard work in the end brings success.

Bert and Jenny were finally married in 1937 in the majestic Rochester Cathedral. She looked adorable wearing a white lace dress and a hat with veil to captivate Bert's family and friends with her charm. Even the grumpy Rebecca was happy giving Bert a peck on the cheek while Alf quietly looked on smiling. All of Bert's family had travelled from Eastleigh as did Tim, Dominic and his new wife. Sadly Fred didn't but he did send his best wishes. After the ceremony, the reception was held in a large hall where everyone dined on good food, wine and beer, and of course there was music. Tim was the best man and made a witty, though cheeky speech, followed by many toasts until everyone had said something. Finally a reluctant Father stood up to make the family toast to bride and bridegroom.

'Dear friends I would just like to say how pleased my dear wife would have been if she were alive to see us here today accepting the beautiful Jenny into our family. Jenny, thank you for joining us and I promise that we will always be good to you,' Father said in a quiet but dignified voice.

He stopped for a second to wipe a tear from his good eye, took a sip of beer, before adding more loudly as becomes a former Sergeant: 'Ladies and Gentlemen please be upstanding to join me in toasting the bride and groom. Bert and Jenny, may you always be happy and remain in our hearts.'

Everyone lifted their drinks to toast: 'Bert and Jenny. God bless them.'

Bert's family present to the newlyweds was a complete dinner service of the finest china from The Boy on an Eagle Pottery. It was a generous gift fit for a king that linked them with Bert's ancestors. Each piece was decorated with hand-painted interwoven green leaves and gold flowers.

Bert and Jenny settled down to enjoy the garden county of Kent with its strange round tower-like oast houses, fields of hops, and fields full of sheep, lines of hops, or miles of fruit trees. They purchased an old house near Rochester with a large garden overlooking the River Medway. It had a large log fireplace in the sitting room and a modern Aga oven in the kitchen that kept the house warm even when outside the snow was deep. Inside the Elizabethan building were low ceilings with ancient oak beams and heavy doors to give it a warm feeling. According to the deeds, the house was built in the sixteenth century by a farmer. It was large having three bedrooms, a kitchen, a sitting and a separate dining room. There was ample storage place including a concealed priest's hole inside the chimney. Traditionally the small room used to hide priests from Cromwell's soldiers during the period of religious intolerance known as the Commonwealth. It was a sad thought that a fugitive hid there in the dark without a window but preferable to imprisonment or death.

It was not long before Jenny planted a large vegetable garden with a lawn surrounded by fragrant roses. Then she established a chicken coop to raise bantam chickens with a hen house behind strong wire netting, while freely in the garden roamed a gaggle of white geese. The thick wire fencing kept out the red foxes that were common in Kent. It must have worked as they never lost any animal to foxes, though the neighbours did. Within a year they had home-made strawberry and gooseberry jam, an ample supply of both goose and bantam eggs and boxes full of fine Kentish apples and rhubarb. Everything and everyone flourished.

When life could not have been better, the honeymoon came to an end when their lovely baby boy Charles arrived in the middle of the night. Now they were a family who lived in their own world enjoying every moment. Another of Bert's dreams had come true.

# 14

## A Tailor and Fascism

When the Blackshirts brought racism to England.

Bert's new job involved attending meetings with the senior management and clients where he was expected to dress like them. So he urgently needed a good quality suit to show his new status as part of senior management. Wanting to look the part Bert asked his manager friend Hugh James where he could get a suit tailored in the East End of London. Hugh recommended Sol Sachs who often did work for one of the very expensive Savile Row tailors, but was much cheaper. Taking Hugh's advice, Bert visited Sol Sachs in his Select Men's Tailors workshop on Stoke Newington High Street. During the first visit he selected the best fashionable British suiting material dark grey with subtle light stripes and was measured for two three piece double-breasted business suits. On the second visit Sol checked how well the half finished suits sat on Bert and what minor alterations were necessary.

Three weeks after his fitting, Bert was informed that his suits were ready for collection. He waited until a day when there were no newly completed aircraft to inspect to take the day off. Then he got up early to drive slowly to London at a time when the traffic was light. Bert hated traffic jams and indeed having to wait for anything. For most of the journey everything looked normal with the shops open and people rushing around from place to place as though chased by someone. On reaching Dalston he found the streets unusually quiet as if everyone had stayed at home. Then he began to notice the shops were firmly closed with their windows shuttered. It made him wonder what was going on as normally the whole area was alive with people and the shops open for business. Even the local costermongers selling fresh vegetables from their barrows on the streets were nowhere to be seen. In fact it looked like a ghost town in some cowboy film. For nothing moved except a few cars going past but none parked by the roadside or stopped. Naively Bert shrugged his shoulders to continue driving up Stoke Newington High Street. He thought that it was probably a Jewish holiday while hoping Sol was in his shop.

As usual Bert parked his Morgan against the curb next to the front door of Sol's Select Men's Tailors. He found the door firmly closed and the windows shuttered, but this did not deter Bert who was determined to collect his suits. So he banged hard on the door loud enough to wake the proverbial dead and waited. How he hated waiting especially in an empty street. After three minutes of pacing up and down he knocked again, this time even louder. Then he heard someone moving inside the shop.

'Who's that knocking so loudly on my door?' Sol asked angrily.

'I'm sorry to disturb you Sol. It's Bert Brown from Kent. I've come to collect my suits.'

'For you my lad it's no problem Bert. Just wait a moment while I unlock the door.'

Then there was the sound of heavy bolts being moved and creaking as the heavy front door slowly opened. Then through the half open door Bert could see the face of old Sol looking very worried.

'It's good to see you Bert. Please an old man by parking your car in my yard. Sadly you've chosen a bad day to visit. Be quick before anyone sees you,' Sol advised.

When Bert drove around the corner he found the gates to the yard open as Sol and his son Jacob let him in. Once inside Jacob bolted the gates fast. Then they went inside the unusually quiet shop. It appeared that today Bert was the only customer.

'Sorry about all these precautions but we're expecting trouble. Oswald Mosley is addressing a mass meeting of his Blackshirts in Dalston Town Hall. If past experience is anything to go by he will rant against all foreigners, especially us Jews and encourage his people to attack our shops. Too often the enraged crowds rampage down the streets like packs of wild animals destroying all in their paths,' Sol explained.

'Surely they can't just run around attacking honest citizens,' Bert exclaimed in horror.

'Sadly they can and do,' Jacob replied.

'Don't the police stop them,' Bert added.

'They sometimes try but often the mob is so large that no one except the army can control them. However, when things get rough the police horses try to tackle the mob. Unfortunately they sometimes arrive only after the damage has been done.'

'I'm shocked to hear this. I've heard rumours and seen the Blackshirts on the march, but until now I never took them very seriously.'

'They're real enough especially when you live in the East End. We're targeted by the fascists even though many of us Jews, Chinese and other refugees have lived here for decades and often for centuries. The ones I really feel sorry for are the orthodox Jews with their black clothes, hats and long beards that can be recognised miles away. Jacob and I are fairly safe as we speak and look like any other Englishman. Even the name of our business was carefully selected not to show our Jewish origins.'

'I just don't know what to say. It is horrible,' commented Bert feeling quite sick.

'In some ways it's our own fault. We failed to integrate with the local population so that we are often identified as money lenders and bankers. If the truth was known few of us are money lenders and most of the bankers are British, French or Americans. For too many the image of Shylock the Jew from Shakespeare's The Merchant of Venice is real. So they think we love money so much that we would exchange a debt for a pound of human flesh!'

'It's only an old play and should not be taken too seriously.'

'Of course you're right Bert but sadly many think it portrays my people. Now during these hard times such ideas tend to encourage resentment and anti-Semitism.'

'I never realised how bad things have become.'

'Well that is enough lamenting about things we cannot change, so let's share a drink and then get down to business. You've come a long way to see us and we must not burden you with anymore of our troubles,' Sol said putting on the kettle.

Then they sat in silence as Jacob served them with a fresh cup of strong tea and some biscuits. Afterwards he brought out Bert's two new suits individually placed on hangers inside a protective linen cover. Then, without saying a word, he took the first one out of its cover for Bert to try. It fitted like a good glove and when Bert looked in the long mirror he saw a handsome smart businessman. It was exactly what he wanted. In fact the best bespoke suit money could buy.

'The suit makes you look like the professional man that I know you are. Indeed it will impress everyone and look good for many years,' Sol said with pride.

'It's fantastic. In fact it's much better than I expected. It transforms me from an ordinary workingman into a man of distinction. Oh thank you Sol, you're the best.'

'I know I am, but it helps when my customer is as well built and dignified as you,' Sol replied with a lovely smile. Sol knew exactly what to say to keep his customers happy.

Then Bert tried on the second suit while Jacob showed him three fine Egyptian cotton shirts that were just his size. In the end Bert decided to purchase three white shirts with detachable stiff collars and three others with attached collars that were white with a smart light blue, vertical stripe. Then Sol insisted Bert stayed for a light meal as they waited to hear the news that the mob had dispersed.

'Bert may I suggest that you drive across to Islington and avoid passing through Dalston. Sometimes, after the mob has gone away, some of the Blackshirts will wait in a pub for the police to leave before starting another riot,' Sol advised.

When Bert left the tailor's shop everywhere was quiet with people again walking around the streets. So he ignored Sol's advice and went back the way he had come, but this time with the Morgan's hood up. Around Dalston he drove down Kingsland Road and along Commercial Street. He noticed there were more policemen with some on horseback in the streets near shops with broken windows and broken glass on the road. For the first time he was aware that a riot or an uncontrollable mob had rampaged down the long road looting and beating up anyone they found, even seriously injuring and maybe killing their victims.

Outside one parade of shops were piles of broken glass being cleared up and on the ground patches of what looked like blood. Bert stopped to ask what had happened only to be ordered by a policeman to move on as sightseers were not wanted. So he drove home feeling sick and wondering what was happening to England. When he crossed Tower Bridge he felt safer knowing he was south of the Thames and on his way home.

On the journey home he felt depressed. How could the former Labour Member of Parliament the Baronet Sir Oswald Mosley change sides and lead the British Union of Fascists (BUF)? Surely someone would stop Mosley and his fascists from destroying democracy and replacing it with a dictatorial state where all power was in the hands of the few. It was said Oswald Mosley had powerful and rich friends who feared a communist or socialist revolution. His position in society was reinforced when he married the outspoken socialite Diane Mitford after her divorce from her first husband, the rich baronet Bryan Guinness. Many of his supporters came from the aristocracy, the rich, and the educated Oxbridge elite. They believed that they had a God given right to rule over the unwashed and undereducated masses. However most BUF activists came from the poor and under educated who were encouraged to believe that their problems were caused by foreigners. Indeed they must be stopped however high the cost. Great orators like Mosley and his wife moulded their audiences to believe that a strong Britain would only come when it was ruled by a supreme leader with absolute power. Mosley suggested he was the man who would modernise Britain to be like Germany and put the common man first. Somehow he managed to convert many of the rich arrogant students who were enjoying life at elite universities and private schools, as well as the nearly ignorant unemployed, to follow him blindly forward. In many rich households, people proudly wore their black uniforms as a mark of their belief that only true blooded Britons should be allowed to rule or even reside in these hallowed isles. The movement grew as the government appeared unable to run the nation and modernise its crumbling infrastructure. Even the roads were inadequate for the growing numbers of vehicles, unlike the wide motorways *autobahns* in Germany and *autostrade* in Italy. At one time Sir Oswald Mosley boasted the BUF had fifty thousand followers, but it was never confirmed. In fact they never won a single seat in Parliament[5].

After the declaration of war in 1940 the British Union Fascists was outlawed under the Defence Regulation 18B and its leader Sir Oswald Mosley imprisoned in the Tower of London[5]. However, Churchill intervened ordering that Mosley be moved to live with his wife in a small house in the grounds of Holloway Prison. The night the BUF was outlawed the nation changed. In many gardens throughout the land men and women hurriedly burned their black fascist uniforms and all documents about the BUF. Most were too scared to be found having anything to do with an outlawed organisation that could be regarded as assisting the enemy in time of war. All knew the price of treason was, if lucky, a long term in prison and more likely hanging. Many of the more militant Blackshirts were arrested in a series of overnight raids and others warned to be loyal to the nation.

Society showed her true colours. The disloyal rich raced to harbours and airports to fight their way onto ships and planes escaping to safety in a neutral or pro-fascist USA. In those weeks the last passenger ships transported the people whose luggage bulged with all of the jewels and as much cash as they could carry. They did not stop to consider their betrayal of both their King and Country. A dockworker muttered to his mate on the dockside, 'There goes Lord and Lady Muck running with their tails between their legs like rats leaving a sinking ship.' His mate laughed but felt sick knowing that the ordinary person had to remain to keep the nation safe.

Some of those who fled their country at her time of need settled in their new homeland. Others returned after the war to regain their position in society and profit from the business opportunities available in rebuilding the nation. Sadly many succeeded to become the new elite and celebrities who exploited the ruined nation. Loyalty to one's flag was something Britain too often fails to reward, but the rich and aristocrat traitors she forgives! Did equality really exist?

# 15

## Tim Flies around the World

Travel broadens the mind. In theory the more we go to new places, experience different cultures and meet different people of all races, the more understanding we become.

*Imperial Airways Caledonia Short S23 Empire Flying Boat landing in 1937 from collection of photographs by H. Meakins.*

Without warning Captain Tim Watkins arrived in Rochester to take delivery of a new C-Class Empire flying boat for Imperial Airways. He had come to Shorts to put the new aircraft through her acceptance trials before taking her on a proving flight from England to South Africa. Tim entered Bert's office early on a February morning when the cold air seemed to blow down from the Medway. The cold air on Bert's face made him look up from his desk to see a tall suntanned Tim standing there resplendent in his Imperial Airways captain's uniform.

'Captain Timothy Watkins reporting as directed, Sir. I've been sent to check out, give her a test flight shake down and take delivery of one C-Class Empire Flying Boat for my employers Imperial Airways,' Tim said saluting Bert with a great smile.

'Well by Jove I'm glad to see you, you old son of a gun.' Bert said first shaking Tim's hand before giving him a hug. For a few minutes they both stood there like long lost brothers meeting again feeling the renewal of the flame of friendship not dampened with the passing of time.

'Bert I'm here for a week to inspect the aircraft and put her through her paces before flying her down to Hythe on Southampton water. Then it's the round of proving and training flights before putting her on the Africa route.'

'I must admit that when I saw the name of the officer coming to collect her I hoped it was you. So I told Jenny to make up the spare bed and kill the fatted calf. On my part I've double-checked every part of the aircraft. I think you'll love her.'

'Do you mean Jenny or the flying boat?'

'Both. Anyway you can judge for yourself as I insist you stay with us. Then we can discuss all that has happened since we last met and make up for lost time.'

'That's great as I didn't book into the local hostelry,' Tim replied.

They spent the rest of the day checking the paperwork, log books, and records of the Empire flying boat. Every aircraft sold was supplied with the latest maintenance manuals, essential tools and a removable set of floating wheels. The wheels were only used when rolling her out of water to check damage and to periodically remove marine growth. The wheels were constructed so that they were easily removed when the aircraft was floating in the water. Lastly there were the compulsory log books for the aircraft as well as one for each of the engines to record all servicing and maintenance procedures. Of course the aircraft was painted in the livery of the airline and fitted out internally as requested. Some aircraft would have more seats than others with different internal configurations. Usually Imperial Airways Flying boats had names all starting with C such as Canopus, Cambria, Challenger and Caribou. They carried seventeen passengers and around two tons of cargo with a crew of Captain and co- pilot, radio operator, flight engineer and one or more stewards/stewardesses.

That evening they sat around the log fire with Jenny, drinking a jug of ale and talking about various things that had happened since the wedding.

'Things at Imperial Airways vary from one moment to the next as the management is changed by government order. Luckily pilots like me rarely have to report to that huge headquarters near Victoria Railway Station. It is impressive but overwhelming. Imperial Airways operates a wide range of aircraft such as the Vickers Velox and Handley Page HP42 Horsa as well as a fleet of flying boats[17].'

'I had heard the rumours that the government wants to control all of the international flights of not only Imperial Airways but British Airways as well.'

'Yes Bert, I'm convinced that in the event of war they will commandeer all civilian aircraft. Then they will unite the two companies along with their smaller rivals. One problem would be that British Airways relies heavily on foreign aircraft. These range from the twin-engine aircraft such as the American Lockheed 10A Electra and Lockheed 14 to the three-engine German Junkers Ju 52 and Dutch Fokker F.VIII and F.XII. So in the event of war or civil strife spare parts would be difficult, if not impossible, to find.'

'So you really think that another war is coming?' Bert questioned.

'Well the actions of Germany in Spain and Italy in Abyssinia are not those of a pacifist. I doubt if they want another war with all of the loss of life and expense that it entails. It's a worry; if there is another war we are not prepared for it as most of our military equipment is old and out of date,' Tim responded with an unconvincing smile.

'Let's hope it won't happen,' Jenny volunteered.

'Well Tim, please tell us about where you fly to and your life in general. I expected by now you would be married and have four children with a big dog named Rex,' asked Bert.

'Well you know I don't like talking about myself, but I will try just for you. When we started to go our own ways I took up flying as a full time job. I was never as good an engineer as Bert so I joined Imperial Airways as a pilot. The fact that I was a certificated engineer with flying boat experience helped me land the job as well as being useful on the more awkward proving flights. It surprises me how few pilots know how an aircraft works or can repair the simplest problem. So I tend to get the more exciting overseas trips to places where ground support often is minimal or non-existent. Of course we have a flight engineer on board but they always like help when things get difficult.'

Over the next few days Tim described his experiences flying from Hythe on Southampton water to the Mediterranean and beyond. From what he said, they flew in all weathers from winter storms that battered the windscreen to hot days when the air in the cockpit stifled his breathing. From Hythe they usually flew via Marseilles and Rome to Brindisi in Italy. Then they crossed to Athens and down over the Mediterranean Sea to Alexandria in Egypt before starting the long journey down the Nile and across the African lakes.

He said something like this:

We take off from Alexandria[17] on the short hop to Cairo, flying low over the pyramids to keep the passengers happy. It is a splendid sight though it can be hidden by thick dust clouds. The ancient sand coloured stone monuments appear to grow out of the desert to point upwards to the stars. I believe that the largest of the three pyramids is the four hundred and eighty-one foot tall Great Pyramid of Khufu built around 2500 BC. While in front of the smaller pyramid of Kharfre is the incredible statue of a cat with a man's head known as the Sphinx. Some guides say the head is that of the Pharaoh Khafre but it is so badly damaged that no one really knows. When visibility is less than a hundred yards we fly by the seat of our pants to land safely on the River Nile at Cairo. Here most of the passengers disembark while others board as we prepare for the dangerous part of the journey. Sometimes we change crew or rotate with another crew already on board. Whatever is the case we usually spend a few nights at Shepherd's Hotel to enjoy a decent soak in a warm bath and many a hearty meal. Meanwhile the ground engineers check and refuel the aircraft in preparation for the next leg. We take off from the River Nile to follow it southwards,

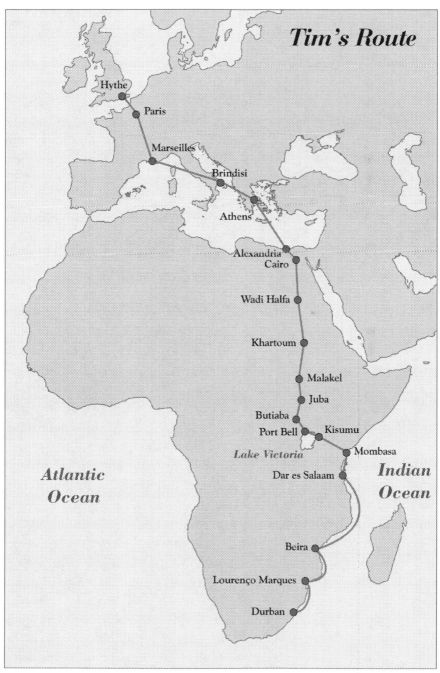

*A Map of Tim's Flying Boat Journey from Hythe*
*in England to Durban, South Africa.*

passing over the vast ancient temples at Luxor and Abu Simbel before landing at Wadi Halfa. There is something majestic about ancient Egyptian temples that are so large and yet so well crafted that it takes one's breath away. Whoever built them must have been not only good architects and skilled masons, but also excellent engineers. Can you imagine erecting a forty foot stone pillar from lying on the ground to being in an upright position among other such pillars, using mostly manpower and primitive ramps? Even today such a task would test the best engineers and scientists.

At each stop we refuel, resupply with fresh food and water, and quickly check the aircraft for obvious damage. On leaving Wadi Halfa, we go down to Khartoum where the Blue and White Niles meet and on to Malakel. After Malakel we leave the desert behind to fly over the vast swamp land known as the Sudd to Juba. When flying over such places the navigation system and George, the automatic pilot, are very useful. In the Sudd there are no landmarks, just miles upon miles of thick aquatic vegetation through which the Nile somehow manages to flow northwards. From Juba the flight path follows the White Nile down to Lake Albert where we land on its south bank at the steamer port of Butiaba. Here crew and passengers stay the night at the Imperial Airways' Budongo Forest Rest House. It is a large bungalow with a huge veranda and outdoor showers situated on a hill overlooking the lake. It is so well run that it feels like being in a fine hotel surrounded by tropical trees and magnificently coloured birds. The evening meal is always the same, that is delicious, freshly caught huge steaks of Nile Perch cooked in butter with rice followed by a desert of freshly picked tropical fruits. I am always surprised that such a delicate tasting fish is over three foot long and a predator of smaller fish – in fact it looks a bit like our Pike. Budongo is in many ways the ideal place for a stopover. The beds are comfortable with their own mosquito netting with a spectacular view across Lake Albert at sunset. Some mornings you can hear chimpanzees drumming on the trees or see the Black-and-white *Colobus guereza* monkeys jumping in the trees as if playing to entertain us. Occasionally a few wild elephants wander through the forest below proving that we really are miles from anywhere in the Rift Valley lakes of Uganda. Everywhere is green you look there is green vegetation and lots of water. It is no wonder that Churchill called this the Pearl of

Africa. The straight forest trees grow a hundred foot into the sky while various flowers add a multitude of colours to the green landscape. My eyes are bombarded by the array of colours that range from the red of the bird known as the Ross's Turaco to the brilliant crimson and blues of a multitude of smaller birds. Then there are the butterflies of every size and shape imaginable. Also, alas, there are a lot of biting mosquitoes and lake flies that make the evenings a bit difficult though a good fire, mosquito nets and the burning of sticks of pyrethrum keeps them away. Maybe I love this place because it is tranquil being a marked change from miles of sand and featureless swamp.

Only when the weather is clear can we take off to fly south eastwards over the African savannah grasslands passing the rugged Mountains of the Moon on our starboard side. The glaciers on the sides of the mountains reflect the sunlight while on the port side are herds of antelope grazing on the savannah. The next stop is Port Bell on the edge of Lake Victoria which can be a difficult landing as the lake is so large that it acts like a sea with tides and a swell that can be unsafe to land on. Luckily the ground team keep us informed over the radio if conditions are unfavourable before we leave Butiaba. At Port Bell we refuel and replenish our food supplies while some passengers disembark and a few join us before we make a slow accent to fly over Lake Victoria.

From Uganda the route takes us southeast to the Kenyan port of Kisumu and then across land to the sea at Mombasa. After Mombasa the journey follows the coast southwards over vast panoramas of pale blue sea, the large coral reefs and sandy beaches where coconut groves magically sweep down to the sea. We land at one or more of the ports along the east coast such as Dar es Salaam, Lindi, Beira, and Lourenço Marques depending on our passengers. This is enjoyable knowing our journey nears its end as we fly down the Natal coast to land in Durban. Sometimes we go on to Cape Town but usually it is served by the West African aircraft. Now we have a few days rest before retracing our route home.

For the first day in Durban most of us stay in our beach hotels catching up on sleep and resting tired bodies. By the second day I become restless wanting to explore my new surroundings. Then I join a guided tour going to this part of South Africa where once the mighty Zulu impis ruled. I like visiting the wildlife sanctuaries north of Durban to see lions, elephant, rhinoceros and herds of antelope that vary from the very small dog like Dik-dik to the mighty Eland and the Greater Kudu. Once at dusk I saw a leopard moving across the ground hunting some unsuspecting animal. Though the leopard is a beautiful animal it has the large cold eyes of a professional killer. Not, in my opinion, the sort of creature to keep as a pet, though I am told some people do. Once I visited a tourist Zulu-style village to watch traditional dancing and listen to the singing and the beat of the drums. There I began to wonder what good our being in South Africa has done for them.

Jenny interrupted Tim to refill their drinks and after sitting down commented. 'You know Tim I never realised just how complicated such an air journey can be. It appears to me to be more dangerous than I thought.'

'You're right Jenny the journeys are a series of short hops that must be carefully negotiated as there is no room for error,' Tim replied before continuing with his saga.

Life on board flying boats is not all fun. Though everyone has their own seat and there is a smoking room and a promenade deck. Every now and then we see the dark shapes of large sharks lurking near the surface in the sea below. It is a timely reminder of the hidden dangers that lurk just beneath the waves in every sea and lake. One found in most African lakes is the huge man-eating ten foot long Nile crocodiles waiting with their bodies half submerged in the water for someone to go for a swim or fall off a boat. Others lay sunbathing on the river banks apparently half asleep with their large jaws open and eyes half-closed. As soon as the water is disturbed these huge prehistoric monsters launch themselves like ships into the water to disappear as they hunt their prey. Strangely both the local fishermen and the women washing their clothes by the water's edge appear unafraid of the danger but probably always kept one wary eye open for danger. However I think the most dangerous of all the wild animals to a flying boat is that curious African creature, the hippopotamus. They occur in large herds grazing on the land at night and wallowing in the shallow lake waters during the day. Though they are hard to see, we must lookout for them whenever taking off or landing on the rivers and lakes between Cairo and Kisumu.

At this point Bert stated. 'I wish I could see a hippopotamus in real life as they seem so magnificent. I read somewhere that they are very dangerous. I think that is because they have large mouths and huge tusks-like teeth that could tear a person to bits in seconds. They probably could cause serious damage to a small boat or even the floats of a flying boat.'

Tim continued.

I cannot recall any aircraft hitting a hippo, but if they had, it would have been badly damaged, if not destroyed. In fact the hippos and crocs could be the reason why so many boats and aircraft disappeared without trace.

Like all good things, Tim's stay ended as he flew away in his flying boat, resplendent in her new Imperial Airways insignia. Afterwards he kept in touch my sending the occasional postcard from all over the globe reporting his latest adventures and showing different lands. Jenny kept every card he sent neatly in an album as a reminder of a true friend.

# 16

## Henry and the Spanish Civil War

The battles between communists and fascists for the control of Spain should have been a loud warning to the world of the horrors of war, but everyone chose to ignore them.

Without telling anyone, Bert's younger brother Henry Brown joined others from Hampshire to travel to Spain to fight with the International Brigades. Like all recruits he made his last will and wrote a letter to his family that he sent to Bert. It read:

Dear Bert,

A group of us Hampshire lads travelled through France to Spain to fight for the Republic against the Fascist Nationalist forces. Our group consists of men from all over Britain, Ireland, France, and even America. At first life seemed simple until we realised that this war is riddled with politics, in-fighting and very harsh discipline. Our forces consist mostly of the anarchists of the *Confederacio Nacional de Trabajo* (CNT) and the *Federacion Iberica Juventudes Liberaties* (FIJL).Then there are the fiercely independent Basques and Catalans. There are also many communists belonging to the Stalinist PCE and the anti-Stalinist POUM. While the republicans and the socialists are alliances of different anti-fascist groups. The Nationalist enemy are also a mixture of groups such as the Carlists wanting the descendents of Don Carlos to be king, the Catholic right-wing party CEDA, the fascist *Falange* and a few monarchists wanting to put Queen Isabella II on the throne. I simply support the ideals of the democratic Republicans against the fascist Nationalist army. Though I'm now beginning to believe that whoever wins this war will have to make peace with all the Spanish regions wanting independence – especially the Catalonians and the Basques[18].

If I die I wish to leave everything I possess to our Father to do with as he feels fit and ask you to be my trustee. I don't want to die but the longer I'm here the more likely it becomes. Some communists are very violent expecting loyalty even unto death. It may be hard for you to understand but in this war being shot for questioning an order is not uncommon and justice a rare commodity only offered to the privileged few.

Lastly I want to say that I will always be grateful to you and Joyce for raising me to become a man. Pray for me and all the rest of our lads in Spain. God bless you and Jenny.

Thank you
Signed
Henry Brown


Inside the envelope was a photograph of Henry with some of his Hampshire pals somewhere near Madrid.

Later another letter arrived describing the defence of Madrid.

It said:


Dear Bert,

This is just a brief note to tell you what is happening.

It was the autumn of 1936 when my unit arrived in Madrid to keep the Popular Front government in power. By now the fascist Nationalists consisted of thirty-four thousand men from the Army of Africa and twenty-four thousand men from the Peninsular Army. All of General Franco's Army of Africa was airlifted from Spanish Morocco to Spain by German *Luftwaffe* aircraft. So we Republicans are outnumbered having to fight with old weapons against a better armed enemy. Then Walther Warliamont of the German General Staff arrived to become the military adviser to General Franco. He established the German Condor Legion consisting of three squadrons of He-51 fighters; a Reconnaissance Group of He-99 and He-70 bombers; and another of He-59 and He-60 floatplanes. This large and very modern air force has overwhelmed our meagre air force to leave us vulnerable to air attack. I have come to learn that aerial bombardment is both very sudden and frightening, as you hear nothing until the bombs explode.

On 1st November 1936, twenty-five thousand fascist Nationalist troops under General Varela reached the suburbs of Madrid where we kept them pinned down. Then the Condor Legion attacked us. Luckily the 11th International Brigade under Soviet General Kleber arrived to support us as we fought from street to street slowly losing ground against superior firepower. Even so I think we inflicted severe casualties on the enemy though they did the same to us. In our forces both men and women fight side by side, some women even lead the attacks and command some groups. From 13th December to 5th January 1937 the Nationalists advanced ten kilometres killing fifteen thousand of our men. Heaven only knows how long we can hold their advance without more men and weapons.

Keep safe Bert,

All my Love and Gratitude

Henry

Henry's letters stopped coming while the radio was full of the news of the battles, political manoeuvrings and innuendo gleaned from observers often far from the front line. After two years fighting the Nationalists conquered most of the land causing the International Brigades to abandon the socialists to fight alone for the little that was left. On 24th September 1938 the International Brigades crossed the Ebro River to disband and flee to France. This allowed fascism its first major victory in continental Europe.

Sometime later Bert heard from Father that Henry had returned home with a Spanish wife, but suffering from bullet wounds to his legs. He could walk, but with a distinct limp. Later Henry and his wife Maria reluctantly explained that the fascist Nationalists killed over seventy-five thousand people while the Republicans killed another fifty-five thousand. This excluded the civilians who died during the bombing of the towns such as Guernica. After the war many ordinary people were arrested, imprisoned and shot by the fascists purely on suspicion of being a socialist. It is estimated that a half a million people died in the war including many women and children with both fascists and communists being equally cruel. Both sides listened to no one but themselves and would destroy the world rather than let it stay free and happy. Henry believed that the only way a caring democracy could exists was where every man, woman and child had equal opportunity and the freedom to follow their beliefs. What they told Bert opened his eyes to the horrors of war that his younger brother had experienced. It made him start to wonder if a blinkered Britain would see the danger of fascism and Germany before it was too late.

# 17

## Short Brothers in Rochester

*Short Sunderland Mark I, T9078 KG-E. RAF No 204 Squadron moored at Bathhurst, The Gambia. This photograph, reference MH6609, is from Imperial War Museum London Collection and used by permission granted under licence waive WAV 2462 of April 2010.*

Suddenly, as if the wool had been removed from their eyes, the British government changed their attitude. They realised that German rearmament program was an actual and dangerous threat to peace. Within days they reluctantly started the expensive task of ordering modern equipment for their badly equipped armed forces. So the ministries produced a series of specifications they sent to manufacturers for the supply of modern weapons ranging from large ships to rifles and aircraft to anti-tank grenades. Among these documents was an order that all new transport aircraft, whether civilian or military, must have a longer operational range. In fact they would be expected to carry more cargo and passengers without the need for stopping to refuel from Britain to America or Cape Town. This would prove difficult to achieve as at the time, for commercial considerations, the operational range of most passenger aircraft was five hundred miles.

One of the few aircraft that met the new specifications was the long range Short S.23 C Class Empire Flying Boats designed for luxury air travel with a length of 88 foot (26.8metres). Twenty-eight S.23 aircraft had been ordered by Imperial Airways to operate on their Empire services. The first Empire flying boat to be commissioned only had a range of five hundred miles at 190 mph while carrying fifteen passengers with two tons of freight. This was not enough. So the airframes were strengthened and the more fuel efficient but slower Bristol Pegasus engines fitted so they could fly fifteen hundred miles without stopping. The demand for flying boats meant that Short Brothers' business was booming with the huge extended hanger full of fuselages under different stages of construction. It was Bert and his inspectors job to examine each one to rectify every fault or sign of poor workmanship. His diligence soon earned him a reputation among the workforce of being a stickler for detail and a man not to be crossed. It was not that he was a bully or even unfair but that he thought that any error however small could prove fatal. As Chief Inspector, he had to certify that every aircraft was in perfect condition since he would be blamed by Shorts or the Air Inspection Department (AID) if anything went wrong. The first C Class to be finished was named Canopus and designed to fly down the coast of West Africa. The second Caledonia was modified to have fewer windows so improving the fuselage's strength to hold the heavier long range petrol tanks needed for the transatlantic mail service. At the time the largest commercial flying boat they built was the Short G Class S.26 Golden Hind that was 101 ft. (30.9 m.) long.

Now there were ten aircraft at different stages of construction in the hanger as they tried to meet an ever increasing demand. It was a slow business as each fuselage was laid down like a ship surrounded by specially built metal frames known as jigs to give support and made to the required specifications. So that any change in size of any part required an alteration in the size and shape of the jigs. The aircraft could not be moved until complete and ready for its seaworthiness tests. The prototype of the military version of the flying boat, the Short S.25 Sunderland made her maiden flight on 16th October 1937. She had a hundred foot wing span and was eighty-five foot long with a previously unheard of range of three thousand miles at 190 mph when fully equipped. After the declaration of war, Shorts increased her speed to 210 mph and added the latest Fraser-Nash rotating gun turrets. There were two machine guns in the front turret, four in the tail and two on the top of the fuselage behind the wings. This unusual shape earned her the nickname the flying porcupine as she proved ideal for anti-submarine warfare and air- sea rescue.

In 1936 to meet the demand for more aircraft Short Brothers and the shipbuilders Harland & Wolff of Belfast formed a new company called Short & Harland. The idea was that the factory was too far from Germany to be easily bombed and would utilise the large skilled local manpower. Unfortunately after the fall of France, Belfast was bombed and the factory nearly destroyed. Initially they built one hundred and ninety Handley Page Hereford two-engine bombers and Short Sunderland flying boats[1].

Then they produced most of the RAF Short Stirling four engine bombers. The original Stirling was developed at Rochester by Arthur Gouge and his team to meet the Air Ministry Specification B12/36 for a four-engine bomber. This stated that it must carry a load of either fourteen thousand pounds of bombs or twenty-four soldiers over long distances. Unusually the aircraft must be easily dismantled into parts for transportation by train and on large trucks! This proved a challenge but with Bert's assistance they produced the Short S31 that was a half-scale model of the proposed new bomber. It had its first flight in September when she reached 180 mph and performed like an aircraft half its size. Once the design was approved a full size prototype L7600 was built. This was so successful that the RAF immediately ordered the L7600 as their main heavy bomber to be called the Short Stirling. The first production the S29 Stirling had her maiden flight in May 1939. She was fitted with four Bristol Hercules II radial engines and capable of carrying a bomb load of fourteen thousand pounds, but only over distances less than five hundred and seventy miles. For longer raids the bomb load was reduced to three thousand five hundred pounds usually made up of seven five hundred pound bombs. Soon the demand for Stirling bombers was so high that parts and complete aircraft were assembled at thirty different sites around the country. The Stirling was an excellent aircraft but handicapped by the RAF's demand that it had to have a dual role being capable of long range bombing and pulling gliders. For the first part of the war the Stirling was the front line bomber until replaced by the faster and larger Avro Lancaster. By the time its construction was stopped, some two thousand four hundred Stirling bombers had been built in three countries. Sadly after the war none were kept in any museum and soon their importance forgotten[1,19-22].

*Short S.26/M G Class Flying Boat and three Short Sunderlands*
*of RAF No 204 Squadron moored on Sullom Voe, Scotland.*
*This photograph, reference MH6666, is from the Imperial*
*War Museum London Collection and is used by permission*
*granted under licence waive WAV 2462 of April 2010.*

# 18

## The Civilian Repair Organisations and Sebro

The problem was not building enough aircraft for the RAF but keeping them operational. So the Ministry of Supply established the Civilian Repair Organisations.

Soon after the outbreak of war it became apparent that the RAF did not have the manpower or experience to repair and maintain all her aircraft. To try to meet this urgent need, the car manufacturer Lord Nuffield was requested to establish within the RAF a number of Civilian Repair Organisations (CRO) and teams to salvage all crashed aircraft throughout the country. Initially he established CROs in airlines, garages, and air training schools but excluded all aircraft manufacturers who were considered too busy building new aircraft.

However, it was soon apparent that a large, well run CRO was required for the more difficult work and should be established near the bomber bases in central England. To meet this need the biggest CRO was secretly established in Cambridge by Short Brothers to be known as Short Brothers Repair Organisation, Sebro for short. Strangely, within weeks of the war ending, most records relating to the work of Sebro were lost due to an 'accidental' fire at Short's headquarters. A number of government actions were presumably carried out under the Defence of the Realm Act or the Official Secrets Act!

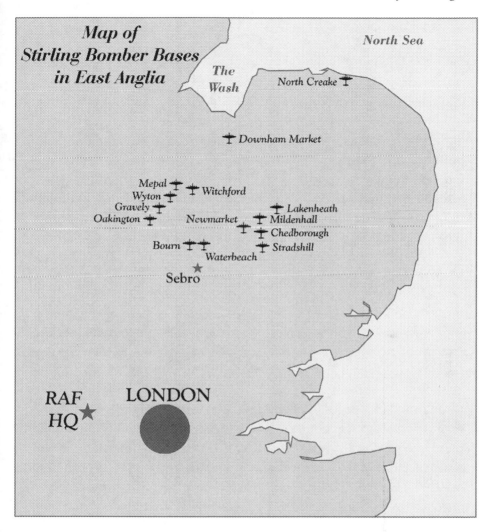

Early in 1939 against Jenny's wishes, Bert volunteered to train as a pilot for the RAF. Bert knew that like his Father before him that it was his duty to fight for his country. Somehow during the RAF medical the doctor 'accidentally' pierced his eardrums so that he failed to be declared fit to fly. One ear could be regarded as an accident, but both were highly suspicious. For many years after every time Bert flew he had very painful earache! When he returned home with his ears still hurting, a disappointed Bert was met by a special delivery motorcycle messenger carrying a top secret letter addressed to him.

It said:

Dear Mr Herbert Brown,

Action to be undertaken under the Defence of the Realm Act 1914 and the Official Secrets Act 1911 as amended in 1939[23].

It is my duty to inform you that you are hereby required to leave Short Brothers Aircraft Works at Rochester to be taken to an university building in Madingley Road Cambridge where rooms are at this moment being made available for you. Within one month you will assemble a team of aeronautical engineers and mechanics that you will train to be operational as soon as possible. Then you will establish a repair organisation in the hangers and facilities being built at Marshall's Flying School south east of Cambridge near Teversham. Your unit will be part of a repair/special requirement facility designed to maintain, repair, and adapt for special uses all makes of RAF and allied aircraft for the duration of the war. The financial management of this project will be looked after by another Short Brothers employee who you will recognise and together you are expected to give us the capacity that sadly our country lacks. The new company will be known only as Sebro an abbreviation of Short Brothers Repair Organisation. Sebro is for all public purposes, now and at all times, to remain a top secret organisation that will not be discussed or written about by you or your men. I need not warn you that the longer such an organisation remains undiscovered by the enemy the longer it will survive. You have been carefully selected for this important position because of your proven expertise of working on many types of metal aircraft and your skill at modifying them whenever required. In your new job you will be expected to be a man of all trades capable of being a team leader and teacher to help us modify any aircraft of our own or of foreign origin for whatever task we decide.

The Prime Minister wishes to remind you that failure in this enterprise could cost us dearly, even the war. We hope that your organisation will give us time to train more aeronautical engineers and mechanics to meet our future needs anywhere in the world. You must always be prepared for all eventualities, however hard and difficult they may turn out to be. Times of civil unrest and war are a proving ground wherein all good men will flourish and show that we British are a nation slow to anger, but when aroused fight back like a lion awaken from a long sleep.

May I wish you good luck and may providence be your guide.

Signed

Lord Beaverbrook for Lord Nuffield

Then there was the following addendum.

Sign this order as having been read and return it in its resealed envelope to the messenger. You may tell your wife briefly why you are moving to Cambridge but no one else. All who need to know have been informed while others must not know anything. Secrecy is important for the safety of both our nation and indeed yourself.

Next morning Bert was ordered to fly from Croydon Airport to Belfast to study the building of the Stirling bomber at Short & Harland factory. Bert was met at the airport by the chief engineer of Shorts who drove him into town. Bert noticed that it was a grim industrial smoke filled city with row upon row of terrace houses and apartment blocks whose skyline was dominated by the large cranes in Harland & Wolff shipyards. Most people he met were friendly and chatted about everything except religion. Sadly the days of the illegal Irish Republican Army was not over though dormant. It was said that the IRA promised to remain active until all Ireland was ruled by Dublin and the British thrown out of every part of the island. The Chief Engineer left him at O'Reilly's Hotel where a room waited for him. He soon discovered that it was less than a ten minute walk to the Shorts works. The hotel was owned by a kindly Mrs Kathleen O'Reilly and her son Connor who were Roman Catholics, born and raised in Belfast. They were quietly Republican in their politics but treated Bert like a member of their family. So he had a clean room, a radio, and good meals as well as pleasant company.

One evening when Bert was drinking a Bushmills Irish malt whiskey at a table near the fire, a fifty year old man rushed in and without saying a word sat down next to him. The man looked as though the Hounds of Hell were on his heels and indeed in many ways they were. In minutes he was followed by three so-called plain clothes policemen who, looking more like a gang of hooligans, burst into the bar pointing their pistols at everyone.

'Listen carefully all you bloody Republicans. Put your hands in front of you palms on the damn tables so that we can see them. Don't even think about moving or getting up. Do it now or face the consequences. I don't care what you think or who you are. You'll do what I say otherwise we'll have a bit of fun. I don't care either way as I like a good fight I do,' one of the newcomers ordered everyone present with an unpleasant grin. He reminded Bert of the bullies he knew when he was an apprentice. On their own such bullies were easy to deal with, but in a group were dangerous. So armed with this knowledge he just sat waiting to see what would happen while quietly fuming with anger.

'Please do exactly what they ask. I think it would be best if we cooperate with these gentlemen,' Kathleen O'Reilly said in a calming, quiet voice mingled with a touch of anger. While speaking, Kathleen tightly placed her right hand on a double-barrelled shotgun concealed beneath the bar. She was ready to use it if things became ugly.

Then it was all too much for Bert. He was shocked and bloody annoyed at being threatened by a group of unknown people without uniform who looked more like thieves than officials. No one was going to threaten him, especially as he was in Belfast on important government business.

'Who do you think you are to go about threatening honest citizens?' Bert challenged the newcomers.

There was no reply just a shocked look on the face of the newcomer as all eyes in the room turned towards the muscular Bert.

'You had better explain yourself or answer to the authorities for your bad behaviour?' Bert continued.

Then, as he started to get up a hand pulled on his arm as if to say don't move. So he didn't move.

One of the intruders, 'Mr Fatty', walked over to point a pistol in Bert's face.

'This is our Belfast boyo not your bloody England. So you'll do exactly what we say or pay the price for your arrogance. Do you understand me mister wise guy?' Mr Fatty said with his foul breath close to Bert's nostrils.

Bert just nodded yes, too angry to talk.

'Has the cat got your tongue boyo; maybe you need a little persuasion to make you more cooperative?' 'Mr Fatty' continued lifting his pistol to hit Bert across the face.

'Gentlemen please leave Mr Brown alone. He's on official business visiting Short & Harland. I believe he's a decent government man, clean, tidy, reads his bible and pays his bills with cash unlike the rest of you,' Kathleen intervened before adding pointedly. 'I think we all could take a lesson from men like him. She hoped to quieten a dangerous situation.

Her soft words worked.

'Mr Brown is it? Have you seen an IRA trouble maker enter in the last five minutes?' he yelled rudely into Bert's injured ear.

'I don't think anyone entered for the last half hour, but I could not be sure as me and my friend have been enjoying a warm fire and drinking a good Irish whiskey,' Bert said still angry and feeling like punching 'Mr Fatty' on the nose. He began to think his uninvited companion was the man they were seeking, though he was at least fifty, had a limp and was much more like a priest than his idea of a terrorist. Indeed he looked more trustworthy than 'Mr Fatty' who pretended to represent the law. Maybe he did!

Bert's comments worked. Immediately 'Mr Fatty' and his men left as rudely as they had come, to run down the street looking for anyone to harass.

'Maybe one day I can thank you for your help by doing you a favour in return,' Bert's companion said with a distinct Southern Irish accent. 'I'm Captain Liam Gallagher who served under Michael Collins, God Preserve His Soul, with the IRA during the troubles I hope are gone forever. At my age and with a gammy leg I can't outrun the fattest Ulster Volunteers. Indeed that's what they're called, though they act as self appointed vigilantes illegal under the British War Act, unfortunately in Belfast some still go unchecked.'

'Liam it's nice to meet you. I'm Bert Brown visiting Short & Harland.'

'Brown is a common English name but even so may I ask if your father or any relative served during the troubles in Ireland as a sergeant in the British Army?' Liam asked.

'For his sins my father served in Ireland during partition, I hope that doesn't cause you a problem?' Bert replied worried about the question, for many of the old sores from the civil war were still unresolved. Most people accepted partition, but a few still wanted a united Catholic Republic of Ireland separate from Britain.

'What a grand stroke of luck it is to be sure. I owe your father a great favour for saving my brother from death for some unauthorised stupidity involving a bomb under a railway bridge,' Liam Gallagher stated.

'What a small world. Father told me about the incident saying that only bastards shoot unarmed schoolboy or hand them over to a firing squad. Well I'm pleased to meet you,' Bert ventured ordering another bottle of Bushmills whiskey and some water.

The rest of the night and for the next few evenings Bert got to know Liam and enjoy his company. Liam had the gift of a clear mind, a wicked sense of humour and a way of speaking that would calm a maniac or make the most devout nun love him. After that first night, the so-called Ulster Volunteers never returned to O'Reilly's hotel and so they talked about the countryside, people and even religion. Neither could tell a Protestant from a Catholic and felt that all who believed in Jesus were, deep in their hearts, good people. It was the disbelievers and atheistic hell raisers such as the Nazis who bring this world to the edge of destruction. Liam's only political comment was that things would have been better for everyone if Michael Collins had not been assassinated. He believed that the American born Éamon de Valera had ordered Collins' death because Collins stood for peaceful coexistence and an independent Irish Free State within the British Empire. Indeed after Collins' murder, de Valera declared an Irish Republic outside the Empire that was neutral and in many ways anti-British[6,8]. Such comments left Bert wondering why so many Irishmen from both sides of the border fought for Britain and the King if de Valera was right and they really hated Britain.

The Short & Harland Aircraft Works was situated on Queen's Island where they produced Short Stirling and Sunderland aircraft as well as the Handley Page Hereford light bombers, and a few Percival Proctors. The diversity of aircraft reflected the government's point of view that the enemy bombers would come from Europe and be unlikely to attack Belfast. While at Shorts Bert learned what was needed to repair a Stirling and recruited some senior engineers to work at Sebro. For the first time Bert came across real wartime security when at every gate to the works all the workers and visitors were questioned and their papers carefully examined. Indeed everyone working there was fully vetted to remove those with pro-IRA or pro-German sympathies who might be tempted to sabotage an aircraft. Every person had, at all times, to carry with them their identity card with a photograph that was checked at regular intervals during the day. Bert was not surprised as there were rumours of IRA activists guiding enemy submarines at night to map the coastline while establishing secret bases to be used when required. However no one Bert met in the security services ever even hinted at such activities. Short & Harland had good relationships with their workers because they employed anyone suitable whatever their religion or place of birth. It made it a happy place to work. If the truth were told Bert was charmed by the beautiful Irish accent, the excellent workmanship and the friendly people. Everyone was helpful as Bert listed the thousands of parts used in a Stirling bomber as they would all be needed when repairing the aircraft. Too soon he finished his work and said goodbye to Kathleen and Liam never expecting to see either of them again. But it is always the unexpected things that makes life both interesting and sometimes highly confusing.

As Chief Inspector, Bert occupied an office in the Madingley Road offices in Cambridge next to his manager Hugh James. Together they planned Sebro around the existing Marshall's Flying Training School outside the city off the Newmarket road. While they were deciding who would do what, the RAF purchased an adjacent large area of farmland that was combined to Marshall's land. This meant that Sebro had one concrete runway for heavy bombers which was extended before a second grass runway was built. In a matter of weeks the whole area became one large construction site erecting a series of large camouflaged hangers and the necessary defence system. At the same time carefully concealed anti-aircraft guns were housed in half-buried concrete bunkers while machine gun posts were set up to cover the airfield and all the approaches. For safety reasons large underground stores were dug and reinforced to house ammunition and spare parts strategically placed away from each other in case of bombing. When the buildings were complete, everything was carefully camouflaged to look like another large farm when viewed from the air. Then Bert moved to the airfield to start the slow process of establishing a large repair organisation out of the smaller Marshall's Flying School. The latter proved useful having the basic tools and manpower Bert needed.

Soon it became clear that Cambridge had been chosen to establish Sebro because it was in the centre of or near most of the RAF Stirling bomber bases in the region. It did not take Bert long to realise his organisation had to be prepared to work on a wide range of aircraft of different sizes and shapes. Probably few jobs would be like the last one, so everything they needed had to be rapidly assembled and mobile. He decided that to be fully operational they would need every size and shape of nut and bolt, windows, undercarriages, fuselage and wheels used in all RAF bombers. The task was daunting as it had never been attempted before because of its complexity.

The first thing they did was to establish who did what. Soon they decided that Hugh James would work at Madingley Road administrating Sebro while Bert became the Chief Inspector organising the repairs at the airfield. As luck would have it both men were good friends from working together at Rochester and so they made an effective team. Hugh proved to be an excellent manager but had little experience of actually repairing aircraft and Bert was happier with his hands dirty than filling in forms and arranging for the men to be paid. To start with, both men shared the clerical work. Bert made lists of all the parts and tools he thought they would require for each aircraft. While Hugh made records of the Sebro employees and all the financial requirements, this included how and when they would be paid. The more Bert looked into the problem of what was needed the bigger it became. So he ended up scribbling notes on pieces of paper while smoking his pipe in order not to forget something. Within weeks a list of a few hundred parts grew into pages requesting thousands of necessary pieces, including specialist equipment for removing broken screws, re-turning metal on high quality lathes and for cutting bent metal from a damaged fuselage. On top of this they would need easily movable heavy duty hydraulic jacks to lift broken parts including engines and wings, easy to assemble strong scaffolding and many drums of penetration oil to loosen old nuts and bolts. In addition each team of engineers and mechanics would need a complete portable workshop so they could work on any aircraft anywhere on the airfield or at a RAF station. Then the lists were typed by his secretary before being sent to the Air Ministry with copies to the RAF. All were marked urgent for their approval and hopefully for the immediate supply of the items.

After the first month, Bert received an unexpected visitor while teaching new recruits how to service a Stirling bomber. He was so engrossed in his work that he did not notice the large black Humber arrive outside the hanger. In fact he was demonstrating how to efficiently replace a damaged undercarriage. As always he placed on a tarpaulin, all the parts in a precise sequence so that their reassembly would be easier. It saved time and ensured nothing was missed. Unfortunately a smartly dressed RAF liaison officer with Lord Beaverbrook for some unknown reason carelessly kicked the tarpaulin sending some of the parts all over the place. On hearing the noise, an angry Bert jumped down from the scaffold to confront the thoughtless officer who had made their work much more difficult.

'Stop that you blithering idiot,' Bert shouted. 'There's no reason for you to make me and my men spend more time repairing this machine than is absolutely necessary. Your stupidity is what I expect from the arrogant bastards who spend their time sitting behind desks in Whitehall while others fight the war. So clear off and don't let me see your ugly face ever again.'

The RAF officer was angry at being spoken to so rudely by a mere civilian and would have reacted except that the older man intervened.

'Mr Brown, please forgive my colleague's carelessness,' Lord Beaverbrook said before adding. 'Remember most people who drive cars can't change a spark plug even if their life depended upon it. I'm afraid the same is true for most pilots and aircrew. The other day I asked a friend if he remembered who built the S6B. He didn't know but he could tell me the name of the RAF pilot who won the Schneider Trophy race. It's as though we remember the celebrity and forget those who made his success possible. Such is life.'

Then he paused to put out his hand.

'Beaverbrook,' he said with the charm that had made him a highly successful business man and now a government minister.

Bert shook the famous man's hand firmly trying to smile while wondering why he was visiting Sebro.

'I had no reason to come here because as you know Lord Nuffield runs the CROs for the RAF, but yours is exceptional. While inspecting a few bomber and fighter bases I was shocked by the lack of aircraft mechanics and qualified aeronautical engineers. When I suggested that soon we would have a country covered with wrecked aircraft with only a few operational, I was told by my RAF liaison officer that your organisation was designed specifically to repair four-engine bombers and other large aircraft. What about the fighters, I asked, to be told that they were much less complex and well catered for. However they complained to me that you have too many spares, indeed much more than you will ever need. What do you have to say to that?'

'Sir they are entitled to their opinion. Let me just add in my defence that each bomber and large transport plane is made of thousands of different components that must all work together if the aircraft is to be fully operational. For example, consider a simple item such as the aircraft wheels. You can clearly see that on the same aircraft the tail wheel is a quarter the size of the two main front landing wheels. Only a few parts are fully interchangeable such as some of the engines, spark plugs, radios and ammunition in any aircraft. If you care to look at these bolts you'll see they are of different lengths and tensile strengths. Some are only tough enough to hold a piece of cowling in place. By comparison these others are so strong that they hold the engine together even when running at high revs for over ten or more hours.'

Lord Beaverbrook discussed with Bert Sebro's requirements until he knew all that he wanted to know. Then walking back to the car he commented to Bert. 'Before this war is over you will be required to repair every sort of aircraft that exists and make special modifications to others. It is a gigantic task but, if what I heard about you is true, you're the right man for the job. Good luck, Bert. If you urgently need anything please feel free to call my office anytime night or day. This is the time when Britain needs more people like you, bloody stubborn, skilled fighters. Only then can we hope to win this war or survive the might of our enemies.'

As Bert watched Lord Beaverbrook's black Humber drove off into the distance he wondered just how much of a poisoned chalice he had been given. Still at least he had the support of one of the senior ministers. The meeting must have been successful as within weeks the supplies arrived by rail, truck and air so that the stores were crammed to overfilling. So they built more stores dispersed around the site. The local town folk were told they were an expanded training facility working in and with the university in association with Marshall's Flying School. Only a few asked any more questions. However anyone who appeared to be too nosy was severely questioned by Sebro's military police. In fact most unwelcome visitors left feeling repentant for asking silly questions, while a few were secretly incarcerated for the duration of hostilities. Even in rural traditionally loyal Cambridgeshire there were enemy agents and informers. Surprisingly many came from the so-called respectable upper class British. The security men were so good that Sebro remained free of saboteurs and fifth columnists for most of the war, though they did have a few close calls.

Within weeks of becoming operational they received their first repair work. A Stirling arrived in pieces on the back of a lorry after damaging her wings during a bad landing. This was the first test of their training and involved removing the engines before checking the wing structure. The old wings had to be repaired and attached to the fuselage to be as good as new, if not better than before. Only when the wings were attached and the fuselage standing on her undercarriage could the engines be replaced and the aircraft again become an entity. Because everyone wanted to work on the aircraft she was looking like new and totally airworthy within two days! So Bert listed her as job number Sebro 01 and wrote against her registration number the comment – a simple job completed well on time. Adding I can now say for certain that we are fully operational. The men at Sebro watched the repaired aircraft gracefully take off to return to her squadron knowing they were ready to face any task. They could never have guessed in a hundred years the enormous burden that was to become their daily work. It would not be long before the men were so tired that their eyes constantly had rings under them and their skin looked a sickly pale colour from lack of sleep. There were times when things were so hectic that they did not go home. Instead they tried to sleep for an hour in a quiet corner of a hanger.

Within a year Sebro was working on all sorts of aircraft not only in Cambridge but also in airfields throughout Kent, Sussex, East Anglia,

Essex, Hertfordshire and Lincolnshire. Now Bert's Morgan proved her worth as nearly every day he drove down country roads to one bomber station or another to discuss how his group could help keep each squadron operational.

# 19

## When the Little Ships saved the Day

The little ships, the unforgotten Homeric catalogue of Mary Jane, and
Peggy IV, of Folkestone belle, Boy Billie, and Ethel Maud, of Lady
Haig and Skylark...the little ships of England brought
the Army home.
Philip Guedalla, 'Mr Churchill'[24].

The war started badly. Within six months the ill-equipped British
Expeditionary Force (BEF) in France retreated after suffering a series
of serious defeats was forced back to the sea. The better trained German
Army supported by Stuka dive bombers and Panzer tanks fought a
*Blitzkreig*, or Lightning war, that destroyed their enemies causing the
demoralised to flee. So it was that the remains of the BEF were cornered
in an enclave around the port and beaches of Dunkirk with no visible
means of escape or defence against air attack. This effectively meant that
the war in Europe was lost even before it had really begun. The news of
her defeated army spread like wildfire across Britain making everyone
expect an invasion and the inevitable fight to the end. Then by a mixture
of good luck and heroism all was not lost as things unexpectedly changed
for the better. People like Bert's brother Henry unexpectedly became
reluctant heroes. According to Henry it happened like this.

'Hello Henry I hope you don't mind me asking, but will you sail your yacht to Southampton and across the Channel to Dunkirk?' asked Lt James Norton of the Royal Naval Voluntary Reserve.

'The Lovely Maria is seaworthy enough to make the trip, but I don't see why I should risk it with the war going so badly,' Henry replied not wanting to be in another war.

'Well I've been asked to secretly approach chaps like you to form a sort of armada of little ships. The top brass think if enough take part we could rescue ten thousand men from Dunkirk. I know it's a lot to ask especially as you have been injured, but if it gets worse we may have to commandeer your yacht.'

'Is it really so bad they need people like me?'

'I reckon that if each boat makes two trips before being sunk and brings back ten people we can rescue even more people. However don't kid yourself that it will be easy since Jerry will try to sink every one of us because they control the skies over Dunkirk. From your experience of fighting them in Spain you know exactly how ruthless they are.'

'Yes I remember Spain, so going to Dunkirk is a personal matter. I will be trying to settle some unfinished business and avenge my friends.'

'I understand but Henry you don't know the half. It appears that either we save as many men as possible or they will be captured. They can't swim all the bloody way from Dunkirk so some of us are going to lend a hand. Will you join us?'

'Well if things are so bad the least I can do is give it a go. Sadly I already know the hell we will be sailing into. So I must play my part even if it is the last thing I do.'

'Thanks Henry. I think that with more people like you we will rescue fifty thousand men and give us a chance of stopping Jerry invading our homes. Good luck. See you in Southampton.'

Henry went home to collect his sailing gear and enough provisions for the crossing.

'I have to go away for a few days but promise I'll be back before you miss me,' Henry said as he kissed Maria.

'You just listen to me Henry Brown and keep safe. You've done your bit so please don't take any more risks than absolutely necessary,' Maria said with tears in her eyes as she understood that he was yet again going into harm's way to help save the nation's army.

A few hours later Henry sailed in his boat among eight other vessels out of the River Hamble to Southampton. There they joined more vessels to follow an ancient Royal Navy gunboat eastwards. Outside Folkestone they saw ships of all sizes and ages arriving from Dunkirk bringing home exhausted soldiers. So Henry's yacht joined the line of small boats sailing the channel. Henry tried to keep calm while following an old Thames sailing barge manned by an elderly bald man and a teenager. Behind him was a line of ships of all sizes, most with engines but some only with sails. By an act of God, the Channel was calm with no large waves but a gentle breeze that let Henry's boat skip along at a decent rate under sail without using his engines.

It was afternoon before Henry's yacht arrived off Dunkirk to queue waiting for his turn to go into the shallow water to pluck the soldiers. He could see many lines of soldiers in the water up to their necks. Nearby larger vessels waited to be able to go in to the mole to embark more people. It was surreal and well disciplined except when under attack from enemy aircraft or shelled by advancing artillery. Then they broke ranks hoping in vain to find any shelter.

For some unforeseen reason, Adolf Hitler ordered his armoured divisions to stop their advance to rearm, so leaving his infantry to overrun the BEF defences. It was a costly mistake as the BEF Rear Guard fought valiantly holding the Germans many miles from the town and the beaches. So Henry's first trip was fairly easy with little enemy fire. He pulled men from those standing in ragged lines up to their necks in water into his boat. Only when his boat was completely full did he reluctantly sail away. Some small ships offloaded their people onto larger ships while others like Henry had to sail across the Channel with their precious cargo. He didn't look back distraught at having to leave so many behind, fully aware that some would never live long enough to take the next boat.

The second trip was scarier. Now the enemy artillery was much closer and bombarding the men on the beaches as he sailed pass half sunken ships and bodies floating in the water. While picking up more men a Stuka dive bomber dropped a bomb nearby that tore a small hole in the hull which he managed to patch. The boat leaked but everyone kept her afloat by bailing the water out as soon as it seeped in. Eventually a very tired Henry reached Dover to disembark his passengers and have a cup of sweet tea. Then feeling refreshed he spent a few hours getting some wood and glue to fix the hole so that she was watertight. Now she was safe enough to sail home. He had done his two trips and now wanted nothing more than rest, but fate had other ideas.

'What are you waiting for?' asked an arrogant RN officer.

'Pardon me. What did you say?' replied an angry Henry.

'I asked what is stopping you from going back to collect more of our men?'

'Because I'm tired, my boat has a hole in her and I don't fancy risking my life without help. Where are the bloody RAF and the Navy when they're needed? There're none of our aircraft over the beaches to protect our lads from Gerry dive bombers or us at sea.'

'Sorry I can't do much about that and I know you have already done your bit,' the officer commented with tears in his eyes.

Then Henry noticed the RN officer only had a left arm.

'It may surprise you but I really would give my other arm to be able to sail with you and save a few more lads. I think you're the bravest group of men I have ever been privileged to know. Nelson would call you the Heart of Oak that is England. God bless you. No one can make you go, but if you decide to give it another try then follow that Yank, I think his name is Paul in his yacht Snow Goose. This is not his war but insists that he must do his bit for his adopted country. Funny bloke, he must be all of sixty, but my God he has guts.'

So, feeling guilty that the old Yank Paul was risking his life to save British soldiers, Henry left in the Lovely Maria to follow Paul's Snow Goose, noting it too had a few scars from previous crossings. The line of little ships sailed together behind a small naval vessel across the water to those beaches full of desperate men trying to get home. Once there they had to wait for their turn to be allowed to go into the shallows. While waiting anxiously Henry talked to Paul. Somehow Paul's calm, warm, American voice cheered Henry.

'Heaven knows how an old New Yorker ended up here being bombed in a small yacht in someone else's war. At my age I should be fishing for my supper off some quiet beach,' Paul commented as a shell exploded nearby.

'It's a strange world that the two of us are helping soldiers escape the war by waiting like sitting ducks. I'm British so I suppose it's my duty, but why are you here?' Henry asked Paul.

'It's a long story. I was on holiday in Europe from my job as a sports journalist in New York when war erupted. While deciding what to do I had a drink at a bar in Southampton and saw others fighting to board ships bound for New York. They looked so disgusting, like a pack of rats fleeing a sinking ship, that there and then I decided to stay and do what little I could to help. So I bought a bungalow overlooking the Solent on the Isle of Wight and found part-time work in a boatyard. Then someone asked if I would sail to France to rescue some stranded soldiers and I said sure, why not. So what's your excuse?'

'Not as good as yours. I'm a solicitor in Southampton who is exempt for military service because I was wounded in the Spanish Civil War. Like you a friend asked me to sail here so I did. I suppose I felt I had to even though I hate war in any form,' Henry explained.

'I like to think that by being here I can justify my living in England but I stayed because I like the place. I'm a widower so have no one to worry about, do you have a family?'

'I've left behind my Spanish wife and my father but I think they understand why I'm here. If I don't make it please tell my family I did my bit.'

'Henry both of us will make it. I promise that I will make sure you get home safely even if it's the last thing I do.'

'Thanks Paul and I will keep a weather eye open for you.'

They had no more time to chat as a Royal Navy launch came alongside when the shelling intensified making it hard for the small boats to stay afloat. In fact most of the larger vessels had left or were leaving loaded with men.

'Gentlemen you may go into the shallows and take off as many of our lads as you can. Be fast and get out quickly as our defences cannot hold the Germans back much longer. Please don't overload your boats for if you sink there will be no one to rescue you,' an RN Lieutenant said.

'Well Henry the sooner we go in the sooner we can get the hell out of here,' Paul yelled out with an endearing grin.

'Dear Lord I ask you to protect us all this day,' Henry prayed out loud.

'I know he will,' Paul replied as his boat sailed off into the shallows.

As Henry neared the now devastated beaches, everything became horribly quiet while the noise of firing suddenly stopped. The only noise was the crying of the wounded and the waves breaking on his boat. Henry knew that this meant that the last BEF positions had been overrun or the Rear Guard surrendered. So he hurried to carry out his task knowing that at any time he would become a target of the enemy aircraft. One by one Henry helped half-naked men into the Lovely Maria until she could take no more. They were all very weak from the cold after standing for hours in the water; many had abandoned their boots and equipment to be able to swim out to any vessel that came by. Most were soldiers except for young William, a civilian like Henry, who had just sailed the Channel to help to have his sailing boat sunk under him. After one look at the bodies lying dead on the beach and the thousands still waiting to be saved, Henry turned away sick with war and man's inhumanity to others. Then, feeling like an absolute bastard knowing there was nothing more he could do, Henry sailed out to sea leaving behind the Hell that was Dunkirk.

All the way back, enemy aircraft bombed and strafed the overloaded little ships. Then Henry's luck ran out as a bullet from a German fighter hit his right arm killing the soldier by his side. Henry had little choice but to lie down on the deck.

'Take it easy sir, while I bandage your arm. It doesn't look too bad but we need you fit enough to take us home,' said a young soldier. He then bound Henry's arm with some torn shirt while William steered the boat in a northerly direction.

'Thank you,' Henry replied as his body shook out of fear and the shock. Strangely the wound didn't hurt but just throbbed like a bad headache after too much cheap wine.

'No problem mate. If we help each other we'll get home. If you don't mind me suggesting, I think we should lighten your boat by burying our dead at sea,' the soldier named James suggested.

'That's a good idea. I think I'm strong enough to steer her,' Henry replied.

'If you feel tired just say the word and I'll do the hard work,' William commented. Then he helped James who was trying to keep the soldiers warm as most wore only their underpants and were shivering from the effects of exposure to the cold wind.

William and James kept everyone cheerful even when they saw a boat on fire or one sinking beneath the waves. Then they passed a large piece of floating debris with the name Sea Goose on it. For a few seconds Henry said nothing but silently grieved for his American friend and looked in the water for survivors. All they found were two men who they pulled aboard. To Henry's delight one was a very exhausted Paul, who on seeing Henry, just grinned.

'My God Paul I'm glad to see you,' Henry said shaking Paul's hand.

'Not as much as I am to see you. We were machine gunned by a low flying aircraft that killed most of my passengers and sank my poor Snow Goose. Bloody fascist bastards shooting unarmed men,' Paul said angrily.

'Even now we're a long way from home and an easy target for any German aircraft on the rampage,' Henry replied.

'You better let me take the helm as your arm is bleeding,' Paul suggested.

'Well just for a while,' Henry responded glad to be able to sit down.

So Paul, helped by William, did the steering while the others bailed out the water gathering inside the battered Lovely Maria. Somehow she stayed afloat just above the waves with water lapping her gunwales. Just as they felt unable to take much more, they heard the noise of more aircraft and in an act of desperation Henry made the sign of the cross praying for a quick death. As the sound grew closer they tried to hide by lying as low as they could inside the boat. Then out of the darkening sky appeared a lone RAF Hawker Hurricane with guns ablaze, attacking a German Stuka that was about to bomb another boat. In seconds the enemy dive bomber was in flames before crashing thunderously into the sea. Behind the Hurricane came two more RAF fighter aircraft, surely sent by the angels from Heaven, to fly low over what remained of the small ships.

Everything changed as if the RAF belatedly kept the enemy at bay before they could attack any of the ships. Just watching the aerial escort lifted the hearts of those at sea. Both ahead and behind the Lovely Maria, Henry saw ships of all sizes limping homewards. At intervals they sailed past the old RN ships stationed to guide them to the nearest port. Everyone felt sorry for the poor devils manning those naval vessels. They had to wait like sitting ducks until the last small boat passed or they were sunk. Surprisingly many of them sailed home, battered but still afloat!

On seeing the White Cliffs of Dover, they felt a tremendous sense of achievement coupled with relief at finding a safe harbour. Even then their ordeal was not over as hundreds of boats vied with each other to find a place to land. It took a few hours before they were allowed to dock at a temporary pier and disembark Henry's precious cargo of weak, semi-naked soldiers. Some like James waved goodbye, while others feeling their feet at last on dry ground walked away as fast as they could.

Then Paul helped Henry to a nearby First Aid tent.

'Henry, take your time and get fit before you go home. I promise I'll phone your family to say you're alive and coming back to them,' Paul promised.

'Thanks Paul and please keep in touch.'

'Don't worry yourself about me because like a bad penny I'm very hard to lose,' Paul said as he disappeared.

Inside First Aid Tent, a medic gently cleaned Henry's bullet wound before stitching it up. Henry felt lucky as all around the tent and on the waterfront were hundreds of wounded on stretchers some without an arm or a leg.

A kindly lady issued Henry with a railway warrant to travel via Brighton to Eastleigh, but after what they had been through together, he was not going to leave his Lovely Maria behind. Though still in pain, Henry climbed back on board his yacht and set her sails to slowly make his way back to the River Hamble following others returning from the crossing. When the yachts entered the river mouth, Henry saw the people lining the river bank cheering to welcome their heroes. As the Lovely Maria neared her mooring, Henry noticed Father and dear Maria waiting for him. Now uncontrollably, tears streamed down

Henry's face. At last he had made it safely back from Hell. He wiped his eyes on his dirty shirt sleeve before throwing the mooring painter to Father who secured Lovely Maria to the landing. In seconds Henry was on the landing running to his Maria as if his whole life depended on her. It was a strange homecoming, for Maria hysterically slapped Henry's face very hard before grabbing him tightly. With tears streaming down her face Maria shouting out loud in Spanish to God thanking him for Henry's salvation. Meanwhile Father watched with a tear in his good eye saying nothing, but his face had the smile of a very proud man whose son had returned safely home covered in glory.

'Henry you must never, ever leave me again. Promise never to volunteer for anything while I still live,' Maria stated firmly.

'Darling Maria I promise never to volunteer or leave you again,' Henry replied before kissing her eyelids tenderly.

'How did you know I was coming home and today of all days?' Henry asked.

'We heard over the BBC that a flotilla of little ships had finished bringing three hundred and thirty-eight thousand men from Dunkirk to England including one hundred and forty thousand French and Belgian soldiers. So Maria and I prayed together for your safety before discussing whether we should come here or not,' Father explained.

'I knew we did well, but never thought we could save so many before the beaches were captured,' Henry commented absolutely surprised that they had saved a whole army.

'While we were still discussing what to do and find out how you were, we had an unexpected phone call. It was a Yank called Paul who explained that he was phoning to tell us that you were alive and well in Dover. When do you think Henry will come home I asked? He laughed saying that it should not be long as he saw your boat sailing westwards out of Dover an hour before,' Father continued.

'Then we hugged each other in sheer delight at the fantastic good news. So I collected blankets, food and drink and we put on warm clothes. Without saying a word Father and I made up our minds to go to your old mooring to wait for you even if it took a week,' Maria proudly intervened.

Father said nothing but looked embarrassed.

'So we took the first bus to come as fast as we could before walking along the river bank – nothing was going to stop us from being here for you. Once we arrived on the Hamble, we joined the others sitting on the river bank to wait through the cold night eating some biscuits and drinking sweet tea,' Maria added.

'Dear Maria spent most of the night making sure I was alright or very quietly chanting some Spanish prayer, while holding her crucifix in her trembling hands. Just as dawn broke and the people around us stirred to make a cup of tea, we saw the outline of what appeared to be sails on the horizon. Very slowly the sails became larger. I think it was over an hour before we recognised Lovely Maria among the four yachts and then we jumped up and down with joy. I felt proud that my prodigal son had returned from one of his wild adventure,' Father said a bit embarrassed at showing any emotion.

'Father was a tower of strength during the wait, but it was worth it when I saw your beautiful tired face. Then I was very angry when I noticed your blood stained bandaged arm not knowing whether to cuddle you or spank your bottom,' Maria added shyly.

'Well let's go home. It'll be good to sleep in my own bed and not worry about the bloody war,' Henry said. He had to leave the landing quickly as he was becoming emotional at the sight of the empty moorings where once his friends' boats were anchored, a few returned later but most were never heard of again.

In the next few months, Henry slowly repaired the Lovely Maria to look as good as new, complete with a fresh coat of paint. However he never wanted to sail across the Channel again. His boat was always a grim reminder of an unusual armada of little ships and above all, of a Yank called Paul who cared enough for his fellow man to risk his life so a few more could be saved. Henry knew that we all, like Father, have our scars from war, some deep inside our souls, some visible for all to see, for no one who has been in any conflict survives unchanged. At times he wondered if any of the men they saved from the waters off those blood stained beaches ever forgot the hell they went through. Many were just lads soon to be retrained to fight in a newer army. Did they even remember those who risked their lives to pluck them out of the cold sea? Those they left behind on the beaches faced years of living in prisoner of war camps or died from their wounds often without sedation. The medics who remained with the wounded were the real heroes, sadly some died during the battle for the beaches. Eventually years later some returned to a strange new world that had mostly forgotten their sacrifices.

Days later Henry was very angry after reading that Dunkirk was a victory – it certainly did not look that way to him. The military called the evacuation off Dunkirk from 26th May to 4th June 1940 Operation Dynamo – Henry thought that only heaven could help Britain if it was an example of good military planning. It reminded him of the bad days in Spain when outnumbered and badly led they survived purely by luck and a prayer. Winston Churchill then sensibly remarked that wars are not won by evacuations [23]. How true. Sadly this was not to be the last British defeat or evacuation. At least people like Henry saved enough of their fellow countrymen to form a new army to defend Britain from the expected invasion. Perhaps this time they would have better equipment as they stood alone against the forces of evil. Now it was clear that Britain was the last stronghold of democracy in Europe and must prepare for a long bitter struggle. However Henry did not have long to ponder upon the situation as he unexpectedly became busy learning how to be a father. For when he returned from Dunkirk, Maria had decided without telling him that she was going to have his baby, just in case he dared go away again. She had been so loving and full of happiness that within two months she had his baby growing inside her but did not tell Henry until her bump started to show. Luckily he was overjoyed on hearing the news, having thought he was impotent or that Maria did not want children. Henry called their newborn son Herbert Jose Brown after his brother and Maria's father. Henry knew he had played his part but he often wondered how Bert was faring repairing bombers in a secret operation so far from family. They kept in touch by writing but it was not the same as having a joke over a beer in the local pub.

Years later Henry received a small brass plate to place on the Lovely Maria stating that she had sailed to and from Dunkirk in Operation Dynamo. He fixed the plate to his ship as a reminder of a strange adventure that had nearly cost him his life. However he often met his friend Paul who turned out to be a journalist and author. Paul promised that one day he would write a short story about their adventures in Dunkirk. He did. It was a novel simply called The Snow Goose[25].

# 20

## Unusual Requests

Often in times of crisis one is expected to do unusual things
without question and for the so-called national good.

Life at Sebro was never dull. At any moment a new task would arrive
often making Bert solve previously unforeseen problems. For example,
one morning a strange but beautiful gull wing PZL P 11c fighter arrived
uninvited at Sebro flown by a Polish RAF pilot. Its unexpected arrival
brought the security men out in force to find out what was happening
as they suspected the unrecognised machine was German. After a series
of questions the pilot was brought before Bert to explain what he was
doing and who he was.

'Well can you please explain what you are doing here?' Bert asked
intrigued by both the young pilot and his unusual aircraft.

'I am sorry to be such a nuisance Sir. Pleaze esscue my mistake,'
the man replied in broken English with a strong Eastern European
accent.

'No problem lad he doesn't sound like a Gerry and is wearing RAF
uniform with the Polish cross on it.'

'Can we leave him with you Bert' asked the security officer.

'Of course you can,' Bert replied with a smile. Then turning to the
Polish officer asked. And what can I do for you?'

'I am Flying Officer Stefan Radvanski a Polish officer in the RAF. I am pilot of Stirling bombers from a nearby airfield.'

'Yes I guessed that much, but how can I help?'

'I have brought my beautiful Polish fighter to you hoping you could store her as I cannot fly her and am not allowed to keep her any longer on our base.'

'And what makes you think I can do such a thing?'

'Another Polish pilot collected his repaired aircraft from here and said he saw some foreign aircraft parked in a nearby field. So I hoped I could place my plane there. She means the world to me as together we have fought our way across Europe to England.'

Bert hesitated for just a few moments as he wondered what he could do. In front of him was a very young brave man who loved his aircraft and was willing to risk his life from Britain. So he decided to break all the rules and let the lovely aircraft stay.

'Stefan I admire you Poles and love the aircraft. So I will let her stay here as long as you promise to come and check on her whenever you can.'

A dumbfounded Strefan just smiled like a boy who has been given a present.

'So be a good chap and park her next to the other foreign planes in the old hanger,' Bert stated hoping that Sefan would be content with his decision.

Stefan saluted Bert before running to his aircraft and taxing her into the hanger. He parked next to two three-engine German Junkers JU 52s and a Dutch Fokker F.XII previously owned by British Airways. Then after a brief chat, the two men parted as friends.

Already Sebro had a number of foreign aircraft being serviced and modified for the RAF Enemy Aircraft Unit based at Duxford. This was another top secret organisation where all types of enemy aircraft were prepared for clandestine operations over enemy occupied territory. The three-engine Junkers JU 52 was particularly useful as it was a common transport used by the *Luftwaffe* and so attracted little attention when flying over Occupied Europe. They were all painted in German camouflage except for a small RAF roundel on both wings. A few had even been rebuilt from crashed aircraft especially the Junkers JU 52 and the Fiesler Fi 156 'Storch' that could land on a cricket pitch. They were regularly used by Special Operations Executive (SOE) together with the reliable Westland Lysander III to take agents behind enemy lines into occupied Europe and bring a few lucky ones safely home.

Often when things were quiet, Bert worked on the foreign aircraft much to the joy of the RAF and especially Flying Officer Stefan Radvanski. When Stefan was not flying he came to check on his much loved old plane. Bert soon discovered that Stefan was a nice young man who had fought the Germans since 1938 when defending Poland. He then flew with other Poles to France to continue their war against the Germans. Some considered him a wild, uncontrollable man; others claimed he had personally shot down twenty German aircraft over France and Poland. It made Bert wonder why he was flying bombers when he was an experienced fighter pilot. However only God knew why the RAF made the decisions they did about foreign volunteers. Stefan was very quiet, speaking in broken English with a heavy distinct Polish accent that sometimes Bert found hard to understand. In time, Stefan's English greatly improved as they became good friends and drank together in the officers' mess, but more often in the nearby Elizabethan pub 'The Barley Mow'. In this old thatched pub, a mixture of local farmers and airmen ate and drank together often laughing like old friends. Everyone tried to relax in a very hard world where life was so short, much too short for most people's liking. The pilots who drank in The Barley Mow came from all over the world. Among them were the two Poles, Stefan Radvanski and Stanislaw Skalski, a Canadian Jim Jefferies, a New Zealander Ron Stevens and many British pilots living many miles from home like Guy Hollis and David Lloyd. The Kiwi Ron Stevens remarked that he felt like a schoolboy when flying with the more experienced, but younger, Poles. He added that the Poles flew by the seat of their pants and could always be relied upon to bring their kite back in one piece. Later Bert found out exactly how true Ron's remarks were. If an aircraft was half destroyed by enemy action, the Poles would fight to bring her home even if it took all night to land her somewhere in England, often just north of Dover or in the Fens. A number of Czech and Free French pilots tended to do exactly the same. It made Bert wonder if the fear of being captured by the Germans was much greater than that of dying in a plane crash.

There was always the same men at the bar chatting up anyone especially women that included Jenny whenever she joined them. They were all young men trying to enjoy life to the full knowing that death walked the corridors where they slept and especially where they flew. Bert could not help getting to know these men and becoming close friends, even though he knew that one day many would not return from a mission somewhere over Europe. In time they became a large unusual family with some Poles joking that they did not fly for the RAF but were Bert's pilots. Bert found such comments embarrassing but was glad that his men at Sebro were appreciated by these brave lads. In the beginning there were very few casualties even when the RAF travelled across Europe to bomb Berlin for the first time. Indeed the time for tears and the gnashing of teeth had not yet arrived but alas it would come as inevitably as night follows day.

On 16th June 1940, Hitler issued Directive 16 ordering the planning of the invasion of Britain. The plans involved landing sixty thousand troops on Britain's south coast between Brighton and Folkestone in *Unternehmen Seelöwe* or Operation Sealion[26,27]. Within weeks the Germans made the plans and started to assemble the required number of barges to transport both men and equipment in ports and harbours on the French side of the Channel. The sudden accumulation of men and barges in the ports was seen by the French Resistance who informed British Intelligence. It was the invasion that Britain had expected ever since Dunkirk. In response the RAF bombers were diverted to bomb the docks and barges as well as all the railways and roads linking Germany to the French coast. It was decided in London that from all indications the invasion would take place between August and October. So they rapidly built a series of defensive lines inland from the sea, while at the same time planting land mines and anthrax/mustard gas spraying devices along the south coast. Then all of the seaside piers were dismantled and the approaches to and from the south coast beaches isolated with barbed wire fences and anti-tank blocks. Under every bridge within fifty miles of the sea, explosives were planted so that when the enemy arrived the British Rear Guard would destroy them in an effort to slow down the invaders. However no one knew if that was possible following the poor performance of British troops in Europe. Whitehall believed that the best defence against invasion would be to sink the German invasion forces while at sea by using all of the resources of the Royal Navy and the RAF. The Royal Navy ships had proved successful when fighting the weaker German *Kreigsmarine*, but the RAF had not done so well against the *Luftwaffe* in France and Belgium.

Since the fall of Dunkirk, the RAF bombers continuously flew sorties over Europe coming back seriously damaged for Sebro to repair. Often Bert went to the nearby RAF bomber base in the evening to stand by the control tower watching the Stirling and Wellington bombers take off and would stay until morning to count them back. Sadly many didn't return, while others were so badly damaged they were taken to Sebro by road. Any aircraft that could not be moved was, when possible, repaired by RAF and Sebro engineers where they landed. Only by working nearly twenty four hours non-stop were they able to keep the RAF airborne as the *Luftwaffe* attacked the RAF fighter airfields.

Unknown to most people in Britain the Germans had decided that it was time to remove the obstacles to the proposed invasion in *Unterehmen Adlerangrill* or Operation Eagle. The first stage started in July when German bombers attacked shipping along the south coast of England and the main coastal ports like Portsmouth and Dover. Then the second stage started a month later in which the *Luftwaffe* was to destroy the RAF fighter stations, along with the fighters that could defend Britain. It was designed to give the *Luftwaffe* complete supremacy of the air. The daily *Luftwaffe* attacks commenced in force on *Adlertag* (Eagle Day) 13th August 1940 when they bombed most of the RAF airfields from Eastchurch to Portland. Every day the *Luftwaffe* flew large numbers of sorties. Each sortie consisted of around fifty aircraft mostly Dornier Do 17 and Do 215, Junkers Ju 88 and Ju 87 and the fast Heinkel He 111 twin-engine bombers. These were escorted by Messerschmitt Bf109 fighters and twin-engine Bf 110 fighter-bombers. That first day a nearly continuous stream of bombers attacked Britain by day and night to be harassed by the RAF equipped with mostly Hawker Hurricane Mk1 and some faster Supermarine Spitfire Mk1 aircraft. It was a fight for survival of Britain versus conquest by Germany in what was to become the Battle of Britain[26,27,28].

Often while working on a damaged aircraft, Bert would see the RAF and *Luftwaffe* fighters above him in deadly combat like ancient gladiators, each desperately trying to destroy the other. Neither side showed any mercy as the one that got away could be the one that next time shot you down. Soon every fighter aircraft that the RAF could muster was scrambled to fight the invaders and as soon as a plane landed, she was re-armed and re-fuelled ready to get back in the fight. Soon the fighter pilots looked tired from lack of sleep as experienced pilots were shot down to be replaced by young recruits with only a few hours training. It was a desperate time and both sides knew it. The daily combat culminated on 15th September when the RAF reportedly shot down one hundred and seventy-nine enemy aircraft in one day. Whatever the real number was did not matter as it effectively knocked the steam out of the *Luftwaffe* bombers who were no longer free to fly over Britain. It was the first time that they had faced such strong opposition, so they responded by increasing their fighter cover. Now the attacks moved away from bombing the airfields to attack other targets. The change started when on 25th August one *Luftwaffe* aircraft bombed London 'by mistake'. This 'error' helped the *Luftwaffe* decide to attack cities. On 7th September three hundred bombers with an escort of six hundred fighters attacked London to start the devastation known as the London Blitz. Within weeks other major cities such as Coventry and Southampton were also heavily bombed as now everywhere in Britain was targeted. The resulting massive destruction of homes and the industrial base of Britain did not break the backbone of the local population as was expected. Instead the people stubbornly dug in their heels to rebuild what was destroyed, vowing revenge and promising to make Germany pay dearly for what they had done. So like a boxer knocked to the ground, the shocked people got back on their feet to stand up ready to fight. The change in tactics had a good side as it allowed a badly damaged RAF fighter command to repair their runways and continue to attack the bombers. They did so with considerable effect.

Now came the hard times when Bert and his men worked flat out repairing every damaged plane, sometimes sending some back into service only patched up. It was when Sebro proved her worth by repairing more aircraft than did all the other CROs put together and even when totally exhausted they never turned down a request for help. Sometimes during the day and at night, their engineers travelled to RAF stations to give all the help they could and assist the RAF's own overworked engineers and mechanics. They went to the Wellington squadrons at Bassingbourn, Born, Tempsford and Warboys; the Lysanders based at Bottisham and Somersham; and of course the Stirlings at Mepal, Molesworth and Witchford. Sebro also ended up helping other bases in Bedfordshire, Cambridgeshire, Huntingdonshire, and Lincolnshire that formed an arc of airfields north of London. On each base Bert met excellent RAF aircraft mechanics who did the majority of the maintenance and minor repairs but were understaffed. Indeed they did not have the necessary heavy equipment or space required to carry out the larger jobs that were inevitably left for Sebro.

As 1940 gave way to 1941 the Cambridge site looked more and more like a scrap metal yard than an operational unit. Everywhere one looked there were the remains of wrecked aircraft that had been salvaged but still regarded as useful. Many of the gun turrets from the ruined aircraft were removed, refurbished and fitted to another to work as good as new. Every part from the wrecks was carefully cannibalized to be used in other repairs even down to the smallest bolt or mirror. Everything that still worked and was undamaged had a value as even the smallest things were difficult to get. Within months Bert's men became experts at stripping down wrecks and removing what was useful before sending the remnants to be melted down to make much needed steel. They regularly received a stream of information from recovery teams and local farmers about most crashed aircraft that they would inspect, repair or scrap. Many were easy to deal with while others turned out to be full of surprises.

It was a Tuesday when Bert was called out to examine an enemy aircraft shot down while flying low over Cambridge. On arriving at the site, he found that the Home Guards had secured the area but on seeing Bert's ID let him and a companion work on the wreck. It was a nearly intact modified German photoreconnaissance Bf 109 fighter where one gun was replaced with a camera. Bert carefully removed the camera with its film still intact. He then used a field phone to inform the RAF Intelligence Unit about the camera and that the fighter could be repaired for the RAF Enemy Aircraft Unit. While waiting for the salvage gang to arrive and the RAF to collect the film Bert and his companion talked to the Home Guard. After an hour an RAF car arrived bringing a young officer to examine the wreck and to collect the film.

'Good morning Sir, I'm Flying Officer Guy de Broyen of the RAF Intelligence Unit and I think you must be Bert Brown. It appears that we have downed another *Luftwaffe* reconnaissance aircraft photographing this area. They were probably looking for the bomber bases or searching for your organisation. I'll have a much better idea of what they were searching for after I've developed the photographs. Though I think you should consider sending some of your men to the bomber stations so that if, heaven forbid, they bomb Sebro we will still have a workable repair system,' Guy de Broyen stated with his usual disarming grin.

'I'm glad to meet you. With a name like yours someone will think you're a foreigner,' Bert joked.

'You're right, it's no joke. My family come from the Northamptonshire village of Puddlestree where they are known as Brown, just like you. Then one day my father discovered that our family arms belonged to the Norman Knight Guy de Broyen. After checking we had a right to use that ancient name he, without thinking of the harm it could cause, changed it by deed poll from Brown to the French de Broyen. You can't begin to imagine the trouble my French name causes me with everyone from the local Home Guard to our RAF security police,' Guy continued.

'Maybe we're related as my family came from Northamptonshire via the potteries and the south coast shipyards,' Bert replied. 'Our crest is a boy on the back of an eagle.'

'That's the same as ours. So we must be some sort of distant cousins. Must remember to tell my old man about your family, he'll be intrigued. Anyhow can't waste any more time chatting to you cousin. Now I must away to my dark room to print the pictures and determine what the pilot was after. Keep safe,' Guy answered.'

With those good wishes Guy drove off into the distance. Bert hoped that the photographs were not of Sebro, but from an uncomfortable feeling in his stomach he knew they were the target.

A week later, Bert was ordered to send some of his men to each of the nearby RAF bomber bases and increase the security around Sebro. Of course he did as ordered thinking it would reduce the distance some of his team had to travel and give him space to train others. Everything became clearer when Guy de Broyen showed Bert some of the photographs the German aircraft had taken before she was shot down. They were pictures of the old Marshal's Flying School and parts of Sebro, but not the more important hidden areas. So the enemy knew they existed but not the exact location. Still one heavy bombing raid on Marshall's would also destroy all or part of Sebro. So the dispersal of some of his engineers to the larger Bomber Command airfields reduced the damage a raid on his base would cause.

'Of course Bert you knew it was only a matter of time before Sebro was discovered by the enemy and attacked. German Intelligence must know we have an efficient repair organisation as we still send so many bombers over their territory nearly every night when some are shot down or badly damaged,' Guy said in a calming tone.

'I know, but I wish they could have been a bit slower on their feet and give us more time to do our work,' Bert responded.

'Well, if it helps, I can tell you that Bomber Command HQ said to me that if it was not for your organization and excellent camouflage they would have found Sebro months ago. In fact they're delighted that even now the Germans do not know exactly where you are situated. Let's hope for all our sakes it remains that way for a long time to come,' Guy added before leaving.

That night in his bed Bert dreamed of his hunter wearing a black Nazi uniform, sitting at a desk plotting his death and the destruction of Sebro. The hunter had the face of the man he first met at *Bayerische Flugwerke* who later interrogated him after his arrest during his motorcycle tour of Germany. He was *Hauptmann* Walter Brandt of *Luftwaffe* security. The shock woke Bert up with such a cry that Jenny had to hold him in her arms for hours before he fell asleep exhausted. It is strange how dreams may sometimes show us what is real or could be happening miles away. For Bert's nightmare was much closer to the truth than anyone could have ever imagined. Somehow both Bert and his adversary Walter Brandt were linked through some mystic force that neither could understand.

# 21

# Heidelberg versus Cambridge

Behind solid oak doors along the darkened corridors of Heidelberg University were very secret rooms. Entry to the rooms and even the building was forbidden except for the few who knew of their existence. Outside Gestapo security guards patrolled the area mostly hidden from view so that no one asked questions. The walls of each room were lined with detailed maps of Europe and the latest photographs of German and Allied Aircraft. These were the places where the *Luftwaffe* and the SS ran their top secret aviation control centre. They methodically and as accurately as feasibly possible recorded the position of every *Luftwaffe* squadron and all enemy aircraft activity. One room was devoted to recording every crashed aircraft whether German or enemy including date crashed, how, type and age. This was after each one was examined at the crash site before being repaired or scrapped. Every foreign aircraft was carefully dismantled to determine exactly where they were built, both the RAF and manufacturer's serial numbers, and if they showed signs of being previously repaired. Sometimes they found new special equipment that provided the latest information about the vital RAF bombing or navigational aids. With this knowledge they hoped to develop mechanisms to block the guidance systems or make them inoperative. All the data from each crash and from air defences were combined in a continually updated estimate of the number of enemy bombers destroyed. This helped them estimate how many were available to attack German occupied territory. The more accurate the information, the easier it was to produce defensive measures and place them where they were most needed. Of course there was room for error as the estimate of enemy aircraft production was difficult to be exact especially when new aircraft were arriving from North America.

One of the offices belonged to Bert's nemesis, SS *Hauptmann* (Captain) Walter Brandt, the former head of security at the *Bayerische Flugzeugerke* in Augsburg. He was a man in his late thirties with cropped blonde hair and deep blue eyes. Herr Brandt was the Chief Investigator in the Aircraft Production, Repair, and Enemy Aircraft Information Unit. The job was much too big for him to handle, but he obtained this position due to his loyalty to the party and above all for his ruthless nature. Now he sat at his large wooden desk worried because the enemy bombing was going relatively unchecked. In his hand was a letter ordering him and his unit to produce more accurate information about the RAF or risk being posted to a less comfortable position. Maybe even forced to fight on the dreaded Eastern Front from which few returned unscathed. It was a daunting task that he did not understand how to solve. So he just sat tapping the end of a pencil on the table as he pondered over the latest data of the number of enemy bomber destroyed and the numbers still operational. None of it made any sense. It meant that the British were either producing many more bombers than he had thought possible or had efficient repair organisations keeping the damaged aircraft flying. He knew he must urgently find ways of reducing the numbers of British bombers nightly pounding German territory. Any idea of failure was unacceptable because the Fuhrer did not like his Berlin or any other German cities being bombed. The Fuhrer had become more difficult to please following the unexpected failed attack on Britain and the heavy losses of *Luftwaffe* aircraft involved.

When the enemy bombing intensified, especially over Germany, *Reichsmarshall* Herman Goering developed and installed better aerial defences. The night fighter defences were re-enforced with new Bf 110D and Junkers Ju88C aircraft fitted with an echo location system. Most of the night fighters were based in France and the Netherlands along the British bomber route to Germany. One of the problems *Hauptmann* Brandt faced was that the number of British bombers reported as being shot down was always much higher than the number of wrecked aircraft located. He decided that this was because some of the enemy aircraft were only slightly damaged and managed to fly home, maybe some crashed into the sea, or the *Luftwaffe* pilots exaggerated their successes to be awarded the coveted Iron Cross. Whatever the reason, the information on the number and types of operational bombers in the RAF had to be more accurate or they risked transferred to more dangerous assignments.

Fed up with trying to solve the dilemma in front of him, a restless *Hauptmann* Brandt walked down the corridor to a nearby large office. He desperately wanted more information. In the office surrounded by detailed maps sat the stocky and dark haired Head of Aircraft Repair and Development of New Modifications *Hauptmann* Willie Weiss. Herr Weiss was a well recognised aeronautical engineer formerly from *Bayerische Flugwerke*. Like Walter Brandt, Willie Weiss was a member of the Nazi Party, but not a member of the *Geheime Staatspolizei*, commonly called the Gestapo. During one of Walter Brandt's more evil moments he thought that if he investigated *Hauptmann* Weiss thoroughly he would find a trace of Jewish or Gypsy blood to explain his darker complexion. For his counterpart was only, in his opinion, also a *Hauptmann* because he was a top aeronautical engineer and not for being loyal to the Nazi Party. He decided that when Weiss was expendable, or he found an equally capable replacement, Walter Brandt would enjoy causing Willie Weiss' downfall.

'*Guten morgen* Willie. I want to find out what you know about any British bomber repair organisation or individual who could be in charge of it?' Brandt asked.

'*Guten morgen* Walter. We have traced most of the well-known aeronautical engineers, especially those with university degrees. It appears most of them work in aircraft manufacture and design or in government planning offices,' Willie Weiss replied. He was not surprised by the question. For some time he had wondered how Britain had increased its production of bombers or repaired so many of the damaged ones. It was the only explanation for the fact that so many regularly bombed German territory.

'I was led to believe that in Britain, most degree holders told others what to do and never got their hands dirty,' Brandt continued.

'That's partly true, but they also have some highly trained certificated engineers. As you know in Britain university places and degrees are reserved for the arrogant and the rich who can afford the fees. I believe that most British engineers have served a six or seven year apprenticeship and attended night school for higher qualifications. Indeed there are only a few universities or higher education institutes in Britain that teach practical aeronautical engineering. The British do not hold engineering with the same respect as we Germans and that is why our machines are always superior to theirs,' Willie responded.

'Yes, we build the best machines in the world and always will. We are tracing the whereabouts of the British aeronautical engineers and designers to know about most of the famous ones. Supermarine's Reginald Mitchell died, Sidney Cramm still works for Hawker, Barnes Wallace is at Vickers in Weybridge, and Geoffrey de Havilland runs his own aircraft factory at Watford. What do you know of any experienced engineers capable of organising and running a large aircraft repair organisation?' Walter Brandt continued striding up and down making a military noise as his boots hit the floor.

'There are a few likely candidates who could, even at the stretch of the imagination, set up such an important enterprise. One of the men who immediately come to my mind is the ex-Supermarine engineer Bert Brown. Do you remember you met before the war when he visited the *Bayerische Flugzeugerke* in Augsburg? However the last time I heard he was Chief Inspector of Flying Boats at Short Brothers in Rochester,' Willie replied. He had purely by chance pulled Bert's name out of the hat and like a lucky gambler had found his man, however *Hauptmann* Brandt was not convinced.

'I don't think that Bert Brown could do such an important job. When interviewed, I found him to be a boring little working class man of no consequence and minimal education. Do you know that he could not even speak any German and probably would not try even if it was to save his life? Still, you had better put his name on the bottom of the list for our agents to trace and at the same time add it to the Death List. I am sure that once we occupy Britain, people like him will not be missed,' *Hauptmann* Brandt remarked clicking his heels together as he returned to his office.

Willie Weiss never liked talking to any of the Gestapo especially Walter Brandt. He was only too aware of their reputation for beating the hell out of a suspect before asking any questions. When wrong, that was much too often for comfort, they never apologised and often left their victims seriously hurt or even dead. It was said that many of their victims helped run the secret anti-government underground that existed in most levels of government and the armed forces. He found such rumours hard to believe but knew that if anyone hurt his lovely wife Angela, he would hate them and destroy all involved. Willie felt that one of Brandt's problems was that he had no wife and was not sure of his own sexuality. However, as requested or more correctly ordered, Willie wrote down Bert Brown's name at the bottom of a list of people to be traced by their agents in Britain. At the time he did not realise that he had set in to motion a series of events directed towards Bert's elimination and the destruction of all major CROs.

Four weeks later, *Hauptmann* Brandt was informed that Bert Brown had disappeared from the Short Brothers Works in Rochester and no one appeared to know where he went. A day later he learned that there were newly expanded repair facilities on most RAF bomber bases and possibly a central Civilian Repair Organisation somewhere north of London. He decided correctly that the vast flat fens north east of London would provide space to build bomber bases and was suitable for landing damaged aircraft. Therefore it would make sense to have a repair organisation near or around Cambridge because it was in the centre of the southern ring of RAF Bomber Command bases. Now he could ask his agents and the *Luftwaffe* air reconnaissance units to search the area for any signs of a large airfield or sites where aircraft could be found.

It was a day when *Hauptmann* Brandt wanted to do something positive as his personal life was in a mess. His secretary, the blond, buxom Greta had refused his advances for the last time, saying that she would prefer to die rather than have his filthy hands touch her. He could not understand the woman as he had only beat her up and raped her the previous night without leaving any marks or causing serious injury. Angry at losing his plaything, he denounced Greta for being a Jew. He knew she would be taken to an extermination camp where her wish of dying would be efficiently carried out. Within minutes of Greta disappearing, he asked the SS lady in charge of women personnel to find him a compliant and submissive young girl to run his office during the day and warm his bed at night. He told her that the girl had to have long blonde hair, blue eyes and be athletic as he wanted someone who he could train to satisfy both himself and his friends. She promised to find someone suitable but warned him that it could take a few days. Feeling restless, he passed the time planning the assassination of another British engineer for Department A4 to carry out. Then, for no real reason, he selected the unimportant Bert Brown as his first candidate.

Luckily for Greta, Willie Weiss overheard *Hauptmann* Walter Brandt telling the Interior Ministry by phone that she was a Jew and should be eliminated as soon as possible. Willie disliked Brandt and any form of racism, so he warned Greta to escape while she still had time. It was risky as Willie knew that if discovered he would be reprimanded, if not imprisoned, as a traitor or sent to fight in North Africa. Such were the ways of the new Germany, some were good but many were very evil. Not needing a second warning Greta withdrew her savings from the bank and travelled first class on the express train to Switzerland. Getting into Switzerland proved uneventful as she still had her *SS* personnel pass, though getting out proved more difficult. In Switzerland she stayed with some German refugee friends who helped her obtain a visa to enter Britain. The only problem was that she had to make her own way there. It took a month to get a seat on a Swiss aircraft flying to Britain via neutral Spain. On arriving in Britain, she approached the British Security Services with information on the German Aircraft Production, Repair, and Enemy Aircraft Information Unit run by SS *Hauptmann* Walter Brandt. The British officers who interviewed her were astounded that such a position was held by a political appointee, so even Germany had an Old Boy network. This partly explained why the Germans had taken so long to find Sebro and the Enemy Aircraft Unit at Duxford. Greta said that *Hauptmann* Brandt had ordered the elimination of a British aircraft engineer who she thought was a Bert Brown. Sadly the intelligence officers did not know about the people who ran Sebro and so did nothing. Instead Greta was handed over to the personnel department to find her suitable work and nearby accommodation. The officer in charge returned to more important matters such as completing The Times crossword. However being very tidy, he placed the details of her interview into a folder, marked it Top Secret and filed it away to be read later when he felt like it.

Within a few weeks *Hauptmann* Walter Brandt heard from his agents where the engineer Bert Brown lived and directed that a V1 missile be aimed at his home. It took a month to get the correct authorization but soon the missile was modified with a longer fuselage to carry more fuel to extend its range. It was only because of a slight navigational error due to an unexpected crosswind that the missile missed the target by a mere two hundred yards. The range was calculated by a mechanism that after a predetermined time cut the fuel lead with a blade. So without any fuel the engine stopped and the *V1* dropped down on to the target. It was a primitive system, but it worked extremely well and above all was cheap.

The first thing Bert knew of the *Vergeltungswaffen* (Revenge Weapon) missile, especially the modified FZG76 commonly known as the V1, was when in the middle of the night his cottage shook violently so that the ceiling creaked and a window broke letting in the cool night air. Startled Bert ran downstairs to examine his home for any damage and make sure the blackout over his windows was still in place. Then he went into the front garden to find out what had caused the strange noise. To his utter amazement, he saw the old lady's house next door had a blackened hole in the upstairs wall from which emerged the tail of what looked like a rocket. Not thinking about the risk, he told Jenny to phone the Fire Brigade before forcing his way into his neighbour Mrs Botrill's house. Once inside, Bert found no sign of life until he heard a quiet sobbing followed by a question.

'Help! Help! Is there anybody down there? Please help me. I'm trapped upstairs. I can't get my bedroom door open as it's blocked by an ugly metal canister-like thing that just dropped out from the sky,' Mrs Botrill muttered while crying. After a few minutes she cried out. 'Dear God protect me a miserable sinner from the hell ticking at my door.'

'Don't worry Mrs Botrill it's me, Bert Brown. Hold on and I'll get you out in a jiffy. There really is nothing to fear but it would be best if we get you out as quickly as possible.' He knew that he was lying but did not wish to worry an already disturbed old lady.

'Thanks Bert. I'm not yet ready to meet my maker,' she replied.

Immediately Bert started to gingerly climb the narrow staircase to find the missile still in one piece partly blocking his way. He managed to squeeze past it and as he did he was frightened on hearing a loud ticking sound, a bit like a grandfather clock. He knew that this meant the timer was still ticking and the bomb could explode at any moment. So realising there was little time to be polite he unceremoniously kicked down the bedroom door. Inside he found the old lady shaking in her long cotton night gown so he covered her in a blanket, picked her up in his arms and raced downstairs and out into the garden. They were just back in Bert's house when the eerie silence was broken by an enormous explosion that ripped the heart out of the old lady's house and broke all of Bert's windows. A shocked Bert looked down at Mrs Botrill's little sad face as Jenny comforted her while they both shed a few tears. Bert thought the old lady looked helpless while holding a cup of sweet tea in her shaking hands.

'Thank you Bert. I've lost part of my house but thanks to your bravery I'm unharmed. May God protect all of us from such evil weapons,' she said again breaking down in tears.

Within twenty minutes the Fire Brigade arrived at Mrs Botrill's cottage to quickly extinguish the fire before spreading a large tarpaulin over the hole in the roof to keep out the rain. Close on their heels came a stream of officials. First to arrive were the bomb squad who wanted to know what caused the explosion and were upset to find that it was a V1 missile with a remarkably extended range. They were closely followed by the RAF Intelligence boffins wanting to know as much as Bert could remember about the bloody rocket, which sadly was not much.

'Bert I'm very angry that you take such risks only to save an old woman! She doesn't matter when your life is so important,' Hugh said angrily as soon as he arrived.

'What did you call me you horrid little man?' Mrs Botrill said with considerable venom. In fact her look could have turned a saint into stone, and Hugh was a nice man but no saint.

'Dear Hugh now you really have put your foot in it,' Bert said with a smile.

'Well what I should have said is well done but don't make a habit of risking your valuable skin,' Hugh answered looking apologetically at Bert and the old lady. 'Well I'm just glad that everyone is unharmed so that we can all breathe a sigh of relief.' In fact he was worried about how he would run Sebro on his own without Bert or an equally capable engineer.

By daylight the extent of the damage became evident. If there had been anyone in the house when the missile exploded, they would have died. However, as fate would have it, no one was injured, even the old lady's tom cat escaped as he had been out on the prowl returning after the explosion. Within a week the villagers and a local builder repaired the cottage to look nearly as good as new. Then the old lady returned home after staying with Bert for a week, but now she slept downstairs near the back door just in case another unwanted visitor arrived. She told Jenny that she would never again look up at the stars with the same wondrous feeling of peace and tranquillity. Adding she would always be afraid that a shooting star could turn out to be another rocket.

After a long discussion between the security men and Sebro's manager Hugh James, it was decided that it was too dangerous for Bert to remain living in the same house. They were certain that the next attempt to kill him might succeed. So Bert was ordered to move to a neighbouring village to live in a bigger house with a large garden. It was selected because it had lots of trees covering the driveway and a large double garage to hide his car when at home. Jenny was pleased to move from the old house as it held some very sad memories. It was in the cottage that she had given birth to their second child a girl they called Catherine who was born prematurely and very small. Sadly she died in her sleep when only two weeks old. The doctor said it was an all too common occurrence nowadays as good food was scarce even in the countryside. So Jenny tried to grow more food and get fresh meat and eggs from wherever she could. She decided that her son Charles would grow strong and if God allowed she would have another baby. Understandably Jenny was distraught and needed a change, so Mr Hitler did them a favour. Once in their new home Jenny slowly returned to her old self, playing with young Charles while waiting for Bert to come home to get a warm cup of tea and a hug. It was what all men really want to be happy and Jenny made certain her man was very content. Sadly Bert's nightmares still returned as he was chased from pillar to post by his nemesis in Nazi uniform. By now he was beginning to think it was the man from Augsburg who helped interrogate him. Of course it was but Bert didn't like the idea of having someone trying to kill him. It only happened in books, didn't it?

# 22

## Planes for Russia

Bert was mystified when he heard that after German invasion of the USSR, Winston Churchill promised the Russian President Stalin that Britain would help them by supplying tanks and aircraft.

So one day he asked Hugh.

'Hugh, is there any truth to the rumours that Winnie has offered to help arm the Russians?'

'From what I've heard through the grape vine he has. Many say it is a clever move designed to help defeat Germany though, like many things Winston did, it presents new problems that he had not fully considered.'

'You can say that again. Just think of the logistics of sending equipment there. If it is true how do you get five hundred Matilda and Valentine tanks to Russia?'

'I heard that some of the cabinet think the whole idea is nonsense. In fact some go as far as saying supplies should first go to our troops in the Far East and North Africa. However they never said it to his face, so as always Churchill got his way.'

'I must say I find Winston a hard man to understand.'

'Don't we all,' Hughie replied returning to his work.

So the already overburdened merchant marine escorted, by the Royal Navy, was expected to transport the war materials across the North Sea through the frozen Arctic waters to Murmansk in the USSR. This was soon to be known as the Arctic Convoys that suffered high losses as they were targeted by the German Navy and the *Luftwaffe*. During 1941, tanks and some fighter aircraft were crated up and shipped from Iceland and Scottish ports to pass German occupied Norway to reach the USSR. It proved to be a hell run where too many ships were lost often with all hands. The first convoy sailed via Iceland on 21st August 1941 arriving in Arkhangelsk ten days later with essential supplies. By the end of 1941 four hundred and sixty-six tanks, food and fighter aircraft had safely reached the USSR.

It was not long before the RAF sent 151 Wing to the port of Murmansk[29,30]. This consisted of Hawker Hurricane fighters to protect the Arctic convoys and train Russian pilots for the 3,000 aircraft that were to arrive over the next three years. Sending the aircraft and the necessary spare parts proved to be a major logistical operation. The first twenty-four Hurricane MkIIB's were prepared in Liverpool and put aboard the converted flat-deck carrier re-named HMS Argus, while fifteen others were crated and put aboard merchant ships. After three weeks at sea the carrier arrived close enough to the Russian airfield at Vayenga (Vianga) for the Hurricanes to fly to their new home. The Vayenga airfield was situated about twenty miles north of the port of Murmansk well inside the Arctic Circle where cold was a major problem. The squadron was not operational until the other crated aircraft and supplies in the merchant ships was offloaded in Arkhanel'sk (Arkangel) and shipped down to Vayenga. Even then some of the supplies were for the wrong model of Hurricane. When the Wing was operational they helped the Red Army defend Leningrad and eventually defeat the Germans in the east. However the move caused resentment, especially in Australia and the Far East, where there was a desperate shortage of fast modern aircraft to defend against an ever increasing Imperial Japanese Air Force. Sadly Churchill had never considered the Japanese to present a serious threat to the British Empire in the same way he feared the Germans. It was to prove another of his greatest mistakes that in the end nearly cost Britain the war in the Far East, and one that the Australians never forgot.

Bert was not involved in the shipments to the USSR except to assemble and supply a series of easily manoeuvrable maintenance and repair shops for the RAF aircraft. This proved to be fairly easy as they were similar to the one's he had designed for the repair of bombers.

The only difference was that they required much less heavy equipment and fewer spare parts. At one point he feared that some of his engineers would be sent to the USSR but in the end they were not. Instead RAF ground crew and engineers were stationed in Murmansk to live under grim conditions, often kept on airfields that were a long way from any towns and isolated from contact with the local population. The few people they met tended to be Russian pilots and engineers, the commissars who watched them throughout the day and during the long nights, and some of the British sailors waiting for their ships to return home. Being sent to Murmansk was like going to Hell as the weather was atrocious and the welcome from the commissars even colder. However in time they made friends among the local population and some even learned to like living there!

In Britain, the propaganda machine started to show films of the gallant Russian workers singing as they worked in factories, in the fields and fighting the enemy. Indeed the British people were asked to support the Russians in the mutual war against Fascism to such an extent that many became communists. Some say this pro-Soviet propaganda helped the small British Communist Party grow and the Soviets to recruit agents within Britain. However the philosophy of Churchill's open support for the USSR was very simple. It was the old adage that my enemy's enemy is my friend. Later Churchill explained that by supporting the USSR in their fight against Germany it made Britain safer from invasion.

Supplying modern fighter aircraft to the USSR instead of sending some to the Far East had catastrophic consequences. It left island fortresses like Malta to be defended only by three old biplanes, The RAF based in Hong Kong were equipped with three slow 140 mph Vickers Wildebeeste torpedo-bombers and two Supermarine Walrus biplane flying boats. Soon these would prove useless against the fast Japanese A6M Zero fighters. The situation in the Far East base at Singapore and in all Malaya was only a little better. Here the RAF 232 Squadron was equipped with ten Hawker Hurricanes and some one hundred and twenty Brewster Buffalo.

Bert was not surprised to read in his newspaper The Daily Express of 26th December 1940 the headline HONG KONG GARRISON FIGHT TO THE LAST. He felt sorry for the garrison who he considered were outnumbered, equipped with antiquated aircraft and used as cannon fodder. In fact it made him feel sick.

'Bloody hell,' Bert said out loud showing Jenny the news.

'Darling Bert you know these things happen, so don't get upset,' Jenny replied.

'I know you're right but the waste of life just makes me want to yell.'

'Then yell if it makes you feel better. It would be preferable to you going so red in the face and having high blood pressure!'

Her sensible comments made him mutter under his breath 'Bloody politicians' and then smile at his Jenny.

Later he heard more news that made him start to wonder if Britain stood a chance when the leaders were so pathetic.

The Buffalo was inadequately armed. After their initial success against some of the slower Japanese bombers, most were shot down or destroyed on the ground. At the last minute the RAF was reinforced with another fifty-one Hurricanes. The surviving aircraft were transferred to the Dutch East Indies when there were no usable airfields left in Singapore. Later forty-eight more Hurricanes were rushed to airfields in the Dutch East Indies onboard HMS Indomitable. They arrived as the Japanese attacked so that most were destroyed on the ground! The troops on the ground and ships at sea defending the region were without adequate air cover and soon devastated by continual air attacks. The Royal Navy Task Force Z consisting of the battleships HMS Prince of Wales and HMS Repulse with four destroyers sailed from Singapore to attack Japanese forces landing in Malaya. Within days they were attacked first by a Japanese submarine and then by land based Japanese bombers. Both vessels were sunk with considerable loss of life even though their destroyer escorts picked up some survivors. It heralded the end of British marine supremacy in the region that had existed for centuries. Simply the British did not have enough modern fighter aircraft to hold back the Japanese[29,30]. The Hurricanes that were so urgently needed by the British and Commonwealth forces during the Japanese invasion of Asia were instead fighting for the USSR! They proved a valuable asset to the Soviets but did that make the loss of the British forces in the Far East justified when the same aircraft would maybe have helped save the day. No one knows for sure and it will always remain a bitter bone of contention between Australia and Britain.

# 23

## The First Thousand Bomber Raids

*All is fair in love and war but to win one*
*must hit the enemy hard where it hurts.*

*Short Stirling bomber flying through German anti-aircraft fire known as Flak.*
*This photograph, reference C2029, is from Imperial War*
*Museum London Collection and is used by permission granted*
*under licence waive WAV 2462 of April 2010.*

For a couple of months after moving into their new house Bert tried to go home early. Of course this was not always possible except when the workload was light and his trained staff did most of the routine work. Then someone in the War Cabinet, or maybe it was in RAF High Command, decided that they would mount an unprecedentedly thousand bomber raid over the main German Industrial areas especially aimed at the Ruhr. Actually RAF Bomber Command knew that they never had that many aircraft operational at any one time. So when such a raid was ordered Bert and his men had their work cut out to find as many operational bombers as possible to fly the exhausting journey to the heart of the German hinterland with a chance of returning in one piece. The main problem of mounting such an enormous aerial attack was to coordinate all of the various types of aircraft taking off from many airfields to fly at different altitudes and speeds. This meant that each aircraft had to be dispatched at carefully timed intervals to reach their target at different times. If done correctly they should form a continual line of aircraft without getting in each other's way. For survival it was important that no aircraft circled the target for any length of time. The longer an aircraft was over the target area the more likely she was to be damaged or get in the way of other aircraft going in for their bombing run. More importantly, the longer the aircraft were airborne the more fuel they used, further reducing their chances of safely returning home.

While planners co-ordinated each squadron for the attack, everyone at Sebro repaired as many bombers as possible. They also helped fit the latest navigational devices such as GEE to improve bombing efficiency. GEE or the Ames Type 7000 hyperbolic navigation system guided the bombers to within a mile of the target[26,27,30]. It consisted of one main transmitter sending out the main pulse and two slave transmitters. By observing the pulses inside the bomber on an oscilloscope the navigator could locate more accurately. The system worked so well that soon the Germans used a similar system when bombing Britain. They had discovered the GEE equipment inside crashed British bombers and modified it for their own use! However it required skill and an uninterrupted signal, so that some aircraft still managed to bomb the wrong target.

In Germany, their planners had greatly improved their air defences by establishing the Kammhuber Line. This was a chain of large sites each one roughly 20 miles long and 12 miles wide. Each site, or Himmelbett zone, contained one Freya radar unit with a 100 km range. The radar controlled a master searchlight and passed information on to many manually controlled searchlights scattered within the area. Later they improved the radar system by adding two Würzburg short range but more accurate radar units. The complete Kammhuber Line consisted of sites stretching all the way across the Netherlands. They illuminated any aircraft caught in the searchlights while sending her position to nearby squadrons of Dornier Do 17, Junkers Ju 88E and Messerschmitt Bf 110G night fighters. The Germans called this highly effective defence system *Helle Nachtjagd* (illuminated night fighting). It worked very well until some German cities demanded that some of the anti-aircraft units be removed from the Kammhuber Line and placed on the approaches to their cities. The effect of the Kammhuber Line was devastating as most of the RAF bombers on their way to and from Germany had to pass over it. The result was that many aircraft caught in the searchlights were severely damaged or destroyed. To help overcome this system, Air Chief Marshall Harris decided that all RAF aircraft would form a steady dense bomber stream. He hoped that the presence of so many aircraft overhead at a time would overwhelm the Kammhuber Line system and their night fighters. As so often in his career, Harris was proved correct. The German system when confronted with so many enemy aircraft at a time became confused as to which ones should be attacked. It was hard for the German night fighters to select a target from so many while facing the massive fire power of the combined bombers' guns. The effect was that the percentage of RAF bombers lost declined with an increase in the numbers of German night fighter aircraft destroyed[27]!

As the war progressed Short Brothers improved their Stirling bomber to carry a four thousand five hundred pound bomb load at 230 mph for three thousand miles at altitudes of up to six thousand feet. So the newer Stirling Mark II and Mark III bombers became the RAF's main heavy bomber until later they were replaced by the larger Avro Lancaster and Handley Page Halifax[1,21,22].

In May 1942 Bert was ordered to send as many of men as possible to the squadrons equipped with Stirling bombers to prepare for Operation

Millennium. This was the code name for the proposed thousand aircraft bombing raid on the city of Cologne. Air Marshall Harris believed large numbers of bombers could devastate major industrial targets such as the Ruhr and in doing so greatly shorten the war. Some people complained it was wrong for the RAF to use German *Blitzkrieg* methods though most wanted revenge for the bombing of British cities. It is a moral argument that with the passing of time and the advent of nuclear weapons has not been resolved.

On the morning of 30th May 1942 all operational bombers, including some from Coastal Command and training units, were ordered to attack Cologne. No two squadrons were to fly along exactly the same air lane at the same time in an effort to avoid confusion. So the bombers were dispatched at timed intervals to form one very extensive bomber stream. One of the main fears was that the younger inexperienced gunners would mistake the smaller British two- engine bombers for enemy Junker Ju88 fighters. Luckily they did not. The main force of Stirling, Lancaster and Halifax aircraft had to survive Cologne's extensive air defences. At the time this consisted of five hundred anti-aircraft guns and two hundred search light batteries. Under this intensive barrage of enemy fire, each pilot had to keep to his allotted altitude, speed and position to prevent the risk of midair collisions or any aircraft blocking those on their bombing run. This proved to be nearly impossible in damaged aircraft with defective instruments, but many still followed their squadron blindly into the attack.

That night Bert watched apprehensively as his friends took off in their Stirling bombers while praying silently for their safe return. The more experienced pilots led the way to fly in the most complex operation the RAF had ever mounted. Stefan waved to Bert as he taxied past, as did Jim and Ron. Bert waved back standing next to the Group Captain until the last aircraft disappeared over the horizon. Then the once very noisy runway full of aircraft taking off was suddenly transformed into an eerie silence broken only by the noises of the safety vehicles returning to their bunkers. Without saying anything the Group Captain led Bert to the underground command room where they could follow the operation.

Inside was a large table onto which each squadron was plotted. Strangely the table was covered with more markers than Bert or anyone else had ever seen before.

'It's going to be a long night Bert. Why don't you go home?' suggested the kindly Group Captain.

'Thanks, but if you don't mind I will stay. I have too many friends up there tonight.'

'Don't we all,' the Group Captain replied. 'Well you may as well stay and help yourself to a strong cup of tea. Then he added. 'If you want to smoke we prefer it if you go outside as it can get very stuffy in here.'

'Anyhow I think the lads looked as keen as mustard to be in action after days, if not weeks, of preparation.'

'Well the Met boys say though it's clear with a full moon over England, there will be thick clouds over the target.'

That night there were so many aircraft in the sky the moonlight appeared reduced by what looked like a massive pattern of gigantic migrating geese. It took over two hours for all of the bombers to be dispatched from bases all over Britain. The slower aircraft took off first to arrive over the target just after the heavy bombers had struck. That night nearly the whole RAF bomber force was in the air attacking Germany. Bert knew that only time would tell if it was a heroic gesture that wins wars or sheer folly that loses them. It was clearly a distinct possibility that the *Luftwaffe* night fighters together with the anti-aircraft guns would decimate the RAF bombers. The RAF Headquarters had estimated a ten percent loss meaning one hundred aircraft would not return. If they ran into stronger enemy resistance the losses would be much higher. If this happened then Britain would no longer have a viable Bomber Command and maybe would end up losing the war!

The organisation and the careful planning for the raid proved successful. During the night the progress of each group was carefully followed and their positions plotted on the large operation tables. Nearby all the aircraft lost was written in chalk on the blackboard at Bomber Command HQ and in their own bases. Most information were only estimates as strict radio silence was in force so the only news HQ received was from radar stations, pilots reporting they were crashing or when an aircraft returned. Within hours of the last aircraft taking off columns of bombers approached the City of Cologne. Some were attacked over the Netherlands by night fighters and crashed or were so damaged they had to return home. Probably because no one had seen so many aircraft at any one time the anti-aircraft guns fired erratically. However, they still managed to set many of the bombers on fire or break them in half. The slower Wellingtons attacked first by dropping incendiary bombs and starting fires to illuminate the target area. So when the main bomber force arrived over the target it was easier for the bomb-aimers to see the fires below. By the end of the night, nine hundred bombers out of the one thousand and forty-seven involved found their target to drop one thousand four hundred and fifty-five tons of bombs, many incendiary (fire) bombs, on Cologne.

'Wake up Bert. The first of our babies is coming home,' the Group Captain said with a huge grin.

'Sorry. I must have dozed off.'

'You certainly did and by the way you snore,' Group added.

'Well what are we waiting for? I want to know the butcher's list and what work my men have to do as soon as possible,' Bert commented wiping the sleepy dust from his eyes.

'Let's go then sleepy head.'

Outside the sun was breaking over the fields announcing the break of day and for a few moments one could hear the birds sing. Then the first bomber returned. Already the blackboard in the operations room showed one reported loss - Captain Sydney Davis. His aircraft C for Charlie had crashed into the sea and the crew was safely rescued. It was an anxious time when those waiting drank cups of strong tea and smoked, trying not to think of what was happening.

The first noise they heard was the distant humming of aircraft engines, like a swarm of angry bees after a storm, long before any plane came into sight. Then the first bomber appeared limping along on two engines with the other two feathered and burned black. By the Grace of God landed as ordered bumpily on the flat grass away from the main runway. Later on Bert found out that she had been hit by a Messerschmitt Bf110 night fighter before reaching the target, so the pilot jettisoned his bombs over the Netherlands and returned home. At least he obeyed orders to bring her home so Bert had another aircraft to repair in preparation for the next raid. Within an hour she was airborne again on the short flight to Sebro. Sadly both the tail gunner and the bomb aimer had died while the co-pilot was severely injured.

Then a second Stirling landed gracefully on the grass with only two engines working and half her tail fin missing. The pilot had been seriously wounded during a frontal attack by an enemy fighter that killed his co-pilot and severely damaged his plane. Then the injured were helped from the aircraft before being whisked away in an ambulance to hospital. Still no aircraft had returned after bombing Cologne making everyone on the ground very tense. The mood on the airstrip was black as everyone worried if the whole mission had been a tragic error. Indeed had Air Marshall Harris sent too many young, brave men to die and lost most of his bombers without achieving anything worthwhile?

An hour after the first arrivals, they heard the unmistakable roar of Bristol Hercules engines pulling the Stirling bombers back home. On the ground everyone felt a sigh of relief as they ran around like headless chickens getting ready to receive their aircraft. Even after a whole night's flying through heavy enemy fire, most pilots managed to land and park their machines where directed. Then, the very moment the engines were turned off and the propellers stopped rotating the doors were flung wide open. Out came their crews like tired snails to walk wearily towards the waiting dispersal trucks and enjoying the feeling of their feet again on terra firma.

Many of the less fortunate were helped onto ambulances while some tail-end gunners were cut free from their turrets and pilots from their cockpits. Once on the ground most aircrew left to get some sleep while the pilots and navigators reported to the debriefing room. Gradually it became clear that most targets had been bombed, if not destroyed. Everyone knew that the full picture would not emerge until later that day after recognisance aircraft had photographed the damage in Cologne and the tally of planes lost was finally confirmed. Luckily most aircraft returned though many were severely damaged. However the loss of too many experienced aircrews was to effectively limit such large raids for the immediate future. Only a few lucky aircraft returned unscathed, but most had only minor damage. Of the one thousand and forty-seven aircraft dispatched thirty-nine never returned and one hundred and twenty were severely damaged. Bert was overjoyed to see that his friends were safe even though their faces showed the effects of flying for long hours over enemy territory. They were exhausted and looked quite ashen with darkened deep set eyes from the strain of night flying.

When the statistics was published Bert was summoned to Bomber Command HQ to be congratulated on supplying so many aircraft.

Then there came the awkward question: 'When could he get the same number of aircraft operational for another raid.'

'Maybe a month if we are lucky, but I'm not promising anything,' Bert replied angrily.

'Calm down old chap, we are not expecting miracles. Just an estimate will do,' replied Air Marshall Harris.

'It is hard to give an exact date. However I can say that if the other bombers suffered as badly as the Stirling then in two months you could mount another mass raid. Please realise that I doubt if you could get a thousand in the air even if miracles sent us a hundred aircraft.'

'Thanks for being so candid Bert,' Harris said scratching his forehead. 'I hope our North American cousins will send us a few bombers in the next few months.'

'I hope so, but what about the crews?'

'Dear Bert, don't teach an old fox like me to suck eggs,' Harris said with a large grin. 'You and I both know that aircrews will be our biggest problem that I hope we are tackling with some success.' He then added. 'We have retrained a few more Polish pilots to fly Stirling as they have proven so reliable.'

Bert left the room disillusioned knowing from now onwards large raids was to be the order of the day. He like Bomber Harris but worried about his stubborn insistence of always being right.

Two days later Guy de Broyen showed Bert some of the RAF aerial photographs taken before and after the raid on Cologne. Before the raid Cologne was a beautiful city criss-crossed by major railway networks and large roads. After the bombing, the railway sidings and part of the city was obliterated. Bert never realised that dropping tons of bombs would be so catastrophic and for the first time pitied the enemy. It was claimed that forty-five thousand Germans were made homeless, and two hundred and fifty factories destroyed but Germany reported only five thousand people injured and five hundred killed. No one knew the truth or would admit to it as both sides wanted to prove their superiority.

By working throughout the day and into the night, Sebro repaired most aircraft leaving those with major structural damage to be worked on later or be scrapped. Within three weeks most were operational and back at their RAF stations. Everyone was proud of their work. Then some of the staff was relocated to work with the RAF all over the land to help keep their bombers flying.

Often repairing damaged aircraft proved very difficult because badly distorted metal had to be straightened or cut away to be replaced by new parts. Damaged wings and tail fins were replaced or at least dismantled, patched up and reinstalled. It took much longer to remove damaged bolts and equipment than making new ones, but as they say beggars can't be choosers, so they just did their best. The work was difficult and time consuming. Sometimes the repaired parts gently slid back into place while at other times they had to be carefully hammered home. The end was always the same. Each repaired aircraft had a final inspection before being flown back to her squadron and they turned their attention towards the next job. Bert kept a photographic record of the more unusual or difficult work to help teach his men how to tackle specific problems. What always surprised him was that so many severely damaged aircraft often with half a wing missing and gaping holes in the fuselage managed to return and some were even flown to Sebro for repair. Of course many were patched up, scrapped where they landed or brought for repair on the back of trucks. Many of them had been temporarily repaired for the short flight to Cambridge where they needed major reconstruction. One of the staff drew a caricature of a tired engineer looking at a metal object with the caption 'No job is ever too small and none too large'. This became their motto so that copies of the cartoon were proudly displayed all over the company for all to see. Even visitors would stop and read it before smiling at the true message.

# 24

## An Unusual Invitation to Eire

If you want a difficult job done thoroughly it is best to do it yourself. Never expect others to do something you will not or are unable to do.

Hitler was angry on hearing the details of the damage in Cologne due to the recent raid from British bombers. First he ranted against *Reichsmarshall* Goering and his *Luftwaffe* before turning his wrath against his intelligence officers. He demanded to know how it was possible for Britain to send a thousand bombers to nearly obliterate a major city like Cologne. Either the German air defences were highly inefficient or the British could repair and build aircraft faster than German intelligence had calculated. If such large raids continued on the industrial heartland of the Reich they would devastate the economy and seriously harm the military strength of the nation. He ended his comments by warning that if these attacks were not stopped certain high ranking officers and their underlings would soon be fighting on the Russian front rather than dining in the finest restaurants throughout Europe. The *Führer's* threat sent a chill down the backs of his audience as Hitler was very generous when happy but acted ruthlessly when upset. As always his forces were expected to win every conflict as failure was a sign of weakness or lack of commitment.

The *Führer's* angry comments caused all concerned to run around finding ways to stop the British bombers flying over Germany, or at least damaging those who dared do so. The initial response was to order every air defence unit to practice until they were capable of rapid, accurate responses to all forms of air attack and the night fighter pilots taught to be ready for combat at a second's notice. Meanwhile the senior air defence officers and air intelligence held hurried meetings to determine how they could stop the air raids knowing failure to do so could prove fatal.

Sitting around a desk in Berlin three men wrote down a list of some of the actions they thought were needed to happen to rectify the dangerous situation.

It read:

Options for the Improved Defence of *Reich* from Air Attack.

1.  All British Aircraft factories and repair organisations must be identified and eliminated by targeted bombing. Those already damaged must be again attacked and destroyed.

2.  The number and strength of night fighter squadrons must be increased and training greatly improved. This must also involve more expenditure on night aircraft location systems.

3.  All anti-aircraft gun batteries and Freya radar units to be reinforced around important targets.

4.  Intelligence must identify key British workers in the manufacture and repair of bombers, where they lived and how they could be effectively eliminated. If the leading engineers could be removed then the aircraft industry in Britain would slow down and even, if lucky, stop working.

At the end of the meeting a directive was sent to *Hauptmann* Walter Brandt to initiate clandestine activities to eliminate all the aeronautical engineers on the Death List. It included Bert Brown who was believed to be in hiding after one attempt on his life had failed. Immediately *Hauptmann* Walter Brandt contacted those in charge of overseas assassinations working in Department A4 who suggested that the best way of killing Herr Brown was at the hands of the IRA. Within days, their agent working in the Spanish Embassy in Dublin, the press officer Senor Juan Gomez found the ideal man for the job. He chose Liam Gallagher, a former officer in the Irish Republican Army who had served under Michael Collins and was a well known Republican. Liam was in charge of a secret group of Irishmen empowered to hunt down all British sailors and airmen who arrived illegally in Ireland. It was even rumoured that everybody he was sent to capture disappeared without trace and never ended up interned in any Irish prison. This was what one expected from the Republican government run by a man who many regarded as a secret ally of German, the Prime Minister Eamon de Valera[8]. Eamon de Valera was born in USA to a Spanish father whose only claim to being Irish was his mother's ancestry and his exaggerated importance in the IRA during the liberation struggle. Like many American Irish and some Republican Irish he distrusted the British to declare the Republic of Ireland a neutral state. It was said that he collaborated with the Nazis, but if he did, it was like the USA by trading with Germany. Perhaps it was a matter of necessity or just a matter of good business.

Senor Gomez collected all the information he could on the potential assassin. It was not an easy task because he did not want anyone to become suspicion of what he was doing. However, within a month he had a file on Liam Gallagher that included commonly visited pubs and reliable contacts. Having started the ball rolling he sent the file, complete with an old photograph of Liam Gallagher in uniform standing next to Michael Collins, in the diplomatic bag to Berlin where it remained gathering dust for another month. Only when it was eventually read by a senior intelligence officer and stamped as being useful was the assassination authorised.

Six weeks later Liam Gallagher was invited to the Spanish Embassy in Dublin to meet with their press officer Senior Juan Gomez. That was what his name said on his business card, but he was actually born Konrad Wisser. After fighting with General Franco during the Spanish Civil War Konrad Wisser was offered Spanish citizenship that Berlin ordered him to accept. Now he was the head of intelligence in Dublin, officially known as the News Agency, for both the Spanish and German Governments. Unknown to Senior Gomez his guest could easily recognise a German when he saw one, having fought them in close combat during the Spanish Civil War. But what the man doesn't know will never harm him, thought Liam with his customary grin. Then he instinctively touched the lucky four leaf shamrock in his pocket hoping it would protect him from all fascists and capitalists.

'Good morning dear sir, please be seated and make yourself comfortable. I'm Senor Gomez. Mr Gallagher I'm delighted that you have accepted my invitation to discuss matters of mutual interests. Would you like a cigarette?' Senor Gomez said offering Liam a cigarette from a large silver box.

There were so many cigarettes in the silver box that Liam took two, one he put behind his left ear and the other he smoked. It was a bit cheeky, but Liam wanted to look like an ill-mannered Irishman with lots of brawn and very little brain. However Senior Gomez was no fool. He knew by reputation Liam was an excellent soldier and a man of his word.

'It's a pleasure Senor Gomez to meet a fellow British hater. For real money I would do most things, but the best of all is anything that will upset the arrogant British until they go red with anger. So what may I do for you on such a lovely day?' Liam Gallagher asked looking Gomez straight in the eyes. Then he leaned casually back in his chair to blow perfectly formed smoke rings into the air.

'I understand you run an organization for the Irish government that hunts down all British servicemen in the Republic. Some say everyone you catch is never seen or heard of again because the peat bogs are full of their bodies,' Gomez said with a smile indicating his approval of such actions.

'Senor Gomez, please don't be fooled by such unfounded and ugly rumours. I've many enemies who spread these evil tales to destroy my good Christian reputation. Indeed it is true my group does arrest and intern all foreigners we find staying illegally in Ireland whether they're British, German or even Spanish. We always arrange that the seriously injured are transferred to the Red Cross to be repatriated under the Geneva Convention regarding Neutral states. If any are stupid enough to try to escape and many do, they simply die,' Liam replied with a serious look that would have convinced his father confessor. 'As you know in a few cases during a war accidents unfortunately happen. That's enough about me, so how may I assist you?"

'I may want you to eliminate a troublesome Englishman with no fuss and leaving no trace as to who did it and why. Can you remove him for us or have I been misinformed about your very special skills?' Gomez watched Liam for any sign of disgust or anger. There was none. Liam looked a hard man who would kill his own mother, if the money was good enough.

'It's a sad day when a good loyal Irishman and a Republican like me can't trust his fellow man to keep his bloody mouth shut. But I suppose now you have some idea about me I had better tell you my side of the story. Every morning when I get up, especially when it's wet or on a cold winter's day, my damaged leg hurts like hell as a reminder of how deeply I hate the British soldier who shot me. If you paid me enough I would go out of your office and kill Mr bloody Churchill himself. I would even enjoy doing it, but let me make it clear I only work alone and at my own pace. I must insist that no one tells me what to do or when to do it as I usually find other people's plans flawed and too dangerous to implement. Therefore, if you want a job carried out, all you have to do is to pay the money up front and arrange for me to meet the target preferably somewhere in the Republic. Then I guarantee that he will be pushing up the daisies as his black British soul burns in the fires of everlasting Hell!' Liam replied hoping he was not too aggressive yet had convinced this clown that he was the ideal assassin.

'Then it is agreed. You will help remove this thorn from our side,' Senor Juan Gomez stated. Then he handed Liam an envelope containing an old photograph of Bert Brown standing in his overalls besides the S6B floatplane.

On opening the envelope Liam was surprised to recognise a much younger Bert. He was the man who had helped him in Belfast, but he made no comment.

'Where do I find this man and more importantly how much do I get paid for doing you this favour? Just to be on the safe side I must insist only on payment in crisp, new American dollars because it's rumoured you sometimes use forged money. So we'll be having none of that malarkey Senor, just the real McCoy,' Liam commented.

'Senor Gallagher please do not insult me by insinuating that I would even think of doing such a dishonest thing, I'm not like the British. I promise you that all our money is genuine, because whatever is rumoured we do not deal in false promises or fakes of any kind. I am authorised to pay you the enormous sum of five thousand American dollars to carry out the job and arrange for Bert Brown, for that is his name, to visit the Republic to retrieve a spy camera. We'll supply you with the British aircraft camera and tell you on what train he will travel on from Belfast to Dublin. Then we will leave the rest of the operation up to you and your men,' Gomez said.

'Senor that sounds grand but let's not go too fast until we both fully understand each other. Before we get into details I want to feel the money in my hand and count it so that there can be no misunderstandings. In the case of subversive activities I have found that, after the dirty deed is done, some people have a habit of failing to honour their promises,' Liam demanded while getting out of his chair as if to leave the room. He was beginning to seriously dislike this Senor Gomez or whoever he was. He had to bite his tongue not to say out loud what he was thinking. It was simply 'you fascist bastard'.

'Please sit down and be patient Mr Gallagher, even I don't have everything in one place,' Senor Gomez replied feeling annoyed at the arrogance of the man. He started to think that after the assassination was carried out he would not mind personally eliminating this Mr Gallagher. He knew such actions could wait as for now he must cooperate with this uncouth Irishman. So he took a wad of new dollar bills from his desk draw, counted a hundred fifty-dollar bills and handed them over to Liam. The latter examined the first one carefully by feeling the surface and holding it to the light. Only when completely satisfied it was the genuine article did he count the others, fold them in a money clip before putting it in his inside pocket.

'Well that's the money dealt with to our mutual satisfaction. Now let's get down and discuss the arrangements for everything must be done exactly as I want it. Your people must somehow arrange for the target, Mr Bert Brown, to contact Mrs Kathleen O'Reilly at O'Reilly's Hotel in Belfast. There he will collect a First Class return rail ticket on the non-stop night express to Dublin and told where and when to meet me,' Liam added.

They spent the next hour discussing when the victim should come to Ireland and how he should be killed. After a lot of argument Senor Gomez agreed that the body should be buried in lime or in a bog to decompose rapidly so it was unrecognisable. It was how Liam was reported to get rid of the bodies of the unfortunate British sailors and airmen he caught hiding in Ireland. Then Liam left the room after picking up a few more cigarettes from the silver box and wishing Senor Gomez the top of the morning. Once outside the Spanish Embassy Liam walked as if on air, he had earned five thousand dollars and had convinced the German Gomez he was their friend. Now for the difficult part of making it appear he had killed Bert Brown without actually doing so.

Two weeks later Bert was sitting in his office sorting out the latest list of spare parts when a small man in a long raincoat appeared. Bert treated him as any other visitor as he must have had the correct documents to pass through Sebro's tight security checks.

'Good morning, what can I do for you?' Bert asked wondering how the man had entered a restricted area.

'Good morning Mr Bert Brown let me introduce myself, I'm John Smith from the Ministry of Air Defence Intelligence Unit. I have been sent here to personally give you urgent secret instructions,' replied Mr Smith.

'Before you say any more Mr Smith please show me your identification and the orders,' Bert replied not fond of being interrupted, especially by a stranger.

John Smith showed Bert his ID card complete with a photograph and all the usual security stamps that showed that he worked for the Air Ministry.

'Herbert Brown it is my duty to inform you that today you must travel to Ireland. There you will retrieve an important missing aerial reconnaissance camera from an Irish contact in the Republic. I hope you realise this is very hush-hush so no one must know what you are doing, not even your wife.'

Bert felt very uncomfortable about too much secrecy without any signs of the usual written authorisation.

'Why should I go when anyone could easily do this simple chore?'

'Don't blame me. I'm just the messenger. You've been selected by the powers that be, so it must be every important. Now be a good chap and don't waste my time by asking any more silly questions,' Mr Smith insisted. Then he handed Bert an official government priority warrant to fly to Belfast that afternoon, the address of Mrs Kathleen O'Reilly of

O'Reilly's Hotel in Belfast and a First Class return rail ticket to Dublin. However, there was still no letter signed by anyone Bert knew.

'You will fly by RAF transport from here to Belfast. Once in Belfast you will contact Mrs Katie O'Reilly who will be expecting you and who will arrange for you to travel to Dublin. The matter is so urgent we have laid on a special flight as you must take tonight's express train to Dublin. Any delay could have catastrophic effects,' Mr Smith stated.

Bert just nodded and decided not to tell the disagreeable Mr Smith that Kathleen would never allow anyone to call her Katie. Bert had been told not to tell anyone, but of course he told Jenny who was now six months pregnant. She cried a bit before telling him to take care and trust no one but his instincts and God.

At exactly 1300 hours an RAF Anson took Bert from Sebro and two hours later Bert was in Belfast. On arriving at O'Reilly's hotel Kathleen was not happy as she pushed him unceremoniously into the back room.

'It's good to see you Bert even in these very dangerous times. Do you know that you have a plain clothes special officer following you?' Kathleen commented.

'Sorry Kathleen I didn't see him as I'm so used to being followed. I suppose it's the price for working on aircraft during a war.'

'Our mutual friend Liam Gallagher left a note for you to show to your shadow. It tells you to take the express night train to Dublin. Once there you're to wait outside the old Post Office for a large white car to take you to the meeting place. He thinks by showing your tail the note it will make your journey safer. Bert be careful as in the Republic there are many anti-British people who would slit your throat for half a sixpence.'

Bert briefly looked at the message before putting it in his pocket while muttering thank you. As he turned to leave the safety of the hotel Kathleen stopped him.

'Please Bert wait. Liam wants you to have this Luger pistol in case things go wrong. He said that on the train you'll be met by Father Sean O'Casey who'll take you to meet him. Sean's a trustworthy man, sadly his brother died at Dunkirk fighting the Germans, and he's a friend to all of us,' Kathleen said slipping the loaded gun into Bert's pocket while kissing him tenderly on the cheek.

Outside the hotel Bert walked slowly towards the railway station being careful not to lose his shadow. Then he broke all the rules by stopping and showing his shadow the letter. The man read it before telling Bert to continue on his journey as if they had never met. Once aboard the Dublin Night Express, Bert sat in the First Class compartment. Now alone for the first time he started to worry. Why should a man he had met only once before want to meet with him rather than with an engineer from Short & Harland to exchange an aircraft camera? Then he decided he could trust Liam. Then there was the strange business of the Luger. Why would he need a gun unless it was for protection and, if so, from whom? However he knew that in foreign lands, especially during a war, caution was the order of the day. As the posters throughout Britain stated 'Careless talk cost lives' and it was probably as true about not keeping your wits when travelling in new lands.

The carriage door opened just as the Dublin Express was starting to move out of Belfast Station to let in a Catholic Priest.

'Good evening my son I trust you have no objection if I share your compartment?' the priest said in a very quiet voice Bert could hardly hear.

'Of course not Father. It will be nice not to be alone and have someone to talk to when travelling for the first time to a City in a new country,' Bert replied.

'Well I'm Father Sean O'Casey, though friends call me Sean and others Father. So take your pick,' Sean said with a sparkle in his brown eyes and a firm handshake.

'I'm Bert Brown. I'm always glad to meet a man of the cloth.'

'Well Bert I think you'll like Dublin. It's a fine old City full of good people and of course the home of Guinness brewed from the waters of the Liffey,' the Father commented.

They sat back to relax as Sean told tales of ancient Ireland and how St Patrick banished all serpents from the Emerald Isle. Father Sean added that they never returned, but the blessed saint did not remove all those human reptiles that poison one's soul.

'How do you sink an Irish submarine?' the Father asked Bert.

'I don't know,' Bert replied.

'Of course you do. You simply knock on the watertight door and being a polite people they will open up even when underwater,' Sean answered with a grin.

'Why do you lick the nose of British aristocrats?' Bert responded.

'This is because they keep their noses high in the air to be what I call toffee-nosed.'

Bert was quiet so Father Sean asked 'Where did I find an Irish bookworm?'

'I don't know.'

'Silly man, it was inside a brick,' Sean replied enjoying the Irish jokes that he could tell knowing Bert was too polite to respond in kind.

For the next few hours Sean told an endless series of Irish jokes that kept them both happy and laughing. Then in the dead of night the lights went out and non-stop Express came to a halt, followed by the sounds of doors being opened and of people running. There was a yell of 'Bert come this way', followed by Bert's shadow saying something like 'Don't go' before giving chase and then the ominous sound of gunfire. As suddenly as the lights had gone out, they came on again as the train gathered speed leaving Bert's shadow behind.

'Well that little charade takes care of your minder by getting him harmlessly chasing shadows. Don't worry he won't be harmed, just hit on the head and sent safely back to Belfast. It's better for all concerned if we're not followed as the road ahead holds many dangers from people we think of as our friends as well as our enemies,' Father Sean continued. His words were a shocking reminder of the danger of what lay ahead. Maybe for all his apparent good nature Father Sean was the Judas Goat leading Bert to his death! But if Bert could not trust a priest then who could he trust?

Twenty minutes later the so-called non-stop express again halted this time to avoid hitting a horse drawn cart that was blocking the track.

'Quick Bert, out we go. This is our stop where our transport awaits,' Father Sean said firmly pushing Bert out of the carriage to land safely on the soft wet grass.

As his eyes became accustomed to the dark he saw the train leave as three armed men took them to a parked black car. They were a vicious looking group of thugs who Bert thought would kill their own mother.

Then Bert was blindfolded and his hands tied in front of him. Feeling like a trussed up chicken, Bert was forced to sit in the back of the car between two rather large men. Then nothing was said for the next few hours as the car sped off over what felt like country roads. As dawn started to break Bert's hands were freed and the blindfold removed. He saw that the car had stopped outside a thatched cottage set in a remote farm apparently miles from anywhere. In seconds a bewildered Bert and Father Sean were ushered into a warm room where by a fireside table sat his old friend Liam Gallagher.

'Bert welcome to my humble home. Sorry about the reception committee, but I can't be too careful as I'm told there's a war on,' Liam laughed. 'Now my brothers it's time for you to go home with my thanks. On your way back I would appreciate it if you take Father Sean home. I want one of you to stay behind to make sure we're not disturbed.'

'Liam, thank God it's you! I was beginning to wonder what was happening. I hope I'm still your friend or has the war changed even that?'

'Bert, don't fret. Nothing has changed war or no bloody war. All real Irish friends are friends for life not just when it's sunny. Which is lucky as it doesn't do much but rain in these emerald isles. First let's have a drink of the best whiskey money can buy and eat before we get down to business.'

So they ate an excellent meal of the best tender Irish beef fillet with fresh potatoes, garden peas and Brussels sprouts. There was even the finest horseradish sauce and English mustard as well as a lot of thick gravy. All this was washed down with a bottle of Old Bushmills Special Old Liqueur whiskey.

'I hope you like the whiskey as it's the finest Bushmills produce and very hard to come by. Eat as much as you can because it could be your last meal for a while.'

'Liam the whiskey is unusually mellow and very good. Indeed the beef is so tender it falls off my knife and tastes fantastic. It appears you Irish don't suffer from rationing like us in Britain,' Bert managed to reply bewildered at his surroundings and wondering what was going to happen. Still he felt better with full stomach and the whiskey.

After the meal Liam explained his predicament.

'The Germans hired me through a Senor Gomez in the Spanish Embassy in Dublin to kill you and hide your body in the bogs. It appears your work is giving them such a headache that they feel they can only cure by killing you. The silly fools think I'm pro-German like some other mindless Irishmen, when as you know I really hate their guts. Let me explain our predicament. I officially work for the Irish Government to hunt down, arrest and intern or kill any soldiers, sailors or airmen from any side who are found in the Republic. So far I have interned three German sailors and one German spy pretending to be a Scotsman. Sometimes during the night their U-boats land agents on our shores that we usually capture before they have gone very far. In my job I find restricted information and a cloak of secrecy helpful to my other employers, the British SOE. When paid to kill you it only took seconds for me to decide that I would personally pretend to carry out the foul deed. It will be done so well that even Churchill will be convinced you're dead, while in fact you're back home safe in the bosom of your family,' Liam informed Bert.

'Well, I'm damned. You work at the same time for both the Irish Government and the British Special Operations Executive. It must be a difficult tightrope to walk but I think you're the ideal man for the job, intelligent and persuasive. I must admit I'm relieved and delighted to see you again old friend, even if it is under different circumstances to the last time we met in Belfast,' Bert commented.

'You can appreciate my dilemma. I must convince the Germans you're dead long enough for you to escape. So here is what we're going to do,' Liam then proceeded to explain his complicated plan. It involved a very realistic photograph of a blindfolded dead man lying in a shallow grave in an Irish peat bog. This would be given to the Germans as proof of Bert's death while he was spirited away to England.

Liam explained that he had developed an effective secret underground railway to convey captured allied servicemen safely across the border into Ulster. It used a simple loop hole in the neutrality agreement that was so straight forward and well accepted that it was never questioned. Under the Neutrality Agreement, Ireland promises to repatriate all the bodies of dead allied personnel together with all captured combatants found to be so seriously injured that they will never again be fit enough to fight. It is one function of the International Red Cross in Ireland to certify that only the very sick and maimed are repatriated. So a local Irish doctor bandages the patient so that only one eye shows and he looks horribly injured complete with blood encrusted bandages. Of course the effect is theatrically managed by using bandages soaked in pig's blood. Some of the 'injured' are made to appear as amputees, others as people blinded from severe burns from a crashed aircraft. It takes time to make the 'invalid' look acceptable when examined by the guards on the border. Each invalid is accompanied by a full medical report signed by a senior Irish doctor, and his name, rank and serial number carefully pinned to his bandages. Indeed everything follows the Red Cross rule book right down to the finest detail and the accompanying documentation. This is essential as it is rumoured there are German informers on the border and in Northern Ireland both at the docks and in the airports.

A few hours later a doctor and a nurse arrived at the old thatched cottage to transform Bert into a war casualty. Liam carefully watched as they strapped Bert's left arm tightly to his chest before bandaging him to look like an amputee. Then they checked to see if he was comfortable before continuing their transformation. Next they covered half of Bert's face with bandages before setting his left leg in thick layers of Plaster of Paris. It was certainly an effective disguise, but bloody uncomfortable.

'Well Bert, always remember that I never hurt anyone who doesn't ask for it. When you get home tell the Security Service that you're on Hitler's Death List and must be protected. I suspect the man who sent you here is a German agent, so if you see him again be warned and if I were you I'd kill the slimy creature. I promise that when this bloody war is over we'll meet at Kathleen's hotel for a few glasses of very special Bushmills. Nod if you understand what I'm saying,' Liam commented softly.

Bert then slowly nodded his head realising that moving was difficult and spoke in a faint mumble. 'I feel like a turkey being prepared for someone's Christmas dinner. It's very itchy, but thanks as I know you're trying to save my life and I will never forget your kindness.'

'Sorry old man if the bandages are uncomfortable but I have included two envelopes inside the plaster cast, one for you and one for SOE. It is unlikely anyone will try to remove the cast before you get to England, but if they do make certain you keep the envelopes because my life depends on it. Before I forget, the camera you came to collect is badly damaged and of no value so I've destroyed it. We must try to keep up appearances so the enemy think you're dead. Now off you go with our friends. Be a good boy and don't do anything I wouldn't do,' Liam joked as Bert was placed on a stretcher and taken outside. There his stretcher was strapped into a bunk opposite another bandaged man next to a nurse in the back of an old ambulance. For the next hour they sped along winding country roads and over at least one humpback bridge that threw everyone around, but no one muttered a word. Twice they were stopped by the authorities at road blocks and the driver questioned. Luckily no one looked inside the ambulance to check if they were casualties of war.

The next thing Bert remembered was lying on a stretcher inside a large hanger waiting for the flight to Cambridge.

'Sir it won't be long before you're safely airborne. Please stay very quiet as it will be uncomfortable when we move your stretcher. It can't be helped as even here, where we are surrounded by security police, the walls have ears. Sadly there are too many curious eyes watching everything and everybody. Once in England you will be taken to hospital to have your bandages and plaster cast removed. We'll try to make you as comfortable as possible but I advise you try to sleep as it will help pass the time,' a young nurse with a lovely soft voice consolingly whispered in his ear. So Bert nodded and tried to sleep or at least meditate on the strange twists and to wonder if his nemesis had been behind this latest problem. He didn't like murder but given half a chance he would kill the nemesis in his black uniform without any qualms.

Three hours later Bert was in an annex at Addenbrooke's Hospital Cambridge having the bandages gently removed. It was a long process as the plaster cast on his leg had dried hard and the bandages were tight. Once free of his bandages his body itched all over, so they covered him with talcum powder. At last he could breathe freely and use his left arm making him feel very glad to be alive.

'Welcome back to the living Bert. We now know that Senor Juan Gomez in Dublin is a German agent and our Mr Smith, the bogus Ministry of Air Defence a traitor who has since been found and dealt with,' said a smiling Guy de Broyen. 'Liam Gallagher even had the nerve to smuggle his latest report to us inside your plaster cast. Crafty old bugger, strangely he holds you in high esteem and says that we must keep you safe.'

'He's just an old family friend,' Bert commented.

'Well that may explain this other package we found inside your cast addressed to your wife. Take it before any officious bastard asks any silly questions.'

That night Bert told Jenny about his Irish adventure and gave her the envelope. On opening the package she jumped for joy as she found it contained five pairs of the latest and very expensive nylon stockings from America. Even more strangely they were exactly her size! It made Bert wonder how much of his private life Liam actually knew and who told him. That night he dreamed of herds of sheep in a large green Irish field and drinking Bushmills whiskey with a lovable rogue at Kathleen O'Reilly's Hotel. Was it a dream or a premonition!

The photographs of the blindfolded Bert lying dead in an Irish bog satisfied Senior Juan Gomez. However in his report to Berlin he embellished the details to suggest he had actually witnessed the execution. So for many months the Germans thought Bert was dead and so forgot the search for Sebro. However, to make his death appear real, British security repainted Bert's British Racing Green Morgan an unfashionable black. Bert suspected it was more because they envied his exciting British Racing Green Morgan than for any real security measure.

Back in Germany Bert's nemesis, *Hauptmann* Walter Brandt, received a commendation from Berlin for eliminating an important enemy of the state. He hoped to be promoted making him less likely to see active service, especially on the deadly Russian Front. Feeling satisfied, he carefully perused the Death List to find others who could be easily removed. He received very little support from his superiors who were busy planning to assassinate Churchill during one of his journeys in Britain or better still, while abroad such as in the USA. They did try to kill Churchill on many occasions in different countries, but luckily every attempt failed. Too often the assassins succeeded in killing one or more of Churchill's many doubles!

# 25

## Bomber Crews and Eggs for Breakfast

It was a time when simple little gestures made one feel very special. This was especially from the young men who every night risked all flying over German Occupied Europe.

Whenever Bert heard the air raid siren while in the pub with his friends, he always wanted to leave. However they often tried to stop him.

'Bert why not stay here with us, you'll be much safer now we have better anti-aircraft guns around the airfield,' said Stefan Radvanski.

'Stefan's right. It's better if you stay. It's a bit late to drive safely home in the dark,' added Jim Jefferies with his soft Montreal accent.

Then the others joined in to demand Bert remained but without success.

'Sorry chaps, but I'm worried about Jenny. She only has our son Charles for company and she's expecting another child. I don't want her to become sick worrying about me,' Bert commented, looking very serious.

They knew how Bert's baby daughter had died after being born too small to survive. Sadly even in the countryside, people died from having an inadequate diet or just the stress of trying to stay alive. Often they reluctantly watched their friend return home, hoping all was well, before going back to have another round of drinks and try to forget the terrors tomorrow would surely bring.

It was a Wednesday morning after yet another top secret special bombing mission, when Stefan Radvanski arrived at Sebro carefully carrying a small cardboard box. He quietly waited for Bert to finish inspecting the port outer engine of a recently repaired Stirling before saying anything.

'Good morning Bert, the lads have asked me to bring you a present for Jenny.'

'Good morning Stefan, I must say it's very kind of them. Well are you going to tell me what it is or must I stand here waiting?' Bert replied with a disarming smile. He was always pleased to see young Stefan whose innocent looks hid his professional ability as one of the best pilots.

'It's only two dozen fresh eggs we've kept for your Jenny. Since you told us she was with child we decided to do something to help. You know that before we're sent on a highly dangerous mission, they serve us a symbolic last dinner with two eggs on our plates. It is their way of saying, well lads we don't expect you back alive or in one piece. Luckily for us they're often wrong. So we told our cooks that henceforth we only wanted one egg and the other was to be kept for our Jenny. At first the head cook made a long face and shook his face. However, with my pleading and knowing we're the officers and aircrew who were not meant to return, he eventually agreed. So please accept our gift and carefully take them home with our love. Remember that as long as we're still alive I promise many more eggs will follow,' Stefan said looking unusually bashful.

Bert was astounded at their generosity for a woman they had met only a few times. It was a gift from heroes who when not flying were seen singing loud, bawdy songs and drinking too much. Above all they were a band of men united in their duty and love of life.

'Tell the chaps, thanks a lot. It's a gift fit for a queen that is very gratefully appreciated,' Bert managed to stutter. Now his face had gone red from embarrassment and yet he was deeply grateful.

At the end of the working day Bert gingerly carried the precious bundle home to present the twenty-four unbroken eggs to Jenny. She was delighted and then, like women tend to do on such occasions, uncontrollably burst into tears. Maybe the tears were for the brave airmen who sooner or later may never return. For Jenny knew that the life expectancy of a bomber crew was only twenty missions and many of Bert's friends had done twice that.

For the next few months the pilots sent a steady supply of extra eggs to help keep Jenny healthy and guarantee that her son was born, large and strong. Soon after the birth, Bert went to The Barley Mow to tell his friends the good news that he had a healthy new son and Jenny was well. Then all present celebrated by toasting the good health of Jenny and her new born son with many rounds of beer.

'Bert you must name the boy Robin after the cheeky and very British Robin Red Breast that visits our quarters. It's a good name, worthy of a warrior like Robin Hood and fierce defender of his territory like the male Cock Robin,' Stefan said. His remarks were accompanied by shouts of 'Here, Here' and 'And so say all of us'.

'We'll see Stefan, but thanks for the idea,' Bert replied not knowing what to say and not wishing to upset his generous friend. So, later that night, Bert told Jenny the lads wanted their baby christened Robin and why. She just smiled and said that it was a good name. However she did not say she agreed as she was determined to name him Bert after his father, her beloved husband.

A few weeks later Jenny went with Bert to the pub to show off her boys. The independent Charles was kept entertained with card tricks and shown how to make hand shadows by Stefan and Ron. Meanwhile everyone wanted to look at the newborn baby to make sure that he was healthy.

'Well he really is a fine bouncy baby. A true Robin Redbreast,' Jim said. 'Already I can hear him sing. He's a real chirping Robin.'

For some unknown reason, probably a touch of wind, the baby made what the pilots took as his first words and so logically christened him their chirping Robin.

So, when the baby was baptised, everyone was delighted when the priest named him Robin Herbert and in doing so kept everyone happy. Then they returned to Bert's home for light refreshments and drinks in the garden by the apple trees. The sun shone brightly, the birds sang and everything looked as it had for a thousand years. For a few hours they were in a green land where peace and good will flourished. Sadly it was a brief but much appreciated respite from the hell and disasters that surrounded them.

Alas time waits for no one. Soon Bert started to prepare for the third thousand bomber raid scheduled to take place on the night of 25/26th June 1942[27]. Even with all the repairs carried out by Sebro and many others, the RAF could only gather nine hundred and sixty aircraft for the raid. However, it was just enough to keep the C-in-C of Bomber Command Air Marshall 'Bomber' Arthur Harris happy. So the raid mostly consisted of five hundred Wellington, one hundred Handley Page Halifax, one hundred Avro Lancaster and seventy Stirling bombers. They added the smaller and slower Bristol Blenheim, Handley Page Hampden, and Armstrong Whitworth Whitley light bombers just to make up the numbers. No one ever explained why it had to be nearly a thousand aircraft. Churchill, Harris or both of them had decided on the number and thus it had to be so.

That night over Germany the RAF losses proved unacceptably high. Of the nine hundred and sixty aircraft involved in the raid ninety-eight were destroyed. Coastal Command lost fifty aircraft while Bomber Command forty-eight reported missing believed lost. In comparison, the slow but strong Whitley and Wellington bombers lost only forty-eight, aircraft. The high rate of attrition troubled the planners making them rethink their tactics. They knew that such heavy losses could not be sustained. They comforted themselves knowing that the raid destroyed or damaged seven thousand houses along with the important Focke-Wulf aircraft factory[26,30]. For Bert it proved a personal tragedy, one that he would never forget. Even in old age Bert remembered the night his friend did not return.

As always he watched the aircraft return to arrange for the repair of those in need of urgent attention. The first damaged aircraft to arrive back was the Stirling F for Freddie piloted by Stefan Radvanski. Stefan brought her down onto the grass away from the main runway with only two engines running and a huge hole in the wing, large enough for a man to climb through. After the engines stopped Stefan clambered out of his damaged aircraft with a bloodied face and a very sad look. Looking very worried he slowly walked up to Bert while his crew were whisked away to the First Aid huts.

'It's good to see you Bert. As you can see it was not just another night over one more target. Instead they were waiting for us with all their defences primed for the kill. It was bloody rough with lot of heavy flack exploding around us as night fighters appeared suddenly from nowhere. Still I managed to bomb the target but on the way home something hit my aircraft with such force that it removed part of my starboard wing. It made the landing a bit difficult, but nothing I couldn't handle. Do you know if Z for Zulu has turned up? I saw Jim Jefferies fighting to keep Zulu in the air having been damaged as he turned for home. Please let me know if he made it? Though something tells me I will never see him again, certainly not in this world. I hope I'm wrong,' Stefan said in a tone that said it all. It would be a miracle if Jim was safe but he hoped he was.

A minute later another badly damaged Stirling bounced along the grass, one wing tipped too low to touch the ground thus breaking it off from the fuselage and swirling the aircraft around. As soon as the plane was stationary, the fire crews covered the fuselage with water to prevent a fire while the crew was pulled out. Afterwards Bert learned they were attacked by a night fighter who shot the pilot dead in his seat so the wounded co-pilot flew the aircraft home. Blood coloured the sad scene a deep red as the few survivors went to hospital and the bodies of the dead were removed. It took Bert nearly an hour to cut the co-pilot free of the twisted metal of what was once the cockpit. The man was given morphine by the base doctor but even so he cried out in pain when eased out to safety. It was just in time as the fuel leaking from the ruined aircraft ignited turning her into a blazing inferno that destroyed everything leaving only a grotesque bent skeleton.

Bert watched the bomber burn thinking it looked like an ancient Viking boat funeral pyre. Later he was shocked to learn from the Station Commander that Z for Zulu was reported as crashing into the sea but, after a careful search, the Air Sea Rescue craft found no survivors. Jim's unexpected death hit Bert like a ton of bricks. Jim had always said that when the war was over they should all go to Canada and visit his home city of Montreal. He said it was the only city in the world where the best of British and French culture happily existed side by side. The city was overlooked by his beautiful Mount Royal with even its own Beaver Lake and a ski jump. As a reminder of home, Jim painted a beaver on the side of Z for Zulu for good luck. This was because they were great survivors out in the wilderness.

Then the sky's opened and the rain came down killing the fires and washing the ground of the blood of the heroes. For God in his mercy let the heavens weep to soak the ground for the grass to grow and everything, well nearly everything, return to normal.

Bert finally drove home muttering under his breath over and over again the words Bloody war with absolute hatred. He always knew war was never a game but a continuous struggle for survival. Even so the thought of his friend Jim Jefferies fighting at the controls of his Stirling as she started her last sharp descent into the cold sea brought tears to his eyes. The tears did not make him feel any better, but made driving through the blackout even more hazardous. After just missing a small lorry in the dim light, Bert stopped for a few moments to gather his thoughts, blew his nose and dried his eyes. He cheered up at the thought of what Liam Gallagher would have said. Something like: 'Any idea of a good war is a stupid mistake! There are no good wars, only bloody conflicts where the good, the bad and the disgusting perish alongside each other without even a flutter of an eyelid or for any good reason. Politicians make wars and we poor sods have to survive their latest ideas and military stupidity'. Somehow it was always the bad people that survived while the kind and decent just disappeared, often without trace. It was as the old wives in England traditionally say 'only the good died young'. Also it was a reminder that they were all just ships that pass in the night. Maybe they did some good during their lives. Maybe they left behind memories to help their friends and family more able to face adversity and struggle through those terrible mires of despair. Probably some were so young they left no memories at all.

# 26

## When Women waited and Prayed for their Men

It was a time of sorrow and hardship. The churches were filled by people praying for the safety of their loved ones and for their return home. While lonely widows tried to raise their children on their own with what little money they had.

Jenny thought the hardest thing about being a housewife during a war was not the shortages or the rationing – it was the uncertainty about what tomorrow would bring. Would it be a time of joy or, heaven forbid, one of sorrow? At anytime she could learn Bert had died or been injured while working somewhere in Britain or even abroad. The only news she received about the war was from the censored radio broadcasts or when a friend dropped by for a chat over a biscuit and a cup of sweet tea. Since moving into their new house near a RAF base, they were safe from intruders but at risk from enemy aircraft. Jenny learned to accept that wherever they lived something could destroy their lives in just a few seconds. Sometimes she wished Bert was working in Windermere with her father Alf, building Short Sunderland flying boats. Her father said among the lakes the risk of enemy attacks was relatively low. Working and living by the lake in a rural community meant that any stranger was quickly identified and regarded as hostile even if innocent, so saboteurs had no chance. Indeed it was probably one of the safest places to live in the whole country.

War was a constant struggle between trying to raise the boys with as much food as she could muster and keeping herself busy. The nights were the worse, especially when Bert did not returned, as sinister shadows formed in her mind often bringing her to tears. Then she cried herself to sleep while hugging her pillow. Many a night Jenny held her old rosary praying for Bert's safety and that he would come home after the last bomber had returned, or from wherever he had been sent. At times like this her Anglo-Catholic beliefs kept her going even when the dark clouds came over everyone they loved. She knew better than to ask about his job or where he went because he could not tell her. Like the angel she was, Jenny never questioned his strange working hours or long absences when he did not even phone her. The only thing she knew for certain was when he finally returned home, she and the boys would always be there with a hug and a kiss.

One day when Jenny was out shopping and Bert was at home recovering from a serious chest infection, he came across her diary. He should not have read it but like the silly man he was did. So he started to read her inner most thoughts that she never told him about.

In her diary she wrote:

Bert has now been away for over a week and there have been no messages. He said he had to go away but as always didn't say for how long or where to. Ever since the flying bomb hit the house next door I have worried that Bert is being targeted by the enemy. When I asked the security man about this he just laughed and said I should not worry my pretty little head over such an unlikely matter. From experience it is when people say silly things like 'my pretty little head' I know they're avoiding answering a serious question. Why do men think that we women, especially young mothers, have no brains and cannot appreciate the difficulties of others? What he then said is something I shall never forget. It was that I must never forget Bert worked on vital war projects that involved him being away from home for weeks on end and I should never question him as to where he had been or what he had done. His work and skills were an essential part of our war effort so he must be cherished and protected from any danger, however small.

Then she had written a few days later:

When Bert returned after being away for over a week I was as happy as any woman can be. He loved me as if his very life depended upon it and kept looking into my eyes with that schoolboy look that makes my legs go weak. No one, even his manager Hugh James, had a clue where he had been only that it was all hush-hush. However he brought me a gift from Ireland, via a friend called Liam Gallagher, of five pairs of expensive American fashion nylon stockings. It was a gift worthy of a princess as they must have cost an arm and a leg to buy and then only if you could find the right spiv to sell you a pair that had fallen off the proverbial back of a lorry! It was a charming thought. However if I ever have a chance I would like to have a few words with Mr Liam Gallagher, if he really exists, to ask him not to keep Bert away from his loved ones for so long. In many ways I'm the luckiest girl in the world with a good husband, two lovely children and a large house in the countryside. So I must count my blessings and be grateful Bert is not off risking his life fighting in some foreign land with so many of the local lads. I always feel safe when walking down the street with Bert especially when the young men whistle and strangers give me unwelcomed looks. I think they take one look at his muscular body to decide someone like him should not be antagonised. Sometimes they even hang their heads in shame.

In the last part of her diary she wrote after Bert's illness when a combination of worry, lack of sleep, and too much smoking made him collapse with pneumonia, the following entry:

At last I have Bert home with us even though he is sick and can hardly walk. Every time I enter our bedroom to see how he is, I notice his eyes wide open as he tries to make an impish smile. The doctor says Bert has been working too hard and needs a lot of love and attention. But I know, God willing, he will be up on his feet within a week and fit to return to work. I know the country needs him, but they must learn to share him with his loved ones. Somehow his work is so emotionally draining that the colour goes from his cheeks and his eyes have permanent dark rings under them. I know he finds seeing his friends fly off into the night, often never to return, very upsetting though he never says anything to me. Once, when his Canadian friend Jim Jefferies died, he told me how he felt, in an effort to explain his red eyes and his unusually sad face.

When shopping or talking to neighbours, I've heard terrible tales about how the rescue teams on the airfields where Bert works have to cut our wounded aircrew free from their damaged planes. A nurse friend says some are so badly wounded that many don't survive more than a few hours and those who do take a great deal of tender care and attention to return to live a normal life. Many are so badly burned or crippled they will always be in pain or in need of help for the rest of their lives to survive in what can be a very cruel world. She says that a New Zealand surgeon Archie MacIndoe and his team performed miracles with his new techniques in plastic surgery to help those badly burned and scarred. She went on to say that the patients called themselves the Guinea Pig Club and were proud of the people at the Queen Victoria Hospital in East Grinstead who tried so hard to make them well. Everyone admires our strong heroes when in uniform, but few think about those who are deformed or crippled. Thank heavens for Archie and his men as well as the others who rebuild the bodies of the maimed.

Last night Bert had another nightmare about his enemy the Man in Black. He woke up sweating but after praying together and talking we have decided to accept him as a real person. Maybe he really is the Nazi Bert met in Germany and at a stretch of my imagination he is the man behind the attempts to kill him. Whatever is true, I believe that God will keep us safe and that Bert's enemy will eventually reap the punishment he deserves. Then Bert calmed down and smiled. Indeed since that night the dreams rarely return though I fear the Man in Black still exists.

A week later Bert returned to work and one evening took me to his local pub to have a drink with his pilot friends. We had a grand time with Bert playing the piano and everyone singing. Two of the young Polish pilots decided to perform in my honour a traditional dance that was both highly impressive and exhausting. Then they sang about home, the girls they left behind, and some rather rude rugby songs I've never heard before. I love being with Bert's friends because they're so full of life and living for the day as they know that tomorrow may not come. What surprised me most was the number of pilots who claimed they owed their very survival to Bert and his men who were the best aircraft engineers in the whole world. All of a sudden it made me feel very proud of my Bert to gain a new respect for his skills and above all for his humility. The aircrew came from all over the world, some thousands of miles from home, considered my Bert their friend. One of the Polish pilots even said they did not fly for the RAF or against Germany, they flew only for Bert. With a subtle blush Bert replied that such a comment could be regarded as treason. He then added affectionately, 'Still thanks a lot you mangy looking lot of bloody mongrels.' They laughed.

As we left the pub to walk the short distance home I put my head on Bert's shoulder as we strolled hand in hand in the moonlight. The stars were very special as they shined down on us. It was as if to give their blessing and promise that Bert would always remain by my side until that awful day when death parts us. Then I will wait patiently until my turn comes to travel that lonely road to Heaven to be united with the one I love. I know it's so because God has promised that for all who believe in him there is room for them in his mansion, and I really do believe his word.

Bert closed Jenny's diary realising what a treasure she was. Tall, thin, often too quiet and sometimes even annoyingly sullen, but a more loving woman never walked this earth. She had learned and accepted that working at Sebro repairing bombers during a war was not a safe occupation. But with her by his side he felt stronger and believed that together they would survive anything, however terrible. Indeed the thought of her unquestioning devotion kept him warm and very happy during the long hard days and nights that lay ahead. However he prayed that the war would not last much longer as already much of the country was in ruins and too many friends had died or been seriously wounded. Would he and Jenny survive the conflict uninjured in body and mind? He doubted it as he would never forget the sound of bombs or the cries of the wounded especially when he cut them out of the remains of their aircraft. Whatever happened he vowed never to abandon Jenny and the boys. Didn't he promise to cherish her in sickness and in health? and he intended to keep that promise. Only time would tell what happened but for now he was content to live in a warm, loving family and work with friends.

# 27

# Britain changed to meet new Challenges

Like the magic of a new day when the summer sun breaks through a stormy night so did women became treated the same as men. The piper at the break of dawn witnessed women of all ages, many for the first time, going out to work for their nation.

In 1940 the Minister of Labour Ernest Bevan called on all women without any children or dependents to look after, to volunteer for work[13,23,27]. He announced that they could do some of the jobs left undone or poorly manned because so many men were away fighting. His request landed on many willing ears. Soon women wanted work, preferably near their homes but even then the number of volunteers was not enough. In December 1941, all unmarried women between the ages of eighteen to thirty were conscripted to work for the nation. In the weeks that followed women queued at centres to be allocated work in factories, First Aid posts, manning Air Raid sirens or on the land and in the forests. Some drove taxis, delivery trucks and tractors, others became bus conductors and even a few ended up as pilots. If there were no jobs available, the administrators found them or created new ones. Indeed modern womanhood was on the move and would never be the same again!

One day Bert put his foot in it.

'Well don't worry about me darling 'cos no one's going to send me women engineers. It was hard enough finding our secretaries,' Bert commented expecting no reply.

'Don't you be so smug, I'm sure a few women would transform your dirty lot into human beings,' Jenny replied with a grin.

'And pigs will fly before that happens.'

'They do in aircraft.'

'Humbug!' Bert commented. It was an expression he had picked up from reading Charles Dickens and one he used when in polite society.

Bert sat down to light his pipe thinking that this was one argument he could never win.

It was not long before Sebro received their first batch of female workers. The first ones were given light but essential jobs as secretaries, cleaners, or cooks, but others became storekeepers and bookkeepers. Still none came to do a man's job. Well that was until that momentous day when four women arrived to be trained as assistant mechanics.

With great reluctance Bert accepted them and was surprised to find out that they had all assembled new aircraft at one of the many factories building Stirling or other large aircraft. Feeling much happier about the turn of events he politely welcomed the ladies and arranged for their separate facilities. Bert unexpectedly found that their arrival turned out to be just what the doctor ordered. The hours of hard work and many sleepless nights had made some of his men a bit sloppy with their dress sense, while still remaining good at their work. The sight of the first four young women assistant mechanics at Sebro was magical. Suddenly the men came to work smartly dressed and well shaven. Even the tea room was clean and tidy, though the pin ups of scanty clad women still adorned the walls. Now swearing was reduced to a few odd inoffensive words like 'drat' and 'sod it' so that if a priest visited he would have been impressed.

Bert's initial fears that young women would not make good engineers was soon forgotten. Within days pretty women in overalls and hairnets had oil smudges on their smiling faces and the dirtiest nails he had ever seen. They even worked as hard as the men. Bert was surprised to find that at the end of the day the ladies were the last to stop working, but the first to wash off the grime and be ready to go home. Their fastidiousness and good manners charmed even the hard hearted partly misogynist

Bert. So it was later that day when at home Bert told Jenny and their maid Maude about his women.

'Well I must say I'm pleased to say that our new young women workers are proving to be much better than expected. In fact their presence has worked miracles in the workshop as my men are more cheerful and, for a change, look respectable. Indeed now the women are now welcome in every aspect of the work even when lifting the heavy engines in and out of the wing mountings.'

'We women keep everyone happy, that's our life's work. You just wait and see we're taking over. Beware one day we'll even have a woman Prime Minister,' commented the usually quiet orphan Maude in her mouse-like voice.

'And I will be King,' Bert unwisely commented.

'And why not?' added an annoyed Jenny.

'The cat's caught his tongue. Don't worry yourself Ma'am as we both know your Bert is a bit of a Philistine. It always surprises me that he caught a lovely lady like you,' Maude said smilingly trying to make her own particular type of joke.

They all laughed. Afterwards Maude walked around with an extra air of confidence.

Whether Bert liked it or not, from then onwards women played a vital role in the workplace and would continue to do so. It benefited all but the young children left to live on their own. Sadly many children had to feed, clothe and entertain themselves and learn from their peers how to survive. It was a time when the joys of childhood were lost as they had to grow up fast to do the household chores that mum once did.

When driving across country, especially during harvesting time, Bert enjoyed seeing ladies with their hair held up in scarves helping to harvest fields of wheat. Some drove the horse and cart while others gathered cut straw to make sheaves. The effect of the women in the labour force was noticeable with more goods available in the shops and national productivity on the increase.

Everywhere information posters stated 'CARELESS WORDS COST LIVES' and 'BE LIKE DAD KEEP MUM! They warned everyone to say nothing of importance as enemy agents were everywhere. Another poster showed two men in hats under a dim light warning everyone that 'IN THE BLACKOUT PAUSE AS YOU LEAVE THE STATION'S LIGHTS;' a simple but vital message as many forgot and were injured. Then there was a picture of a pretty girl wearing trousers and holding a pitch folk with the caption 'FOR A HEALTHY HAPPY JOB JOIN THE WOMEN'S LAND ARMY.' Another rather Russian looking poster showed in the foreground a woman standing with her open arms raised while aircraft flew overhead and in the background were buildings. On this was printed 'WOMEN OF BRITAIN COME INTO THE FACTORIES.' Perhaps the most effective was the famous 'DIG ON FOR VICTORY' poster showing a man with a fork under one arm carrying an armful of vegetables. Everyone including the King was seen gardening, while people had miniature farms in their back yards or grew vegetables in window boxes. Some of the lucky ones were able to buy government supplied live baby rabbits, chickens, and geese to rear for food or just to produce eggs. The demand for such animals soon outstripped the supply, but that always happens during any crisis. The important thing was that for a change everybody wanted to grow their own food.

Everywhere one was bombarded with information, some important but others not so relevant. Vitally the nation was mobilised to win the war or at least make a bloody good attempt at doing so. The BBC radio continuously broadcast special programmes designed to increase production by keeping the workers happy in the workplace and at home. Ernest Bevan had his own radio show called 'Worker's Playtime' broadcast from a different factory canteen every day 'Somewhere in Britain' that was a mixture of music, comedy and government announcements. On radio he always personally thanked people for their good work and encouraged them to continue the struggle on what he called the Home Front. Within days of its first broadcast, the show became popular to be accepted as part of the working day. The show included the very popular household names such as Else and Doris Walters, Percy Edwards, Charlie Chester and Bob Monkhouse. At home the people listened to other programs such as 'Hi Gang' with Vic Oliver and to 'Big Hearted' Arthur Askey with Richard 'Stinker' Murdoch in 'Band Wagon'. The most popular programme was Tommy Handley's 'ITMA (It's That Man Again)' that was full of quick-fire jokes and ridiculous characters such as Colonel Chin-strap, Mrs Mopp and

Claude. These radio shows brought smiles to the faces of a nation tired of war and weary of hardship.

The newspapers and films showed pictures of King George and the Queen visiting bomb sites in London, the two Princesses changing a car tyre, or Winston Churchill holding up two fingers in his famous V for Victory sign while smoking an extremely expensive cigar. It portrayed an image of everybody working together to do their bit for victory. The other side of the coin was unfortunately all too visible where the criminals and cheats exploited everyone. The illegal traders termed 'spivs' or 'wide boys' could be seen throughout the nation in pubs and on the corners of dark streets. There they sold from suitcases bottles of whisky, cigarettes and ladies nylon stockings at exorbitant prices. They thrived because rationing meant such items were impossible to buy in the shops. Some shopkeepers exploited the shortages to make a quick profit. When there was nobody around, some shopkeepers sold things for an extra five shillings without a ration coupon from what was known as under the counter. Of course it was illegal, but few cared about that and even less reported the shopkeepers. It is hard to blame the shoppers when life was hard. The average ration per person was so severe that few were happy living on such a paltry diet. In one week the ration for an adult was four ounces of bacon or ham, eight of sugar, two of butter, eight of cooking fat, two of tea, one of cheese and tow ounces of jam. Meat was rationed by price so that the best cuts were too expensive for anyone to afford except for the very rich. In theory eggs were available but in practice they were not. Even in the countryside eggs were kept for those with enough money to afford the inflated prices. Items like bread, vegetables and fish were not rationed and for many people these became the staple diet.

During the night, even while the bombs were exploding all around, gangs roamed the damaged houses and shops to steal whatever they could find. The shortages of luxury goods meant that nearly everything, however damaged, had a good second-hand value and could be sold without any questions asked. The theft of personal effects became so common that many people would not leave their damaged homes in the fear of all their belongings being stolen. To stop the robbers, the government passed laws making it a hanging offence to steal from bomb-damaged sites, but few were caught and still less- executed.

Occasionally the police would find old warehouses filled to the roof with stolen or looted goods that they confiscated and were later distributed to the displaced people. It was like Dickensian times when many people like Fagin and their gangs robbed everyone. They thrived like never before supplying their ill gotten gains to the rich as well as anyone with the money and no morals. Some people whose children were off fighting for King and Country purchased black market goods. Even those items obviously stolen from the docks marked Government Issue to be shipped abroad for the forces were sold under the counter. The most popular items were chocolate, cigarettes, petrol, ration books, silk stockings and identity cards. This business in ID cards became so common that the police became seriously concerned. This was because the ordinary ID card had no photograph and could easily be forged by crooks and enemy agents to pass undetected. So they put photographs on all special ID cards issued to the top men and people working in sensitive areas to tighten security.

With the help of the new women workers the rate of the repair and refurbishment of aircraft increased. Things went so well that even RAF Bomber Command stopped complaining about how long it took to get their bombers back into action. Now Bert had placed well trained, experienced engineers in all bomber stations even those who had no Stirling bombers. It proved to be a good move and was well received by all involved. In many cases some of his men rotated between working in Sebro and at the RAF stations.

It was about this time that Bert was asked to meet an old associate, the aircraft designer Barnes Wallace at the Vickers Works in Weybridge, the home of the Wellington bomber. The journey down to Weybridge took nearly all morning but Bert found it exhilarating and a change from his normal routine. It was early afternoon when Bert drove into the Vickers yard to be met by Barnes Wallace waiting with his hands in his pockets.

'Welcome, Bert. I hope you don't mind me calling you by your first name, as you're now as senior as me?' Barnes said smoking his pipe.

'It's a pleasure to see you again sir. If I remember correctly the last time we met was after the 1931 Schneider Trophy race,' Bert replied.

'Yes I believe it was. However Bert I must insist you call me Barnes.'

Barnes explained his latest work was designing weapons to destroy hard to hit targets. He then mentioned modifying Stirling, Wellington or Lancaster bombers to deliver specially designed very powerful bombs. All the design work and testing was done in secrecy under his direction and Bert would only be needed, when the time came, to advise them on the different ways of modifying bomb bays to hold the weapons. Until then Bert was to carry on as normal. Indeed most of Barnes Wallace's ideas were tested in his own back garden with the help of his son until they were perfected enough to get official support. He explained that one of his ideas was to make a bomb bounce across the water like a pebble to hit targets like dams. Barnes explained that he had made a table tennis ball do just that in a bath tub in his backyard. Then with the help of his son he had even made a heavy golf ball do the same thing. Only time would tell if any of his ideas would come to fruition but he hoped a few would succeed.

Meanwhile Bert and his men were kept busy as gradually the RAF front line bomber became the Avro Lancaster and the Handley Page Halifax as the slower Stirling was given a supporting role. The newer bombers could carry larger bombs over greater distances than the Stirling. Of course when the Stirling was designed no one thought that its shallow bomb bay was a disadvantage because there were no gigantic bombs until the early 1940s. The two main features pilots loved about the Stirling were its manoeuvrability and useful things like a small observation window in the right hand side of the cockpit, so the pilot could see the runway. With the arrival of newer bombers, Sebro had to get different spare parts and modify their equipment especially for the American Boeing Consolidated B-24 Liberator bombers supplied to the RAF. Still the struggle continued as the war went on.

# 28

## The War goes from Bad to Worse

Bad planning and poor command cost the allies their Far Eastern bases.

By March 1942 all of Bert's fears had come true. Now he read in the papers the disasters befalling an Empire struggling to survive. First the gallant Hong Kong had surrendered on 25th December 1941. Six weeks later Bert read of the surrender of the huge garrisons in Malaya and Singapore on 15th February to a triumphant Japan. For Bert the last straw was when Rangoon fell on 8th March 1941. Now all Britain was in shock. Now in desperation the Allies fought to save India, Australia and New Zealand. What little that was left of the ill-equipped allied forces retreated to the Naga Hills from Burma while the Australians defended Port Moresby in Papua New Guinea. It was a time of desperation. It was a time for prayer. Above all it was when the cream of the youth held the thin red line[5,23,24].

As 1942 ended, all around Cambridge the ground was covered with a thick layer of snow reminding everyone that the war was far from won. Inside the hangers at Sebro the air was so cold that the cold metal became brittle and had to be slowly warmed before they could work on it. Bert insisted that every thirty minutes his workforce warmed their hands over an open brazier or had a warm cup of tea. This reduced frost bite and the fingers becoming too numb to function safely. However, the fuel required for heating and cooking was strictly rationed so in an attempt to keep warm most people wore many layers of clothing. During those long winter's nights many around the country simply froze to death as hardship dug deeper and deeper. The old, the weak, the sick and the destitute were among those who suffered most of all. A few lucky ones found work and shelter by doing menial tasks while the younger ones often falsified their ages to enlist in the armed forces where food, clothing and shelter was provided. Even in combat, few combatants had to suffer the hell of living without food and shelter that the dispossessed did in Britain.

On special occasions, such as when celebrating Stefan Radvanski's 21st birthday, Bert played the piano and they drank bottles of the best French champagne taken out of hiding for such an occasion. It was surreal. Stefan and his friend Stanislaw started fighting the Germans during 1939 in a desperate attempt to defend their homeland Poland when only seventeen. Somehow they made their way to France fighting every inch of the way until eventually, ending up in England in their Polish fighter planes. These two young men knew more about war and fighting the *Luftwaffe* than anyone else in the room. Indeed they were proven war veterans and yet only just legally men. In an effort to escape thinking of home and family, they tended to live life to the full and worked even harder than they played. Even in England they had problems. Firstly few could speak English and those who could often had a heavy Polish accent. So in the early days the Polish air crew were issued with special identity papers in case they were arrested by overzealous Home Guard and police on the suspicion they were German spies. It was only during a celebration or after a funeral that they showed their true nature. On such occasions they drank home-made vodka which they somehow distilled on base, while singing Polish songs and performing exhausting folk dances. Indeed they were very popular and in the eyes of their colleagues a special breed of heroes. Many knew they may never see Poland again, but vowed to fight the German invaders to the bitter end, and they did just that. Indeed before the war was over Stefan was awarded a DFC with bar and mentioned in dispatches for his bravery.

The news from North Africa was not better where Rommel's *Afrika Korps* pushed the Allies back towards Egypt and the Suez Canal. Bert smiled when he read that the Soviet Army was managing against all odds to give the Germans a taste of their own medicine. Slowly the Soviets were holding back the massive German advances to maintain control over the important besieged cities of Moscow, Leningrad, and Stalingrad. Only time would tell if the Russians in Europe and the Allied forces in the Middle East and India were strong and determined enough to defeat fascism.

After the Japanese surprise attack on the Pacific fleet of the US Navy anchored at Pearl Harbour on December 7th 1941, the USA declared war on Japan. Then on 11th December 1941 Hitler and Italy declared war on the USA. It proved to be a major error that cost them dearly.

Within weeks, the first contingent of American men and aircraft started to arrive in Britain. The American aircraft greatly boosted the airpower based in Britain available to harass the Germans. Unlike the British bombers, the US aircraft tended to be larger, designed to fly high and had gun turrets all over them. Their size had one major disadvantage as they needed long concrete runways to take off and land. So they were allocated the most modern RAF bases where there were long runways and the British aircraft dispersed to smaller airfields. For example RAF Alconbury and Bassingbourn airfields were transferred to 8th USAAF equipped with Consolidated B-24 Liberator and Boeing B-17 Flying Fortress bombers. Meanwhile a new base was opened at Graveley for No 8 group RAF, the Pathfinders, flying the large Lancaster bombers and the smaller de Havilland DH98 Mosquito fighter bomber[26].

The Americans brought with them nearly everything they needed. It was all new and big but sadly untried. Likewise most American aircrews had little combat experience and no idea of how they were expected to behave in rural England where most were stationed. The first arrivals were very warmly greeted with village reception committees, dances and speeches. The younger generation was delighted to see these men with their strange accents and wild behaviour. They introduced to Britain their own style of dancing and music that was as lively as it was exciting. The Americans generous nature was a ray of sunshine in a bleak world where there were few luxuries. Not surprisingly lonely women flocked in their large numbers to dance with a Yank as they called all Americans. They were like a field of flowers sparkling in the sun doing everything to attract the inquisitive bees and with any luck become united, even if it was for only a few hours against the wall of the village hall. Both sexes had needs they readily fulfilled without thought of what tomorrow may bring. Soon most women knew that Yanks made good lovers who were generous giving them perfume, stockings, and money. It was not always a happy time. On many occasions the Yanks were beaten up by husbands and boyfriends returning unexpectedly on leave to find them in bed with their wives. Sometimes groups of jealous local lads attacked any Yank they found walking alone. Nobody wanted to lose his woman to a Yank or have her end up with an unwanted pregnancy. Some lucky women married Americans, but many were already married. So unfortunate pregnant women secretly left their homes in the dead of night to quietly deliver their child or risk their lives having abortions in illegal clinics.

The Americans introduced their new energetic dances and swing music that soon became enjoyed by all and a part of British life. One of the most popular American musicians was the brilliant Glenn Miller and his fifty piece Army Air Force Band. He came to Britain with his songs like Chattanooga Choo-Choo, I've Gotta Girl in Kalamazoo and Moonlight Serenade. It was not long before both he and his music was simply adored by the whole population. Without doubt the two tunes that stayed in the memory of all who heard him play were Little Brown Jug and his immortal signature tune In the Mood. Dance Halls around the country resounded to the American sounds as the young danced the jitterbug with great enthusiasm, the same way their elders had loved the Cha-Cha-Cha. When Glenn Miller disappeared on a flight from England to Paris, the whole nation mourned him as though he was their son. Indeed he was the one American who all of Britain simply adored.

However the relationship between the British and the Americans soon developed into a love hate relationship that has never disappeared. It was not long before the ration weary, poorly paid British developed a strong dislike towards the newly arrived, wise guy, Americans who flouted their money for all to see. Many British people believed that the US was only fighting the war because they had been humiliated at Pearl Harbor, or as some people said caught with their pants down. In fact most Britons could not forgive the US ambassador to London from 1938 to late 1940, Joseph P Kennedy for telling President Roosevelt that

Britain would be overrun by Germany and should not be supported. He was also accused of trying to meet with Hitler to develop a German-US understanding without the approval of his own government or indeed Britain. As one local vicar told a newly arrived American officer 'Sir, we are glad to see you over here to help us fight the common enemy. But may I ask you simply one question, why did it take you so long to come?'

Wiser heads advised the American commanders to teach their men not to upset the locals. They did not listen. So the distrust of Americans grew, especially as more arrived in Britain wanting a girlfriend or the things they had back home. Unfortunately an American private (GI) earned three pounds and eight shillings a week while his British counterpart earned only fourteen shillings, a fifth of what the GI was paid. This was at a time when a pint of beer in a pub cost a shilling. Soon matters further deteriorated when the British discovered that on every US base there were special shops, the Post Exchange (PX), where only Americans were allowed to buy subsidised duty-free alcohol, cigarettes, nylon stockings, and perfume. So the US government fuelled the flood of luxuries used to seduce many ration hit British ladies into their men's arms while causing disgust among the British and Allied servicemen. Sadly many an allied sailor died while serving on the Atlantic convoys that were bringing tons of unnecessary luxuries to US bases instead of vital supplies. It showed how little the US government and their military in particular understood or cared about the sensitivities of their allies. So when a ship was badly damaged at sea and had to be made lighter to prevent it from sinking, the first items the sailors jettisoned were always those crates marked For the Use of US Personnel Only.

Officially Bert had little to do with the US Army Air Force as they came with everything they needed from complete spare engines to nuts and bolts, which were a different thread to those used in Britain. The British screws had a Whitworth Standard thread that was incompatible with the American Unified Coarse thread so were not interchangeable. They also had their own well organised mobile mechanical workshops. Bert was so impressed with them that he copied a few ideas to incorporate into his own mobile workshops, especially those to be sent overseas to Malta and Cairo to service the RAF in the desert war.

# 29

## Bert's nemesis strikes again.

The biggest danger to security is when everything is calm and people relax.

Everything was going well as Bert and his men carried out their work without too much interference from anyone. That was until, without warning, the enemy arrived to wreak havoc for Bert's nemesis still roamed free.

It started as a normal quiet evening as Bert walked around Sebro. It was his nightly routine to check that everything was where it should be and no equipment left out. He normally walked from his office in the main hanger to check that the night shift had clocked in and the blackout was firmly intact before driving home. As usual there was nothing noticeably amiss so he lit his pipe and continued his walk stopping occasionally to chat to the security men. It was what he had done a hundred times before without any problem. However this night was different. Unknown to Bert death lurked in the shadows looking like just another part of an aircraft that someone should have removed.

It was not.

The apparent broken piece of metal was an explosive device connected by carefully hidden wires to a small hand held detonator in the nearby bushes. For some unknown reason, the assassin hiding in the shadows did not detonate the bomb until Bert was walking quickly away from it. This meant that when it exploded to send deadly shrapnel all over the runway it did not kill Bert. Instead it threw him up in the air and across the ground to lie unconscious, badly injured, but still very much alive. The explosion shook Sebro causing alarm bells to ring bringing the security men and the emergency services to investigate what had happened. For a few minutes it was chaos as they first thought the base was under attack. Then they found Bert lying face down in the white snow stained red with the blood oozing from his wounds with bits of metal embedded in his body. The ambulance arrived bringing the nurses who tenderly placed Bert on a stretcher and tried to stop the bleeding before rushing him to Addenbrooke's hospital to receive urgent attention. He looked so badly injured that few of his colleagues expected him to live.

Not far away from where they found Bert, a security man spotted an intruder running from the bushes. He appeared to be carrying a small detonator that could have triggered the explosion and making for the fence.

'Hey stop or I will shoot,' the security man yelled out.

He was joined by others who chased the intruder until he was climbing the outer security fence. The assassin fired his pistol at the pursuers sending them into hiding as he climbed further.

'Stop now or I will fire,' the head security man shouted.

Again the assassin fired at his pursuers.

It was his last mistake. In seconds a volley of rifle fire hit him pushing his body into the barbed wire fence. Though death was immediate it took the guards twenty minutes to pull the body away from the fence for identification.

Later it was discovered that the intruder was James Thomas, a newly employed delivery man for a local shop who was bringing goods to Sebro. Sadly no one had bothered to carefully check his ID papers. They on closer examination proved to be rather poor forgeries. A raid on his lodgings did not prove much except that he had few personal effects and had left nothing here to prove who he was. Some weeks later the Intelligence officers managed to find out that he was from an important family and well educated. He was classified as unfit for military service being blind in one eye. Further investigation showed that he had been a member of Mosley's Blackshirts working for Germany by collecting information and carrying out acts of sabotage. Within a month the secret service unearthed and arrested four other enemy agents belonging to Thomas' group. One of them was a priest who guided German bombers to their targets over London by signalling to them with a lamp from his church tower!

In hospital Bert proved to be a very obstreperous patient who was not good at taking orders even when he knew he should. On gaining consciousness, he tried to get up even though he was covered from head to toe with layers of bandages. Then a young orderly's strong arm pushed Bert back down onto the pillow.

'Now you must be a good chap and rest. You've had a serious accident and need time to heal,' a nurse said as she injected his arm with a sedative that made him sleep.

Later Bert was taken to the operating theatre where the surgeons had to locate and remove a large piece of shrapnel from his back and many smaller metal splinters from his left arm. Luckily nothing had damaged any nerves or hit any vital organ, but it was still a matter of time before anyone would know if he would ever return to work. After the operation, he was placed in the Intensive Care Unit closely watched over by the nursing staff while guarded by one or more security men. No one was going to take any more risks and determined to keep Bert alive. In Intensive Care he was given blood transfusions and pain killers while his bandages were regularly changed. Within days he started to heal though his whole body ached as he lay there on the bed confused wanting to do something. Soon he started to move about until an elderly doctor read him the riot act.

'Please behave yourself otherwise we will have to restrain you,' the doctor warned.

'I'll try but I need to be doing something,' Bert replied.

'Sir you're bloody lucky to be alive. If you had been a foot closer to the bomb you would be dead or more seriously injured,' the doctor warned him.

'What bloody bomb?'

'The one you missed that was powerful enough to blow up a car, so heaven knows how you survived.'

Bert was shocked to find out that he of all people had been careless. Bloody Hell he thought the horrid Man in Black is still after me. Then seeing that the doctor was puzzled by his reactions Bert commented. 'So that is what happened. Thanks for telling me doc as I wondered why there was so much fuss.' Bert's charming smile cheered up the doctor.

'Now you know how lucky you are, maybe you will start being more cooperative or else I will order the nursing staff to ignore you. They have a lot to do so try to be a good chap,' the doctor quietly suggested.

Bert just nodded. He was shocked to know he had been a bloody nuisance, so he decided to be more cooperative. Everyone said he was lucky to be alive with all his limbs still attached! Indeed when he looked around the ward there were other patients with one or more limbs missing and one blinded by fire. So he calmed down to silently meditate. Then he thanked God for his deliverance. He prayed to quickly get better and be allowed to go home to his family.

It was four weeks before Bert went home and then under strict medical surveillance. A nurse stayed with him making sure he had his medication, his bandages changed and above all that he stayed in bed for the next two weeks. He was pleased to be home with Jenny and the boys, but was no longer his former self. Gone was his self-confidence. Now he doubted if he would survive the war where the enemy could be lurking behind every bush or just around the corner. He worried that next time the assassin would succeed and then what would happen to Jenny and the boys? She would have to survive on his meagre savings and what little she could earn. Now his eyes hurt so he could not concentrate on anything not even to read a much loved book. It made him feel worthless and helpless like a baby. At times the room revolved; or with eyes closed, he had visual disturbances where there was a spectacular firework display worthy of the brightest 5th November Guy Fawkes Day. Only there were no hot potatoes and sausages baked in the bonfire or beer to wash it down with. When asleep he was troubled by flashing coloured lights and evil dreams, or devils chasing him across fields and bombs exploding all around. Afterwards he awoke sweating like the proverbial pig knowing that he was slowly going mad or at least losing his sense of reason.

On good days Bert played happily for hours with the boys in the garden. On others black clouds gathered causing him to doubt his value to Jenny or indeed to anyone. How could he have been so stupid to ignore all advice and use the same routine when inspecting the works at the end of each shift? His meticulous and methodical ways had handed the assassin an exact timetable for his own destruction. Anyhow he was of little importance, being just a glorified mechanic doing a job like hundreds of others, so why should the enemy pick on him, especially when on paper, Hugh James was the actual manager and therefore the boss? Was the effectiveness of Sebro in keeping so many bombers in the air important enough for the German High Command that they had to destroy it? This had been the third attempt on his life. He could not help worrying just how many more were still to come before they eventually succeeded. Surely against such odds sooner or later his luck must run out. He consoled himself by one of Father's sayings that one should be like a cat and have nine lives.

It was a very miserable day with the rain keeping everyone indoors. Things were quiet as the doctor had left with the nurse saying that Bert only needed to take things slowly. According to the doctor Bert was healed and what happened next was up to him. Then Guy de Broyen arrived.

'Good morning young man and what may I do for you?' Jenny asked the unwelcomed uniformed visitor standing at the front door.

'Good morning Ma'am. I have come to see Bert Brown on a personal matter,' Guy replied softly as he understood Jenny wanted to keep Bert safely at home.

'Must it be today? He's very tired? Why don't you come another day next week?'

'I don't want to appear rude but I must insist on talking to my cousin Bert.'

'Oh you're his distant cousin Guy! Then I suppose you can come in but do not upset him,' Jenny said leading Guy to where Bert was sitting in an armchair smoking a pipe.

'Hello you old skiver,' Guy said giving Bert a schoolboy grin and looking very smart in his new Squadron Leaders uniform.

'Good morning Guy, come to gloat or just to show off your new uniform. Sorry mustn't be rude. Congratulations on your well deserved promotion,' Bert said suddenly feeling happy Guy had come. It was as if the black clouds had disappeared and nothing was going to stop Bert from being glad to be alive. For the first time since his accident he missed work and the companionship of his pilots and workmates.

They were all a good humoured bunch even when all around was more danger than he had experienced. And yet he had never heard one of his friends complain about their injuries, their losses or indeed the danger of their work. It made him realise that he should stop feeling sorry for himself and rejoice at being alive.

'Well thanks, Bert. I must say you look much better than I expected, in fact, pretty good for an old man. You know Sebro isn't the same since you so unexpectedly went on leave.'

'You sound like my doctor who insists I should get off my backside and do something instead of cogitating like an old woman,' Bert commented suddenly wanting to do more.

'How good are you at walking?' Guy asked seriously concerned for his cousin's health.

'I'm getting pretty good at walking on the old pegs. When it's not raining I walk around the garden and go down the road with Jenny to the post box. At first it was exhausting but now I like it and need the exercise to make my muscles work normally. Yesterday, I had a letter from my father who reminded me that being injured was just like getting old. Not very pleasant but something one can overcome with fortitude and help. He should know, having been shot a number of times and only has one eye. Dear old Father, never complains about anything but simply gets on with life,' Bert remarked surprised to be discussing such things with anyone other than Jenny.

'That's splendid news. I always knew no one could destroy an old warrior like you.'

'Not so much of the old thank you very much, you're just a mere youngster.'

'Sorry. Anyway I had my reasons for visiting you other than seeing how you are.'

'I thought so as you're too busy to waste time visiting a silly old fart.'

'What bloody nonsense! Last night I was wondering if you would like to spend a few days by the sea with me to watch Barnes Wallace's new toy. He would like your support for his new device. It seems that the Men from the Ministry are very sceptical and so he needs all the professional help he can get. He told me that you had both discussed the new bombs he's developing. Barnes reckons his latest device could destroy the heavily guarded Ruhr dams and help shorten the war. Well what do you say to a holiday by the sea?' Guy pleaded with his best schoolboy grin.

'It depends on if Jenny and the doctor say I can go. If they do I would love to feel the wind in my face and the sweet smell of sea air. I've always liked Barnes because he's a nice man with no airs and graces. I believe he's a real design engineer who rolls up his shirt sleeves to do whatever is required and never minds getting his hands dirty. He's such an original thinker that I'm certain there's little I can do, but you know I'll do whatever I can.'

Guy explained they would go by car to the coast and if things went well, later on they would go to a Lancaster squadron to supervise the modifications of the bomb bays for the latest of Wallace's creations. From past experience, Barnes's work was always good original science and innovative engineering. His strange geodetic construction of the Wellington bomber adapted from his work on airships made her expensive to build but difficult to destroy. The strong fuselage was built as a series of duralumin rings forming an external skeleton or monocoque construction. Though the Vickers Wellington was slow with only two engines, it was so strong and so successful that over ten thousand were built to be used throughout the war all over the world.

After Guy left and the children had gone to bed, Bert and Jenny sat in the garden looking up at the stars as the first of the night bombers took off into the sunset. It was a beautiful sight and yet indicated another round of death and destruction in which the bomber crews would risk their lives to destroy the enemy. On both sides children would lose parents, women lovers and the world its peace.

# 30

## Barnes Wallace and the Bouncing Bomb

As a child I was taught that necessity is the mother of invention. Brilliant men like Barnes Wallace proved it to be a fact by developing extraordinary weapons. Maybe his bouncing bomb that destroyed dams was the most famous of them all. Others say it was the Wellington bomber or the huge bombs that destroyed underground bunkers.

Chesil Beach in Dorset was used to test new weapon systems because it was secure, being guarded by the nearby Royal Navy base at Portland. The eighteen mile long pebble and shingle beach was two hundred yards wide and part of a large tidal floodplain. This meant that the average distance between normal high tide mark and that at low tide was about thirteen yards. So that at low tide the beach was exposed allowing nearly every part of an experimental apparatus used during high tide to be easily recovered. This was important as it prevented secret parts from falling into the hands of the enemy[31].

After an enjoyable night in a local hotel, Guy and Bert drove down to a long, winding road that followed the inhospitable part of the coast. Every hundred yards they passed heavily manned road blocks, machine gun posts and Military Police. Bert thought that if the enemy wanted to know when an important guest was arriving, or a top secret operation was going on, all they had to do was watch the activity on the beaches or above them on the high cliffs. They probably did. However the security men kept everyone whose name was not on the approved official visitors' list away from the area.

On arriving at the observation point above Chesil Beach, Bert found Barnes Wallace pacing in the shallow waters with his trousers and shirt sleeves rolled up to keep them dry. Looking down from above Bert noticed a group of six men in raincoats watching from the dry grass. They included two senior uniformed RAF officers and four Ministry of Supply bureaucrats. The latter ruled everything, sometimes for the good but often not. The Men from the Ministry were a force to be reckoned with. They too often put obstacles in the way of any new project, usually on the grounds of the cost. Their problem was everything must be found in a recognised reference book or personally ordained by someone senior, preferably Churchill himself. Indeed they were the same men who, decided after examining Frank Whittle's jet engine that it had no real use in modern warfare and refused it financial backing. Of course they took advice from a rival A. A. Griffith and decided to support Griffith's engine instead. However at the end of the day, the Whittle jet engine proved superior. If they had been a bit more adventurous, Britain would have had an operational jet fighter flying in the RAF as early as 1940[32].

Bert noticed that Chisel beach had a series of flags marking out the distances on the ground. Then he saw a radio operator and Barnes Wallace huddled over a transmitter talking to the pilot of a lone Wellington bomber flying low above the ground. The first thing Bert heard was the noise of aircraft engines growing louder as the Wellington approached with a large round object suspended from her bomb bay that he presumed was the new bomb. It made her look like a pregnant duck Bert thought realising just how difficult it must be flying such a large object with such a heavy load strapped beneath it. As they watched the spherical bomb was dropped from about a hundred feet on to the sea only to watch it sink unspectacularly to the bottom without even one bounce. An hour later the plane loaded with a new bomb flew lower at an altitude of sixty feet at 200 mph. This time the spherical bomb hit the sea to skip a couple of times along the surface before sinking like a lead balloon.

'Bert I'm glad you're here. I would like your opinion on how I can get my bomb to hit its target. As you can see it's spherical, a bit like a large golf ball, and should bounce along the surface until it hits that wreck over there just above the waves,' Barnes said looking very apprehensive. 'It is just a matter of finding the correct speed and altitude for my bomb to be dropped.'

'A bit like skimming stones over the water to skip up to three or four times,' Bert added hoping to sound well informed.

'Yes, what we schoolboys used to call Ducks and Drakes,' Barnes answered.

'I know it works with small flat stones but why try using heavy spherical objects?' Bert asked puzzled by the logic.

'I got the idea from reading about Admiral Nelson's Navy. Then the naval gunners aimed their guns to send the cannon balls so low that they bounced on the surface to strike the enemy just above the waterline,' Barnes continued.

'So I expect you built models and tested the idea.'

'Yes you know how I like to work. When I get an idea I always privately test it to avoid embarrassment on the occasions it goes wrong. First I tried it out in my back garden assisted by my son with a small catapult, a metal bath full of water, table tennis and golf balls. The best results came when I used those golf balls with a dimpled rather than a smooth surface. When the tests were successful I requested permission to build a model of a dam in a water tank at Weybridge. Then fired golf balls at it the model dam in the tank. The hard part was carrying out hundreds of tests recording every minute detail such as speed and angle of impact. I only stopped when sure of the exact speed and angle of impact needed to make the golf balls bounce along the surface to hit the dam wall. Normally the balls should rebound on impact but because they're spinning they hug the dam wall to sink to the required depth before exploding,' Barnes said as a smile crossed his face. He was rightly proud of his latest idea, that is if he could show the powers that be that it worked.

'Is this the first test you have made dropping the model bombs from an aircraft?'

'I wish it was. Sadly it's the sixth or seventh. With each failure the Men from the Ministry of Supply become more critical and less supportive,' Barnes remarked.

'The last attempt was much better,' Bert said. He was trying to cheer everyone as he was only too aware that all great ideas have teething problems.

'According to my calculations the bomb must be dropped exactly at sixty feet above the water at 240 to 250 mph,' Barnes muttered. 'The pilot must have been flying too fast or maybe he was afraid of going into the sea.'

Bert thought, one could not blame the pilot for being cautious when at that altitude it would be very easy to crash with little or no chance of survival.

'Wallace I think we've time for two more runs before it gets too dark. If the bloody thing doesn't bounce and hit the target we'll consider it non-operational and should be scrapped, or at least modified,' said the older of the Ministry Men in a very severe tone.

'You know we can't afford to spend any more money on experimental toys on our already overstretched budget,' another man said.

'You know Bert now I've to fight an army of accountants and bureaucrats. Even Air Marshall Bomber Harris says the bouncing bomb is the maddest idea he has ever heard. Luckily Air Marshall Portal supports the project but only if I can prove it works,' Barnes said. Then he continued walking around the shore with his trousers rolled up to his knees. He looked more like a man going to build sandcastles with his children than an excellent engineer.

'Knowing you I'm ready to bet a week's wage that you'll succeed? You always do,' Bert remarked encouragingly as they waited for the next test.

'Thanks old friend, I pray you're right,' Barnes commented walking towards the radio.

At the next attempt Barnes told the pilot to fly exactly at sixty feet doing 250 mph at the very moment they released the bomb. From data collected in hundreds of experiments at Weybridge, Barnes Wallace calculated that for the bomb to bounce the airspeed and altitude from which it was dropped were critical. He was always meticulous in everything he did, some would say even pedantic as all his designs were tested to perfection. Only when they passed all the required tests was he happy with a job well done. Suddenly things became grim as a cold wind started to blow sand into everyone's faces. This made the Men from the Ministry shuffle around looking even more disgruntled with their heads covered with thick woollen scarves. Soon they knew that the weather would deteriorate further making the sea surface choppy and unsuitable for the experiment to continue.

On the third attempt the Wellington flew low over the sea to approach the flags marking the start of the bombing run. The aircraft appeared to fly dangerously fast above the waves so any squall could prove disastrous, even fatal. Still she came on looking abnormal with the ugly round bomb sticking out from her belly. Just past the first marker the spinning bomb was released to hit the sea surface and proceeded to skim on top. There followed one bounce, then a second and a third until it hit the target and sank to the bottom as it was designed to do. The experiment had worked and even the disgruntled Men from the Ministry smiled as the success meant they could go home and more importantly get warm.

Typically Barnes Wallace radioed the pilot to thank him for a job well done before coming to discuss the meaning of this success with the observers. Everyone agreed his bouncing bomb worked, but it would require specially modified aircraft and training aircrew to make the bombs bounce even under enemy fire. The Ministry Men agreed the project could continue but only if he could achieve the same result from large cylindrical rather than spherical bombs, preferably to be dropped from a faster low flying Avro Lancaster. This was because manufacturing the round bomb was too expensive when a simple cylinder would be ten times cheaper. Even then Barnes required Air Marshal Harris approval for the RAF to deploy the weapon. So Barnes Wallace returned to the drawing board and went to meet Bomber Harris who eventually approved of the idea.

Years later Bert dined with a retired Rear Admiral who said any idea of a heavy iron cannonball bouncing along the surface of the water was pure balderdash. According to him the things were so bloody heavy that if they missed the target they simply fell to the bottom of the sea. Then he lit his pipe while accepting that light ping pong balls could skip along the surface of water, but a heavy iron cannonball never! Maybe the bouncing bomb was a bit of luck, but Bert preferred to call it an act of sheer genius by a very nice man who knew how to get his hands dirty.

# 31

## The Pathfinder Force

With my lights I will lead you to victory.

*A train of two hundred and fifty pound bombs next to the Stirling bomber N6101 at 1651 Heavy Conversion Unit at Waterbeach, Cambridgeshire. She was the first Stirling built by Short & Harland in their Belfast Factory. Photograph is from the Imperial War Museum London Collection under licence waive WAV 2462 of April 2010.*

The arrival of the USAAF aircraft large bomber formations had a huge effect on the war. With more heavy bombers there was a reciprocal increase in the damage inflicted on industry throughout all German occupied lands. To maximise their effect, it was agreed that during the day, hundreds of high flying American bombers would pound the German war machine while the RAF bombers operated mostly at night. The idea was to bomb the enemy continuously so that they had no sleep and would give up or at least have greatly reduced industrial output. Unfortunately the Allies did not understand that even if the German people wanted to make peace Adolf Hitler would never allow any surrender. As far as he was concerned his people would prefer to die fighting rather than suffer the ignominy of a second surrender and all the deprivation that would follow.

Even when the British bombers were using better navigational systems, often their efforts did not have the desired effect as too many bombs still missed the targets. Sometimes when the first bomber mistook a decoy target for the real thing the following aircraft bombed the same area. It became clear to the planners that the most successful raids were those led by experienced pilots with good navigators who could bomb or at least be very near the designated target. After much angry debate, a special Pathfinder unit known as Group 6 was formed using some of the most experienced bomber crews. It was intended that one or more Pathfinder aircraft would fly ahead of the main bomber force to identify, locate and then illuminate the targets using incendiary devices and marker flares. Not everyone welcomed the formation of the Pathfinders, as many in Bomber Command were angry at losing some of their best men and worried about the consequences of the pathfinders marking the wrong site. All objections were overruled and the Pathfinder Force (PFF) established. Initially the PFF were equipped with modified Stirling and Wellington bombers. Later they were replaced with the new, smaller and much faster DH98 Mosquito.

The next necessity was to develop better ways for the bombers to locate their target in all weathers. This was important because even when equipped with GEE navigational system they were only directed to within a mile of their target. Often the problem was that dense low cloud formations obliterated the target from the navigator's and bomb aimers' view. In such conditions an accurate raid proved impossible. So the boffins developed a new system called Oboe that used two ground radar stations to guide the bomber exactly to the target. When first used in a raid on March 1943 it worked exceptionally well. Unfortunately this system only had an effective range of three hundred miles and worked with only one aircraft at a time. So the Oboe system was used by the Pathfinders to illuminate the target area for the following bomber to find.

To overcome the limitations of Oboe, the scientists developed H2S. Unlike Oboe the H2S system was mounted inside the bomber to allow the navigator to clearly locate the darkened or dense cloud covered cities below. The bomber fitted with H2S system transmitted radar pulses downwards that bounced off the ground to be recorded on a fluorescent screen back inside the aircraft. The strength of the pulse recorded on the screen depended on the material it hit. Water and land absorbed most of the pulse sending back only weak responses while buildings absorbed very little thus reflecting strong echoes that lit up the H2S screen. At last the navigators and bomb aimers could clearly distinguish between open fields and built up areas. In fact the H2S screen showed an accurate image of what was below even through thick layers of dense cloud and smoke. Suddenly the accuracy of the bombing raids dramatically improved resulting in inflicting severe damage to German industry and communications[26,27,30].

There followed the development of many other systems to reduce the losses of aircraft during the raids. The newer bombers were better armoured with more fire power to protect them from the menace of night fighters. Then, wherever possible, long range fighter escorts were used to protect the more vulnerable bombers. Next the boffins developed Window consisting of hundreds of bundles of metal foil. These bundles were dropped from decoy bombers to confuse the enemy radar by sending a large number of signals to reflect on their screens. It worked so well that when it was used during a seven hundred and ninety aircraft bombing raid on Hamburg, only twelve aircraft did not return, when normally at least sixty would have been lost.

Inevitably many of Bert's pilot friends were posted to the Pathfinder Group 6. As expected their casualty rates were higher than the other bombers because the enemy night fighters soon learned to attack them. This problem was only partly overcome when the Pathfinders changed from flying large bombers to using the smaller, faster, low flying and more manoeuvrable de Havilland DH98 Mosquito. The Mosquito was designed by R. Bishop with two Rolls Royce Merlin engines to have a low radar profile. It was built mostly from moulded plywood that was non-reflective making it hard to see on radar. The early versions mistakenly were built without any guns. They were later added when it was realised its speed of 380 mph did not give the pilot enough protection from enemy attack. It was not long before the well armed models were used in special low level missions to attack specific targets. They were so accurate that they could breach a prison wall, destroy a Gestapo building or other targets, even in highly populated areas such as towns and cities.

At last the night bombing raids were accurate enough to inflict serious damage to the enemy. However the RAF bombers still had only very limited defences against enemy aircraft. So they had a higher casualty rate than the USAAF whose larger aircraft flew at high altitude with more guns and fast fighter escorts that sadly the RAF lacked. The situation was not rectified until the RAF had enough faster, long range fighters to escort their bombers. On many occasions Bert expressed his disgust that our bombers were not given the same protection afforded to the American ones. His outrage was enjoined by many senior RAF officers so much so that the Ministry of Supply initiated projects to purchase and design faster long range fighters to escort the bombers. Unfortunately the best of the new jet fighters such as the de Havilland Meteor came into production too late to alter the situation. The immediate response was to supply the RAF with some American fighter aircraft to guard her bombers. War is about surviving and to survive one must adapt, innervate and invent weapons to be stronger than the enemy. One such weapon was Barnes Walllace's Bouncing Bomb that Bert hoped would work.

# 32

## The Bouncing Bomb and the Ruhr Dams

A high profile daring raid looks better after the propaganda machine hides the real price. The bouncing bombs damaged two Ruhr dams but at a terrible price.

It was spring 1943 when Bert started to work on the special mountings to hold Barnes Wallace's nine thousand two hundred and fifty pound cylindrical bouncing bomb in the reliable Avro Lancaster. It was a rush job as everything had to be ready within twelve weeks. He really did very little other than to advise the RAF engineers. The first thing they did was to lighten each of the Mark III Lancaster Type 464 bombers by removing some of the protective armour plating and the mid-upper gun turret. This was to compensate for the extra weight and the drag from the large bomb. This made the aircraft easier to take off but more vulnerable to damage from hostile fire. The bomb mounting had to be simple enough to be easily released, while so strong that it would keep the heavy weapon in place throughout the long flight to the Ruhr. After much discussion the cylindrical bombs were secured inside the bomb bay using clamps placed on either side. Attached to each bouncing bomb was a small electrical motor that spun the bomb at the correct rotation rate just before it was released. This small device was very important because if the bomb did not spin it had little or no chance of bouncing. After a few modifications, a system was installed in the eighteen Lancaster bombers of 617 Squadron led by Wing Commander Guy Gibson.

In preparation for the raid, a select group of ace pilots and aircrew were taken to a new squadron. There they were secretly trained to fly at sixty feet above the ground over different terrain. They were not told what they were training for or why it was at night and often very low over water. It was most pilots' nightmare, but they were all experienced at attacking unusual targets so never questioned their orders. Much of the intensive training was flown over the Eyebrook Reservoir because from the air it looked similar to the targets. This involved the aircrews learning to fly in all weathers at less than sixty feet over the hilly landscape and the lake. At first the local population were shocked by being woken at all hours of the day by the noise of heavy bombers approaching their sleepy hollow. However in time they accepted it when told they were training for an important mission as everyone knew strange things happened in war. Anyone who asked too much was subjected to hours of intensive questioning until they were too scared to cause any more trouble and allowed home. It was felt that the mission had to be kept top secret to prevent the Germans increasing the defences around the targets that were already formidable. Already in private, some experts considered the proposed attack suicidal and too expensive. Indeed they doubted the dams would be seriously damaged and even if they were, many of the aircraft would never return. It was a tremendous gamble with only a slim chance of succeeding. However Air Marshal Harris and his planners decided that the raid must take place, even if only one dam was breached. This was because it could affect German productivity and maybe more importantly it would be an important propaganda coup.

During the last few weeks before the attack the planners studied the maps of each dam to note the positions of enemy defences and any hazards. Simple objects such as power lines and unexpected hills could destroy a low flying bomber and were carefully marked on the maps. It was then decided that the three main targets should be the Möhne, the Eder and the Sorpe hydroelectric dams. This was because these three dams stored over four hundred million tons of water supplying much of the power needed by the Ruhr industries and were part of the flood-control system for the Weser and Ruhr Rivers. The planners believed that their destruction would release an enormous wall of water to race down the valleys flattening or at least severely damaging the factories below. It was calculated that the best time for the raid was when the water levels were at their maximum and around full moon when the visibility would be good. Therefore the best time for the raid code named Operation Chastise would be on the night of 16th May. It was not until the morning of the raid that the crews were given their targets and then isolated so that no news could be leaked that may warn the enemy.

Two weeks earlier Barnes Wallace had provided the bomb aimers with a simple wooden device to be aligned with the two towers of the Eyebrook Reservoir Dam. This device was to help them know the distance from the target that the bomb should be dropped for maximum effect. This he hoped would help the bomb to be dropped at the correct distance to bounce and hit the dam. He then stood back knowing that there was little more he could do. From then onwards it was a matter of wait and see.

On the night of 16th May the bombers were divided into three groups. The first bomber to take off at 2128 hours was from Formation 2 consisting of five aircraft that would fly the longer northern route to the Ruhr. They were followed by the other aircraft at ten minute intervals. Next to leave was Formation 1 with nine bombers followed two hours later by the reserve force Formation 3 of five more planes. The aircraft had been ordered to fly at no more than a hundred feet above the ground to avoid enemy radar. This was made more complicated by trying to fly around all heavily defended areas. Wing Commander Guy Gibson's aircraft G for George was the first to arrive over the Möhne dam having encountered no problems. Once there he flew across the reservoir and dropped his bomb. It did exactly what it was supposed to do and skipped along the surface to sink when hitting the dam wall. It may have exploded but nothing was visible from above and no damage reported. So Gibson circled G for George around the dam to guide the other planes onto their target while drawing the anti-aircraft fire. The second Lancaster M for Mother piloted by Hopgood was set on fire by enemy flak so that the bomb overshot the target as the damage plane crashed. The next two bombers released their bombs hitting the dam but without any noticeable effect. After each unsuccessful attempt the code Goner was radioed back to base. Then the last bomber of the group J for Johnny piloted by David Maltby successfully dropped her bomb to bounce and sink against the dam wall. When nothing happened everyone was devastated that after all their efforts they had failed in achieving their objective. They had failed to take into account the fact that the effects of the damage to the weakened dam wall would take time to become apparent.

A few minutes later Guy Gibson saw a three hundred foot breach suddenly appear in the dam wall to release a torrent as tons of water streamed out of the breach. Exhilarated Guy signalled back to base that the Möhne dam was breached. The man-made flood raced down the river causing devastation. Later reports indicated that over a thousand people died in the flood water and industrial output was severely reduced throughout the Ruhr.

Then Gibson guided the other aircraft as they attacked the Eder Dam which was breached and with all their bombs used returned home. The three aircraft that attacked the Sorpe Dam failed to cause any damage partly because the area was covered in thick fog. The waters from the Eder dam did not cause as much damage as those from the Möhne Dam but still they reduced the Ruhr electricity generating capacity. Importantly the Sorpe Dam was not seriously damaged and continued to function. Of the nineteen aircraft involved in the raid, two never reached their target and eight were lost. In all fifty-three airmen died in one of the strangest and bravest bombing missions of the war.

Back at 5 Group Command everyone was delighted at the result. Only Barnes Wallace was upset when he was shown what he considered were the very high casualty figures. In fact the results were better than many expected as Bomber Command thought the attack might fail and only a few aircraft would return. But the very humane Barnes felt personally responsible for the death of too many young men.

Later Wing Commander Guy Gibson was awarded Britain's highest award for bravery the Victoria Cross and many of the crews decorated for their part in the dam raid. The breaching of the dams was important psychologically, but the long term effect on the war was minimal. Within a few months the Germans had repaired the damaged dams and the Ruhr returned to normal production! Many people have said that the raid was only partially successful, whereas a few more attacks at regular intervals would have been devastating to German industry. Perhaps similar raids should have been made on the other dams but they were not. In fact on the night of 18<sup>th</sup> October 1944 British bombers attacked Sorpe dam using the huge five ton Tallboy bombs. They missed the target. The result was some large craters in the surrounding countryside. The critics forget the huge cost in both lost planes and trained aircrew from the dam raid that could not be justified on a regular basis. Maybe those few months of reduced German productivity in the Ruhr would prove critical! No one will ever know. However it boosted the morale in a Britain tired by war, as well as shocking Germany. The raid using the fantastic bouncing bombs proved that anti-torpedo netting and good anti-aircraft guns was not enough to safeguard most dams from aerial attack.

# 33

## With the Americans came unusual challenges

Now different aircraft arrived from the USA and Canada to challenge the most capable engineer because of their size and different types of screw threads and bolts.

Some jobs presented special problems involving modifying known techniques while others meant making special equipment. Often Bert helped make parts for captured German and Italian aircraft so that they could be flown by the RAF on secret missions. But soon this became routine, unless the captured aircraft had special modifications or contained secret equipment. In such cases Bert had to call in the RAF intelligence boffins, such as Guy de Broyen. Everything they found in an enemy aircraft was carefully recorded especially details of their armaments and the frequency at which their radio was set, as well as any navigational and bomb aiming devices.

One job they hated was dealing with aircraft that had crashed landed near built-up areas or on an operational airfield while still carrying their fused bombs. On one occasion Bert and his men were called to an RAF fighter station in Kent where the runway was blocked by a USAAF Boeing B-17 Flying Fortress with a collapsed undercarriage. It was shorter than a Short Stirling but heavier being designed to carry a huge bomb load. In fact it could carry a 2000lb bomb or a load of 6000lbs. By comparison the Stirling could take eighteen bombs no larger than 250lb. This aircraft would not have been a problem except it had landed on a small fighter air base where there was no heavy duty crane to lift it.

When Bert arrived, he walked around the broken aircraft to inspect the damage and decide whether to try to lift up the whole aircraft or cut it into smaller more easily manageable pieces. As the aircraft showed few signs of structural damage other than a collapsed undercarriage, Bert decided that they would lift her and fix the undercarriage so she could be moved off the runway.

'Sir we will try to lift her up so that we can repair or replace her undercarriage. Then we can at least move her off your runway,' Bert told the worried Station Commander.

'If you can it would help a lot. I've placed some of our fighters on the grass apron ready for takeoff and must hope that any landing will see the aircraft on the runway. If not there will be a hell of a bang,' the Station Commander replied.

'Is there anything special that I should know about the aircraft?'

'The crew had returned from a bombing raid and reported no problems before they went back to their base. I must say they were in a bit of a hurry and not very cooperative.'

'Don't worry yourself about it as some of the youngsters tend be ignore the niceties of good manners. Let us hope they haven't forgotten anything important.'

'Such as?' the Station Commander asked.

'Well they could still have a few bombs aboard?' Bert commented feeling concerned.

'If they did will that present any danger?'

'Should not be a risk as long as they are not fused. If they were they could have exploded when the undercarriage collapsed.'

'Good luck. I will send over our bomb disposal expert just to be on the safe side.'

The first thing they did was to lift the plane off the ground using hydraulic jacks so that they could repair the undercarriage. It was not easy as part of the fuselage was on soft wet grass making the jacks sink into the earth. Unfortunately the crew had left to go back to their unit abandoning their plane for someone else to deal with. No one warned Bert the bombs were still aboard and fused ready for dropping. So any large shock could make them explode. It was a stupid mistake, indeed very likely a deadly one.

Unaware of the hidden danger the Sebro men started their work. First they lightened the fuselage by removing the engines one at a time. This proved fairly easy as the aircraft was new and the holding bolts accessible. Then the hydraulic jacks were placed under each wing and slowly started. It was a long process as at each stage the body of the aircraft was held up by rapidly placing scaffolding under each wing to take some of the strain. Then the jacks were repositioned with metal plates beneath them to reduce the chances of them digging into the soft ground. After two hours the fuselage started to lift from the ground and as it did everyone had a terrible shock.

'Run men, run as though the Devil's on your tail,' Bert yelled seeing that the bomb bay was open and out had dropped two large bombs.

'Dear Jesus the bugger nearly fell on me,' shouted a mechanic called Patrick.

'It wouldn't have hurt you as you're much too thick,' his mate replied.

Everyone laughed nervously.

Then they waited for two minutes in case they exploded.

'Go and get the bomb disposal experts to check them before we get back to work,' Bert ordered the still shaking Patrick.

In minutes they assessed the situation before carefully removing the bombs after making them safe. This included another ten bombs still in their racks inside the open bomb bay. It took two hours before all the bombs were made safe, their fuses removed, and the remaining bomb cases taken away.

'Bloody Yanks! It's bad enough leaving their wreckage for someone else to remove, but how could they fail to tell anyone she contains twelve fused bombs,' remarked a very angry bomb disposal officer.

'I agree,' replied a concerned Bert. 'Thanks for your help. It could have very easily become a tragedy." He looked around the aircraft before adding. "Is it safe to continue our work?'

'I think so, but you should be very careful in case she holds other hidden surprises. I'm a bit pissed off because we don't normally deal with friendly bombs, only enemy ones.'

'The aircrew probably forgot or didn't realise how dangerous keeping their armed bombs was,' Bert commented.

'They're just a load of bloody cowboys! Too ignorant, wet behind their ears, and dangerous to be allowed to fly. Sometimes I wonder just whose side these bloody Yanks are on?' the man angrily added.

'I bet you they would be scared stiff if they were told how close they were to blowing themselves up when they crash landed with fused bombs aboard. Maybe someone should tell them,' Bert commented with a grin.

The bomb disposal man laughed before adding. 'I'll phone their base to speak to the pilot and tell him how lucky he was. That will take the wind out of his sails or at least make him piss in his pants.'

It took another four hours before the seventy-four foot long USAAF B 17 Flying Fortress had a workable undercarriage. Then the eight ton aircraft was gently pulled off the runway to a nearby parking area. The base commander was delighted to hear his runway was clear again though he had used the grass to keep most of his fighters airborne or standing by ready to be scrambled. To everyone's amusement when the B-17 was safely parked the USAAF salvage team arrived to take over. Better late than never Bert thought, as he collected his men and equipment to let the Yanks clear up their own mess. None of the Yanks said thank you or apologised for their mistake which made him angry. It was a standing regulation that all damaged bombers jettisoned their bombs and fuel before landing. This reduced the risk of accidents to everyone on board and those on the ground. Obviously someone failed to drive into the thick heads of the pilot and crew of the B-17 why this was important. Maybe they didn't know how dangerous the work had been, but their apparent arrogance did not make them any friends. Indeed it increased the already deep hostility that many felt against the Yanks.

Sometimes accident happened that were not anyone's fault. Occasionally an aircraft would skid on landing to veer away from the runway towards the support staff waiting on the ground. Usually everyone ran away from danger but sometimes people were crushed under the aircraft's wheels or cut to pieces by the propellers. Strangely, when rotating at full pitch, the propellers cannot be seen and present a real danger to those on the ground. This was a serious problem especially at night or when the light was poor. Every engineer and all ground crew knew the risk, but many unfortunate civilians did not. On one occasion a badly damaged Stirling came in to land too fast, skidded on the wet runway to race headlong into a hanger. The result was one great explosion and the destruction of aircraft, hanger, crew and some ground staff. Luckily such incidents were very rare. The pilots who made such mistakes usually paid for them with their lives. More often a damaged aircraft could not clear the trees when trying to land, so they either crashed or trimmed the trees down to a safer height! Sometimes they landed with branches stuck in their undercarriage as a reminder just how close to disaster they had been. Others hit electricity cables or telephone wires or ended up nose down in a muddy field.

It was not uncommon after a major bombing raid to find aircraft landing on one wheel or with half a wing. Some pilots still managed to perform a perfect three point landing while others ended up with one wing torn off lying on their side or unusually with the aircraft's nose buried in the soft grass. Sometimes the impact on landing was too much for the damaged fuselage so that it simply broke in half spewing out everything and everyone inside. If they landed on the grass the aircrew often escaped with minor injuries but were badly hurt if they landed on hard concrete. However well the planes were built, there was a limit to the structural damage they could sustain.

As the war continued Bert's file of photographs showing damaged aircraft grew. The stronger Wellington and Stirling bombers often had major parts missing but still returned to base. The pilots called it flying on a wing and a prayer. Others called it skill, while many just put it down to luck or their mascot. Whatever the reason, the return of all aircraft however damaged was important even if it took weeks to make them airworthy. Just the spare parts and scrap metal were worth more than their weight in gold and equally as hard to find. So the nation donated their aluminium cooking pots to making engine gaskets and old iron fencing was melted down to make steel. Every yard of silk was used to make parachutes while the best cotton was reserved for covering aircraft like the Hurricane and the gliders. In fact anything that could be recycled was and many new roles were developed for old things. Used tyres were retreaded even if they were worn down to the canvas. Most things that looked new were cleverly made from anything available. It was a time when scrap merchants sprung up everywhere as the demand for metal in any shape or form increased. Some less honest people stripped the lead from church roofs while others collected old brass shell cases and anything made of copper. Gradually the raw materials needed by industry were supplied and the essential machinery and parts produced. One old man was heard to joke to a man who was parking his old car on a piece of empty land.

'I wouldn't park her there my lad as when you get back the wheels and probably the whole car will be gone and sold for scrap.'

Needless to say the man parked his car somewhere safer.

# 34

## The beginning of the end

*A group of British 'Red Beret' paratroopers assembling in front of a row of Short
Stirling aircraft and in the top left can be seen a glider. They were preparing
for the attack on the bridges crossing the Rhine in a series of battles code named
Operation Market Garden.*
*This photograph, reference CL1154, is from Imperial War
Museum London Collection and is used by permission granted
under licence waive WAV 2462 of April 2010.*

The Allies decided to invade Italy after defeating Rommel's *Afrika Korps* in North Africa. This presented different problems such as how to land enough troops at the same time, occupy enemy territory and keep them supplied. It was clear that most of the troops and their equipment would be landed from the sea onto defended beaches. To succeed they had to be supported by heavy naval and aerial bombardments. Ideally the paratroopers would be dropped ahead of the main invasion force to blow up enemy communications so making the landings less dangerous. But how could they land enough men and equipment silently and quickly? The answer was to copy the German landings on Crete and use gliders. So the planners built three main gliders that were cheap and could land both men and equipment on any flat area.

The Allies used three gliders [26,27,30]. The British Airspeed Horsa could carry twenty-five men or less men plus a jeep or small anti-tank gun. The General Aircraft Hamilcar was bigger but not so manoeuvrable. It was designed to hold a small tank or seven tons of men and equipment. Lastly there was the smaller American Waco CG-4A Hadrian glider that carried thirteen troops. Most of the gliders were towed behind specially modified four-engine bombers such as the Stirling[20,21] or the Douglas DC-3 Dakota. Their original use in Sicily was not effective as only twelve out of one hundred and forty-four gliders landed near the target. So it was necessary to improve glider pilots training and find more reliable ways of towing and releasing the gliders at the correct moment.

It was not long before Bert was required to see what could be done to improve the pulling harnesses for the gliders and their safe release. The mechanisms involved were not difficult but the organisation very complicated. To launch twenty gliders at a time, they had to be arranged on a runway in pairs with their tow ropes neatly coiled on the ground in front of them. Then they were attached to the bomber tug aircraft that would pull them towards their target. Timing was essential if the troops inside the gliders were to live and be released exactly at a point from where they could glide down nearer to the target. The slightest cross wind or poor navigation could prove disastrous. After many operations it became clear that the slow gliders were too often hit by enemy gunners and an inefficient way of getting men to the target. However, they were still used to fly in light artillery and supplies, while the main force of men was dropped from aircraft to parachute down on to the objective.

From February 1944 Bert was involved in the exercises to test the effectiveness of transporting paratroopers in gliders towed by modified Stirling aircraft. On 6th February the 3rd Parachute Brigade was dropped from ninety-eight transport aircraft. Then at the end of March two hundred and eighty-four aircraft were used to deploy a whole Brigade by parachute and using gliders. As the weeks went by, training became very important for both the towing aircraft and glider pilots. This included night flying and teaching the pilots to distinguish between the various surfaces they would have to land on such as fields, and roads. They needed to know how to recognise and avoid the latest German anti-glider mines and other obstacles that could prevent a safe landing. With the help of the latest maps and intense training the airborne armada was ready for D-Day. Their part of Operation Overlord (D-Day) was called Operation Tonga.

Just before 2300 hours on 5th June 1944 six Handley-Page Halifax bombers took off towing six Horsa gliders followed by two hundred and thirty-nine DC-3 Dakotas and Stirlings pulling two hundred Horsa and four larger Hamilar gliders[23,26,27]. Within days of the paratroops landing, all their objectives were achieved. The bridges over the Caen Canal and the Orne River that led to the east were captured and German defences eliminated. Between 5th and 7th June, eight thousand five hundred airborne troops were deployed with only eight hundred casualties. The attack on the Merville Gun Battery was not so successful. It was captured and some of the guns only partially destroyed. When the Battery was recaptured by the Germans they succeeded in firing some of the guns. However, the allied gliders proved a success in helping the landing of the massive invasion forces on to the beaches of Normandy and assisted their break out to the east. Then the aircraft were used to drop supplies to the ground forces and bomb enemy positions. They dreaded low cloud formations that sometimes covered the drop zone that made delivery of essential supplies often impossible. Later this proved to be a serious limitation in other airborne assaults, especially at Arnhem where many supplies landed on ground held by the German army.

Three days after D-Day Bert returned home to be greeted by his loving family and the news that the allies had broken out of the beachhead to advance into France. Everywhere people smiled. They felt that at last the end was in sight as the allied troops marched into Europe to destroy the Nazi regime. That night when the boys were asleep Bert and Jenny sat in the garden looking up at the skies and enjoying the June warm air.

'It's strange, after days of watching the skies full of aircraft it now feels like something is missing. No more drone of engines or long dark shadows, just a star lit sky. It makes me feel romantic and pleased to have you home again,' Jenny commented with her head on Bert's shoulder.

Then a lone aircraft crossed low overhead from a reconnaissance mission to refuel before returning to France.

'Just remember my love that the war still goes on and many of our friends are taking the fight into Germany. Now I know we will win and most of the hard work is over,' Bert replied giving her a kiss to celebrate the beginning of a new world.

However what Bert did not know was that by a stroke of good luck his nemesis had disappeared. It happened like this.

SS *Hauptmann* (Captain) Walter Brandt was ordered to Berlin to receive the Iron Cross for his services to aviation. While there Walter enjoyed himself spending hours in night clubs and at parties totally ignoring the regular air raid sirens. He had heard them so many times before and yet had never experienced even the sound of a bomb bursting nearby. The warmth of the well-endowed woman he was with and the bottles of champagne took his mind away from thoughts of war. Now he was celebrating his Iron Cross that he proudly wore around his neck. The women loved a hero and he intended to get as many as he could in an effort to make up for lost time. For now the woman called Karla he met in a sleazy night club would keep him warm throughout the night in return for a few marks. He relished the thought of ravishing her nubile body especially as her hand stroked his leg. Even when he saw the flashes of bombs exploding nearby he drove on towards a night of unparalleled passion and fulfilment. They had not gone very far down the road when a large bomb exploded a few feet away. The explosion was so great that it vaporized the couple so that afterwards there was no trace of them or the car.

A week later SS *Hauptmann* (Captain) Walter Brandt's name was placed on the ever growing list of persons reported as being absent without leave. When he was found he would be court marshalled and probably shot. Back in Heidelberg the dark haired *Hauptmann* Willie Weiss was happy. For the first time in years he no longer had *Hauptmann* Brandt looking over his shoulder to brag about his Iron Cross. Willie thought that Brandt could stay away forever and he would not be missed. In fact he smiled at the thought. He did his duty by saying that he was reluctantly reporting *Hauptmann* Brandt as being absent without leave adding that he hoped he was safe. Willie did not mean a word but to say anything else would have looked like disloyalty, if not treason. Therefore he started to put into action those projects that Brandt had stopped. The first thing he did was to implement his plans for the production of fast, jet interceptors such as the Heinkel He 162A *Volksjäger* (People's fighter) operational in December 1944. Then he supported the Junkers 8-263 rocket-propelled fighter, the Messerschmitt Me 262A jet fighter that was now produced even though it first flew in 1940 and the Arado Ar 234B-2 bomber. It was the right move that proved too late as Germany was already facing defeat on all fronts and her factories subjected to regular bombing. He hoped like so many of his colleagues that a strong defence of Germany would force the invaders to agree to a cease fire and a settlement that left his nation intact.

Meanwhile in Cambridge Bert relaxed knowing the worst part was over.

'You know Jenny that for the first time I believe the war will end within two years,' Bert said sipping a cool beer.

'If you say so my love,' Jenny replied cautiously. For too many times before people had talked about the end being near and it had not ended.

'The change came when the Americans came. Then their bombers and long range fighters inflicted even more damage on Germany than we could ever have done on our own.'

'I thought you didn't like them.'

'I don't like the way they look at you as if you were some piece of meat available at a price,' Bert replied grumpily.

'Forget them. They're just young men about to face death who are far away from home and in need of female company.'

'You may be right Jenny, but they had better keep away from you.'

'Darling Bert you worry too much. I'm a big girl with all the man I can ever need,' Jenny replied giving his arm a gentle squeeze.

'Still I'm impressed by their engineers and aircraft.'

'Is that all?' Jenny said trying to tease him.

'No it isn't. I admire their bravery and commitment to destroying the fascists.'

'It's funny that four years ago we all thought they support fascism,' Jenny commented while pouring Bert another beer out of the bottle.

'Maybe we should thank the Japanese for attacking the US fleet in Pearl Harbor and forever changing the direction this war was going.'

'Oh Bert you can't say that. Think of all the innocent people who died there,' the sentimental Jenny retorted.

'Did they care when thousands of our people were annihilated under the German mass bombing raids on our cities? I can tell you they did not. Remember their Ambassador Joseph Kennedy told President Roosevelt that Germany would win the war.'

'Bert you know he was just another silly man,' Jenny retorted going red in the face.

'The fact remains the US has helped save our bacon and shortened the war by years. Only one thing really worried me,' Bert replied looking very serious.

'And what is that?'

'Just how much the Americans are going to charge us for what we have borrowed and whether we will one day regret sending them so much information on jet engines along with aircraft information.'

'There is no sense in worrying about things that we can't control. Though knowing Churchill he would sell us all just to keep his America happy.'

'Dear Jenny you have taken the words out of my mouth. When this war is over we will have an election and chuck Churchill out. He was never elected as Prime Minister and much too often makes important decisions without consulting his cabinet.'

'Bert, we all know he is the typical British Bulldog a fierce, fearless bully. Too much an arrogant aristocrat for my liking, but we must all agree a magnificent leader,' Jenny wisely added.

Then they raised their glasses to toast.

'God save our brave men fighting for our freedom and our American allies.'

The Jenny added, 'We must not forget all the others from all over the world who have stood shoulder to shoulder with us since 1939.'

Everything started to improve as the war moved to Europe and the Atlantic convoys proved more successful. The presence of the USAAF aircraft in Britain increased especially during the build up to the invasion of France in 1944. The tide was turning and the vital role of Sebro slowly diminishing. Now aircraft repair was still important but the engineers did not have to work so hard and the staff started to smile. Not only did they still work on Stirling bombers, but also on the Consolidated B24 Liberators used by the RAF and the USAAF. The end had not come, but the beginning of the end was in sight. There were no more attacks on Sebro or personally against Bert Brown, so that they lived to survive the war that had seemed once so close to being lost.

They never forgot their friends often keeping in touch or meeting on special occasions. Whenever one or more met they enjoyed each other's company. They rarely, if ever, discussed the dark days when defeat was so real that the very word was only mentioned occasionally and even then it was whispered. At the end of the war many of the RAF aircrew remained in the service, joined civilian airlines or returned home. Sadly many of the Poles who went back to Poland were arrested and disappeared as the communists took over. Some stayed in Britain to work as airline pilots, study at university or become farmers. Most of the aeronautical engineers found work in the aircraft industry, building a new generation of aircraft or maintaining the newly emerging civil airlines that again criss-crossed the world carrying mail and people to every corner. After the war because of lack of orders for flying boats and a difficult financial situation Short Brothers closed their main factories to centre all their work in Belfast. Eventually they were taken over by the Canadian company Bombardier Group of Montreal but still manufacture aircraft.

After the war, many of the former pilots, aircrew and engineers watched silently when the RAF Battle of Britain Memorial Flight flew overhead. This became a traditional event at most air shows, royal events and memorial days such as Remembrance Sunday, Battle of Britain Day and Armed Forces Day. Usually they flew an Avro Lancaster bomber,

Hawker Hurricane and Supermarine Spitfire for all to see the remains of the wartime RAF. Sadly no Short Stirling bombers were preserved though their memory is not forgotten by those who remember the first British four-engine single wing bomber.

# Postscript.

What happened next to Bert is the subject of another book. Basically when the war drew to an end life changed sometimes for the better and for some people for the worse. The consequences of the agreement by Presidents Roosevelt and Stalin during the Yalta Conference to isolate Britain by dividing the liberated countries into areas of influence were to prove devastating. Effectively Germany was to be divided into three zones one American, one British and One Soviet. Only after French protests did there become a French zone made up of parts from both Britain and American ones. Europe became divided by what was to become known as the Iron Curtain while the USSR and the USA competed for world dominance. Even the few areas under British influence such as Greece became a battlefield for political ideologies.

With the end of the war came the financial and political settlements. Britain was bankrupt owing the USA the War Loans of $586 million in cash and $3,750 million credit for purchases of war materials. This was equivalent in 1945 as £145million and £930 million respectively. During difficult negotiations the US set an interest rate of 2% on the loans and stated that they must be repaid in 50 instalments. During that period six payments were deferred due to Britain's financial problems. In the end the final payment was made in December 2006. The argument over the then high interest rate charged to an ally was to haunt Anglo-American relationships for decades. This was made worse by the American demands that Britain supports the US on most international policies. One factor that made matters worse was the fact that the US maintained military bases in Britain where all concerned came under US and not British Law.

After the war Britain struggled with rebuilding her ravaged economy and changing from the production of war materials to making goods that could be exported for much needed foreign exchange. Unemployment grew as did the need for social reform. In a desperate bid to save the nation many companies were nationalised including airlines. The nation was confused by demands to support their former enemies while suffering severe poverty and hardships. During this time Bert found work as a ground engineer servicing the aircraft airlifting food and fuel to Germany. It was the time of the soviet blockade of Berlin when the allies started the Berlin Airlift which ended in May 1949.

Immediately afterwards Bert joined British Overseas Airways Corporation (BOAC) as a fleet engineer responsible for the building and introduction of new aircraft for their expanding network. He found many colleagues already working there including Tim who still flew Short Flying Boats. Both men remained friends and together were responsible for developing new aircraft to link the whole British Empire by air to London. There were many problems to be tackled and dangers overcome. Due to limited finances BOAC had to use and buy wherever possible British built aircraft. This posed a problem as there were few British aircraft being manufactured. In 1947 Bert went to Canada to build a fleet of twenty-two new aircraft based on the American Douglas DC-4 to be known as the Canadair CL-4 or Argonaut. In the meantime BOAC purchased Hermes 4 aircraft from Handley Page. By 1950 both planes were in service alongside the Lockheed Constellation and Boeing 377 Stratocruiser. In that year BOAC earned Britain a much needed $4 million dollars.

In March 1949 BOAC had to absorb the assets of the nearly bankrupt British South American Airways (BSAA) and its associated airlines. This followed a series of tragic accidents to BSAA aircraft. First in 1948 a BSAA Avro Tudor IV their Tudor IV Star Tiger disappeared between the Azores and Bermuda. In 1949 the Tudor Star venture crashed killing three passengers at Rio do Janeiro and two weeks later the Avro Tudor Star Ariel carrying seventeen people disappeared between Bermuda and Jamaica. The British government intervened as now BSAA was losing money and nearly bankrupt. So in March 1949 BSAA was merged into

BOAC bringing with it new routes to South America, a fleet of aircraft with unhappy histories and large debts. The BSAA debts were to be repaid by BOAC in instalments with interest to the government. It was to be such a burden that for many years BOAC made an operating profit but after paying the BSAA debts was always in the red. Strangely when BOAC was privatised as part of British Airways all debts were written off.

From 1950 onwards Bert was fleet engineer for the Hermes going on dangerous proving flights across the Sahara Desert. They flew via Tunis non-stop to Kano in Nigeria, then to Lagos, Accra in the Gold Coast (now Ghana) and Sierra Leone. The Hermes was very successful until in May 1954 when one of the fleet named Horus crashed in the Sahara Desert. Then Bert and a team of engineers flew to Tunis and by land searched for the crew. They were all alive except for the flight engineer. A later enquiry blamed the crash on a navigational error that meant the aircraft ran out of fuel though others said it was the effects of a dust storm. With the introduction of new aircraft with longer range and the ability to carry more passengers a new era of air travel was born. Soon BOAC needed larger and faster aircraft so in 1952 they introduced the first all jet powered airliner the De Havilland DH106 Comet 2. It was fast with a crew of six but only carried 22 passengers. In early 1954 disaster struck when unexplainably two Comets crashed having disintegrated. The service was withdrawn. They were later replaced by the Bristol Britannia 100 and 300 series and the Douglas DC-7C. Now the Britannia 300 had a loner range and could carry 139 passengers a vast improvement over the smaller aircraft. In time the studies on the De Havilland Comet 2 showed it had crashed due to a new phenomenon known as metal fatigue. The lessons learned from that investigation make modern air travel much safer.

By 1962 BOAC was one of the leading international airlines with a reputation for reliability, excellent engineering and the motto 'BOAC Takes Good Care of You'. Bert now had to learn to deal with new dangers faced by terrorism and metal fatigue. He flew around the world starting new routes or arranging for local airlines to work. This meant a passenger leaving London could within three days fly to nearly anywhere in the world on scheduled airline flights. New jet aircraft were introduced starting with the DH Comet 4 and Boeing 707 followed by the Vickers VC 10, the Boeing 747 and the Concord. In 1964 Bert retired but the airline he had helped build continued from strength to strength.

In 1972 BOAC Chairman Sir Keith Granville inaugurated the Polar service from London Heathrow to Japan to supplement the flights from London via Sydney and Fiji to the western seaboard of the USA. It was a golden age that sadly has long since gone. For after the complete merger of British European Airways (BEA) with British Overseas Airways Corporation (BOAC) to form British Airways (BA) in 1973 it was privatised. The new BA cancelled many routes to countries where they made little or no profit to concentrate on the valuable ones such as to North America, South Africa, Hong Kong and Australia. The global concept of BOAC had died never to be reborn.

# HISTORICAL INFORMATION

*The Supermarine S6 N248 being prepared for display at the Goodwood Festival of Speed. It was flown by Flt. Lt. Atcherley in the 1929 Schneider Trophy Race. Picture taken by Dominic Meakins*

*Reconditioned Twin Cockpit Spitfire Trainer Mark IX at Shoreham Airfield. Picture taken by Author*

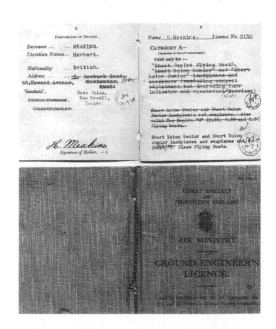

*Air Ministry Ground Engineer's Licence C.A. Form 9. Note that the war time address in Cambridge is obliterated and there is no reference to his being certified to work on Stirling and Liberator aircraft. It only refers to the Short Brothers Rochester Scion Junior landplanes and seaplanes and 'C' Class Flying Boats.*

*Herbert Meakins at*
*Supermarine in 1934.*

*Herbert Meakins retiring*
*from BOAC in 1965.*

# Bibliography.

1.  Mike Hooks, *Shorts*. Stroud: Tempus Publishing, 1995.

2.  Ivor J. Hilliker, *A Solent Flight*. Southampton: Kingfisher Publications, 1990.

3.  Alan Smith, *Schneider Trophy Diamond Jubilee. Looking back Sixty Years*. Poole: Waterfront Publications, 1991.

4.  J. Rudyard Kipling, *Dedication*. In *The Five Nations*. London: Methuen & Co, 1903.

5.  Henrietta Heald (editor), *Chronicle of Britain and Ireland*. Farnborough: Chronicle Communications, 1992.

6.  Tim Pat Coogan, *Michael Collins*. London: Arrow Books Ltd, 1991.

7.  www.en.wikipedia.org/wiki/Michael_Collins_(Irish_leader)

8.  Tim Pat Coogan, *De Valera: Long Fellow, Long Shadow*. London: Arrow Books Ltd, 1995.

9.  www.en.wikipedia.org/wiki/%C3%89amon_de_Valera

10. www.en.wikipedia.org/wiki/History_of_Ireland

11. J. Rudyard Kipling, *Return*. In *The Five Nations*. London: Methuen & Co, 1903.

12. John McRae, *In Flanders Fields*. London: Punch, 1915.

13. John Bastable (editor), *Readers'Digest Yesterday's Britain*. Pleasantville: Readers's Digest Association, 2003.

14. Bennetta Jules-Rosette, *Josephine Baker in Art and Life: The Icon and the Image.* Urbana and Chicago: University of Illinois Press, 2007.

15. www. rjmitchell-spitfire.co.uk

16. en.wikipedia.org/wiki/R.J.Mitchell.

17. Harald Penrose, *Wings across the world. An Illustrated History of British Airways.* London : Cassell, 1980.

18. www.en. wikipedia.org/wiki/Spanish_Civil_War

19. www.en. wikipedia.org/wiki/Short_Stirling

20. www.historyofwar.org/articles/weapons_short_stirling_bomber

21. www.raf.mod.uk/bomber command/stirling

22. www.stirling.box.nl.

23. Winston. S. Churchill, *The Second World War.* London: Pimlico, 2002.

24. Philip Guedalla, *Mr Churchill.* London: Pan, 1942.

25. Paul Gallico, *The Snow Goose. A Story of Dunkirk.* London: Michael Joseph, 1941.

26. Chaz Bowyer, *The History of the RAF.* London: Hamlyn, 1979.

27. Guy Wint, Peter Calvocoressi and John Pritchard, *The Penguin History of the Second World War.* London: Penguin, 1999.

28. Len Deighton, *Battle of Britain.* London: Jonathan Cape, 1990.

29. Peter Jacobs, *Hawker Hurricane.* Marlborough: The Aviation Series The Crowood Press, 1998.

30. Ralph Barker, *The RAF at War.* Alexandria, Virginia: Time-Life Books, 1981.

31. en.wkipedia.org/wiki/Barnes_Wallace

32. en.wkipedia.org/wiki/Frank_Whittle

Other reference materials used.

*Janes's Fighting Aircraft of World War II*. New York: Crescent Books, 1989.

Herbert Meakins, Personal papers and photographs. (unpublished).